Jimi Hendrix Turns Eighty

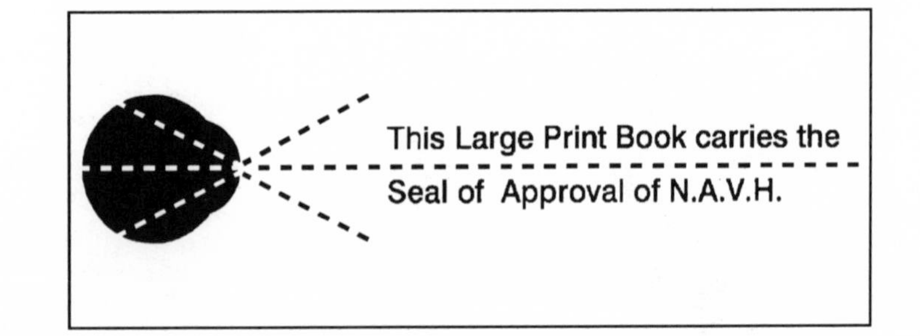
This Large Print Book carries the
Seal of Approval of N.A.V.H.

Jimi Hendrix Turns Eighty

Tim Sandlin

THORNDIKE PRESS
An imprint of Thomson Gale, a part of The Thomson Corporation

Detroit • New York • San Francisco • New Haven, Conn. • Waterville, Maine • London

This is a work of fiction. Names, characters, places, and incidents either are the product of the author's imagination or are used fictitiously, and any resemblance to actual persons, living or dead, businesses, companies, events, or locales is entirely coincidental.

While the author has made every effort to provide accurate telephone numbers and Internet addresses at the time of publication, neither the publisher nor the author assumes any responsibility for errors, or for changes that occur after publication. Further, the publisher does not have any control over and does not assume any responsibility for author or third-party Web sites or their content.

Thorndike Press® Large Print Laugh Lines.
The text of this Large Print edition is unabridged.
Other aspects of the book may vary from the original edition.
Set in 16 pt. Plantin.

LIBRARY OF CONGRESS CATALOGING-IN-PUBLICATION DATA

Sandlin, Tim.
Jimi Hendrix turns eighty / by Tim Sandlin.
p. cm. — (Thorndike Press large print laugh lines)
ISBN-13: 978-0-7862-9502-9 (lg. print : alk. paper)
ISBN-10: 0-7862-9502-3 (lg. print : alk. paper)
1. Hendrix, Jimi — Fiction. 2. Retirement communities — Fiction. 3. Old age — Fiction. 4. Baby boom generation — Fiction. 5. Musicians — Fiction. 6. Large type books. I. Title.
PS3569.A517J56 2007b 2007000355

Published in 2007 by arrangement with Riverhead Books, a member of Penguin Group (USA) Inc.

Printed in the United States of America on permanent paper
10 9 8 7 6 5 4 3 2 1

I wrote this book for my father,
Red Sandlin, who showed me
you can age with dignity or rage
or laughing all the way.
It's your choice.

And the young men who entered
Johnson 8 & 9 in the fall of 1968.
The scattered and the dead.

And as always, Carol and Leila.

ACKNOWLEDGMENTS

Call me strange, but I read the acknowledgments of every book I read. I think the thank-yous matter. Here are mine:

Kyle Mills, Dr. Bruce Hayse, Kyle Hong, Amanda Gersh, Curt Pasisz, Deborah Bedford, and Henry Levinson.

Dean, Carin, and Kiva McConoughy-Munn.

Flip Brophy, Jake Morrissey, and Susan Petersen, who didn't give up.

Drew and Nancy, the coolest women in L.A.

Scottie and Michael, role models for my daughter.

The folks who run Pearl Street Bagels and the Jackson Hole Center for the Arts, for giving me a place to write.

Parts of this story were written in St. John's Hospital and the St. John's Living Center here in Jackson. I would like to thank the wonderful staffs of both places, for patience and putting up with stupid questions.

And Carol, who makes it possible.

It takes life to love Life.

EDGAR LEE MASTERS,
Spoon River Anthology

AUTHOR'S NOTE

The only thing I know for certain is that this book will be true, someday. Librarians of America will move it from fiction to nonfiction.

On a clear October afternoon, a gentleman, who was seventy-two but in such good health he could have passed for sixty-two, prepared to putt a golf ball across the thirteenth green at one of the many courses lying ten miles inland from the Pacific Ocean in that stretch of green peninsula between Santa Cruz and San Francisco. The hole was a bit more than five feet from the gentleman's golf ball, not a gimme but certainly a putt he expected to sink. He hunched his shoulders and squinted down the shaft of his putter, bringing the ball into sharp focus. He flexed his knees and swung an air-putt between his toes and the ball, adjusting for force. He shifted his head to look at the hole, where a man he didn't know well stood with his hip cocked to one side and a hand on the flagpole, waiting. At that moment, something went wrong. True north jumped three degrees to the left.

The gentleman was not dizzy. He was not

faint. It was as if the green and the land it sat upon shifted under his feet, sidewise. The gentleman stumbled and kicked the ball. The man holding the flag, ready to lift it away, said, "What?"

"Did you feel an earthquake?"

"Not me." The man holding the flag turned to a third man who waited at the lip of the green, beside a sand trap.

"You feel an earthquake?"

"What earthquake?"

Guy Fontaine, the putting gentleman, was fairly new to California. He'd moved there from south-central Oklahoma to live in his daughter's guest cottage, and, like any newcomer, he'd been waiting, holding his breath, so to speak, for his first earthquake.

But, from all his daughter and son-in-law had told him — exaggerating the way locals will with outsiders — he'd never heard of the earth moving aside. The ground had simply shifted from here to there.

Guy bent over from the waist, picked up his Titleist, and strolled across the green toward two rented golf carts. He slid the ball into the right front pocket of his pants. He sniffed the air, which was still new to him — the salt of it, the smell of wind blown over thousands of miles of water. It was a beautiful day, but not beautiful in the sense that he'd been raised.

In Oklahoma, down along the Red River, a day like this would have thrown the locals off. That's what Guy felt — thrown off. The humidity wasn't right. Or the barometric pressure. Something did not fit his perception of how air should feel.

He slid his putter into the bag on the back of his cart, settled into the driver's seat, and tightened his Velma-Alma Comets ball cap. Then he shifted the gear rod into reverse and stepped on the accelerator pedal. The man still standing with his hip cocked and one hand on the flag said, "Hey." He looked at the third man, who shrugged.

They didn't know Guy well, having been paired with him by the club pro only that morning. Separately, they had each decided his Oklahoma accent was a bit put-on. He played golf well, for a man his age, and the Californians didn't think a man with a broad southern Oklahoma accent would be able to play well. Neither of them had been born in California, but they'd lived there long enough to know how to stand while you wait for a colleague to choose his iron, and Guy didn't stand that way. He was too attentive. They could not understand how a man without California golf mannerisms could be three strokes ahead after twelve holes.

And they didn't know what to think when

Guy shifted into forward and drove the cart away. They watched him cut across the number four fairway, bounce over a cat track, past the clubhouse onto the access road. As they watched, Guy signaled with his arm held out straight, parallel to the road, that he intended to turn left. Then he turned left.

The man standing on the lip of the thirteenth green moved his putter from his right to his left hand and dug into his pocket for a cell phone.

Guy drove maximum cart speed up the access road, past mailboxes, and under a gated archway with a sign announcing the name of the golf course and the fact that the public was welcome to play there. He zoomed, if eight mph could be called zooming, by a barn where city people who owned horses could keep them fed and exercised. The next building was shaped like a barn, too, but, instead, was a store where these same city people bought regional wines and organic fruit. Gourmet cheeses. Brand-new butter churns that look old.

Guy swung right onto the state highway that cut through a pumpkin farm where a farmer sat in what looked like a miniature tractor, forearms draped across the steering wheel, staring at Guy through Vuarnet sunglasses no farmer in Oklahoma would dare wear. The pumpkins were swollen to a bursting, waxy orange, like pumpkins in grocery stores or on TV. To Guy, they seemed ready to pick, but he wasn't sure. He was used to watermelons or pecans and didn't remember anyone in this area growing pumpkins. He made a mental note to ask Lily when pumpkins were considered ripe for picking.

Cars formed a line behind the golf cart, impatiently waiting to pass. Some took a risk and shot by between approaching cars. A hybrid SUV far back in the line honked its horn. The driver was from Santa Barbara and not accustomed to waiting.

Guy signaled a bent arm right turn and moved his cart onto the entrance ramp leading to the Harbor Freeway. He hummed a tune that practically anyone in Oklahoma could have told you was called "Boomer Sooner." The words went like this: "Boomer sooner," repeated seven times, then a hard "OKU," followed by "I'm a Sooner born and Sooner bred and when I die I'll be Sooner dead, rah Oklahoma, rah Oklahoma," then a repeated "OKU." Had Guy been the sort of man who smoked cigars, this would have been his moment.

The slow-moving cart left a fair level of jumble in its wake, once it reached the interstate. Cars swerved left, around him, causing drivers in the passing lanes to brake without warning to those cars behind them, whose drivers reacted somewhere between alarm and panic. A few brave souls blew past Guy on the shoulder. More than a few horns were honked and curses shouted. The problem was made worse by the people swerving, honking, and simultaneously reaching for cell phones to report a golf cart on the freeway. Cell phone use in a crisis is the American way, but it causes as many mishaps as it prevents.

In Guy's mind, the honkers were neighbors from Waurika and Addington, beeping greetings as they passed by on their way to Wichita Falls. He smiled and waved. Since it was football season, he flashed the Down with the Longhorns signal at the cars with Oklahoma plates, which, so far as Guy could see, was all of them. He shouted, "Hello, Bartholomew," to a black man he knew who worked at the post office in Ringling. He swerved to miss an armadillo crossing the blacktop in front of Jake's Hush Puppy House where Guy knew they sold more silver bourbon than hush puppies. Guy didn't care what Jake sold. One of his favorite expressions that he used so often it drove Lily nuts was " 'To each his own,' said the old lady as she kissed the purple cow."

He was both surprised and pleased by how

well his 1958 Bel Air purred along the highway. The clunk in the transmission had healed itself, and the vinyl car seat felt warm in the sunlight. The radio was playing KOMA Oklahoma City, a song about a man named Big Bad John. He should reach the Red River soon. He thought he might take off his shoes and socks and walk in the dry riverbed. It seemed like that kind of a day.

Red and blue alternating light flashed against the inside of Guy's bifocals, and a California Highway Patrol car pulled alongside. The highway patrolman made a sweeping arm movement intended to mean "Stop the cart, now."

Guy smiled and gave the anti-Texas sign, which is done by holding the index and little fingers out, over the fist, pointing down. Pointing up has the opposite meaning. The highway patrolman, who had never been in Texas or Oklahoma, interpreted the sign as Hawaiian for *shaka.*

He rolled down his passenger-side window and shouted, "Pull the cart to the side of the highway."

Guy Fontaine came back from Oklahoma. He found himself driving a golf cart on the Harbor Freeway. His first thought was "Uh-oh." His second thought was "The battery on this golf cart is dying."

Guy turned a hard right and might have driven across the ditch into the fence had the battery not given out altogether. He sat, waiting, keeping both hands visible so the patrolman would not feel threatened.

The patrolman pulled his car to a stop on the shoulder, checked Guy in the rearview mirror, then got out and walked toward the cart with his left thumb hooked on his belt. On the highway, cars burst forward like a river coming over a knocked-flat dam.

Guy gazed across the field toward where he knew the Pacific Ocean was. He bit his lower lip, wondering what he should do next. His best bet, he figured, was to fake normalcy.

Guy turned to face the approaching highway patrolman. "Pretty day, isn't it, Officer."

This seemed to set the patrolman back a notch. Guy figured judging day quality wasn't part of the man's regular job.

Guy said, "Have you ever walked barefoot in the Red River? There's never any water in the riverbed, this time of year. The sand is soft and warm as a tropical beach." He stopped, took off his ball cap, and looked at the patrolman. "You don't even know where the Red River is, do you?"

"No, sir, I don't. Show me a driver's license, please."

"Since when do you need a license to drive

a golf cart?"

"Since you drove on the interstate highway. Driver's license. Please."

Guy dug for his license, which was still from Oklahoma. He hadn't bothered changing it over yet. "Is there a problem? Something I can help you with? I'm not certain I have my registration and insurance on me."

The patrolman looked at the photo on Guy's license and said, "Step out of the vehicle, sir."

"I know for certain I wasn't speeding."

The patrolman took off his sunglasses and stared at Guy. "Get out, now, sir."

"You're not going to play along, are you?"

"No, sir."

Guy turned and swung his legs out the open door. He sat, watching traffic flash by in the fast lanes. Guy knew this was one of those moments where life changes from one way of doing things to another, and never goes back again.

The patrolman said, "Sir."

Guy looked from the speeding cars to the patrolman. "Is there any hope of you not telling my daughter about this?"

One

November 2022

Henry Box's heart is skipping beats. Henry, who will soon change his name to Sioux, leans forward on both elbows and, casually, hoping neither of the other men at the picnic table notices, he touches fingertips to neck. *BA-dip, BA-dip, BA-dip.* Nothing. After an agonizing second in which Henry must decide whether to speak up or die quietly, his heartbeat returns. *BA-dip.*

"I think I'm in fibrillation," Henry says.

Ray John Mancini doesn't look up from the letter to the editor he is writing on a keyboard so small he types by thumb. "If you're going to fall over, go to the infirmary. I'm working here."

On the far side of the redwood table, Nicolas Lessac studies the front page of the *San Jose Mercury News.* Nicolas wears an ascot. His half-lens glasses hang by a silver chain. "According to this story, Jenna Bush has the highest approval rating of any president in thirty years, in spite of Gulf War VI."

Ray John coughs his disgust. "Jenna has no room to brag. There hasn't been a president since Carter wasn't hated by more than half the country. He was too boring to hate."

"Doesn't anyone care that I'm fibrillating?" Henry asks.

Ray John looks across at Nicolas, who sniffs and turns to the obituaries. Ray John says, "No one cares, Henry."

The three men are seated around a newspaper-cluttered table located at the end of a stepping-stone pathway that skirts an ornamental pond at the rear of a property known as Mission Pescadero. In the foreground, across the green, closely cut lawn, a group of twenty or so women are taking a yoga class presided over by a thin-as-a-broom-handle, freckles-across-the-bridge-of-her-nose instructor named Dixie Lichens. One woman, older than the rest, sits propped in a wheelchair at the edge of the group, her eyes clouded as a roadkill deer.

Henry, behind prescription sunglasses so dark they appear black, stares at Dixie's chest while she balances on her belly with her hands pressed at her sides, her chest perpendicular to the mat, and her face lifted up to the sky in a maneuver known as the *cobra.*

Her bird voice calls to the ladies spread in a semicircle around her. *"Keep those toes pointed straight!"* Even though with his glasses on Henry is too blind to pass a driving test, he clearly sees nipples straining against spandex. The girl has no breasts to speak of, but she does have choice quality nipples.

"The object is to create an arch from heel to head!" Dixie shouts.

Henry finger taps Ringo Starr's drum solo from the *Abbey Road* album on a Pro Class Frisbee. He's wearing the lucky sweater he's worn so long he can't recall why it's lucky. Any wife would have thrown it out years ago. He says, "Are you aware that Blue Cheer was the first group to smash their instruments onstage?"

Ray John — black turtleneck, fedora, upper lip curled by scorn — says, "That is a blatant lie."

Henry continues as if he hasn't heard. "I remember, like it was yesterday."

Nicolas glances up from the obits. "Since when do you remember yesterday?"

"January 1967," Henry says. "Winterhaven. Randy Holden rearing back like he's got a baseball bat instead of a guitar."

Ray John snaps. "It was Leigh Stephens. If you must wallow in the old days, at least get your facts straight."

Henry blinks behind his glasses. "Randy Holden."

Ray John has written so many letters to the editor, he can browbeat and type with passion simultaneously. "Randy didn't screw off The Other Half and join Blue Cheer till late '68. Leigh Stephens was lead in '67. And it was the Fillmore."

"Winterhaven."

"How can you be so stupid? I was at the gig, for God's sake."

"You were still smoking banana peels when Blue Cheer played the Fillmore."

"Winterhaven."

Nicolas counts the dead — two older than him, four younger. Not a bad day, considering. One of those younger was thirty-two and an educated reading of certain code words lets Nicolas know the man committed suicide. Nicolas says, "No one alive today cares whether it was '68 or '69."

Henry and Ray John both say, " '67."

Ray John throws Henry a look meant to be condescending and continues on his own. "I left Berkeley the summer of '69. Radicalism was dead by then."

"No one cares when radicalism died, either."

"I care." Henry's voice takes on the melancholy plaint he falls into whenever he speaks about his roots. "I was living in the Haight by '66. I was disenchanted before disenchantment became cool."

Dixie performs something called a front fold — *"Align that pelvis, girls!"* — which involves pressing the facial cheekbones against the knees. Even though the women around her are in their late sixties and seventies, more than a few of them keep right up with Dixie. Henry thinks this is impressive. His is a generation of women for whom stretching is a lifetime commitment.

"Half the time you gentlemen claim anyone who remembers the '60s wasn't there," Nicolas says, "and the other half you're arguing about who played lead in the Great Society."

"Darby Slick," Henry says.

Ray John nods his agreement. "You're jealous because you came on the scene after it was over."

Nicolas sniffs. "I personally, myself, was at Stanford, studying when whoever it was in Blue Cheer smashed his guitar on whatever stage he was on."

"Too far away for the authentic experience," Ray John says.

Henry feels for his pulse again. "You have no idea what it was like at the beginning," he says. "No one who wasn't there understands."

Two

The archway double doors that separate Mission Pescadero from the outside world swung open and a threesome entered, tightly grouped, like a herd of spooked elk. Guy Fontaine, in a dress shirt buttoned to the neck, even though it was warm. His daughter, Claudia, mid-forties, maybe older. Her husband, Rick, a building contractor with middle-aged crown baldness. Claudia was nervous, the type of nervous that makes some people talk even when no one is listening. Henry could not make out the words from across the quad, but she seemed to be pointing out things that were obvious. People do that with the very young and old. *"Look, Bobby, lunch is on the table."*

The newcomers walked up the entry path past a half-naked-woman statue the Mission owners bought at a Trout Unlimited silent auction. Claudia checked out everything and the men nothing. Rick exuded the air of a healthy person in a hospital — damned if he's going to take note of anything. Guy kept both hands shoved deep in his pants pockets. He had the posture of one who has recently taken a hard blow to the spine.

They stopped at a lone, ancient eucalyptus tree on the bank of an ornamental pond to watch the twenty elderly women doing their front folds. They were close enough now for Henry, Nicolas, and Ray John to make out Claudia's words.

"See how darling these girls are. They haven't given themselves up to despair."

Guy stared at the point where the tree met the earth. He didn't give Dixie so much as a glance.

"What do you wager he's an involuntary?" Nicolas said.

Henry took off his sunglasses and, closing his eyes against the brightness, scratched his eyebrows with the tips of his fingers, breaking loose a snow squall of dandruff. "I wonder how many times he's heard *'We're doing this because we love you'* in the last week?"

Ray John said, "If he asks my advice, I'll tell him to kill his family."

After some searching, the new people found the door to Administration and went inside. Ray John and Nicolas returned to angry letters to the editor and current events in the newspaper. Henry continued staring at the door to Administration, remembering his own admittance. His conservator cried. She made herself the one the clerk brought Kleenex and chamomile tea to. The manipulative bitch.

"I'll wager they took his money," Henry said.

"And car," Ray John said. "You can spot the poor slobs who have just been told they'll never drive again."

Dixie's voice piped through her thighs. "Heels apart, Sunshine, toes together. Your eyes should be looking at your navel." Dixie's eyes were looking several inches south of her navel. Henry wondered if she was too proper to say *snatch,* or she assumed her elderly charges couldn't double over that far.

"I'll sign this one Pepé Le Pew," Ray John said. "Those sons of whores in San Francisco will never catch the irony."

"You think the fog is finished for the season?" Nicolas asked.

Henry sniffed the air, as if he'd learned to smell fog before it becomes visible. "The fog is never finished for the season. There's government machines offshore that make it, to keep us disoriented."

"You're paranoid," Ray John said.

"And you're consumed by rage. I'd say that makes us even."

The door at the top of the ramp leading into Nursing Care opened and women too old to have been teenagers in San Francisco in the '60s were wheeled parade-like into the sunlight. They reacted like lizards on a rock. The old women blinked, slowly. They lifted their faces, if they could. Turned their arms palm up, if they could. Even after the other four senses have dulled and died, we humans can still feel sunlight on skin. Their keepers in blue uniforms and neon rubber shoes stood around the half-naked-woman statue, hands in pockets, eyes glazed, bored to the verge of imitating their patients' catatonia.

Ray John hit Save and read his own words aloud: "We are the invisible minority, cast aside by a culture aimed at satisfying only pubescent desires. What makes us unique from other minorities, such as blacks or homosexuals, is that we were once like you and, someday, if you survive, you will join us. A landlord or employer would never treat a black man with contempt if he was certain of becoming one. How can you treat the aged as nonentities, knowing where you yourself are going?"

He turned to Nicolas. "What do you think?"

"My initial reaction is that you are urinating upwind."

"Someone has to fight for us. Teenagers control America."

Henry said, "I don't trust anyone under sixty."

The session came to a close and the yoga women relaxed, breathing through their nostrils, hands on their hips, thumbs forward, except for one stone-hard woman with Asian features who stood the other way, thumbs back. This woman walked to the older, glaze-eyed woman slumped in a wheelchair at the edge of the group. The younger one murmured quietly to the older one in the chair. She tucked a beach blanket around the unused legs. The older one spoke, sharp and low, and the Asian woman's face snapped back as if she'd been slapped.

Dixie drifted over to the wheelchair, rubbing a towel along her arms. She said something to both women. They looked at Dixie with all the compassion you would give a drowned rat.

"What's the catfight about?" Nicolas asked.

Ray John spit. "The usual. Suchada hates everyone young, straight, healthy, or happy. Phaedra just hates everyone, including Suchada."

Guy and his family came back out of Administration, accompanied by Alexandra Truman, giving the standard initiate tour. Alexandra's look reminded Henry of a style he thought of as flapper, although he couldn't quite remember why. He thought flappers, like Alexandra, wore straight-across bangs and bowl cuts. Smutty eye shadow. Her lips had been professionally puffed, and she walked with her shoulders back, tits to the fore.

"Mission Pescadero was established in 2010 as the premier continuing care retirement community in the Half Moon Bay area. Our guests — we call them guests because that's what they are — lead vibrant, creative lives within the context of loving assistance tailored to individual needs."

Alexandra dressed like a young bureaucrat from ten years ago, back when she was a young bureaucrat. Shaft skirt above the knees, sleeveless blouse, cloggy shoes on two-inch heels. Lapis lazuli bracelet. When she was young, Alexandra had pierced her tongue and nipple, but that was long, long ago. Now she had become the type of administrator who will happily fire any employee who breaks the personal hygiene code, which excluded holes in the tongue, nose, or lips.

She pointed out the stonework over the dining hall entrance. "Those words embody the true spirit of Mission Pescadero."

Claudia read the inscription cut in sandstone. "*Independence. Dignity. Respect.* Isn't that wonderful?"

Alexandra continued the pitch. "We like to think of this noble tree as the symbol of our spirit." She and the tour group stood in a line, looking at the eucalyptus as if it held a message. None of them looked up, above eye level, so if the tree did hold a message, for them, it was contained in the peeling bark.

"We have yoga on Tuesday and Thursdays. Tai chi Wednesday. A sock hop every Friday night featuring a rock band made up of our own. They play golden oldies from back in your day," Alexandra said.

Claudia took offense. "I listen to adult contemporary."

Alexandra missed it. "Isn't that the same as lite jazz?"

The tour wandered on around the pond. Alexandra showed them Contemplative Corner and the chapel. Claudia pointed out the ducks.

"Look," she said. "Ducks. I wish we'd brought saltines to feed them."

Guy crossed his arms over his chest, hugging his elbows, holding on.

Henry said, "He knows they're geese and not ducks, but he'd die before he'd tell her." Ray John cleared his throat with a sound that came out as a low growl.

Rick checked out the thick walls and the bell tower at the front corner. He said, "It's built like a fort."

Alexandra said, "Our architect modeled the compound on a classic Spanish mission."

Rick said, "Looks more like your classic state prison to me."

Alexandra ignored the prison remark. "That door leads to a world-class exercise facility and the sauna and hot tub."

"Did you hear that?" Claudia said. "They have a hot tub."

As they reached the picnic table, Alexandra said, "And here are some of your fellow guests. Gentlemen, I'd like you to meet Guy, Claudia, and Rick."

Nicolas touched his ascot. Ray John seethed. Henry played it neutral. Everyone waited for further introductions until they realized Alexandra had forgotten the names of the men at the picnic table. She made a sound that could pass for an apology, knowing they knew, and plowed on. "I'll let you in on a little secret, Guy. There are four-point-five girls here for each boy. These fellows are more popular and in demand than they've ever been before."

Claudia took off her glasses and cleaned them with a special tissue made just for that purpose. She said, "Lily died seven months ago and Guy is stuck in stage three of the grief process. He's not interested in girls."

Henry tried to recall stage three. Bargaining. Or maybe denial.

"Lily was the only woman he ever loved," Claudia said. "He's devastated."

Ray John looked at Guy. "Is this your daughter-in-law?"

Guy spoke for the first time since they entered the gate. "Daughter."

Ray John said, "Tell her to go fuck herself."

Claudia gasped. Rick pretended he hadn't heard. Nicolas and Henry tried not to smile.

Alexandra said, "This is going in your file, Buster."

Guy shrugged and said nothing.

Three

Dear Roderick,

I'm in the library, typing on this antique Dell computer they have in here. It's quiet this time of morning with everyone outside taking advantage of the lack of fog. They just brought a new patient through on the tour. That idiot Alexandra Truman of the big hair and little brain fawned him and his family into and out of the room. Miss Iron Crotch doesn't waste time on the library. She'd rather get the new meat onto the quad, where she can show off her tree and whoever is out there doing activities. Alexandra loves showing activities. Makes her feel more like she's running an exclusive spa than a holding tank. She wouldn't dare take new people over to N.C. N.C. is nothing but a greenhouse for breathing corpses.

I only caught a glimpse, but the new

patient is tall and has most of his hair. Sexy little sideburns. His eyes weren't quite focused but I imagine that's because they've got him on anti-anxiety meds that don't mix well with blood pressure or reflux pills or whatever else the poor man takes, not to mention they've stolen his life away from him, which does strange things to people's focus. Most of the ones who were alert before their families hijacked them come out of it in a couple of weeks. A few give up and slide slowly into the moat. This guy didn't strike me as a man who has given up. But that may be wishful thinking.

My only prayer is that this one isn't another Haight survivor. What we don't need around here is one more chow hound changing his name back to Wolf or Cowboy and talking about The Boss Man all day. Trying to grow a ponytail. Telling any woman who won't sleep with him she has hang-ups. It's amazing how their brains stay fairly intact while their language regresses fifty years. If one more turkey neck tells me to "Keep on truckin' " I'm going to spew all over the Happy Face bastard.

Not that my neck doesn't belong on

poultry. And the skin under my arms — why, Roderick, it just hangs there like wet crepe paper. Let me tell you, there is absolutely nothing noble about growing old. You think when you're a twenty-five-year-old chick, dancing barefoot in a tapestry, wraparound skirt and silver dangling earrings, that old age will be about the same as now, only without the passions and sexual politics and the pressure of maintaining your looks, but it isn't. The motivational blockheads don't tell you about bursitis in your wrist keeping you awake all night. And the passions are just as awful as ever — worse, since there is so little hope of change for the better. I know women whose day at the beauty parlor is the only thing they have to look forward to. Pathetic.

Okay, I'm not basking in the carpe diem. God knows, I try to bask, but, hellfire, Roderick, you can't fake joy. There's a poster in Administration telling us we will live longer if we are perky, positive, and punctual, but, from my observation, the crabby hang on years after the meek inherit the Great Whatever. Maybe you just notice the complainers more.

I'd better go. Willow Kubliak is edging around the diet and nutrition shelf, waiting for me to get off the computer. Willow and I are about the only ones here without our own computers. I don't know why she always wants to use the library e-mail when I'm on it. I told one of the candy stripers that I'd never owned a computer and she looked at me like I'm an alien mutant. She said, "How is that possible?" I should go on TV. Or make a sign that says NEVER OWNED A COMPUTER and hang it around my neck and go spare change in Ghirardelli Square. I'd make a fortune.

Anyway, I must sign off, my darling Roderick. Take care and do what the doctors say. I'm sure they're fools, but they mean well enough. Don't forget to chew your food fifty times before you swallow and always brush your teeth and don't forget your mother.

All my love,
Mama

Four

Guy Fontaine sat on the end of his new twin bed, feet pressed to the floor, hands on his thighs. His right hand held a remote control aimed at the plasma TV he brought from the cottage behind his daughter's house in Foster City. There was a bedside table and a built-in chest of drawers. A small bookshelf. A microwave oven stacked on a matching mini-fridge with a doll-sized ice tray in a doll-sized freezing compartment. The walls were key-lime-pie green, and the ceiling continued the motif in a meringue white tinged in brown. A cheap clock/podcast receiver sat on the bedside table beside a framed photo of Lily as she looked at thirty, soon after Claudia was born. Before Martin. Over the bed, a painting left by the last resident showed a unicorn standing on the shore of a lake, being tended to by three naked women with strategically placed hair.

Arthritic moans seeped through the walls, and bedsprings squeaked. Coughing. Lots of coughing, and flushing. The building hummed with life, while Guy appeared frozen in time, wax-like, except for the thumb on his right hand, which, every two seconds, squeezed the Up button on his remote.

The station numbers ranged from 2 to 146 with gaps in the middle for premium channels Alexandra Truman had assured him he may receive if he paid an added fee. Even without premium, Guy had 120 choices for entertainment, not a one worth more than two seconds of his time.

The cycle, 2 to 146, took four minutes to complete, as long as Guy remained constant. Four minutes to see all there was to see, then he started over. It occurred to Guy that the rest of his life would be played out in four-minute cycles. Guy found comfort in the idea. All that was required of him was to make it through four minutes at a time, a certain number of times, before he would be clear of the whole mess.

Even though he told himself it no longer mattered one way or the other, Guy couldn't help but wonder how long that would be. He was a healthy man of seventy-two. At least, he thought he was until Claudia dragged him to the weasel-faced geriatrician in Palo Alto. His Oklahoma M.D. had poked a stiff index finger into Guy's scapula, grinned, and predicted Guy might live to ninety, with a minimum of luck. Dr. Symmes in Palo Alto said Guy was depressed, probably multi-infarct, and no longer competent to care for himself or his finances. Dr. Symmes looked at Claudia and Rick as he said this. The only words he spoke to Guy were, "How are we feeling today, Mr. Fontaine?" The doctor didn't wait for an answer, which is probably for the best since Guy had a tendency to flash anger whenever a bonehead used first person plural as ingratiation.

One thing Guy knew without doubt, Lily would have hated this bedspread. Violet swirls behind a pattern of blood-red roses and green, thornless stems. The moment Guy saw it on the Sam's Club shelf, he thought, *Lily will be appalled,* followed by *Claudia will choose it.* Claudia chose everything that went into Guy's room at Mission Pescadero. When he drove the golf cart down the Harbor Freeway he lost his right to make decisions. In Sam's Club she held the bedspread toward him like a waiter presenting wine. Claudia spoke loudly on account of she believed Guy was hard of hearing.

"What do you think, Dad? When you lose bladder control, stains won't show too much, you think?"

Flip, the cycle started back on channel two. Two was San Mateo Chamber of Commerce, three came from somewhere within the bowels of Mission Pescadero. It announced club meetings — chess, bird — activities — concerts, visiting Brownie troops — and menus — breakfast, lunch, and dinner. Birthdays. Guy had been told they televised the Christmas skit so shut-ins over in Nursing Care didn't have to miss anything important. Thirty-eight was Weather, forty, Food, 116, Rodeo. If Guy ever hesitated in the two-second interval routine, it would be on those three channels. The satellite dish came with twelve all-sports networks, including poker, European off-center sports like soccer, rugby, and cricket, NASCAR, and one called Classic, which showed games where everyone already knew the winner.

Ten years ago, Guy watched any football, basketball, or baseball game, no matter who played. If nothing was on ESPNs 1 through 6, he turned the sound to mute and watched X-games. Sports was his career — writing about them for a small daily in southern

Oklahoma. He had a title — sports editor — and his own desk. Free tickets to any event within two hundred miles, which took in the university in Norman, and the Dallas Cowboys. He expressed life through sports metaphors.

But somewhere along the line, Guy lost his passion. He realized the athletes were children with nothing to offer him. Arrogance had become a virtue. When did that happen? First, he stopped watching contests in which he had no emotional stake in the winner. Then, a lifetime of caring deeply came slamming to a halt last New Year's Day, in the hospital, sitting next to Lily as she took air in through rubber tubes while a machine tracked her heartbeat. The linebacker on the team Guy loved above all others started taunting the opposing boys. The taunting was not friendly competition but mean-spirited, nasty words picked up by the network microphones and broadcast to millions of viewers.

Guy said, "I cannot admire that child, no matter what team he plays for."

Lily blinked, her eyes on the ceiling.

"I don't care if he wins or loses," Guy said, and he turned off the television.

Lily's voice was a whisper. "You could have done that forty years ago." Her hand moved a quarter of an inch — much like Guy's hand on the TV remote ten months later — and she pushed a button, releasing morphine into her system. Guy watched her eyes soften.

He missed her.

Five

Guy Fontaine fell asleep at dawn and missed breakfast. So, at noon, when he crossed the quad to lunch, he was walking into the dining hall for the first time. Second time, if you count the tour with Claudia and Rick in which Alexandra stressed the prestige of table service. The dining hall was nearly empty then, just a couple of English-as-a-second-language busboys filling shakers with sea salt. A Hispanic woman, who was old enough to be a resident but wasn't, knelt on her knees, scrubbing the floor beside one of the back tables. She nodded at Guy and Guy nodded back.

Alexandra glared at the woman on her knees, or maybe she was glaring at the spot on the floor. Guy could tell something in the setup ticked off Alexandra, although she kept the displeasure out of her voice as she delivered her spiel. "Most assisted living centers serve cafeteria style, with rotating numbers on the tables so no one eats first two days in a row. We were the first establishment of our kind on the Coastside to institute table service at all three meals."

Guy's daughter, Claudia, said, "That is so wonderful."

The old Hispanic woman grasped a dining chair and pulled herself to her feet. Alexandra stalked over to inspect the work. She said, "Inez," and pointed to the chair itself. "Can't you see that stain?"

Inez said something in Spanish.

"Are you people blind or what?" Alexandra said.

Inez dropped back to her knees and sprayed 409 on the chair.

Alexandra stalked back to Guy and his family. "I don't know which is worse," she said, "old men who pee themselves and sit in it for hours or Mexicans who can't clean it up." She leaned toward Claudia, confiding. "Normally, I'm not prejudiced, but it must be something ethnic. White women can smell rancid urine. Why can't Hispanics?"

Now, the next day, Guy Fontaine walks into a crowd where everyone knows the ropes and each other and no one knows him. High school hell, all over again.

There are twelve tables, six six-tops lined on either side of a center aisle with a small stage down at the end, for entertainment. Kitchen bat-eye doors to the left, drink station featuring Peete's coffee to the right. The walls have been painted a poached catfish color. There are photographs of peninsula naturescapes framed in metallic silver — beaches, rocks, giant redwoods. Guy thanks whatever God he believes in the motivational poster motif that saturates Administration hasn't been extended to the dining hall. In his old age, he's come to hate cute ways of saying BUCK UP. A life can't be put back together by eight words or less.

Most of the chairs seem reserved in some system Guy can't catch on to. He approaches a table occupied by three women in flowing skirts and longer hair than you generally find on older women, and an incredibly thin man with snow-white hair down to his butt, bicycle shorts, and a basketball jersey. A rubber-tipped cane made from some twisted hardwood leans against the table. The man nods acknowledgment, not quite welcome.

Guy touches an empty chair and one of the women screeches, "Sunshine sits there!"

Guy apologizes.

The long-haired man says, "Sorry, mate."

Guy moves to the table across the aisle where the man who told him to tell Claudia to fuck herself tips the only open chair up to show that it is taken.

Guy stops to look around. Everyone seems to know what is expected of them. No one seems to care whether he is there or not. Then he sees one of the other men from the picnic table signaling him to come over.

"This is Wanda Bretschneider, and Ike and Marta Pitcairne." The man who waved Guy over introduces a stocky woman brooding over her thumbs on her coffee cup and a tiny couple holding hands and huddling together, smiling. Guy has seen couples like them in southeast Oklahoma. They want almost desperately to befriend outsiders but they've been with one another so long they've lost the knack.

"I'm Nicolas Lessac."

"Guy Fontaine." The two men shake hands, awkwardly, neither a natural hand pumper. Nicolas's hand is a bit soft for Guy's small-town background, and he's never really trusted men whose glasses hang off little gold chains.

Nicolas nods to an open chair in front of a napkin in a napkin ring, a water glass, stainless steel silverware, and two canned peach slices swimming in a monkey dish. "This seat's vacant. Judith Frost passed through the tunnel last week and no one has taken her space."

Guy sits down. He pours himself water from the community carafe and drinks half a glass in one pull. "Is *passed through the tunnel* Californian for *died?*"

Nicolas more or less chuckles. "They took her to Nursing Care. There's a maintenance tunnel between the buildings, from A.L. to N.C."

"A.L.?"

"Assisted Living. People who can no longer make it here are taken over through the tunnel. Alexandra thinks it would traumatize the residents, seeing our cohorts wheeled across the quad."

Ike and Marta smile big and nod, then retreat into themselves, afraid they have come on too strong. Without moving a muscle, Wanda gives off an air of effrontery. Guy thinks about it and sees that by taking Judith's seat, he has offended Wanda. They must have been friends.

"Yesterday, the woman told me to sit anywhere. I didn't realize the chairs are assigned."

"They're not, but I pity the person who

lands at the wrong table." Nicolas leans toward Guy as he speaks. Guy sees this as a man about to give him the lowdown.

"The tables are based on where you were in 1967," Nicolas says.

"Waurika, Oklahoma," Guy says.

"That table where they tipped the chair up on you is the Berkeley radicals. You met Ray John yesterday. He acts pissy, but, at heart, he's a pussy-cat. Next to him is a loosely grouped bunch from San Francisco. Mission District, mostly, some south of the slot. Then there's Sausalito, a lot of Sausalito party girls ended up here. The table with all the walkers and wheelchairs is North Beach."

"Who decided all this?" Guy asks.

"It evolved over the years. The table with the fellow who calls everyone *mate* is Haight-Ashbury before the summer of love. Next to them are the Haight newcomers, which means summer of love or after."

"That would be 1967."

"You're catching on fast. The confusion comes because after Reagan sent the National Guard into Berkeley in '69 a lot of radicals lost their idealism and drifted across the Bay to join the peace, love, dope, and sex movement. They qualify for either table, but those tables hate each other. It makes for hard feelings."

Guy watches as Ray John raves at the women at his table. Ray John seems irate, his face flushed, his hands waving like panicked birds. Guy does not come from a tradition of hands moving during speech. Based on movies, he sees it as an ethnic, urban form of communication.

Nicolas cocks his head to one side, in a thoughtful pose. "I guess all the tables hate each other, if you want to be technical, but Berkeley and new Haight hate each other more than what we would call the norm."

"Why is their hair so strange?"

Nicolas repeats the soft chuckle — more an ironic throat clearing than a chuckle. He developed it at Hewlett-Packard as a defense against bureaucracy. "The men are trying to grow it back out, like it was before they joined the establishment."

"What?"

"Before they got jobs. Mortgages. Insurance. But hair only grows so long, when you're older, and then it stops and the ends split."

Marta says, "It turns frizzy." Ike nods. His head is bald as a trailer hitch.

"The New York table is over by the kitchen," Nicolas says, "although they've passed into something of an East Coast table the last year. They still feel vastly superior to Californians, and the Northern Californians feel vastly superior to Southern Californians. Then there's neighborhoods in L.A. that lord it over other neighborhoods in L.A. Everybody is better than somebody."

"I suppose Texas would be at the bottom," Guy says.

Nicolas repeats his chuckle. "The neatly groomed bunch are your midwesterners who accidentally got old on the coast here. I imagine that's where you would have ended up, left to your own."

"Did you attend an institution of higher learning?" Marta asks.

"Eastern State. It's in Wilburton."

"Oklahoma?"

Guy doesn't answer. How many Wilburtons can there be? Instead, he studies the midwesterners for something in common with himself. On the whole, they're heftier than the east or west coasters, and they are dressed neatly, but it's a Wal-Mart neatness compared to the others' studied casualness. The midwesterners seem more aware of the dangers of letting yourself go.

Nicolas says, "That table over by the drinks bar doesn't eat meat. There's a fruitarian, a vegan, an ovo, a lacto, an ovo-lacto, and a macro-biotic pescarian, who even I don't count as a real vegetarian. Every woman there thinks the other five are immoral food harlots."

"What table is this one?" Guy asks.

"Stanford graduates," Nicolas says. "At least, it used to be. We've been whittled down by an even more upscale continuing-care home that opened in Woodside."

"Valet wheelchair parking in the rec room," Ike says.

"We don't know that for sure," Marta says.

Nicolas goes on. "Wanda here went to Caltech, in Pasadena."

Wanda does nothing to confirm or deny the fact.

Guy studies two tables at the very back, each occupied by two women. "What about them?"

"The two on the right had husbands in Vietnam. Frances's husband went MIA and Georgia's died years later of Agent Orange syndrome or something Georgia blames on the war. They both think the rest of us are villains and cowards. Whatever you do, don't get them started."

Wanda speaks. She's been so silent till then that Guy is surprised she can make sounds. "You weren't in Vietnam, were you?"

Guy says, "No, I wasn't," but he doesn't

explain why. Most men in the Mission would explain why, when asked that question.

"You look like you were in Vietnam," Wanda says.

"I wasn't."

There follows an uncomfortable silence. It's as if Wanda has accused Guy of something, but he's not sure what. Looking like a person she doesn't like? That doesn't make sense.

Hispanics stream from the kitchen carrying lunch plates with silver lids stacked on trays held up in their left-hand palms. The right hand carries a tray stand. Each tray has six plates, lunch for one table, even though not all the tables have six people.

Guy studies the other table of two women. One is older, eighties at least, in a wheelchair. She wears an obvious wig, the color of rusted iron. The other is Asian, small, crew cut, and wound tight as a golf ball string.

"What about those two?" he asks.

"That used to be the gay and lesbian table before a couple homes exclusively for retired gays opened in San Francisco. Most of them moved up there and the ones who stayed couldn't stand sitting with Phaedra and Suchada, so they left for location tables."

As Guy watches, the small woman leans across and holds a handkerchief to the wheelchair woman's nose. It doesn't take a lip-reader to tell the younger one is saying "Blow," and the older one is blowing.

Marta says, "Phaedra should have gone through the tunnel long ago." Marta squinches down, even smaller, afraid what she said may offend someone.

Nicolas draws his napkin from its napkin holder and wipes his silverware. "Suchada would strangle Alexandra if she tried sending Phaedra across. It's easier to wait for the old bra-burner to die."

"Maybe after they're gone, I'll move over and start an Oklahoma table," Guy says.

"But then you'd be alone," Marta says.

Guy forks a peach slice and slides it across his tongue. It's been on the table so long it's not cold anymore. Maybe it never was. Guy thinks but doesn't say, "That's the point."

Six

Lunch is broiled fish with slaw of some purple tint and the rice-pasta concoction an advertising agency once called "the San Francisco Treat." Unsweetened iced tea and a hard roll. Apple crisp for dessert. Suchada cuts Phaedra's fish into bite-sized morsels.

She says, "There's a new one over with Nicolas Lessac. He's watching us."

Phaedra, whose diabetes-induced glaucoma keeps her locked in a world of fog and shadows, glares in the direction where she thinks Nicolas might be. "Is he gay?"

Suchada looks Guy over again — tall, gray hair, pressed slacks and a clean button-down shirt. He forks slaw and sniffs it, as if trying to decipher the secret ingredient. "He's a flaming heterosexual."

Phaedra holds her iced tea with both hands while Suchada strips a straw for her. "What's Nicolas doing?"

"Wiping silverware with his napkin. Probably telling the new one what bitches we are."

"Nicolas Lessac is seventy-five and doesn't know he's a fag. I find that obscene."

Suchada pokes her fork through Phaedra's fish. It seems to be cod, or whitefish. Maybe an ocean perch.

Phaedra stabs at Suchada's hand with her fork, missing badly. "Don't touch my food. How many times have I told you not to touch my food?"

"We wouldn't want you to choke," Suchada says.

"Next thing, you'll be chewing it for me. I'm not a baby."

Suchada doesn't rise to that one. "You want ketchup?"

Phaedra's voice is a buzz saw. "On my fish?"

"The last time we had broiled fish, you had me put ketchup on it."

"Stupid!" Phaedra splutters, struggling to find words strong enough to express her outrage. "That is a blatant lie. You make these ridiculous statements and think I won't know better because, in your mind, I have no memory. I do have memory and I have never put ketchup on fish in my life."

Suchada doesn't challenge Phaedra, but Phaedra knows Suchada thinks she is right and is only staying silent to keep the peace. Phaedra shifts her weight from side to side in her wheelchair. Her head dips, then jerks forward. Her hands quiver.

"I cannot believe you think I ever put ketchup on fish."

"I only based my question on what you asked for last time."

"Don't condescend to me, young lady."

"I am not condescending."

"I made you."

Suchada braces herself. How many times has she heard the speech she knows is on the way?

"You were a child when I picked you off the street. You were nothing. You don't have an opinion I didn't give you. Not a thought."

"Nobody is disagreeing with you, Phaedra."

"I was famous, and I did you the favor of creating your personality, and now you treat me like a burden."

"That's not true."

"I was the keynote speaker at the Third Congress of Women. I delivered a blistering rebuttal to John Irving's contention that the women's movement needed male support."

"It was a brilliant speech."

"I hate male feminists. Male feminists are worse than pigs," Phaedra says. "I took that bastard down a few pegs."

"You were my hero, Phaedra."

"Were?"

"Are."

"That's a lie. To you, I am nothing but a burden."

"Hero."

"Burden."

"Hero."

The sad thing about Phaedra's rant is that it's true. Forty-three years ago, when Suchada was a teenager named Betty, Phaedra swept into her life like a tsunami. Tall, graceful as a dancer, eyes on fire — hell, her entire body was on fire. Phaedra was an original. She was everything Suchada's mother-the-housewife wasn't. Suchada owes the shape of her existence to Phaedra. The question is, how long is she supposed to pay?

Phaedra forks a chunk of fish and tosses it into her open gullet. She swallows without chewing and says, "Burden."

Seven

Henry shuffles in late and almost misses lunch. He stands at the door, trying to take his pulse in such a way that no one will notice. Blinks. Switches from his outdoor to indoor glasses, looking like a boy caught in an old man's body, trying to decide whether to enter a swimming pool or not. Jesus the waiter catches Henry's attention and drops a plate off at his usual seat at the early Haight table. Henry nods his thanks.

He cuts between Sausalito and North Beach, where people are already eating. Men nod hellos; women don't. Henry picks up a carton of whole milk and a cup of coffee, then wanders to his place at the table. He sits between two women, both calling themselves Sunshine. Winston, the table patriarch who is not only the oldest but also the only one who didn't sell out and go establishment during the middle years, refers to them as Sunshine #1 and Sunshine #2.

Sunshine #1 is in the middle of a story about a man whose apartment was so filthy, rats came and went like roommates.

"He gave the rats names," she says. "It was on Geary, down near the Fillmore." She means the original Fillmore and not Fillmore West. Everyone at her table takes this for granted, while one table over, the late Haight table, someone would have asked which. "Scuz was living with Lactose Larry for a while but Larry got so he couldn't stand the mold on everything. He rented a bed by the hour from two hookers with strange names," by which she means they were black. "They had a hotel room on Sutter."

Lucinda, who spent the middle years of her life teaching poetry and creative writing at Pomona State, says, "Trippy."

Winston nods Henry a greeting. "G'day, mate." Winston is the one with butt-length white hair and a basketball jersey. While the others had been having careers, Winston worked as a bicycle mechanic in the summer and a chimney sweep in the winter. He is famous for having been to 1,536 Dead concerts. Since Winston is now in a room full of retired professionals who, for the most part, wanted to be like him, he views Mission Pescadero with a certain sense of superiority.

"Scuz heard if you eat nothing but brown rice for six months you get a natural high," Sunshine #1 says.

"I tried the brown rice diet and what you get is malnutrition that makes you feel like you're stoned," Willow says. Willow weighs 180 pounds. She started her career in orgone therapy, then Jin Shin Do massage, and finally biofeedback. After her client list dried up she sat on her couch, watching daytime television, smoking medicinal pot, and eating until her kids committed her to the Mission.

Sunshine #2 says, "The new man tried to steal Sunshine's seat, but I stopped him."

Henry knows what he is supposed to say, so he says it. "Wow."

Sunshine #1 says, "Scuz found a box of Styrofoam trays in a Dumpster, and he ate his rice out of those so he wouldn't have to do dishes, but he left them lying around all over the place and rats invaded."

Willow says, "Scuz gave me crabs once."

Lucinda says, "Heavy."

Henry fork-cuts his fish into six pieces as a Chinese gentleman named Hu wheels his wheelchair over from North Beach and talks quietly to Winston. Henry, only two seats away, can't hear the words. Hu passes folded bills to Winston, who passes a Sucrets tin back to Hu. An observer at the late Haight table would not have noticed.

Willow says, "He dosed me with acid."

"Who?" Henry asks. Hu's head jerks, as if he's been caught out.

"Scuz," Willow says. "The little prick dosed me and gave me the crabs. I was so P.O.ed I stole his Moby Grape album. It was a bad trip, all the way around."

Sunshine #1 nudges her apple crisp over to Willow. "Dosing people with acid totally messes up a person's karma."

Winston picks up his cane and taps it on Hu's tires. Besides dealing drugs, he is also resident wheelchair mechanic. "There's times it's the only thing to do. When the person you're dosing needs their doors kicked open."

Henry folds his fish pieces into his napkin and tucks the napkin into the side pocket of his sweater. He says, "I disagree strongly. Acid is too intense for some people and you shouldn't trick them into taking it."

Winston pulls a spoke wrench from his cutoffs pocket. "It's people who can't take it who need it most."

"Stealing the Moby Grape album is where

you went wrong, karmatically," Lucinda says. "You'd have done better by cutting off Scuz's dick."

Henry checks his pulse, this time on his wrist. "Cutting off dicks doesn't hurt karma?"

Sunshine #1 giggles. She'd been a famous model in her late teens. She was part of the Twiggy look, which lasted about six months. During those six months so many people told Sunshine #1 she was beautiful that she developed the self-image of a hot chick, and never lost it. After the modeling career went south, Sunshine #1 married a mall developer and spent the middle years shopping. Sunshine #2 never got over the unfairness of it all.

Sunshine #1 says, "Cutting off dicks never hurt any girl's karma."

Henry knows better than to ask who Scuz and Lactose Larry are. It doesn't matter. And it doesn't matter whether Sunshine #1's story took place last week or fifty years ago, although Henry is sure it didn't happen between those two time periods. Nothing that happened in between matters enough to talk about now.

Sunshine #1 says, "Last I heard, Scuz moved to Boulder and joined the Rainbow family."

Lucinda says, “I was with the Rainbows for a while, but my feet were too tender to go barefoot in the Colorado winter, so I hitched to Humboldt and got my master’s instead.”

Henry pockets his carton of milk and pushes away from the table. “Time for me to move out.”

Winston braces himself on his cane as he leans down toward Hu’s wheel. “You’re not leaving us?”

“I have some reading to do.”

Sunshine #2, who was a schoolteacher in the middle years, wrinkles her nose at the word *reading.* Her dream is to live the rest of her life without reading anything longer than a shampoo bottle.

“There’s an African drum ceremony after lunch,” she says to Henry. “Kids from Pacifica High School. It should be a trip.” She reaches across and brushes dandruff from Henry’s shoulders. “We could dance.”

He stands to go. “I think I’ll pass. I’ve never much enjoyed white kids playing African drums. Too much like vacation Bible school.”

“Well, then.” Sunshine #2 smiles. “Onward through the fog.”

Henry says, “Onward.”

“Lactose Larry died in 1980,” Willow says.

"Aneurysm."

Lucinda says, "Bummer."

Henry stands under the dining hall fake adobe archway to switch back to his sunglasses. He walks across the quad, making a slight detour to knock on the eucalyptus trunk. Henry has been a wood knocker for as long as he can remember, and live trees hark back to the original intent of wood-knocking, which was to awaken sprites. Henry knocks wood with the reverence others cross themselves.

He enters Residential and turns from the elevator to the stairs. His room is on the third, top, floor. There are two elevators and a generator in case an earthquake or power shortage cuts the electricity, but Henry takes the stairs for exercise.

Henry has a theory that it doesn't matter so very much how long you live. Nothing short of immortality matters in the long run anyway, and Henry doesn't buy into immortality faith systems. For him, what matters is the quality for the last ten years before you disappear. Long-term sickness, sadness — his particular problem — or poverty is to be avoided, if possible; therefore, walking the stairs is better than riding the elevator. He shares this theory much too often, so that while many of his friends and co-residents agree with him, they wish he would include tedium in the sickness, sadness, and poverty category.

Henry enters his room at the end of the hallway. The walls are decorated with Hendrix and Firesign Theatre album art. His bed is covered by a sleeping bag instead of sheets and the bedside table lamp has an ultraviolet lightbulb, by which he's been hand-copying *On the Road* into a Big Chief tablet. He empties his jacket pockets of fish and milk onto the turntable top of his RCA Victor record player.

"Mr. Scratchy, I brought lunch."

Henry reaches into his billfold for a tiny key that originally came with a Barbie diary. He unlocks an illegal lock on the closet door. Locks are not allowed at Mission Pescadero. Each room comes with a safe the size of a *Webster's Collegiate Dictionary,* and according to Alexandra, that's all the privacy anyone needs. Even then, she has a master code she claims to use only when the resident dies.

Henry pops the little lock and slides the closet door open six inches. A cat — yellow, bald patches, three legs and a stump — hops out of the closet, mewing softly.

"Fish today," Henry says as the cat slaloms

in and out between his ankles. “They had apple crisp, too, but you wouldn’t have enjoyed it.”

Henry arranges a napkin on the floor and the pieces of fish on the napkin. As Mr. Scratchy lunges for the fish, Henry opens the milk carton. He reaches into the closet for the bowl in his dirty-clothes hamper and pours in half the milk. A litter box is hidden behind book boxes on the far end of the closet. The litter Henry disposes of on the quad grounds, a little each day, like Stalag 13 prisoners getting rid of tunnel dirt.

Mr. Scratchy is highly illegal. Banishment illegal. A resident caught with ecstasy or guns is put on probation and his family notified. A resident caught with a pet is subject to instant eviction.

Mr. Scratchy attacks the fish. Henry sits on the end of the bed and drinks the other half of the milk. He says, “My mother used to make an apple crisp you would have wept for, it was so tasty. Warmed up and topped with heavy cream, my God, it was wonderful.”

Henry kicks his loafers off, crosses his right ankle over his left knee, and leans on his left hand. “I wish you could have known my mother.”

Eight

Rocky Gingrass is at the library computer, doing what she does after lunch.

My Very Dear Roderick,

I saw your father yesterday. Gap Koch was stoned on whatever they feed those people in N.C. He'd peed his pants. Couldn't hold his head up. When he saw me he said, "Hey, sweet thang, you're cute as a button." In other words, he was exactly in the same shape as he was the day I met him. It was as if fifty-two years of being a corporate lawyer and throwing power around like donuts in a food fight never happened.

Gap didn't recognize me, of course. That's not because he's demented and doped out of his head. He hasn't recognized me since the day you were born.

Here's something odd, Roderick. I don't know if it was his urine-soaked pants, or maybe his breath, or maybe the fall air coming off the coast, but something — I'm sure it was a smell — yanked me right back to that drive out here from Alabama the September after our high school graduation. I remembered details I thought were lost. More than details, the feeling came back. I felt so intensely like I did at eighteen and on the road that tears puddled my eyes. Driving across Kansas with my feet out the open window, running out of gas in God-squat, Wyoming. In Utah I bought brown spray paint and painted dust clouds over the back wheels of Gap's VW bus. Nothing garish or psychedelic like hippie vans. We were subtle.

We had six hundred dollars saved up from summer jobs hidden in the roof lining above the driver's seat. It felt like a fortune. Gap wanted to join a commune because he'd heard the girls ran around naked in California communes. That was as far as his fantasy life went. I wanted to live in San Francisco where I could go barefoot while wearing a flowing white dress and real flowers in my hair. It's almost impossible now to believe how naive children were back then. I dare say there's not an eighteen-year-old alive today who thinks people in general are beautiful, much less that we are on the verge of the Age of Aquarius.

Gap and I landed in Oakland, not knowing the difference, and we went to this place that was like a clearinghouse for kids on the street. They gave us an address where they said we could crash down by Golden Gate Park in San Francisco, only when we found the place these black kids on the front steps wouldn't let us go into the building. They told us to get lost. So we slept in the van that night, in a Longs Drug parking lot, and the back of the bus smelled like Gap did yesterday. Two weeks of sex in a sleeping bag smells like an old man pissing himself.

Guy wanders in the open doorway, looking out of his element, like a man who's never been in a train station finding himself in one. He knows the basic pieces of what he is supposed to do, but not how they fit. Rocky glances up at him, takes in the pressed, tucked-in look that says Guy is not from California and has never asked anyone for spare change.

She says, "You need a hand?"

"No, thanks."

Guy circles the room, clockwise, studying the books and art. He stops in front of a print of Monet's bridge in the park. He runs his hand across his forehead, pushing up hair that doesn't need pushing up, an old habit from years of wearing a cap.

Guy says, "You were here yesterday."

Rocky is surprised he remembers. He appeared poleaxed yesterday, and poleaxed people rarely recall faces. "I'm here every day, after lunch."

"Why?"

"I don't see that as your business."

Guy nods, as if she has made a valid point. He drifts from the painting to the next bookshelf. An entire set of the Foxfire series, all sixteen volumes. A few duplicates or even triplicates. The books seem to be about self-reliance and mulching.

Rocky feels like she should make up for her rudeness. "Are you looking for a book?"

"A medical book."

"Any special medical book?"

Guy works his way down the shelf, past the collected works of Richard Brautigan, including *The Abortion* in hardback, and Baba Ram Dass. "I'm not sure."

Rocky stops typing, mid-word. "When people die or go through the tunnel, their books often end up here. That's not the wall for medical books, unless you think *Be Here Now* is about health. You don't look like the sort who does."

Guy walks to the next wall.

Rocky says, "I'm writing my son an e-mail."

Guy knows she didn't have to tell him and appreciates that she did. "Will he write back?"

"Roderick is in a place. A home, kind of like this, only not really," Rocky says, as if that answers Guy's question.

"Lily used to write our daughter every Friday night, but Claudia didn't write back. She called on Mother's Day."

"Claudia's the woman you were with yesterday?"

Guy nods again. "We have a son in New York. Martin. He doesn't write or call."

Rocky hits Save, gets up, and goes to the bookshelf to the right of the windows. Guy trails after her. Rocky holds out her hand.

"Roxanne Gingrass, but everyone here calls me Rocky, so you might as well call me Rocky, too."

They shake. To Guy, Rocky's hand feels like an old bomber jacket that's been worn for decades. To Rocky, Guy's hand is smooth bark, say an aspen. His fingernails are clean but cut by clippers instead of scissors. The back of Guy's hand is a topographical map of blue veins.

"Guy Fontaine," he says.

"Is that your real name?"

"Guymon."

"Are you trying to self-diagnose?"

"This doctor in Palo Alto made some tests, but he wouldn't tell me the results."

"They never do, not for older people." Rocky pulls a book from the shelf. "This might be what you're looking for."

She hands Guy the AMA *Guide to Your Family's Symptoms.* He opens it and finds boxes of type and arrows with Yes or No written in them. The page he opens up to is headed "Abnormal-Looking Bowel Movements."

"What kind of person looks at his own bowel movements?"

"Almost everyone over seventy can give you twenty minutes on yesterday's poop."

"Not where I'm from, they can't." Guy pages through the book. "Dizziness." "Numbness or Tingling." "Constipation." None of the headings apply to him. "I don't know where to start."

Rocky tips her head to look up at Guy, who is a foot taller than she is. "If you don't mind me knowing your symptoms, I can help. Some men mind and some will tell you more than anyone would want to know."

"I thought I was somewhere I wasn't."

"You blacked out?"

"I thought I was driving a Bel Air south on a section road in Cotton County, Oklahoma, but in reality I was in a golf cart on the freeway up by San Bruno."

"Oh, my."

"That's what I thought when the highway patrolman walked up."

"How long did you think you were someplace else?"

Guy tries to remember. "Ten minutes, maybe. Or fifteen. Time does odd things when you're hallucinating."

"Do you hallucinate often?"

"Never before or since."

Rocky takes the book from Guy and flips to the index. "Let's see." She studies the topics list while Guy looks down at her forehead and hairline. She has bangs, of a sort. Kind of a whorl that starts at the peak of her head and swirls like a satellite view of a hurricane. He wonders if he smells badly. He hasn't wondered about that since Lily went into the hospital the last time, and the idea that he cares comes as a warm surprise. Rocky is short, small-boned. Lily was farm-girl stocky, not fat or even overweight, although he has trouble seeing her in his mind now. Already, so soon after her death, when he calls up her face he sees a familiar photograph and not Lily herself.

"How about 'Forgetfulness and Confusion'?" Rocky asks.

"Forgetfulness, I suppose, if you mean forgetting where I was. I didn't feel confused until afterward."

"We begin where it says *Start here.* 'Has the confusion or forgetfulness developed suddenly during the past few hours?' "

Guy leans toward Rocky to look at her finger on the page. She smells like post oak leaves on the ground. "It was last month."

" 'Yes' would have meant a head injury. See here" — she points — "but 'No' leads us to 'Are you suffering from heart or lung disease, or diabetes?' "

"Not that I know of. I had a checkup in Oklahoma City, after Lily . . ." He drifts off but Rocky knows what he means. "Before I moved here to live behind my daughter's house, in the guest cottage." The word *cottage* feels pretentious on Guy's tongue. No one from home lives in *cottages.* It's a fairy-tale word. "Dr. Cummings said I didn't have any of those problems."

" 'Are you taking medication?' "

"I don't believe in taking pills."

"My God, Guy, you are either a liar or a freak."

He can't tell if she's serious, so he plays along. "My granddaughter thinks I'm a freak."

" 'Have you recently been drinking alcohol?' "

"I was playing golf."

"And?"

"I don't drink when I play golf. I hardly ever drink anyway, except maybe a Blue Ribbon back when I used to watch ball games."

"Let's move along then." Rocky's beginning to think Guy is a liar — an elderly man with no physical complaints who doesn't drink? Not likely. " 'Has anything traumatic happened lately?' "

"My wife passed. That was traumatic."

"How long ago?"

"Does the book ask that?"

"I'm asking that."

"May second. On a Monday morning. She had renal cell cancer that spread to her brain, then her heart filled up with water or something. They never told me exactly what she died from."

Guy looks so much like a lost Saint Bernard that Rocky wants to touch him, but she doesn't. She thinks he wouldn't get it.

"No wonder you're confused. You're supposed to be confused. It's normal."

"That's not what my daughter's doctor said."

"He said what your daughter wanted to hear." Rocky moves her finger to the far right side of the page, the boxes without exit arrows. "Here's what it comes down to, according to the book. You are either absent-minded, hysterical, or demented."

Guy shifts his weight back on his heels, away from the oak smell of Rocky's hair. "Which do you think it is?"

Rocky tilts her bifocals to focus on Guy's eyes. They are a rinsed blue, like the sky at the horizon over the Pacific. It's the first time she's had an excuse to make close eye contact in several years, and she's forgotten the side effects of eye contact. It isn't particularly pleasant.

"God, I don't know. What does demented look like?"

Nine

The elevator doors open with a *Bing!* Guy steps off and turns left. He is wondering whether the golf cart meltdown indicates absentmindedness or dementia. He's fairly certain he's not hysterical. Hysteria is a condition Guy connects to women, for vague hormonal reasons. If he were hysterical he couldn't analyze what he is so well. And if the incident was caused by dementia, do those things go away on their own? He's been as clear-thinking as ever, since the one lapse.

But he's never been absentminded in the past. Lily couldn't look a number up in the phone book, set the book aside, pick up the phone, and punch in the number. Between the setting aside of the book and the picking up of the phone, she inevitably forgot the number, so, in order to make a call, Lily had to prop open the book and place her fingertip under the number while she punched buttons. Guy used to tease her about it. He knew the phone numbers of almost everyone they knew.

So what was the golf cart deal about?

Guy counts three doors down the elevator side of the hallway, turns the doorknob, and walks in on Winston, both Sunshines, and Willow having sex.

The tableaux is stunning. Arms, feet, hair, all akimbo. Guy can't quite figure which body parts go to which bodies. They are so *old* — senior citizens should never be seen naked — and yet their postures are young. Orgies are beyond his frame of reference. He's never ever even seen a picture of one. He can't get over how parboiled their skin is. It hangs in places skin should not hang.

Winston lies flat on his back with his long, white hair fanned in a semi-halo across the pillow. He has skeleton tattoos on both arms, disappearing onto his chest, where Willow sits like a sunbathing seal. She has a horizontal flesh fold across her thigh Guy has never seen on a woman before. Sunshine #1's hands, arms, lower legs, and face are a cracked leather brown — the tennis tan — yet the rest of her body is newsprint white. Sunshine #2 has frizzy black hair and a Chinese character tattoo on the small of her back, which Guy catches a glimpse of before she pops up between Winston's legs. The three women seem to be cavorting on Winston, as if they see themselves as slim wood nymphs.

Willow sucks air and covers herself with her hands. The Sunshines look at Guy humorously, their eyes a challenge. Winston moves Willow's crotch so he can speak.

"G'day, mate."

"I thought this was my room," Guy says.

Sunshine #1 giggles. Her hair is straight and gray, streaked with white, parted in the middle. Her ribs are thin as bicycle spokes. She says, "Care to join us?"

Guy's face must show his horror because all three women burst into laughter.

Guy says, "No, thank you."

"There's pills on the bureau there," Winston says. "Take one and come back in a half hour."

"Maybe tomorrow." Guy backs out as quickly as possible without insulting the women.

Guy stands in the hallway, near hyperventilation. A Hispanic woman comes from the end-of-the-hall stairwell, carrying a vacuum cleaner. Guy recognizes her as the woman cleaning urine stains in the dining hall yesterday. He thinks, *What the hell was that?*

He'd known California would be different, but this is beyond the pale. The thing that amazes him almost as much as walking in on four naked senior citizens is walking into the wrong room. He'd been dazed when they took him to his room, yesterday, and hadn't paid attention coming out today, but still . . .

The Hispanic woman turns on the vacuum. As she pushes and pulls, she glances at Guy, then down at her machine. Now he has to go somewhere. It won't do to lurk around the hallway with her watching.

The door he barged through was 212, across from 213. Maybe his room is 213, the other side of the hall. That makes more sense than the other possibilities, such as turning left when he should have turned right. Guy doesn't want the cleaning woman to see him knocking on doors like he's lost, so he taps lightly on 213, hears nothing, and opens the door to find Ray John and Lucinda sitting on the bed, smoking a joint. They, too, are nude.

"Come in and close the door," Ray John orders.

Guy does as he is told. He knows the joint is marijuana, he isn't seventy-two and wet behind the ears, but it seems unlikely for a naked man and woman to be smoking in broad daylight.

Lucinda sits with her legs in a position that back when Guy was young was called crisscross applesauce. He supposes it has a yoga name now. She speaks in the contracted rush people speak in when they're holding their breath.

"Have-a-hit."

Guy doesn't answer. He's hypnotized by the St. Christopher medal dangling from her left breast nipple.

Lucinda says, "It's killer shit."

Guy says, "I'm allergic to killer shit."

Ray John holds the joint pinched between his thumb and index finger. "Then why the hell are you here?" He looks hostile. Guy gets the idea he's barged into an emotionally charged situation. At least, Ray John is charged. It's hard to tell about Lucinda. It feels to Guy that something more is going on than two naked people smoking dope.

"I'm looking for my room," Guy says.

"This isn't it," Ray John says.

"I knocked but no one answered."

"Ray John's deaf as a post," Lucinda says.

"I am not."

Lucinda plucks the joint from Ray John's fingers and sucks on it, hard.

Ray John says, "If you heard a knock, why

didn't you tell him to get lost."

"I wanted to see who was at the door."

"I have to leave now," Guy says.

Lucinda keeps her eyes on Guy as she hands the joint back to Ray John, who takes his own hit. Lucinda says, "I hope we'll see you at the sock hop."

"Sock hop?"

"Tonight, in the rec room. We all get trippy and dance. You look like you need some fun."

With a *whoosh,* Ray John releases a cloud of smoke.

Ten

This wasn't Guy's first experience at misplacing a room. Back in the 1980s, hotels went to entry key cards instead of real keys and stopped printing room numbers on them in case the guest got mugged. "For Security Purposes," the note that came with the key card said. Guy traveled often at that time, to sporting events, and twice he forgot his room number and had to go downstairs to the desk and ask the clerk what room was his. Both clerks were good-natured about it. They teased him — one a bit more than Guy thought necessary — but they understood how these things happen.

What Guy did not realize is that, in your thirties, a moment of forgetfulness is considered comic while that same faux pas, in your seventies, is taken as proof you've gone feeble. He explained his predicament to the secretary in Administration whose name he remembered from yesterday as Glenda. He even called her Glenda so she would know his memory was good. Glenda was an iridescent, deep black color as opposed to simply black the race, and she was reading a *Modern Mate* magazine. She marked her place with a manicured finger as Guy finished his story.

"You see, Glenda, I didn't pay attention yesterday and now I've forgotten my room number. Could you look it up for me?"

"I'll have to check with Miss Truman." Glenda reached for the intercom.

"Why?"

Glenda pushed a button. "Alexandra, will you come out here. We have a man —" She looked at Guy, having already forgotten his name.

"Guy Fontaine."

"Guy Fontaine. He seems disoriented."

She released the button before Guy could get out, "I am not disoriented. How can you say that?"

"Miss Truman will be with you in a minute."

"Surely you have my room number on file."

"I'm not allowed to give out personal information."

"Even if it's my own room?"

Glenda did not answer. She went back to

her magazine, as if he didn't exist. Guy fought off the urge to act up, maybe show her a soft-shoe shuffle. He could do a pretty mean "Me and My Shadow," which might get her attention, but would probably only confirm her disorientation claim. There's nothing more irritating than being dismissed as intangible.

Alexandra Truman came from the inner office in a jade-green blouse and black skirt. Basically the same outfit as yesterday only in a new color. Guy saw she had three piercings in her left ear, two in the top helix and one in the bottom. He hadn't been alert enough to notice them yesterday.

"Why, hello, Mr. Fontaine," she said, as if she had come upon him unexpectedly. "I trust we are settling in comfortably." Guy tried to recall where he had heard the combination of inflections. Or no inflections. The voice running down sentence instead of up.

"Fine, except I wasn't paying attention yesterday and I forgot my room number when I went to lunch just now."

Alexandra crossed her arms over her chest. Her eyes narrowed, clinically. "Are we experiencing dizziness?"

"I don't know about you, but I'm fine. I just forgot my room number."

"Do you know where you are?"

Where you are. All flat. No question at the end, and that was how Guy got it. Public television for children. Way back. Claudia loved Mr. Rogers like Santa Claus but Martin threw toy trucks at the screen whenever he said, "Welcome to the neighborhood," in that Alexandra lack of lilt.

Guy said, "The third ring of hell."

Glenda glanced at Alexandra, not getting the literary reference. Alexandra's upper lip twitched. "Sarcasm is a defense mechanism we do not appreciate, Mr. Fontaine. Tell us where you are and what month it is, or I shall be forced to call Dr. Beaver."

Guy wondered what the implied threat was. She said *forced to call Dr. Beaver* as if it were an unpleasant last resort. *I'll tell your father. March to the principal's office this minute, young man. The boss wants to see you.* What would happen if just once he called the bluff?

"Mission Pescadero Continuing Care Center," Guy said, "which isn't in Pescadero, by the way. November. Your name is Alexandra. This is Glenda and she's getting married. I can name all fifty states and their capitals. Can you?"

Alexandra didn't react. It was the nonreaction of a trained professional. Her lack of reaction was the reaction.

"I can name every book in the Bible, including the thirteen from the Apocrypha. Let's start there, since any old coot in a coma can do Genesis through Leviticus." He stood straighter and said, "Judith, Esdras, First and Second Maccabees —"

"That will be enough," Alexandra said.

"If I recite the Gettysburg Address, will you tell me my goddamn room number?"

Alexandra crossed to an old-fashioned Rolodex on Glenda's desk and spun it three-quarters of a turn. "It's perfectly natural to feel out of place in a new environment, but you don't have to vent hostility. We are here to serve your needs, Mr. Fontaine, and when you behave in a disoriented or aggressive fashion, we must quickly determine what those needs are. My questions are standard procedure."

"I'm not aggressive, *Miss* Truman. I just want to go to my room and lie down."

She looked up from the Rolodex. "Then you are dizzy."

"Is everyone who wants to lie down after lunch dizzy?" He appealed to Glenda. "I'll bet you'd give anything for a nap about now." Glenda nodded. "But that doesn't mean you're dizzy."

Alexandra drew a card from the Rolodex.

She held it by the tips of her fingers, farther from her eyes than a woman would with twenty-twenty vision. She said, "Glenda, will you buzz Eldon." To Guy, she said, "Your room is 312. Does that ring a bell?"

Guy immediately saw his mistake. Wrong floor.

A stocky black man who was more a cigar-ash shade than purely black walked through the door. He wore a sienna brown uniform and crepe-soled shoes. A tag on his breast read ELDON.

Alexandra said, "Eldon, will you escort Mr. Fontaine back to room 312 in Residential."

"I don't need a babysitter," Guy said. "All I needed was the number."

"And what would your daughter think if I let you wander the grounds alone and disoriented?" Alexandra said.

"I wandered for seventy-two years without my daughter's permission. I can wander now."

Alexandra stuck the card back into the Rolodex. "It's policy, Mr. Fontaine. My policy. Eldon, show Mr. Fontaine to his room."

ELEVEN

The sex is not satisfying to Ray John. He doesn't achieve climax although Lucinda comes twice before she complains of soreness.

"We're through now," Lucinda says.

"All right."

Modern medicine no longer makes erection failure a hassle for elderly men, as long as they plan ahead. They can get it up, but they cannot always get it out — the opposite of junior high.

"Did you enjoy that?" Lucinda asks. She likes being told she's good in bed.

Ray John lies. "It was nice." The bottom line is Ray John is past the point of having satisfactory experiences. He will never again be in a situation with nothing to complain about.

Lucinda cuddles against Ray John's collarbone and breathes into his chest hair. Lucinda likes the cuddling part of sex almost as much as the sex itself. "We'll finish you off tonight. Before the hop. The timing should be perfect," by which she means the Esaulis will still help Ray John start but it won't keep him from finishing. The women of Mission Pescadero know their pharmacology.

"Whatever you want," Ray John says. "I could go either way."

Lucinda snorts. "What an awful thing to say."

"It's the truth. I always speak the truth, no matter who it affects." Like most people, Ray John wouldn't know the truth about himself if it walked up and bit him. The truth is, he was so desperate for sex — especially sex with Lucinda — for so many years that now he feels it would be a moral failure to pass it up even though, for the most part, he finds the huffing and panting undignified. He can't stop wanting it even when he no longer wants it.

Lucinda licks the skin between Ray John's collarbone and shoulder socket, searching for salt. "Listen, Ray John."

Ray John's spine stiffens. He has a near phobia of sentences starting with *Listen.*

"You're not getting hung up or anything?" Lucinda asks.

"Define *hung up.*"

"Middle-class morality. The curse of our parents."

"My parents are dead. They can't curse me."

"Yes they can, and you know it." Lucinda blows gently across his chest. With one eye open and one closed, the hair looks a bit like cattails in the breeze. "When we were making it, you said my name several times, as if you're attached to me."

"I was only being thoughtful. I'm not attached, not in any negative way, if that's what you mean."

"I spent forty-two years in monogamy prison. Don't ask me to go there again."

Ray John can deal with this. He's learned with Lucinda, you never make demands, never let her see expectations. "You're breaking up with me?"

"Of course not, silly. I just want to make sure you understand the terms here. We have fun and God knows I love you."

There's that word. *Love* is even more loaded than *Listen.*

"But I love of a lot of people," Lucinda says. "You and I are not mixed up in an exclusivity scene."

"Oh." Ray John thinks about the first time he saw Lucinda Mays — Country Joe and the Fish, the Green at Golden Gate Park, a rare warm St. Patrick's Day. Lucinda dancing in a yellow silk dress with a fringe hem. Bare shoulders and arms. She wore a green wreath in her blond hair and hordes of Mardi Gras beads around her neck. Barefoot, arms extended, sun on her face, Lucinda spun around and around to a song about a girl named Sweet Lorraine. Ray John can still hear the music. He can still see her face strobing by. Never, in his capacity for knowledge, could he believe that face would ever grow old.

Ray John says, "You want to hump other men, but you don't want to stop humping me?"

"I prefer the term *spread my love to* instead of *hump.*"

"It's that new guy. Guy. You've got the hots for the new guy Guy." Ray John likes saying *guy Guy.* It brings Guy down a few inches.

"I'm speaking in general."

"The guy wasn't in Haight. He's probably never been in Haight."

"I'm not going to marry him, for God's sake."

"I'd be shocked and amazed if the hick can even name the original Chicago Seven."

Lucinda raises up on an elbow and looks into Ray John's face. "You have no idea what women want, do you?"

"My dream is you're not going to tell me."

"What I want has zip to do with being able to name the Chicago Seven."

Ray John blinks, quickly, searching for a back track. "What I meant was, he doesn't have much in common with us."

"That's what makes him a challenge."

Lucinda slips out of bed, lifts her panties off the mini-refrigerator, and walks into the bathroom. Ray John marvels at her lack of self-consciousness. Even at the height of free love, Ray John wasn't comfortable naked. Everyone else would be stripping for a skinny dip and he'd find an excuse to go back to the microbus.

Lucinda reappears in the bathroom door, a loaded toothbrush in one hand, panties in the other. "Besides, I'm talking people in general, not simply the new guy. We should both see new people. Monogamy is so" — she searches for the word — "Eisenhower."

Ray John sits up in bed, the sheet casually covering what he wants covered. "You want me to ball other chicks?"

When Lucinda shrugs, her hair ripples across her bare neck. "If anyone will have you."

"Lots will have me, don't you worry on that score. You know Queen Alexandra's favorite statistic — four point five girls to every boy."

"Alexandra is only counting residents. The odds even up when you throw in staff." Lucinda starts brushing her teeth.

"You mean like the gardeners and orderlies? You think orderlies have the hots for you?"

Lucinda speaks through toothpaste froth. "I don't see why not."

She turns back into the bathroom and spits. Ray John takes the opportunity to slide on his boxer shorts. "You're an old woman, that's why not. Old. You are only beautiful inside your head and, with the lights out, my memory. Men who didn't know you back in the day see you and think nothing but *old*."

Her voice comes from the can. "That's not true."

"Those orderlies see you as dead. They see all of us as dead."

Lucinda walks back into Ray John's room. "I weigh exactly the same as I did in 1966."

Ray John has to admit Lucinda's held up better, for her age, than any of the other Mission women who are now paying for going braless through their rites of passage. But the key words here are *for her age*. No young person could conceive of Lucinda as she had once been.

"I watch the gardeners watch me," Lucinda says. "They look at my body and they see a woman."

"A dead woman. Worse than dead. Some of those perverts would screw a dead woman. None of them would screw you."

Lucinda stands on one foot and steps into her panties. Her hair flows across her shoulder and parts on either side of the St. Christopher medal. She smiles at Ray John. "Want to bet a hundred dollars on that, bucko?"

Twelve

Rocky dreads the Friday-night sock hops. As far as she can tell, everyone dreads the Friday-night sock hops, except maybe the guys in the band who, if they stay awake long enough, get lucky afterward. Rocky dreads the sock hops for the same reason she dreaded sock hops back in Opp, Alabama, nearly sixty years ago — call it the alienation of crowd loneliness — and she shows up now for the same reason she showed up back then, because the only thing worse than going to a sock hop is not going. Something interesting might happen, and if you aren't there, you miss it. At Mission Pescadero — or Opp, Alabama, in 1963 — an interesting moment is a godsend, worth any amount of boredom while waiting for it to come.

Folding chairs normally used for on-site funerals are lined against the recreation hall side walls. Punch-and-carrot-stick-quality food at the back. Stage up front between two potted palm trees. Eldon Gaede, a nurse from N.C., and an orderly known as the Squealer because of his tattletale tendencies cluster together near the side door. Chaperones, just like in junior high, only at Mission Pescadero they're called attendants. Rocky sits midway down the east wall, knowing that if she waits from now to Easter, no one will ask her to dance. It was that way in Opp, in junior high. It is that way now.

She sits next to Darcy Faye Gardiner, who tells her about a Trips Festival in 1966. Nothing that counts has happened to Darcy Faye since 1966, even though she claims the festival opened doors to possibilities she never dreamed existed.

"I opened the door and there it was. Edge City," Darcy Faye says.

If that's true, thinks Rocky, why didn't she follow up on the boundless possibilities? Why open the door if you're not going to go somewhere?

Darcy says, "There was a sign on the punch that said 'ELECTRICIANS ONLY, THOSE WITH FEAR, DRINK THE OTHER,' but silly me, I didn't get it. I thought maybe they'd spiked the grown-up punch with Everclear."

The band is called Acid Reflux — lead, bass, keyboards, and drums, with an occasional female vocalist, when they ask her to sit in, named Sparkle Plenty. Sparkle Plenty's father named her after a character in the Dick Tracy comic strip. Unlike almost everyone else in Residential, Sparkle goes by her real name.

Darcy Faye holds Rocky's wrist with both her hands. Darcy Faye has widespread seborrheic keratoses and whenever a new patch sprouts, she is certain it's melanoma. She rushes to get it cut out, but now she's used all her Medicare for biopsies, so the Mission doctor, whose name is Beaver, is only willing to acid-burn off the more furry bumps. Darcy Faye's face looks like a potato that's been stored under the sink too long.

"The ballroom turned upside down," she says. "Can you wrap your mind around that? Upside down. I found myself crawling across the ceiling, like a gecko."

"I doubt it," Rocky says.

Right in front of Rocky, Nicolas is doing a modified Frug with Willow. Shaking his hands, bouncing on the balls of his feet, bobble-heading in his ascot, Nicolas gives off the vague impression of Snoopy in a Christmas special. Willow slips into a dance Rocky knows as the Pony. Nicolas looks from Willow to Rocky and winks at Rocky, as if to say, *Get a load of this.*

Acid Reflux is playing "Hey, Joe," eighteen minutes of asking someone named Joe where he's going with that gun in his hand. They are doing the Deep Purple long version, as opposed to the Jimi Hendrix version, or a dozen other versions Rocky can — but would never — name.

Guy Fontaine wanders up the gap between the sitters and the dancers. He carries a paper cup dwarfed in one hand and has the aspect of a lost child. He stops between Rocky and Nicolas, and, without taking his eyes off Acid Reflux, says, "You think they know any rock and roll?"

Rocky looks from Guy to the band. Tom Gypsom, the drummer who claims to have once roadied for Sopwith Camel, is singing the "Hey, Joe" howling part, closing his eyes, living the emotion.

"They think they are playing rock and roll," Rocky says.

Guy wrinkles his nose. "I'd call this white boy blues. Or maybe rhythm and blues. I wouldn't call it rock and roll."

"You're talking Top Forty," Rocky says.

"I am?"

"These guys hate golden oldie radio. You won't hear much 'Teen Angel' or Bachman

Turner Overdrive coming out of them."

"Pep bands used to play 'Shotgun Driver' at basketball games. Made me wary of Bachman Turner." Guy glances at the empty chair beside Rocky. "You mind if I sit down? You're the only person here I know."

Rocky is surprised by Guy's forwardness. Maybe he isn't so much the lost child after all. Maybe he's an extrovert temporarily shut down by the shock of institutionalization.

"I didn't think we'd see you tonight," Rocky says.

"Was either this or *Survivor XXXIX.*"

Rocky and Guy sit, watching the band, who, to Guy, are dressed for Halloween. Mick, on keyboards, has the Paul Revere and the Raiders thing going. On bass, Chicken Little, a poet from North Beach by way of San Francisco State, wears a Nehru jacket. Nehru jackets were popular for three months in 1967 and the butt of nostalgia flashbacks ever since. Guy can't decide if C.L. is making some kind of retro joke or he actually thinks the jacket is cool. That's the trouble with camp. You can't tell who is in on the joke and who is the joke.

Fairly Fast Freddy, on lead guitar, is into Joe Cocker in rehab. Fairly Fast is another one of those names too many people assume. In the hippie world, things that start as unique become clichés in less than a week. Until recently there'd been a Fairly Fast Eddie, who died, and a Fairly Fast Joe Bob, who went through the tunnel and is now Catatonic Joe Bob. Although it isn't said aloud, most Mission residents welcome the attrition of men named Fairly Fast.

Darcy Faye leans across Rocky and touches Guy on the forearm. "Are you okay? We heard you lost your way this afternoon."

"I forgot my room number. I didn't lose my way."

"Sunshine said you walked in at an awkward moment."

Sunshines #1 and #2 are hopping around in a group of women dancing together down by the stage. Almost all the women have flowers in their hair — daisies, daffodils, a couple of irises. Sunshine #1 has an orchid. The Sunshines are not speaking to each other in that loud way people have of not speaking to each other when they want universal awareness of the fact that they aren't speaking. At dinner, Sunshine #2 had been talking about the first time she slept with a man who was wearing an adult diaper.

"Chicken Little went and dropped his

bell-bottoms and I couldn't believe my eyes. He looked like a starved sumo wrestler. I laughed so hard he lost his stiffie."

"*Dropped* his bell-bottoms," Sunshine #1 said. "Not *went and dropped.* Say it right."

#2 knew #1 was right, but #2 had been a schoolteacher and couldn't handle being corrected. She said *went and dropped* was vernacular — slang — and Sunshine #1 should put banana pudding in her mouth and shut up. Sunshine #1 said #2 had hang-ups, which is about the worst accusation you could make at the early-Haight table.

Rocky says, "There's a pool you can enter for five dollars. Name the hour and minute we'll see Sunshine #1's tits and win the pot."

"That generally happens?" Guy asks.

"Every Friday night."

A woman back at the snack table slaps a man who is elderly even by Mission Pescadero standards. His glasses fly, but no one moves to help.

Guy watches with interest. "Who's the Colonel Sanders lookalike?"

"He thinks of himself as Mark Twain," Rocky says.

"Mark Twain didn't wear a white belt."

The man who looks like Colonel Sanders

but thinks of himself as Mark Twain drops to the knees of his linen suit and crawls under the snacks table, feeling for his glasses. Three women Guy recognizes from the New York table comment on his manners and the size of his ass.

"His name is Julian, but a few months ago he decided he'd rather be called Mr. Natural," Rocky says. "He told me he once smoked a joint with Sneaky Pete." They watch Mr. Natural hit his toupee on the bottom of the table. "You can't believe anything any of these old goats say. The ones who can remember lie."

Mr. Natural finds his glasses and turns, under the table, to crawl out. Rocky says, "There's something wrong with his liver so he has breath would stun a wharf rat, but he doesn't know it. He's the only man in here the girls don't chase."

Darcy Faye does the droop across Rocky thing again, to get Guy's attention. He tries not to look at her keratoses, but not looking feels more obvious than looking. "Are you seeing anyone?" she asks.

"Seeing?"

"Dating."

Guy's eyes go slick. He takes a drink from his cup, then stares down the chair line at Suchada and Phaedra. "My wife passed on recently. I don't think I'll see anyone anytime soon."

Darcy Faye pats his arm. "I've found frequent skin-to-skin contact helps the grief process."

Guy says, "Not mine."

THIRTEEN

Phaedra tugs her rusted-iron wig down, causing the sudden loss of much of her forehead. "You know what I need."

"What do you need?" Suchada unscrews the cap off a pint of Black Velvet hidden in her nylon jacket.

"The disgusting details. When I was your age, I never missed a disgusting detail." Phaedra shakes her head sadly. Due to degenerative posture, her head appears to be hanging off her neck, dangling from side to side. "But now. The eyes have betrayed the body. Swear to me, Suchada, you'll never grow as old as I am now."

"I have no intention of ever being as old as you," Suchada says, which isn't quite the same thing. Suchada pours two fingers of Velvet into Phaedra's plastic cup with the built-in straw and heavy-duty lid they got in a Burger King promotion years ago.

"I could spot disgusting behavior from a

block away," Phaedra says. "And not just men. Women, too."

"That's one of your gifts," Suchada says.

"Damn right." Phaedra is in a rare good mood, brought on by Black Velvet and the knowledge that she made it through another week. Even though Phaedra has never held down a job, she puts stock in weekends. To her, a strong woman does not get drunk on weekdays. Waiting till Friday night before getting plowed out of her skull is proof she isn't an alcoholic.

"Willow just ran from the room, weeping," Suchada says.

"I'll bet someone called her fat." Phaedra takes a long pull through her straw. "I'd have done it myself if she'd come over to suck up to us."

Suchada blots the dribble off Phaedra's chin. "It was Ray John." Suchada sips at her own spiked teacup. She cuts her whiskey with green tea, while Phaedra drinks hers straight. "Making Willow cry is like drowning puppies. It doesn't take any skill."

"I'd have knocked that silly hat off the pretentious bastard," Phaedra says.

"Rocky is hitting on the new man."

"I never trusted Rocky Gingrass. We were on a committee together once, when Barbara Boxer ran for president. I never could prove it, but I swear Rocky went potty during a conference call."

"Darcy Faye is telling him about the first time she took LSD."

Phaedra grunts and dips her head to her straw.

Suchada continues. "Henry Box is being publicly melancholic. Staring at his hands in his lap. Looks ready to cry."

"Henry is always one step from the chasm."

"But he's such an exhibitionist depressive. I don't mind a person falling into despair, but do they have to do it in front of me?"

"Show some empathy, Suchada."

"What?"

"We haven't all had the pampered life that was given to you on a silver plate."

"I cannot believe you are defending Henry."

"He's too pathetic to hate." Phaedra makes the sound of sucking a cup dry. "Henry Box offered me his seat on the cable car once, after I was gassed at a war rally. Before I found out the antiwar movement was sexist as a Georgia country club."

"Would he have offered you his seat if he'd known you're a dyke? Oh, my God, Sunshine #2 is flipping off Sunshine #1."

From across the dance floor comes *Peace*

Peace Peace, chanted by a circle of women around the Sunshines.

"I don't think Henry cared whether I was a dyke or not," Phaedra says. "I looked a mess, and smelled of tear gas. He certainly wasn't trying to seduce me."

"Winston and Hu are sneaking outside to smoke pot."

"What's Winston wearing?"

"Striped pants. Madras shirt. Top hat."

"The Australian act is an affectation, you know. He's from Waterloo, Iowa. Been married five times. He was a trust fund baby but he wants everyone to believe he lives by his wits and charm."

Suchada pours herself another finger of Velvet. To hell with the green tea.

"What a cockeyed freak Winston is," Phaedra says. "That whole chimney sweep career of his was a result of loading up on MDA and going to *Mary Poppins.*"

"I never saw the movie."

"There's dancing chimney sweeps, and Dick Van Dyke speaking in this bizarre accent. Thank God Winston didn't go to *Sound of Music* that night. He'd have become a singing nun. Don't be stingy with the refreshments. I paid for the bottle, remember."

Suchada pours the last of the Velvet into

Phaedra's cup. "How's the urine pouch holding up? You need a change?"

Phaedra's glazed eyes flash anger. She's isn't so old not to know when her buttons are being pushed. "I'll tell you when I need a new pouch."

Frances Ian walks past, wearing a polyester pantsuit. She comes so close even Phaedra can make out the MIA/POW badge pinned to her flat chest. Frances is wearing White Linen perfume and has a strange way of walking, as if she were on a boat.

Phaedra shouts, *"It's been sixty years, Frances. Give it up!"*

"She heard you," Suchada says.

"Screw her. If I was married to Frances I would have gone MIA myself."

There is a flurry of activity at the front double doors. The New York women split and move aside. Mr. Natural leans forward, like warming himself on a space heater.

Suchada says, "Sparkle is making her entrance."

"How bad is it?"

"You remember Janis's outfit on the *Pearl* album?"

"Feathers, as I recall."

"Put that outfit on an eighty-year-old bag lady."

Phaedra lifts her head and sniffs the air.

"Blindness is a total curse, Suchada. Death is better."

Fourteen

Rocky approves of the way Sparkle holds her microphone, lightly, with her fingertips, the way women hold a mike and men don't. Straight men, anyway. Male rock stars squeeze a microphone like they're jerking off.

Sparkle shouts, "How you old folks doing?"

Not the opening Rocky would have chosen. She doesn't buy starting with a question, not since she saw John Lee Hooker come out one night and scream, *"Can you dig it?"* for forty-five minutes, after which Rocky couldn't dig squat.

Sparkle grins at her crowd. "How about it, is the Metamucil kicking in yet?"

This brings a few chuckles and a yodel from the North Beach crowd. The Sunshine controversy is forgotten.

Rocky is impressed by the outfit. Sparkle found it in a San Mateo costume shop —

Half Price After Halloween! — specializing in album covers. It is precisely Janis on *Pearl.* Red satin nightgown under a flowered, billowy robe. Pink boas flowing from her hair. Suchada exaggerated when she said "eighty-year-old bag lady." Sparkle isn't a day over sixty-seven. She has the face of a post-debutante who spent a lifetime wading through slop and came out on the other side with a sense of humor. Sparkle channels Janis. In the good way.

Now she turns to the band and says, "Let's make some noise."

Whonk! Whonk! Whonk! Whonk! Whonk! Tom, Mick, Chicken Little, and Fairly Fast Freddy hit it, all together. Sparkle ducks her chin, closes her eyes, and lets out a slow moan.

"Cry" — stretched four beats — *"Baby! . . . Cry"* — another four count, then, *"Baby!"*

Rocky checks out the dance floor. Sparkle has done Grace Slick and Little Richard in the past. This is her first shot at Janis and even though she isn't the original, she is a damn sight closer than any old woman has a right to be.

"Honey, welcome back home."

The aging hippies stand silent, lost in a communal flashback. Even Guy takes notice.

"She sounds like Big Mama Thornton," he says.

Several heads swivel. "You heard Big Mama?" Rocky asks.

"In Arkansas, she played with Clifton Chenier," and without knowing it, Guy's place in the community pecking order shoots up several notches.

"She must have been about this woman's age," Guy says. "We thought she was ninety."

"Black women can hit the high notes after menopause," Darcy Faye says. "Sparkle is the only white chick I've ever heard who can keep up."

Over across the way, Lucinda goes into the weaving arms psychedelic swimming through music thing. Henry closes his eyes and hangs his arms forward, zombie style. Two sisters from Sausalito perform a dance step up, step back, step up routine. Rocky is reminded of that old question: What's it all about? Answer: The Hokey Pokey.

At the close of "Cry Baby," Sparkle turns to the band and smiles. "Let's kick some aged butt." Fairly Fast Freddy grins and leans into the "Me and Bobby McGee" intro.

That gets 'em going. Sparkle comes dangerously far out to the front of the stage.

She bends to flash antique cleavage, then she rips into the words.

"Busted flat in Baton Rouge, waiting for a train . . ."

The crowd howls the way crowds have always howled when they recognize a song, as if they absolutely must right now tell the band *I know this one! I know this one!* Sunshine #1 tears her top off and everyone checks their watches. Nicolas yelps with delight. He nailed the tits pool. Others start shedding clothes. Shoes first, then bras and support stockings. Finally shirts and blouses. Two midwestern women ask for help climbing the snacks table, where they dance like go-go girls in vinyl boots. Winston lights a joint. An adult diaper flies onto the stage.

Every voice in the place hits the line, *"I'd trade all my tomorrows for one single yesterday."*

Rocky looks for the chaperones. No one in sight. No doubt they are outside smoking cigarettes, the pastime of chaperones from the beginning of time.

Henry hip-jerks to the light switch panel by the doors. He begins to flip lights on and off. Dark. Light. Dark. Light. Dark. Not much of a light show, but it does make a nice geriatric strobe effect. More clothes drop to the dance floor. More joints are lit. Arms fly hither and yon. Heads shake, like babies making themselves dizzy, the innate way to get high. Everyone not in a wheelchair is standing, even Guy. Even the Vietnam widows, although they aren't dancing.

Acid Reflux finishes "Bobby McGee" and tears right into "Get It While You Can." Sparkle is in a zone. Pain shrieks from every line of the song. Smiles become loopy grins. Tears leak down faces. Darcy Faye Gardiner whirls like a dervish. Rocky closes her eyes and feels the way she felt in 1966, in the Avalon Ballroom, when she was free and life would never end. Only it isn't the same feeling. This joy comes with the crushing awareness of loss. Imagine looking at a group photo of your kindergarten class and knowing how and when each child will die. Rocky begins to cry.

The guitar licks dribble away. Then the keyboards and bass. Finally, drums. Sparkle's voice chokes off in mid-groan. Rocky opens her eyes to see Alexandra Truman striding across the stage. Every article of clothing, every muscle of Alexandra's body, evokes sensibility. Alexandra walks straight to Sparkle and tears the microphone from her hands. For a moment, it appears Sparkle might put up a fight, but the moment passes. Sparkle turns back into a woman who is given the senior discount without showing an ID.

Murmurs skip across the crowd.

"What's she doing here at night?"

"Shit."

There are plenty of *shit*s, and people reaching to replace clothes. Eldon and the Squealer stand at the side of the stage, at the base of the steps. Eldon bends down to pick up Lucinda's wraparound skirt and hands it to her. She smiles a thanks.

Alexandra stands there like moral rightness itself, glaring until she has full attention. She lifts the microphone to her lips. "This sock hop is over."

Boos erupt throughout the room, the loudest coming from New York and Berkeley. Rocky has her own flashback. How many times has she been present when grown-ups pulled the plug on a good time. It has been that way forever. It will be that way forever. People not having fun cannot stand seeing others have fun. In Alexandra's case, it is worse than not being able to stand the seeing of it. Someone — no doubt the Squealer — must have phoned Alexandra at home or wherever she spends her Friday nights and brought her all the way down here to poop the party.

"In fact," Alexandra says, "I would say you people have lost your right to any sock hops in the near future."

More boos. More grumbling. Rocky herself hisses. A cardboard juice box flies through the air and bounces off Tom's snare drum with a *whack.*

"Privileges must be earned," Alexandra says.

Guy takes note of Alexandra's liver-colored lipstick. Did she put it on before coming out to shaft her charges, or is that the shade she sports whenever she is off duty? In Guy's experience, women who wear lipstick the color of body organs tend to be carnivorous.

"You are behaving like children and therefore I shall treat you like children." Alexandra taps an impatient pump. "Is that what you want?"

Ray John may have started the clap, or it could have been Phaedra. Whoever started it, the rest of the room soon reverberates with the slow beat of rhythmic applause.

Alexandra's face flushes a bruised red grape color. Her mouth slits like a gash, and for the first time in memory, she raises her voice. *"Don't make me tell your children!"*

The clap protest sputters a slow death. Alexandra stares her charges down, one at a time. Most look away, at the floor. A few, like Rocky and Phaedra, stare back. Guy looks at the side door, working out the odds of escape.

Once she regains authority, Alexandra huffs a breath into the microphone. "That's better," she says. "It's about time you people learn how to act your age."

Silence. Eerie, weird silence, like holding your breath in a graveyard. Rocky looks from face to face. The joy of a few minutes before has been replaced by masks worn by those with no control over their lives. Sulking pouts. Imagine teenagers in antediluvian bodies.

Henry Box's pants hit the floor. The crowd turns as one to see Henry at the back of the room, by the light switches. He shuffles in a circle, then bends down to touch his knees. That is as far as Henry can bend.

Both Sunshines raise their skirts and drop their drawers. Suchada is drunk enough to go next. Then Winston.

Alexandra barks, "Stop it."

Nicolas, Lucinda, Darcy, the midwestern go-go girls. Sparkle Plenty. Behind Sparkle, the band forms a line, leading with their butts. Hu struggles upright, out of his wheelchair, turns with help, and drops his corduroys, revealing his catheter tube.

"Peer pressure makes you do strange things," Rocky says, dropping her capris.

Guy says, "Not me."

Within moments, everyone except Guy, the Vietnam widows, Phaedra, and three others in wheelchairs are bent over, their bare rear ends aimed at Alexandra. No one counts, but she must be facing fifty old assholes.

Alexandra turns to Eldon. "One smirk and you're fired."

"Yes, ma'am." Although it is all Eldon can manage to fake indignation, the Squealer is horrified. Nothing in his past prepared him for this sight. His last job was in a muffler shop.

Alexandra says, "Fuck it all, anyway," and she walks offstage. At the side door exit, she turns and speaks to Eldon.

"Cut the electricity."

"Yes, ma'am."

Alexandra walks out.

Fifteen

For as long as Guy could remember, which was a long time in spite of claims made by his daughter, he had found refuge in sleep. In college at Wilburton he was shocked to discover not everyone lies down at night, closes their eyes, and falls straight to sleep. He was amazed. Why not? Why stay awake when you'd rather be asleep? He didn't see the point in tossing and turning, and, like anyone else for whom a skill comes easily, he could not understand it as a gift others don't have.

Only twice — when Lily was first diagnosed and the week before her death — had Guy known what it's like to stare at the ceiling and listen to the clock against his desires. After Lily died, there were two sleepless nights, then the gift came back. Guy rediscovered his refuge.

But now, months later at Mission Pescadero, he no longer looked forward to nightfall. Getting to sleep wasn't that difficult, although it took a half hour instead of two minutes. The problems came at two, four, and six a.m. Two o'clock, he awakened suddenly, heart pounding, night terror in the stomach. After a trip to the can, he lay there for an hour, either too hot or too cold, not even close to sleep. Sentences beginning with *The economy* crawled unwanted into his head. Global warming. An argument with Lily thirty years ago, in which, to this day, Guy swore he was right. A girl he could have kissed but didn't. The OU–Texas game in 2012. Money. The never-ending war. *Where is Lily now and what will become of me after I die?*

The same thing happened again at four and six, until 7:30 in the morning, when he finally went down hard until ten when he awakened, feeling hungover and unrested.

Friday night after the sock hop, Guy got four hours of sleep spread over ten hours of being in bed. Saturday and Sunday were no better. By his appointment with Dr. Beaver Monday morning, he felt strung out. Trashed.

The nurse Guy recognized from Friday night told him to undress and put on the paper nightshirt and sit on the table. Guy did these things, always cooperative. He sat on the end of the table, legs dangling, a long while, thinking about an aunt of his in eastern Oklahoma who refused to see a doctor and lived to the age of ninety-four. She said if she ever went to a doctor she would die and, sure enough, that's what happened. Her last words were, "I told you."

Dalton Beaver blew in wearing dark slacks, square-toed boots, a shirt with an alligator on the breast, and an unbuttoned white doctor's tunic. He glanced at Guy, grunted to himself, and sat on the stool on wheels. He flipped open a fairly thick file. Guy thought two things: First, *He looked at me but didn't see me,* and second, *Why is my file so thick when this is our first appointment?* The fairly thick file meant he and Dr. Beaver were not starting with a clean slate.

Without looking up from his reading, Beaver said, "You must be Guy Fontaine."

"And you must be Dalton Beaver."

Dr. Dalton Beaver gave off an odor Guy did not usually connect with doctors' examination rooms. There was a faint smell of rubbing alcohol, of course, and the mint room deodorizer doctors must buy at bulk rates. But as he dangled his legs off the end of the table, watching Dalton Beaver pump up the blood pressure cuff, Guy noted something different. Clove, maybe. Or an abundance of dryer static-cling sheets.

"My son, Josh, went out for lacrosse." The doctor talked with his stethoscope in his ears, ostensibly listening for Guy's beat. He did it so quickly, Guy suspected fakery. "I told him to go for basketball or soccer, some sport that would give him an edge later in life. He wants to run for Congress when he grows up. Can you believe that? I told him being a former lacrosse player won't get you votes."

He put the stethoscope away and rolled up the cuff.

"What's the blood pressure?" Guy asked.

"It's fine."

"What's the pulse?"

"Your pulse is fine."

"I want the numbers."

"Never mind the numbers, Mr. Fontaine."

"I deserve to know."

"You would only misinterpret them if I told you." Beaver clipped a device intended to measure oxygen saturation in the blood onto Guy's pinkie finger. Once again the off smell wafted into Guy's nostrils. Asparagus sweat, perhaps.

Dr. Beaver studied the pinkie device and grunted. "I hear you had quite the adventure Friday."

Guy thought he was referring to the group

moon. "I wasn't part of that."

Beaver glanced at Guy's file. "Says here you were found wandering the property, disoriented and lost."

Guy placed his hands flat, palms up, on his thighs. He pictured the color blue. The hands gesture and mental imaging were anger management techniques Lily taught him, back when his son Martin was a teenager. "There is no truth in that statement."

A brief smile flickered across the doctor's face, not a smile, actually, more an eyebrow lift. An outward sign of inner skepticism.

"I was not disoriented," Guy said. "I forgot my room number. I'd only been in the room the once and I didn't pay attention when I left for lunch. You people are making more of this than what happened."

"Come now, Mr. Fontaine, you did nothing to be ashamed of."

"I'm not ashamed."

"What you did is perfectly normal for a man with your condition."

Guy concentrated on his breathing. Lily would not want him to make matters worse. Some doctors like their patients and some don't, and kicking the jackass's ass out the window might affect the relationship. "And what condition is that?"

Dalton Beaver flipped back two pages in the file. "Dr. Symmes diagnosed you as a probable multi-infarct dementia. I'd say your adventure Friday confirms Dr. Symmes's findings."

"Just like that, I'm written off."

"You are not *written off,* Mr. Fontaine. There are many options we can explore to make your remaining time comfortable."

Remaining time. Guy stared at the doctor with the alligator shirt. He could tell that in Beaver's mind, he was a lost cause.

"Listen, Dalton."

"Dr. Beaver."

"I've been doing research on the computer in the library and I don't think I have dementia at all."

Beaver made a put-upon sigh sound. "I strongly believe it should be illegal for anyone over sixty to go on the Internet."

Guy plowed on. "Absentmindedness to the point of hallucination is completely normal after a major trauma, such as losing your wife. It's a natural defense against grief and is almost always temporary."

Beaver swung the stool around to look at photos of his children framed on the wall. Josh was the spitting image of his father, down to the deeply cleft chin and giraffe-like eyelashes. Ginger's looks ran closer to her mother — a professional hostess. Dalton wondered what his life would have been like if he'd stayed in private practice. Contract work with a care center seemed so simple when he went into it. Predictable hours. Captive patients too old to complain in any official capacity. Medicare takes care of the bills and doesn't ask questions. He'd thought it would give him time to be a soccer dad.

"Okay," he said. "Let's pretend I'm not a highly trained physician and twenty minutes on the Internet has made you a medical expert. What is it you want, Mr. Fontaine?"

What did Guy want? He wasn't used to being asked that question. "I would like you to send me home. Back to Oklahoma, where I can take care of myself around my own people, where I won't be an embarrassment to my daughter."

"You think that's why you are in continuing care, because you embarrassed your daughter?" Beaver checked page one. "Claudia."

"She talked me into selling my house in Waurika and coming to live with her, but now I'm more trouble than she expected. She says I sap her energy. Claudia doesn't understand letting me go home would get me out of her hair, the same as locking me in here."

"Did you see any locked gates when you came in, Mr. Fontaine?"

"You know what I mean."

Beaver began to write with a pen given to him by a drug salesman. He hadn't had to buy a pen since med school. "And where would you live in Oklahoma? You told me yourself you sold your house."

"I could buy another one."

"With what? You've been declared legally incompetent to manage your own affairs. Somehow, I can't imagine your daughter letting you squander her inheritance on another house."

"But it's my money."

"Not anymore."

Beaver scribbled while Guy looked on. Beaver was no doubt agreeing with the Palo Alto quack. When she took control of Guy's assets, Claudia had assured him it was only a technicality, that his money was still his. His self-confidence had been rattled by the golf cart incident and he'd trusted her judgment more than his own, that day.

Beaver clicked his pen in and out quickly, like firing a semiautomatic weapon. "One of the primary symptoms of your disease is denial you have it."

"Saying I don't have it proves I do?"

"That's a bit of an oversimplification, but, basically, yes."

"I read on the Internet that anger or depression are the signs of dementia."

"Those also."

"So any reaction I have to being told I'm senile proves I am senile."

Beaver entered the charge codes on the billing sheet. He was getting bored with this one. When he was young, dementia had excited him, but now he'd rather talk about his kids. He resented that Guy had kept the entire appointment centered on himself.

"That's true, isn't it, Dr. Beaver?"

"Have it your way. I don't argue with patients."

"What about cheerful acceptance? If I agree with you that I am senile, does that prove I'm not?"

"Not necessarily. You could be lying. The senile are notoriously sneaky. How are you sleeping? Do you need a prescription?"

Guy rubbed his hands on his thighs, palms down, knuckles toward the doctor, which went against Lily's basic rule of anger management. But holy hell, how do you get the attention of a man who thinks you're as good as dead, without hitting him?

"Are you an alcoholic?"

"Of course not."

"One of the symptoms of alcoholism is denial, and yet" — the journalist in Guy could not believe he was saying *and yet* — "you must admit that not everyone who denies being an alcoholic is one. The same must be said for dementia."

"I'm going to make a note that I offered you sleeping pills and you refused." As he wrote the note, Beaver said, "Your denial goes far deeper than denying you have the disease."

"What else am I in denial about, Dr. Beaver? You tell me."

Dalton Beaver stood to leave. "I believe in the practice of tough love, Mr. Fontaine."

"*Love* is an odd word choice for what you practice."

"Here is the hard truth. You are in deep, deep denial if you think there's a chance in hell of you ever going back to Oklahoma. You are in continuing care now. My care. Adjust your attitude, Mr. Fontaine. You aren't going anywhere."

Sixteen

Mid-morning on a pleasant day in November, the men of Mission Pescadero gather around the redwood picnic table on the quad, beside the goose pond, to discuss weather and current events, and, in Ray John's letter-writing case, the dream of influencing those events. Except on Tuesday and Thursday, of course, when no matter how depressing, outrageous, or mean-spirited the government is that day, group focus rests on Dixie Lichens's tits.

Today is Tuesday. Dixie is resplendent in a silver lamé leotard. She seems to have lost a pound or two over the weekend. Her sternum strains against the lightly freckled skin between her shoulder hollows. She brings a rich intensity to the stretching process.

"Pull those hamstrings, ladies! You can do it! Come on, Lucinda, put some muscle into it!" Dixie speaks in exclamation points. Her breastless nipples push against her sports bra, like twin thumbs opening her chest cavity.

Henry Box holds his breath, remembering a twirler he once stalked without her knowing it in what was then called junior high. Now it's middle school. Missy Thompkins had been a high school sophomore, which put her a generation ahead of Henry the eighth-grader. Missy's thighs winking from her pleated velveteen skirt represented the wonderful, creative possibilities he thought awaited him on the far side of puberty. Puberty itself came late in high school for Henry but the creative possibilities he'd hoped for never quite materialized.

Today, Henry, Ray John, and Nicolas are joined by Winston and Guy. Five old codgers gathered around a stack of reading material with nothing to do but gripe: the coffee clique. Guy is quiet, distracted. There's some chance he isn't aware of Dixie's tits. Henry takes him as a man who has been in a situation for several days and is just now figuring out what it means.

Winston, for his part, leers at Dixie like a hod carrier on his lunch break while justifying his role as Ancient Mariner turned Pussy Hound.

"Those chicks were the height of sexually

active back in the old days, and then they drifted away from their own bodies, not even knowing they were drifting." Winston's shirt is off, tossed across his cane on the table. On this cool yet sunny November day he wears cutoff corduroys and he's barefoot. His visible skin is brown and cured as an old-style baseball glove. One foot is propped on the end of the bench as he uses a pocketknife to shave a corn off the outside edge of his large toe. "No matter how free they pretended to be out on the street, they dreamed of monogamy, and when they found it, they didn't know what to do next."

Henry leans on his forearms to look down the table, past the men, toward the yoga girls. In contrast to Winston's beach attire, Henry wears his sweater, a long-sleeve button-down shirt, and wool trousers. And he is still cold. Henry has been cold since the day he turned sixty. "I was married twice and neither of my wives dreamed of monogamy."

Winston snorts a laugh that Henry takes, correctly, as derision. "Sure they did, or they wouldn't have married. As modern women they were torn between what they were supposed to want and what they wanted, so they failed at both. That's the curse of our generation's female."

Nicolas says, "Imagine sex without consequences. Centuries from now those twenty years between the pill and AIDS will be remembered as the Golden Age of Civilization."

Ray John pulls his fedora down over his eyes. "Bullshit." Ray John is in an even worse mood than usual. He is upset over his hundred-dollar bet with Lucinda because he knows he will lose. He knows he has goaded the girl he's loved from afar for fifty-whatever years and up close for two into sleeping with someone else. Was that stupid or what?

Winston says, "There's twenty-seven women over there and I've shagged eighteen of them."

Shagged? Henry tries to recall a time when *shag* meant something. Maybe during the nostalgia waves of 2020, but you should have an actual social experience for nostalgia to refer to, and he can't remember *shag* ever being real as opposed to kitsch.

Ray John is working the *San Francisco Chronicle* Sunday crossword puzzle in ink. He says, "It's immoral to keep score."

Winston laughs and cuts into dead skin on his toe.

Henry watches the women rise from their workout pads to assume standing stretches.

He wonders who in the yoga class has not slept with Winston. Suchada, for certain. Some of the old vegan bunch, maybe. Marta Pitcairne, who is so married she can't clean her teeth without Ike loading the toothbrush.

Winston plows on, bragging. "I used to think forty was the peak age for female lustiness, but I've changed that to seventy."

Dixie has her arms stretched high overhead, palms together. She lifts up on her toes and the leotard fits like skin on skin. The sun glistens off her body. Henry feels suddenly nauseous. He emits a choked sigh.

Winston is more interested in his own theories than heartbreaking beauty. "Many if not most women go without sex for years. Forget it completely. They may waste the rest of their lives not thinking about how good it can feel unless some man does them the favor of flipping the libido switch back on."

Ray John speaks without looking up from his puzzle. "You're a goddamn saint, Winston."

Winston misses the gibe. He often mistakes sarcasm for compliments.

Henry is impressed by the way Ray John flies through the crossword. He has never understood the crossword puzzle phenomenon in the senior community. How is it that a person who can't remember the last time they changed underwear or even which side of the road you're supposed to drive on can blow through the most complex crossword puzzles? Young people can't do that.

Winston says, "Willow's been so insatiable lately, I'm thinking she may have Alzheimer's."

"What's that supposed to mean?" Guy says. It's the first words he has spoken since sitting at the table.

Henry explains, embarrassed by the truth. We're on a sensitive subject here. "One of the early signs of Alzheimer's is increased libido."

Guy says, "I don't believe you."

Henry shrugs. The last thing he's about to do is disagree with anyone about anything.

"It's true." Winston folds his knife, one-handed, and stands to stuff it into his cutoffs pocket. "As a woman's mind regresses, the sense of touch becomes more acute. It's not just sex, I've seen Alzheimer's women cry from ecstasy in a bubble bath. Or a satin nightgown. You put one in a satin nightgown and she thinks she's gone to heaven."

In Guy's mind, he sees Winston with Lily, the way he was with the Sunshines last week. "You're sick." His hands form fists on the table. "You're all sleazy perverts."

Winston turns from the yoga class to face Guy. You can tell he's thought about this. "Hell, mate, it's all the poor women have left. Think about the time there between finding out they have the disease and forgetting they have it. They are terrified, and who can blame them? The sense of touch and the need for love both explode."

Winston's shoulders twitch and his hands pull at his ponytail. "The families treat them like zombies from *Night of the Living Dead.*" Winston's voice changes to his version of a Marin County Junior Leaguer. *"That's not really Grandma, dear. She doesn't know what she's doing."*

Henry recalls a family visit he witnessed in the rec room. He was watching the governor's race debates — Daisy Barrymore against Senator Kobe Bryant — with some others, including a stroke victim named Angelica who has since gone through the tunnel. Angelica's son and daughter were visiting, sitting on either side of their mom, each holding a hand.

"We're cleaning out her room," the daughter said. "Getting rid of all those photo albums and the crotcheted knickknacks. I always hated that stuff."

"You could sell her books on eBay," the son said.

The daughter said, "The light in there is perfect for my GyroGym."

They both watched TV in silence, until the son said, "I only hope after she's gone, I don't remember her the way she is now."

Later, when the son and daughter had returned to their lives, the debate ended and a commercial came on for a drug that shrinks prostate glands. Angelica turned to Henry and spoke aloud, in the twisted way of a woman relearning speech. "Did I die and no one told me?"

Nowadays, Angelica wakes up every morning and asks for her husband, Jody, and every morning an orderly tells her Jody died years ago, and every morning the news hits Angelica just as hard as it did the first day she heard it.

"What about men?" Guy asks.

"What about men?" Winston says.

"Do they turn into sex maniacs, too?"

Winston looks to Ray John and Nicolas for help. He says, "I'm not interested in men."

Ray John says, "Men get pissed."

Nicolas nods. "Abusive, like all the firewalls are down. They'll be in the dining hall and out of nowhere start yelling at their wives. 'You want to suck his dick, go ahead, suck his hard cock while I'm still alive to see it. That would make you so happy. Suck him, *now.*' "

"Either that or they stop talking altogether. They stay in their rooms and won't come out," Henry says. "We had one gentleman watched game shows with the sound turned full blast the whole last three years of his life. Never said a word to anyone."

That gets Guy's attention. "You've been here three years?"

"Five."

"Jesus."

Winston sits back on the bench, only now he's facing in toward the table instead of out toward the women. "The most sensual of all are the early onsets. Forty-five years old and they can't find their kitchen without a map. Those women come in here knowing they may have five years to live and in three they'll have the memories of a newborn. Early onsets need love more than anyone else on earth."

Henry looks at Dixie, standing on one leg with the other leg parallel to her body, her foot tucked next to her ear. He wonders if she thinks about coming down with early onset Alzheimer's. Right now, Dixie is alight with life and energy. The magic word *poten-tial.* But then, only a heartbeat ago, all the women in Nursing Care had been filled with the same light.

He says, "I think Guy is right. There's a valid ethical question here."

"I didn't say there's an ethical question. I said you people are sick."

For a change, Ray John doesn't spew cynicism. Some things are important to these old men. Taking advantage of the helpless is a question that hits close to them all. "It's a judgment call. If they're so far gone you're skirting a statutory situation, you have to say no, whether they claim to know what they want or not."

Winston nods. "None of us needs to screw vegetables."

A small private plane flies over at low altitude. All the men except Guy cover their cups. So many boomers are dying these days and having their ashes scattered over the ocean that you never know who's going to end up floating in your coffee.

Winston begins his morning ritual of cracking each knuckle on each hand. It's the reason he isn't usually encouraged to join the clique. "The best sex I ever had was with an early onset named Casey Kasandris. She was a screamer. The chick came if you brushed the inside of her arm with a feather." His eyes fade into the unfocused stare of a man viewing fond memories. "She's over in N.C. now. They don't even bring her outside on nice days anymore."

Seventeen

Casey Kasandris. How far gone was she, after all? Once in the so-called blue moon, Casey wondered that herself. The remainder of her days and nights were spent lying on her back in a crank-up bed, visiting with ghosts and rabbits in the ceiling. Her past played up there. Like an interactive home movie, she saw herself as a girl, or maybe it was another girl's past, a girl from the books she read as a child. Those girls were more solid than she was. She saw the childhood of Laura Ingalls in her little house on the prairie and thought it must be her own.

As Henry, Guy, and the boys talked outside, Casey tried to follow what was going on near but not quite on the extra bed in her room. Others hovered there. Not ghosts, she was almost certain.

Alexandra Truman had Dalton Beaver backed up to the bed, her pelvis pressed against his. Alexandra's arms draped across

Dalton's shoulders. Her hands caressed the hair on the back of his head, just above the collar of his light pink shirt. His arms hung at his sides, fingers twitching.

Dalton pulled away from Alexandra. "I can't."

"*Dal*ton."

"Soon," he mumbled. "I promise."

Alexandra lowered her arms. She blew air, exasperated. "This racing to the edge of adultery then stopping before you've technically committed the sin is unseemly."

Dalton blinked, quickly. "*Unseemly* is a strange word, right now."

"It means wanting to cheat on the Hobbit is the same as cheating on her." Alexandra called Dalton's wife the Hobbit for two reasons: Melissa's head was large in proportion to her body and the name of a fictional being dehumanized her.

Dalton pouted. "That's not true. I have never cheated on Melissa and I can't start now. You have to give me more time."

"Time for what? You're either with her or you aren't. Working yourself into a frenzy then faking virtue is so high school. You're like a virgin giving hand jobs."

Alexandra stood, knuckles on hips, giving Dalton the evil eye. She enjoyed her evil eye. The secret was in how long she held her silence. Nothing made men so uncomfortable as a silent evil eye.

Sure enough, Dalton rationalized his behavior. "Melissa and I lead separate lives. We have nothing in common except the children, and soon she will see how empty our marriage is and let me go. The end will be her idea."

"And that will make you feel better?"

"I have to be able to look Melissa in the eye and say, 'I did not void the contract.' "

Alexandra's voice dripped derision. Only a high-level administrator could sustain such a level of disgust. "Listen to yourself, Dalton. You always have to be the good guy. You can't stand not being in the right, even when you're fucking around on your wife."

"Don't use that word."

"Fucking, fucking, fucking. It's time for you to make a choice." She waggled her hands, palms up. "Me. Or the Hobbit."

Dalton visibly squirmed. Sweat beaded along his hairline. Men in general and doctors in particular will climb metaphorical walls to avoid an ultimatum. "She'll take Ginger and Josh if I leave her now."

"Grow a spine, Dalton. Your kids are too old to be taken away."

"Melissa is a sneak. She'll manipulate

them into hating me for breaking up the family."

Moments like this were the times Alexandra wished she could smoke in the Mission. She was the boss, for God's sake. She should be able to smoke anywhere, anytime. What was the point of being boss if you had to obey the rules? "Kids that age are supposed to hate their parents. I hated mine. I still do."

Dalton's lower lip went puffy, his eyes damp. She'd cut him where it hurts, as she'd known she would. "My kids don't hate me."

"Sure they do. Nobody likes you except me." Alexandra almost smiled. "I'm all you've got, Dalton."

"You're exaggerating."

Alexandra was ready to forgive. She'd proven she had the power to bring him to tears. Now was the time for reward. "I've seen your patients look at you. They think you're the Devil," she said in a way that conveyed approval.

He picked up on the new tone. For some reason, she wasn't angry anymore. "They call you Queen Alexandra."

Husky voice. "I am Queen Alexandra."

Her right arm snaked back over his shoulder and they oozed into one of those drawn-out, openmouthed kisses that can be fun if it's you kissing, but are disgusting to look at. Alexandra's hand traveled down Dalton's chest and across his belly.

Casey said, "I am here."

Alexandra would have been less surprised if the bedpan had spoken. "What's that?"

Dalton was on the verge of saying to hell with principles. "Nothing. Don't stop now."

Alexandra stepped back from Dalton and turned to the other bed. "You told me she's a vegetable."

"She is." Dalton burped a nervous laugh. "Casey has all the mental function of a sweet potato."

"Sweet potatoes don't say 'I am here.' "

Careful not to move any closer to the bed, Alexandra studied the woman she'd forgotten was in the room. Casey was only fifty, not much older than Alexandra herself. Their hair was nearly the same shade of brown. Casey's eyes were open, blinking at the ceiling. Her arms against the blankets looked thin as chopsticks.

"I went to a lot of trouble to put her in a double room with no roommate, all because you told me she's brain-dead."

Dalton circled Alexandra to get a better look at Casey. "I don't think I used the words *brain-dead.*"

"You said she had the self-awareness of a house plant. I don't mind doing this" — she threw an arm toward the empty bed — "in front of a plant, but not some woman who can spy on us and knows what she sees."

Dalton bent over Casey, and with his blunt thumb and index finger, he spread her right eye. He looked down into the pin-prick of a pupil. Casey gave no reaction.

"I'll have to adjust her medication."

"You mean to sedate her even more? You would sedate a potato?"

Without moving the thumb and finger stretching Casey's eyelid, Dalton looked over at Alexandra. "Hell, Alexandra, what is it you want?"

Her voice caught an edge. "I want a place where we can be together without you having to put the witness in a coma."

Dalton released Casey's eye, but it didn't snap shut. He felt the papery wrist for a pulse. "We sedate this entire building and you know it. Don't play innocent with me."

"I know you calm down the troublemakers."

"We calm down all of them." He lifted Casey's hand and looked at her nails. They glowed the proper shade of blue. He manipulated her arm to check flexibility in the joint. "You want to wake her up? She won't know where she is, she'll be confused and frightened, and we'll be forced to find another place to meet. The Mission can't afford to leave a room empty for our pleasure, and I'm not the type for janitors' closets."

Alexandra wondered why a semiprivate extended care room was romantically thrilling in Dalton Beaver's book but a janitor's closet lacked class. Seemed like splitting hairs, to her. "If you'd leave the Hobbit, we could do this in a hotel, like normal adults."

A knock at the door made Dalton jump as if he'd been hot shot. The door opened a crack and Glenda said, "Miss Truman?"

Alexandra straightened her hair. "Yes."

The door opened another inch, not enough for Glenda to see the occupants of the room or what they were up to. "We found it, Miss Truman."

"I'll be right there."

The door closed, without a click. Alexandra adjusted various undergarments. "I have a fire to put out."

Dalton's heart fibrillated. He hated surprises. "How did that girl know where to find you?"

Alexandra tilted her face to peck Dalton on the cheek. "She made a lucky guess."

Eighteen

A Clark's nutcracker glides out of the eucalyptus and lands not ten feet from where Nicolas sits reading the *Gray Fox Times,* a slick magazine aimed at aging boomers. Each month the cover features a movie star or rock legend of a certain age who is still vibrant and healthy. Proudly active in both the professional and sexual sense. *If I can keep going, so can you people out there in assisted living.* The unattainable role model. The nutcracker two-hops sidewise at a forty-five-degree angle, moving both toward and away from the picnic table full of old men. The bird's eye is on Henry.

Nicolas speaks as he reads. "What a fascinating article. It says here that more seniors are defrauded by relatives than professional conservators."

"Depends on the definition of *defrauded.*" Ray John has completed the crossword and is staring off into space, in the general direction of the arched openings atop the bell tower. He's thinking about what a gyp love is. "Conservators work the system, so their stealing is legal. Relatives simply steal."

Henry feels in his corduroy jacket pocket for a muffin left over from breakfast. It's called a sunshine muffin and is chock-full of carrots and nuts. A fruitcake without fruit. "My conservator came by on my birthday last month. She brought a banana cake and stayed for lunch. I thought she was being social, but yesterday I got an 820-dollar bill for the visit."

Henry carefully breaks the muffin into three equal pieces and tosses one toward the nutcracker. "The banana cake was twenty dollars. I can't believe I'm paying twenty dollars for a banana cake."

Winston holds his cane out, parallel to the ground, aimed vaguely in Dixie Lichens's direction. He bounces the cane tip off the gravel walkway. "You should refuse to pay. Tell her to shove her cake up a dark place."

"The woman pays my bills." Henry underhands another bit of muffin the nutcracker's way. "She charged me thirty dollars to write herself an 820-dollar check. Next month, she'll charge me thirty more dollars for writing herself a thirty-dollar check. I'm going to die paying for that banana cake."

He eats the final muffin morsel. "I hate bananas."

Guy resists the urge to wipe dandruff off Henry's glasses. "I don't understand."

"Conservators legally suck us dry," Ray John growls. "On the other hand, Hu's son drained a million from his bank accounts, and gave Hu no reason at all." He punches a swan-neck deformed finger toward Guy. "Which do you see as the defrauder? The conservator, or the son?"

Guy considers the question while the nutcracker beaks up muffin and flies back to the tree. In the background, he can hear Dixie going for the big finish. *Breathe through your diaphragm, girls. Deep breath. Count five. Exhale. Count five. Concentrate on the wonder of air.*

"I couldn't tell you without knowing what a conservator is."

Ray John says, "You tell him, Henry. You're the man has one."

"When I turned seventy-three, I bought myself a motorcycle."

"You?" Guy doesn't hide his amazement.

"Don't scoff." Henry turns his pocket inside out and shakes away the remaining crumbs. "A Honda 250. I enjoy whale watching and I needed a way to get up and down the coast. But the man who owned the motor-cycle shop called a woman in Oakland who pays him to let her know when someone my age buys a bike. She took me to court, saying I was wasting my money and she could take care of me better than I could myself."

Guy feels gorge rising in his throat. "A stranger did this?"

"I never saw her before the day in court. The judge gave the Oakland woman control over my money and she threw me in here. I get an allowance. She charges two-ten an hour to pay my bills and balance my check-book."

Henry dusts off his fingers. "You have to realize, I was an accountant after I left Haight. I've been balancing checkbooks for five decades."

Some switch deep in Guy's head or psyche or wherever switches reside clicks. Call it the had-enough switch. "I don't see how this is possible. You must be leaving some-thing out."

Henry spot-checks his pulse. It seems ragged today. "A geriatrician in Palo Alto gave me a competency test. I scored thirty, which is the highest score possible, but Dr. Symmes said I was 'maintaining a superficial façade of functionality.' " Henry has said "superficial façade of functionality" so often his voice twists the words, giving them layers of meaning.

Guy is quick on the uptake. "Dr. Symmes?"

"Sounds like you've met the slime-bucket doctor," Ray John says.

Guy says, "I've met the slime bucket."

"Darcy's conservator charges four hundred to drive her over to the beauty parlor," Nicolas says. "He won't hear of her patronizing her regular place."

"That's still better than what would have happened with a daughter-in-law," Ray John says.

"You don't know that." Henry checks his big-number watch. It's almost time for his ten o'clock pills. "Not all children rob their parents."

Neither Henry nor Ray John have children. Henry thinks his life would have been better with children. Ray John thinks his life would have been worse. That is the difference between Henry and Ray John.

"Why didn't I know about this?" Guy's voice is angry, but because he's from Oklahoma, where anger sounds like indifference, the others don't know him well enough to notice.

"They're called guardians in other states," Nicolas says, "and it's been going on forever, as far as I know. Wasn't till the mid-'90s college kids started looking at professional conservator as a career. They were originally supposed to help old folks without families make health choices. Now you wear a Speedo on Maui and somebody's going to slap a competency exam on you."

"What's the iron twat got hold of?" Winston asks.

Alexandra steps out of Residential, followed by Eldon Gaede, and together they cross the quad. At the same moment, a lanky, careful man in a pea-green uniform comes through the front gate.

"Looks like a raccoon," Guy says.

Henry rises to his feet. "Mr. Scratchy."

Alexandra, Eldon, and the uniformed man converge near the goose pond, exchange a few words, then proceed, Alexandra a bit ahead of the men, toward the picnic table. Alexandra holds Mr. Scratchy by the scruff of the neck. The cat hangs like groceries in a plastic bag, only the yellow eyes proving he is still alive.

Henry lets out a choked sob. Guy looks across at Henry's face. The skin is a splotchy mosaic of pink and pale. His mouth is open.

At twenty yards and closing, Alexandra goes into her ream job. "When you accepted our hospitality, you signed a contract, Henry

Box. You knew the rules. You agreed to abide by those rules."

Of all the bad things that Henry imagines can happen at this stage of life — and Henry imagines bad things almost continuously — this is the worst.

"How could you take advantage of me like this, Henry? How could you be so aggressive?"

Guy can see that beneath the fury, Alexandra is having a grand time of it. This is the part of her job she relishes.

"You knew the consequences of your actions." Alexandra plants her feet and holds Mr. Scratchy at arm's length, away from her body. "What do you have to say for yourself?"

Henry's voice cracks, high, like a child's. "I'll do whatever you want, only leave me Mr. Scratchy."

"Don't be infantile, Henry. Of course the animal has to go." Alexandra turns and deposits Mr. Scratchy in the hands of the uniformed man. His cap says ANIMAL CONTROL and his breast pocket flap says ANDY. Mr. Scratchy's three legs pump against Andy's chest. Andy smiles at Henry, embarrassed by the inevitable heartache brought on by doing his job.

"Are you evicting me, too?" Henry asks.

"You know the policy." Alexandra does the thing where she blows air up, lifting the bangs slightly off her forehead.

"Let me gather my belongings, and I'll take Mr. Scratchy with me."

"No can do, Henry. You were placed under my care by a court order and there's no leaving until your conservator and I arrange a transfer to another facility. The process takes several weeks. Your animal must be removed today."

Silent tears course down Henry's cheeks. A drop hangs off the tip of his nose, but he makes no effort to brush it off, so Nicolas reaches across and touches the teardrop away.

Alexandra crosses her arms over her chest. Speaking in that Mr. Rogers drone, she says, "You have no one to blame but yourself."

"Give the man his cat."

Guy has also risen. He comes around the picnic table and, without asking, lifts the cane from Winston's grasp. "It's Henry's cat. Give it to him."

Alexandra's eyebrows harden into a flat line. "This does not concern you, Mr. Fontaine. Do not compound the situation."

Guy holds the cane waist-high, in his right hand, as he moves toward Andy and the cat.

"You should treat people with proper respect."

Alexandra says, "We have a rule against animals in continuing care. Henry knew the rule and he knew what I would do if he broke it."

Guy continues on toward Andy, who glances at Alexandra, unsure what to do. Eldon steps closer to Alexandra's side. Rocky appears at the library door. The yoga women leave their mats.

Alexandra reaches for Guy's left shoulder. "We all know this is your dementia acting out, Mr. Fontaine, but if you do not back away, I will be forced to have Eldon restrain you, physically."

"Watch your head," Guy says.

Andy lifts one hand up to protect his head while holding Mr. Scratchy with the other. Guy feints toward Andy's chin, then two-hand swings the cane like a five iron, driving into Andy's media collateral ligament. Andy makes a sound similar to a stabbed tire and falls to the ground.

Eldon steps forward. Guy pokes the rubber tip of Winston's cane into Eldon's throat and says, "Don't."

From this point, actions flow fairly quickly. Alexandra shouts, "Get him, you dumbass." Lucinda whacks a pint bottle of sparkling

Evian into the spot where Eldon's spinal column meets his skull. Mr. Scratchy tears the sleeve off Andy, taking a fair amount of skin with it, and disappears into the juniper bushes in Contemplative Corner. Winston says, *"Far fucking out,"* and takes off for his room in search of weapons.

NINETEEN

Hands pull Guy back to the picnic table, where he stands beside Henry Box, watching the yoga women remove their watches and jewelry.

"That was dynamic," Henry says.

Guy repeats what he said earlier. "You should treat people with proper respect."

Henry says, "Right on."

Sunshine #2 and Willow sit cross-legged on the ground at Guy's feet and link arms. Sparkle and most of the Sausalito contingent form a linked semicircle around them.

"What are they doing?" Guy asks.

"Nonviolent direct action," Henry says.

Senior citizens pour from Residential. The ones who think they can get back up afterward squat on the ground around Guy and Henry while the others stand along the edge of the outer circles. No voices are raised. Very few even speak. The only orders given are by Sunshine #1, showing the midwesterners where to line up between the picnic table and the back wall.

"You'll cover this side," Sunshine #1 says.

Marta Pitcairne asks, "From what?"

"Pigs."

Phaedra says, "Revolution is the festival of the oppressed."

Suchada says, "Germaine Greer. Where do you want us in this thing?"

"Put me up front, close to the bitch," by which Phaedra means Alexandra, who is the very definition of apoplectic.

Alexandra looks down on the rapidly forming concentric circles between her and the picnic bench. She wraps her painted fingernails around Andy's upper arm. "Get those two out of there."

Andy doesn't budge. "I'm animal control, lady. Those are people."

"Andy, you are the classic example of a coward."

"You want me to look for the cat?"

She turns to the other side. "Eldon, you're head orderly. Break up this mob."

Eldon rubs the back of his head. "Did you just call me a dumbass?"

Lucinda, who is sitting at Eldon's feet, says, "I'm sorry I hit you with my water bottle."

"Is that what it was?"

"Normally, I follow the path of nonviolence. I don't know what came over me."

Eldon looks down at the old woman in Danskin tights smiling up at him. To his amazement, she winks.

Initially, Dixie Lichens is dismayed to find herself abandoned by her class, but as the women swing into action, she is impressed by the efficiency of movement. The complete lack of uncertainty. Not once does anyone question whether this is a good idea.

Dixie bounces across to two women watching from the sidelines. She says, "This is so cool."

The woman in the luminous Dacron pantsuit, red tennis shoes, and heavy eye shadow says, "You'd think it was planned."

The other woman, whose weight is above what Dixie looks at as a reasonable target, snorts in disgust. "I wish I had a gun."

The other woman says, "This isn't about Vietnam, Georgia."

"Of course it is. It's exactly the same bull hockey they pulled then. The spoiled brats throw a fit every time they don't get their way."

From across the lawn comes the sound of voices raised in song. *"All we are saying, is give peace a chance."*

The heavy woman turns in disgust and

stomps off.

Dixie listens to the song, which seems to be the same line repeated over and over. She finds it both beautiful and vaguely familiar. "I don't get it. How is what they're doing about Vietnam?"

Dalton Beaver strolls down the Nursing Care wheelchair ramp, listening to his cell phone. He is so concentrated on whatever is being said that he makes it almost to the infirmary before the situation at the far end of the quad sinks into his consciousness.

Alexandra spots Dalton and hand signals Get-your-butt-over-here.

As Dalton passes the eucalyptus, a waif of a woman in a white wool nightgown and blue terry cloth bathrobe pushes her walker through the Nursing Care doors. Eighty-five, at least, with severe curvature of the spine, cheekbones that could break through sod, and hands so arthritic they look like claws, the woman inches down the ramp and out into the sunlight. Her striated lips appear to be chewing. Or fluttering. Definitely moving independently of her mouth and intentions.

As he approaches Alexandra, Dalton whines into the phone, "It's work, Melissa. My job. I've got to go." He clicks off his cell phone. "Why are they singing?"

" 'Cause they're a bunch of babies throwing a temper tantrum." Alexandra holds out her hand, palm up. "Give me your phone."

Dalton holds his cell phone tight. He's afraid Alexandra might call his wife. "What for?"

"What do you think what for? To sic the sheriff on these idiots."

Dalton passes the phone to Alexandra. "Do you know the number?"

"Nine-one-one, you fool."

"Don't touch the Redial."

Winston limps from Residential with an aerosol can in his left hand and another can under his right arm. He comes along the pathway, making decent time, considering, till he catches up with the slowly advancing waif.

"Need some help there, Judith?"

"Get over and stop that woman from phoning the law. We need twenty minutes to organize."

"You got it."

"I'll catch up when you're done."

Back at the picnic table, Guy asks Henry, "Who's the bent-over one on the walker?"

Henry squints across the quad. "Judith Frost. She went through the tunnel last week."

Guy sees himself as a man who's lived a

rich life, but this is the first time he's ever struck a person in uniform. After the initial horror, he feels a tingle of satisfaction.

"Folks back in Waurika don't fight authorities," he says.

Henry says, "If the authorities are wrong, we have to fight them."

"Not in Oklahoma."

Winston underhand tosses an aerosol can to Ray John, who, uncharacteristically, catches it. Side by side, they advance on the power elite.

From her place back by the midwesterners and less experienced revolutionaries, Sunshine #1 calls, "If you kill them, we're no better than they are."

Dalton's complexion changes for the worse. "Kill them?"

Andy says, "If you don't need me anymore, I'll be leaving," and he does.

Guy surveys the various orderlies, gardeners, and kitchen staff hanging back, well out of range. "I'm having trouble following this."

Henry nods Winston's way. "Bear spray."

"What's that?"

"Winston bought a case of bear deterrent. It won't kill anybody, but Winston says it's stronger than legal Mace."

"What's he going to do with it?"

"Liberate Mission Pescadero." Henry's

face shines with a brightness you rarely see on a depressive. To Guy, he looks ten years younger. Hell, sixty years younger. Henry's big ears and ridiculous haircut give him the face of a kid on the morning of his prom.

Winston says, "I'll take the phone."

Alexandra hesitates, her index finger poised over the Send button. "Are you threatening me?"

In the seconds of silence, Mr. Natural hits it for all he's worth. *"One, two, three, four, we don't want your fucking war!"*

Rocky taps him on the leg. "That's done with, Mr. Natural."

"Oh."

Ray John aims his nozzle at Dalton Beaver. "We are arresting the two of you for crimes against humanity."

Alexandra snorts. "Oh, horseshit."

"This country is no longer worth diddly," Winston says. "Welcome to the sovereign state of Pepper Land."

Dalton says, "I'm going to pull your Ambien. You'll never sleep again."

Ray John zaps him with two seconds of directed mist, enough to put Dr. Beaver into a fetal position, dry heaving. Alexandra quickly steps away from Dalton and the residual spray lingering in the air.

"You're next," Ray John says.

She stares at him, back across the crowd at Guy. She looks up at the bell tower, then back to Guy again. She says, "I swear to God, you will live long enough to regret this." She hands Dalton's phone to Ray John.

A cheer goes up from the crowd.

TWENTY

As "Give Peace a Chance" echoed from the Mission walls, Suchada got off the ground and walked over to Ray John. "Where you planning to put the hostages?"

Ray John's heart pounded from the adrenaline rush of laying out a doctor. "We'll lock them up."

Suchada said, "Where?" She pointed out there are no rooms with locks in Mission Pescadero, at least none that can be locked by a key. Alexandra's office door locks, but anyone on the inside can unlock it and walk out, so that didn't do them any good.

"Maybe there's a straitjacket over in N.C.," Winston said.

Dalton, by now, had made it to his hands and knees and was crawling for the pond. Eyes the red of fresh blood. Lungs of a late-stage asthmatic. Drool. Judith Frost humped her walker past Dalton without so much as a glance his way.

"So, it's started," Judith said, her voice clear and unslurred. Not the voice you would associate with Nursing Care. "What's it over?"

"Henry's cat," Suchada said.

Judith nodded. Her hands lifted the walker a quarter inch off the ground, then let it drop. The residents had unhooked their arms and were clapping at the appropriate beats. *"We shall not be, we shall not be moved!"* The gardeners talked among themselves. No one down there had gone back to work.

"That's as good as anything else." Judith jutted her chin at Alexandra. "Stick her and the one you gassed in the dispensary. You'll find the key in Dalton's desk. Top drawer on the right."

Judith's attitude rankled Ray John. Spraying Dalton had given him a cool sense of control. He was in no rush to give it up.

He said, "Who died and left you in charge?"

Judith glared at Ray John. Her mouth chewed. Her heavy eyelids fluttered. "I put me in charge."

Nicolas stood along the edge of the North Beach crowd, close enough to be considered part of the gang, yet detached enough to look upon the chanting old-timers from a separate height. Nicolas wasn't sure he was having fun. Granted, life at Mission Pescadero could be blindingly boring, but Nicolas had reached an age where boredom wasn't so awful. In his experience, most alternatives end badly.

For one thing, he had no experience at seizing institutions. He didn't know enough to remove his watch and class ring, to locate a handkerchief in case the Boss Man breaks out tear gas. Back at Stanford, Nicolas's roommates had taken over President Lyman's office and the off-campus headquarters of Operation Rolling Thunder. He'd been aware of the day thousands crossed the bridge to the Berkeley Induction Center and got themselves beaten, run down by cops on horses, gassed, and thrown in jail, but that wasn't nearly as exciting as the microchip. Nicolas had been punching cards to program a vacuum-tube-driven computer big as a bus. Taking over an induction center was small potatoes compared to the discovery of a chip that held memory.

With both Hewlett and Packard long dead, Nicolas had been forced into retirement by managers who weren't even born when the chip was created. And the same information that first took a bus-sized computer and then a chip can now be held in a drop of water. Nicolas was satisfied to play out the string without surprises. He had no wish to spray bear repellent in the establishment's eyes.

"Whose side are you on?" Sunshine #1 asked.

"What's that?"

"You're wearing a look of disapproval."

"I was wondering how this will affect lunch."

Nicolas and Sunshine walked around the crowd as the song dribbled away and the singers pulled one another to their feet. They joined a group clustered around Judith Frost.

Sunshine #1 said, "You're looking good."

Judith's mouth worked itself into a tiny smile. "I feel good."

"You're in better shape than last week, when they took you through the tunnel."

Judith snorted a short laugh. Nicolas thought of it as a cackle. "I stopped taking their pills. Hid the little buggers under my tongue till I could flush them down the can. You'd be surprised how much better you feel without Beaver's plant food." She gave Winston a shove to the shoulder. "Go make sure the clown doesn't drown. The media will blame us if Beaver turns up dead from that idiot's gas job."

Winston — with Alexandra in tow — walked off to fish Dalton Beaver out of the pond.

Ray John said, "Wait a minute." He couldn't understand how he went from instigator to idiot. "I know what I'm doing. I was at Berkeley on Bloody Thursday."

Judith inched her walker in a ninety-degree circle until she faced Ray John head-on. "I remember you on Bloody Thursday. You're the pissant we sent out for pizza."

"I certainly don't recall anyone named Judith Frost," said Ray John.

Judith chewed air and nodded her head. She seemed about to say one thing, then changed her mind and said another. "You were in Berkeley in '69, hey?"

"Yes, and I'm aware of standard procedure for the support of demonstrators."

Judith stuck a fist in her own sternum. "Selma, '65. Columbia, '68. And Paris. Madison, '70. Copenhagen, '71. Wounded Knee, '73. Gdansk, Seattle, Guatemala City, Havana, Cape Town in '07 and '17. You want me to go on?"

Ray John did what he could to show defiance, but it was too late. Judith had established her superior legitimacy.

"While you were clocking in and out and

firing off angry e-mails to your congressman, I was being clubbed in Jakarta. Operations don't go the way they did in '69, in Berkeley. They call it Bloody Thursday because one kid got himself killed. One death doesn't make the papers now. Attica is today's model, and there's no such thing as demonstrators. You disagree with the government now and they brand you a terrorist. And they'll be more than thrilled to crack your skull on concrete."

Judith rotated her walker back even more deliberately than she had when turning toward Ray John. With her chin tucked down on her chest, she looked up, making eye contact with each member of her audience. "You want to lead the revolution, you lead it. But don't come crying to Judith when half your people are shot up."

Judith focused in on Nicolas. "We'll have company in ten minutes. I need you to push eight wheelchairs over to the front gate. Cram the chairs in tight and lock their wheels down good."

"With people in them?"

Judith turned to Rocky. "You do it. This one's a fool."

"I can do it," Nicolas said.

"Don't let anyone through that door who isn't willing to kick the crap out of a grandma. And you" — Judith chose Willow — "you make certain any cop who is willing to kick a grandma knows damn well they're being recorded for the nightly news. Round up every camera you can find. I want digital, video, cell, Hu has a wristwatch high-tech enough to shoot *Star Wars XIV.* Cover the front and back exits and the two loading docks. There's one off the kitchen and the hearse garage in Nursing Care. Can any of you old farts climb steps?"

To Nicolas's surprise, several hands were raised. Judith gave the nod to Mr. Natural and Lucinda. "You two get up in the bell tower. Take your phones and make sure the batteries are good. First sign of the law, call her." Judith stuck a thumb at Sunshine #2.

Ray John thought that when he liberated Dalton's phone by way of Alexandra, he put a stop to law enforcement's imminent arrival. "How do you know the law is on the way?" he asked.

"There." Judith nodded toward the Administration door where Georgia stood beside Glenda. Glenda had a hand hooked over her belly, the way women stand when they are pregnant. Georgia was talking into her wristband phone. "You didn't gas everybody."

Twenty-One

Ten minutes to the moment later, Deputy Sheriffs Bobby Christmas and Esteban Vasquez throw open the double front gate to discover two rows of wheelchair-bound senior citizens, four across, two deep, and behind them another thirty or so elderly men and women packed tightly as urbanites on a rush-hour cable car. Two Treo camera phones are uplinking the deputies — one, from the background, in the left hand of an overweight woman in a midriff-baring teddy — Willow — and the other from above, held by a skinny longhair with no shirt balanced on a stepladder — Winston.

As the doors open, a man in a FREE SQUEAKY FROMME sweatshirt, green wool pants, and a fedora — Ray John Mancini — cuts loose. *"We are people of this generation, bred in at least modest comfort, housed now in universities, looking uncomfortably to the world we inherit."*

Hu shakes his fist. *"Vote with your feet, vote from the street."*

Bobby Christmas says, "Jesus Christ."

A woman with turkey vulture posture and plumage — Judith Frost — clears her throat with the growl of a midsized terrier. She speaks: "The residents of Mission Pescadero have liberated this continuing care center facility as a symbol of freedom for the aged and powerless."

Bobby Christmas looks for a way over or through the mess. There isn't one. "Come on, lady. My job is hard enough without hags busting my balls."

"I resent the use of *hags* to characterize a normal stage of life," says Sunshine #2.

"Power to the old people," says Sunshine #1.

Ray John plows on, relentlessly. *"When we were kids the United States was the wealthiest and strongest country in the world; the only one with the atom bomb, the least scarred by modern war, an initiator of the United Nations that we thought would distribute Western influence throughout the world."*

Esteban Vasquez is interested in Ray John's singsong. The rhythm is familiar, like the Declaration of Independence, only the words are new. *Kids. Atom bomb.* "What's that he's saying?"

Many of the old folks shrug. Rocky knows, but she won't tell.

Judith also knows the answer. "The Port Huron Statement."

"Oh, Christ," says Bobby.

"What's it mean?" asks Esteban.

"It's the manifesto of our generation."

"As we grew, however, our comfort was penetrated by events too troubling to dismiss."

Phaedra and Hu are positioned dead center in the front row of wheelchairs. Because only five A.L. residents are in chairs, Nicolas had to fill the last three spots from Nursing Care. Two of these are, for all practical use, catatonic women. The third is Gap Koch, who thinks they are waiting on line for a ride at Universal Studios.

He says to Bobby, "Bring me a grape soda pop, boy, and I'll give you a new quarter."

Bobby says, "Christ," for the third time. He can't take his eyes off Phaedra's bald crown.

"Not only did tarnish appear on our image of American virtue, not only did disillusion occur when the hypocrisy of American ideals was discovered, but we began to sense that what we had originally seen as the American Golden Age was actually the decline of an era."

Phaedra leans in toward Bobby. "Scat!"

Bobby blinks twice — *blap, blap.* "What's that?"

"You're out of your depth here, young man. Time to call backup."

Esteban agrees with Phaedra, but before he can beat a retreat to the county SUV and radio, he has to ask the right questions. "You folks have any weapons in there?"

"I'm not saying," Judith says.

"I am," says Sunshine #1. "Of course not. You can't change the human spirit at the point of a loaded gun."

"Why don't we desist with the talking, Sunshine," Judith says.

"If you treat people like that, Judith, karmatically, you are no better than Alexandra."

"How about hostages?" Esteban says.

Judith says, "Maybe," and she gives Sunshine #1 a look. Sunshine #1 pretends to zip her lips.

Esteban goes up on his toes to check out what quad is visible through the doors and over the crowd. He sees a couple of gardeners milling around by the Administration flower bed. A beautiful young woman in a silver lamé leotard. A pregnant black girl.

"My grandma's a housekeeper here," he says. "Inez Vasquez. Could you ask around, make sure she's okay?"

"We'll do that," Judith says. "You go call someone with more authority."

A chill zips down Bobby's spine, the sort of chill people usually blame on a cat walking over their grave. Bobby's chill is brought on by the thought of calling Lieutenant Monk.

He says, "Cyrus is not going to be happy."

Phaedra uses her best snarl. "You tell Cyrus we're waiting."

Crowd noise of the sports-event sort seeped through cracks and into the dispensary, where Dalton Beaver sat on a step normally used to reach high shelves. Alexandra Truman paced.

"I wonder what's going on out there," Alexandra said.

"They're no doubt planning ways to torture and kill us." Dalton bent over a regulator connected to a stainless-steel oxygen tank. He turned a dial, then flipped a switch.

"I cannot believe they took my phone," Dalton said. "Why didn't you fight for it? A physician without his phone is powerless."

"Hell, they would have gassed me, too. That prick Ray John was itching for an excuse." Alexandra walked along the medication shelves, counting pint bottles of pills. Inhalers. Ampoules for diabetics. "My mother would marry you to get the key to this room." She stopped at a strewn pile of packaging in the corner. "What's all this here?"

Dalton attached a split rubber tube to the regulator. "Samples."

"Drug salesmen leave these prescription medicines with you?"

Rather than answer the obvious, Dalton inserted rubber tubes into each nostril.

Alexandra stopped her exploration to watch him. "Do you give the free pills to your patients?"

Dalton inhaled oxygen-rich air deeply into his burning lungs. It didn't help as much as he'd hoped. "I don't believe in giving patients medications they don't pay for."

Alexandra picked up a blister pack of Vitasec. It seemed like a lot of cardboard and plastic for only three pills. "We should find a way to charge for it."

Another round of cheers from outside.

Dalton pulled an elastic band around his ears, which gave him the luxury of hands-free assisted breathing. His voice came like speaking through a head cold. "If Melissa calls and I don't answer, she'll take for granted I'm with you."

"Why should the Hobbit take for granted we're together?"

"Melissa is crazy when it comes to you. If she finds out about us being locked up together, she'll say we planned it."

"As in we tricked the residents into kidnapping us just so we'd have an opportunity to fuck?"

Dalton winced at the word he didn't like to hear. "That's how her mind works. She'll say if I respected her I would have made sure we were held prisoner in different rooms. She'll divorce me and take my children, and she'll tell everyone at the club it was my doing."

It occurred to Alexandra that there is absolutely nothing sexy about a man with rubber tubes up his nose. "Dalton, you are more interested in who gets blamed than you are in what happens."

Guy on his hands and knees crawled through a space between thorns in the shrubbery, following the theoretical flight of Mr. Scratchy. Henry sat, one skinny ankle over the other skinny knee, his hand cupped at his chin, on a concrete bench positioned to face the sandstone chapel located across the far corner of the quad. The bench was built in such a way as to convey a mood, thoughtful and Greek, as opposed to the rest of the Mission, which was meant to look Spanish. Had the Mission been a real mission, the quad would have been called a plaza and there would have been a church up by the entrance and bell tower. The spot now occupied by the chapel would have been cubbyholes where they locked the Indians up at night so they couldn't run back to their former lives.

"My relationship problems can be traced to the day my father committed suicide," Henry said.

"I'm sorry to hear that. It must have been hard on you." Guy worried about black widows and brown recluse spiders. He was new at crawling through damp, low places in California and wasn't certain where danger lurked.

"I never met him." Henry felt for his pulse. He thought he might be skipping beats. "He killed himself on his honeymoon. Dad and Mom were in Yellowstone Park and Dad jumped into a boiling thermal pool." Henry paused, distracted by the shape of the shadow creeping down the chapel wall. He was almost certain it was past time for his ten o'clock pills, but he'd taken his watch off during the excitement and left it on the picnic table.

"What's the cat's name?"

"Mr. Scratchy."

Guy brushed back a caterpillar bag and squinted down the gap between shrubbery and wall toward a drain opening. That was about the only place the cat could be unless it had doubled back toward Residential.

"Come out, Mr. Scratchy. Come out, come out."

"They'd been married four days, only it's not what you think. Mom was already three months pregnant." Henry wiped his glasses on his shirttail. No matter how hard he cleaned, they always had eyebrow dandruff on the lenses. "Mom never said so, but I got the idea it was a shotgun wedding."

He put the glasses back on, two-handed, carefully fitting the ear pieces over his ears. "Dad chose death over having me."

"I think I see him," Guy said.

"I firmly believe Dad's suicide affected my ability to maintain an interpersonal relationship."

Guy bent way down with his cheek touching the dirt and dead leaves. He squinted up the drainpipe to where Mr. Scratchy had somehow lodged himself, face out, toward Guy. Pulling pets from stuck places was something Guy knew about, as opposed to nonviolent direct action. Crawling on all fours through shrubbery kept Guy away from the insurrection while he figured out which side he was supposed to be on.

Mr. Scratchy hissed.

"I'm not sure if I can get him out of this hole," said Guy.

"I was married twice," said Henry. "The first was an alcoholic. She drank Yukon Jack and cranberry juice for breakfast. And the other one cried herself to sleep every night for a year. They both cheated on me."

Guy reached for Mr. Scratchy, who backed up and spit through broken teeth. "Maybe you'd be better at getting Mr. Scratchy to come out."

"He would scratch the heck out of my arm if I tried. That's how he got his name."

"I wondered about that."

"My second wife never forgave me for driving her to adultery. She said I was distant."

Guy stated what, to him, was obvious. "Women who cheat always blame their husbands."

"That's true. I hadn't looked at it that way."

Guy reached up to his elbow into the drainpipe. Mr. Scratchy dug his claws deep into the back of Guy's wrist. In pain, Guy yanked his arm out of the hole, dragging

Mr. Scratchy from the pipe by the claws embedded in Guy's arm. Guy quickly wrapped his free hand around Mr. Scratchy's neck.

"Gotcha."

"Mr. Scratchy is the only pure relationship I've ever had." Henry reviewed his life, testing to see if the statement was true. "Except for maybe a one-night affair I had with Sunshine #2 back during the Summer of Love. We made it under the stage at a Mothers concert, then walked up to the Coit Tower." He stood to look at movement at the front gate. The crowd, which had been drifting away from the entrance, was surging forward again. "The love was real and good, but we were both on acid. I don't think Sunshine #2 remembers being with me."

Guy back-crawled from the bushes, holding Mr. Scratchy by the scruff of the neck. Mr. Scratchy fought being dragged, but with only one hind leg, he couldn't tear into Guy with the fervor of a four-legged cat.

Guy made it to his feet without releasing his hold on Mr. Scratchy. "Here's your cat."

Henry nestled Mr. Scratchy in his arms. Mr. Scratchy broke into a noisy purr. Henry nodded toward the gate. "Someone is coming."

Twenty-Two

Here's the deal with Cyrus Monk. Father, Vietnam. That should tell the story. Cyrus Monk, Sr., returned from the conflict overseas and announced to his pretty wife and toddler son that he was but a husk of his former self. He stayed in either his room or the garage for two months, then one Sunday night, the three of them drove to an Arby's Roast Beef where a group of college kids in red, white, and blue tie-dyed undershirts publicly denounced Cyrus Sr. as a baby killer.

"I crave to be a heroin addict," he said, and he went about the business of making his dream reality. He abandoned his family in a basement apartment on the wrong side of San Jose and hitched to a squatter town called Slab City, out in the desert south of Twentynine Palms. Slab City is the largest congregation of disability-check cashers in America, a sort of haven for veterans and nonveterans alike, living under the shadow of post-traumatic stress.

Cyrus Sr. moved into an empty antique Mini-Winnie without air-conditioning. He lived on objects found around and in the Salton Sea. He died by driving a stolen International Harvester forklift off the end of the pier at Sonny Bono State Park.

Cyrus Jr., who at his father's death became plain Cyrus, spent his childhood in an ethnically diverse neighborhood. His mother held down two jobs — one at Furr's Cafeteria and the other cleaning Intel offices at night — to keep Cyrus clothed, fed, and in school. Every morning when she woke Cyrus and every evening before she caught the bus to work, Eileen Monk would ask Cyrus two questions: "Why are we poor?" To which Cyrus answered, "Because Daddy was ashamed to be in the world." And "Who made Daddy ashamed?" To which Cyrus answered, "Hippies."

Therefore, the aged rebels of Mission Pescadero could not have chosen less sympathetic law enforcement. And while Nicolas does not know that Cyrus's father met his death in much the same fashion as Henry's — self-inflicted, in water — Nicolas instinctively knows the man who steps from the county SUV like Clint Eastwood here to put an end to this foolishness is not an ally. We're not talking the spaghetti-Western Clint, either, all stogie and death, but the twentieth-century version. Hat on straight as a level. Brand-new cowboy boots. Yellow sunglasses. This is Dirty Harry.

"Esteban," Cyrus says. "Get off the phone. Your mama can wait."

Esteban files the mama crack in the place where slights are kept pure. It was Cyrus's long-running needle, just for him. Esteban once left a stakeout to drive his mother to the hospital for her B-12 shot and Cyrus never let it go.

"I'm talking to a woman inside. Says she's an administrative assistant."

Bobby nods good-naturedly at Cyrus. Cyrus is Bobby's hero and role model, but not pal. Cyrus scares Bobby spitless.

Cyrus squints at the crowd in the doorway. Phaedra is eating a nectarine. Hu has put on a stretchy nylon headband decorated with a marijuana leaf pattern. He pulls up his pants leg and empties his urine bag on the travertine patio tile, where Bobby stood earlier. The others are shuffling back into postition. No one except Nicolas seems unnerved by Cyrus's arrival.

"She say anything I might give a damn about?"

"The residents are upset over a cat."

A look of infinite disgust crosses Cyrus's face.

Esteban simultaneously listens and talks. "I think. This woman I'm talking to — Glenda Peters — says they disabled a doctor with some kind of nerve gas and they've locked up her boss." Esteban listens a moment longer. "Alexandra."

Cyrus Monk walks across the street the way men in new cowboy boots walk on pavement. Leading with his crotch. He takes in the extreme longhair on the ladder with the camera, and the two wheelchaired women who are asleep.

"What sort of nerve gas?"

Esteban relays the question and waits. "She doesn't know."

A chant kicks in from the Sausalito sector. *"One, two, three, four, we don't want no conservator."*

"Bobby, fetch me my Taser, from the car." Cyrus doesn't wait for Bobby and the Taser. The back of his neck prickles from a need to hit hippie flesh. "Who all's in charge here?"

Judith speaks from the first upright row behind the chairs, between Suchada and

Nicolas. “Each individual is in charge of his or her self, but I have been chosen as spokesperson for our community.”

Cyrus squints an eye at Judith, wondering why they chose the scrawniest bird in the flock as their spokesperson. He takes for granted she’s a lesbian. “Tell these individuals they have two minutes to break up and go back to their business.”

“Or what?” Ray John says.

Cyrus turns his attention from Judith to Ray John. God, he hates old men in ponytails. He’d love to kill them all. As Bobby hands Cyrus the Taser, Cyrus says, “Or I’m going to hurt a whole load of senile freaks, starting with this one.” He points the gun at Hu, who is grinning up at him in an irritating way.

Nicolas can’t take his eyes off the Taser. Black, evil, four yellow racing stripes. It looks like a serious staple gun. Nicolas has never been in extreme pain before, not once in seventy-five years, and he has developed a fear of pain bordering on phobia. He has the same fear of love and hunger, for the same reasons.

Suchada says, “You would give an electric shock to a man with a heart condition?”

Hu’s grin spreads to the point of idiocy.

He bobs up and down and hums a happy tune.

"I'll blast him out of his shoes," says Cyrus.

"Is whatever satisfaction that will bring you worth the resulting lawsuit?"

This sets off the Sausalito chorus again. *"The whole world is watching. The whole world is watching."*

Cyrus glances at the cameras, wondering if they're on a live feed or just recording. He slips the Taser into a leather holster on his belt. "How do I know he has a heart condition?"

"All men his age have a heart condition."

Up on the ladder, Winston is thinking about selling his footage to an independent documentary filmmaker. He plans to hold out for creative control of the sound track. He could lay on some Who. Or Animals. British rock fits well with riots. Winston films, the crowd chants, the deputies wait, and all this time Hu's stupid grin is grating on Cyrus. The lieutenant is not a man to suffer fools. Nor can he stand being the butt of jokes.

"What are you smiling at, you crippled half-wit?"

Hu bobs his head. "You're standing on the wet spot."

Cyrus looks down at the patio tile where Hu has so recently flushed his urine bag. The fluid, made darker by a hepatic liver, oozes out in a rough amoeba shape around Cyrus's Tony Lamas. Cyrus cannot abide that from a hippie in a headband. He grabs two fistfuls of Hu's shirt and yanks him up. Hu's hands, grown strong from years of wheel propulsion, grasp the handles of the chair, so Cyrus lifts both Hu and wheelchair off the ground.

Phaedra jerks to the side and forward and sinks her teeth into Cyrus's wrist.

Cyrus drops Hu and his chair and slaps Phaedra in the ear hole.

Suchada leans across Gap and nails a half brick into Cyrus's widow's peak, causing him to yelp and fall back a step.

Suchada says, "Two minutes isn't up yet."

Bobby and Esteban hurry to Cyrus's side, each taking an elbow. Bobby wonders what choice he will make if Cyrus orders him to shoot somebody. Esteban thinks the old lady with the brick is pretty cool.

Hatred is more enduring than love. Cyrus's hatred glows with the timeless intensity of a class O star. However, first, foremost, and more vital to Cyrus than hatred, he is a professional lawman. Head of San Mateo County Coastside Operations, answering to the sheriff over in Redwood City. Much as Cyrus would enjoy going stark nuts and stomping, zapping, and clubbing the whole bunch, the professional in him says, "No. Not yet."

Instead, he buys cool-down time by inspecting the tooth holes on his wrist. Five across the top, four on the bottom. Blood seeps down his arm and drips off his elbow.

"Crap," he says. "I'll need a rabies shot."

From the edge of his peripheral vision, he hears Phaedra's cackle.

Cyrus pulls the Taser from its holster and turns, slowly, to his enemies. It matters to Cyrus that they see him as coldly efficient, as opposed to crazed by bloodlust. Bloodlust is effective for scaring the piss out of horny teenagers, but these are not horny teenagers.

"I don't care who has a heart condition, you people are moving aside," says Cyrus.

He flips off the Taser safety and looks up into the nozzles of five cans of bear repellent. Each can is held at arm's length by a man or woman who has wanted to blast a cop for over fifty years.

"Nonviolence only goes so far," says Ray John.

"Right on," says Sunshine #1.

At that moment, the KHMB News Watch news van rolls onto the scene.

TWENTY-THREE

Up in the bell tower, Mr. Natural thumb-flicks his butane lighter. Lucinda Mays leans toward the four-inch flame and lights their second joint of the siege. She maintains as much angle as possible, not facing the flame head-on for fear Nr. Natural's breath might detonate a gas flare.

"This is heavy material," Mr. Natural says.

Lucinda isn't sure if he's talking about the pot or politics. Inhaling marijuana smoke for all she's worth, she breathes a drawn-out "Yeah."

Lucinda is squatting on the balls of her feet, painting PEPPER LAND in red finger-nail polish across the bottom of a flag she and Sunshine #2 made in crafts. It's the Joni Mitchell *Blue* album cover painted on a Depends Fitted Brief for adults.

"You think *Pepper Land* is one word or two?" Lucinda asks.

"I believe strongly that Pepper Land exists so that one may spell it any way one so damn chooses."

Mr. Natural hovers at the arched opening, in his linen suit, playing zoom in-and-out games with a thirty-year-old video recorder the size of a suitcase that once belonged to Fairly Fast Joe Bob before he went through the tunnel. Mr. Natural has the camera focused — at least, he thinks it's focused — on the two sheriff's department SUVs parked across the street. He hears, but cannot see, the action at the gate below.

Lucinda settles back on her heels to admire her work. "There was a time Willow and Sunshine #2 based their hair, clothes, and attitude toward men on Joni Mitchell. Sunshine #1 was the opposite. She said Joni was a Melanie wannabe."

"Melanie performed at Woodstock. She sang a torch song to her bicycle, as I recall."

"I can meet a woman my age and tell you within ten minutes whether or not she ever based major decisions on Joni Mitchell lyrics."

Lucinda passes the joint to Mr. Natural, who takes it without moving his right eye off the viewfinder. "I can do that trick with men and R. Crumb comics."

"The girls on Haight loathed R. Crumb."

"That is precisely why we liked him."

Standing suddenly makes Lucinda dizzy, but she marks that up to dope, not blood pressure. She's been standing quickly all her life. She attaches the Pepper Land flag to a ten-foot fly pole Ray John's ex-wife bought at a garage sale back when she had illusions Ray John would fish away his retirement.

"You know the black dude?" Lucinda asks.

"What black dude?"

"The orderly Alexandra keeps on a leash, like a bodyguard."

"Eldon." Mr. Natural zooms in on Cyrus Monk's front windshield, then goes wide angle on the street. Like Winston, Mr. Natural is aware of the commercial possibilities of an extended revolution. "The spade gentleman is cool. He caught Hu and I with a lid in the chapel and didn't confiscate it. We tipped him a J."

"Do you think he's cute?"

Mr. Natural glances over at Lucinda. "I've never thought a male person was cute in my life."

The noise level downstairs rises to a crescendo, then dies out. Lucinda says, "He's got a nice ass."

Mr. Natural doesn't hold the joint like a joint. He holds it like a cigarette. "Lucinda, he's forty years younger than you."

"If I was a guy and Eldon a chick, forty years would be nothing but a challenge. You've slept with women forty years younger than you, back before you got swamp breath."

Mr. Natural is so stunned he forgets to give the joint back. He sees himself as modern. He firmly believes in equality for women, but sometimes these old broads say the weirdest shit. "But what about Ray John?"

Lucinda finds a crack between rocks at the archway, just the right size for wedging the fly pole butt. She wedges the pole and sends the Pepper Land flag flying. Another cheer rises from the street.

"Aren't the two of you, like" — Mr. Natural searches for the word — "an item?"

"Don't bogart."

Mr. Natural passes the joint. "Sorry."

"Ray John and I are dear friends, but I am free to do what I want, when I want." She inhales smoke and speaks through held breath. "With whomever I want."

Only a creative-writing teacher would have nailed the *whom.*

"Oh," says Mr. Natural.

"I could blow you, this minute, with a clear conscience."

"Are you going to?"

"Of course not. You're old enough to be my daughter's father. I'm just saying I could if I wanted, with a clear conscience."

While Mr. Natural works out the implications of *daughter's father,* the KHMB News Watch news van parks behind the sheriff's department SUVs.

"Somebody's here," Mr. Natural says.

Cyrus and one of the deputies cross the street to the news van. The other deputy lags behind.

"They're leaving," says Lucinda.

Mr. Natural presses his eye to the viewfinder. "No, he's preventing the TV nerd from getting out of the van."

Lucinda leans forward with her hands on the arch opening. "He looks like my grandson."

"The cop looks like your grandson?"

"The TV nerd driving the van. My grandson spikes his hair up like that. Makes his head look like a jack."

Mr. Natural tries to picture the TV kid's head as a jack. "With or without the tire iron?"

"You never played jacks? It's a game. You bounce a ball and pick up jacks."

"I thought you meant a car jack."

"Jesus, Mr. Natural, nobody's head looks like a car jack."

The TV kid tries to open the van door, but Cyrus palms it shut. On the other side of the front seat, an older guy — navy blue coveralls, hearing aid — stares straight ahead, as if he's damned if he'll get involved.

Cyrus's voice floats loud enough to hear from the bell tower. "I told you, son, there's no story."

Lucinda can't hear the TV kid with the spiky hair's answer, but she has the feeling it's whiny. After another thirty seconds, the van growls to a start and rolls away. Cyrus stands, hands on hips, staring at the Mission doors. He spits, walks to his SUV, and he, too, rolls away. The deputies get into their SUV, but they don't roll anywhere.

Mr. Natural turns off the video recorder. "Looks like the other two are hanging out."

Lucinda flips the roach out, over the street, where it lands with a bounce on the pavement, in front of the deputies. She says, "I've got a brutal case of munchies. You know what's for lunch?"

The group mood is upbeat. Playful. Imagine a college cafeteria after the football game in which our brave boys triumphed. Bantering and flirtation fly between rival cliques. Loud laughter from Sausalito, the party table. A minor food fight involving butter pats sailing from North Beach to New York and back. The vegan offers the fruitarian a fig. Synchronized pep cheers from the San Francisco table.

"What do we want?"

"Cornbread!"

"When do we want it?"

"Now!"

Even the waiters are lighter on their feet as they burst from the kitchen bearing trays filled with sloppy joe.

Over at the Stanford table — which should be called something else since only Nicolas, Ike, and Marta actually went to Stanford — Guy Fontaine watches the dining hall goodwill with the slight distance of a sports writer. He knows why fans feel good after victory. They are happy because he, Guy, cracked a cane across the kneecap of authority. He acted out their dream, and now, through the miracle of sports transference, they feel like winners.

Judith Frost of the puffing cheeks, striated lips, and shaking hands holds court at the Stanford table. Although no one introduces her to Guy, he can tell she is in charge. These people, gathered around her like linemen around their quarterback, have taken control from Alexandra and given it to Judith.

"I want two people and a camera on each exit at all times." She twists her turkey neck to spray spittle toward Wanda Bretschneider. "I want you, personally, to track down Colin the maintenance man. He hides in the tunnel, drinking his lunch. You need to check out the generator and get back to me with a fuel estimate."

Guy assumes Wanda is known for her mechanical skills. It strikes him that, should the revolution be driven by senior citizens, it won't be driven by men.

"I need to see that nurse, passes out pills over in N.C.," Judith says. "Her name is Kirsten or Kristen, I never figured which. Nicolas."

Nicolas freezes over a bite of sloppy joe.

"I want you to go exploring in Alexandra's computer. Find me some dirt."

"I can do that," Nicolas says.

"Don't talk with your mouth full. It's disgusting. Tell Mick to set up his sound system out by the tree."

"Are you bringing back the sock hops?" Nicolas asks.

"Did God make you stupid or was it environmental?" Judith points a shaky finger to Ike Pitcairne, who, along with Marta, has been doing his best to stay invisible. "You, bring me a groundskeeper."

Guy finds himself watching Rocky brood over her lunch at the San Francisco table. Rocky hasn't joined in the cheers or the flying butter games. Her eyes are lowered to her plate, but she isn't eating. To Guy, she seems pensive. Lily would sometimes get pensive, back in Waurika, even before the cancer. Not so much depressed as braced, as if she was expecting bad news. Guy always wanted to do something to put her at ease, but hard as he tried, he never had much of an effect on Lily's mood. It's frustrating to love someone and not be able to make her happy.

Rocky raises her eyes and looks across the room at Guy. They hold the look a moment, then Guy waves, sort of a mocking rodeo queen wave. Rocky doesn't wave back.

Guy himself, while not wallowing in group fun, still feels better than usual, considering Lily is dead and he may be senile and he's trapped in assisted living in California. For the first time since the golf cart social blunder, he can see the people around him. He thinks this is because he hit a human being, which is an odd reason to see more clearly. The last time he hit someone was in high school. A senior made a split finger sign to Lily during a safe-driving assembly and Guy decked him. Lily was properly impressed, but Guy doesn't recall the fight changing his vision.

Now he wants to take part. He feels as if he started this upheaval and he should help with it. To give it the sports metaphor, he would be the kicker who makes a tackle.

Guy pictures the Mission from a defensive standpoint, remembering details he hadn't been aware of before. He sees the bell tower and the arcades before Residency and Administration. He wonders if there's a ladder tall enough to send someone into the tree. The north and south walls are thick enough to put people on, but only people with balance and legs. You could post sentries over the chapel and up on the Residency fire escapes.

"What if they climb the fire escapes?" Guy asks.

Judith's owlish glare makes Guy nervous. He feels like an outsider. She's probably been planning an insurrection for months. Heck, maybe they all have. They sure didn't hesitate when it came time to link up and sing.

"You're the Okie who whacked the dogcatcher," Judith says.

Guy lets the Okie crack slide. "Guy Fontaine."

"Here's the deal, Guy Fontaine. We can't

stop an all-out military assault. If that lieutenant sheriff with the stick up his butt decides to land a helicopter on the quad and attack, guns blazing, we're screwed. But he won't."

"If I was in charge, that's what I would do," Guy says.

Judith puffs her cheeks like a bullfrog in heat. "Only if you didn't care what anyone thinks, which, from what I've heard about you, might be true."

Guy can't help but wonder what she's heard about him. Do the comatic women in Nursing Care wake up at night to gossip?

"Our power is our age," Judith says. "Killing people in their seventies and eighties is bad public relations. Beating up the old and helpless doesn't look good on TiVo. Or podcast, cable, satellite, and photo phone."

She leans toward Guy. Guy has an awful feeling she might touch him.

Judith says, "Whoever controls the broadcast outlets, controls the continuing care center. You understand?"

"Not a bit."

Judith chews her lips and cranes her head from shoulder to shoulder. She seems to be deciding if Guy is worth the trouble of an explanation. "Your children locked you in here, right?"

"My daughter. Claudia."

"Stole your keys and then your money."

Guy nods.

"Took your freedom."

"She said she had to because she loves me."

Judith clucks. "Kids don't know much about irony, do they?"

"You have to be over sixty-five to get it."

"So, now your daughter doesn't want any reminders of what she did. She wishes you the best, but only if you stay out of sight, and getting stomped on TV isn't staying out of sight."

"You think she'd mind me getting stomped if it's not on television?"

"She wouldn't even know. The last thing your daughter is going to ask you is whether or not you've been abused this week."

Over at the Haight tables, Henry and Ray John get into it over the location of the Diggers' free dentist in December of 1969. Henry claims it was on Clayton Street. Ray John says Jordan. Various women take sides based more on loyalty to Henry or Ray John than any memory of free dental work in the sixties.

Judith and Guy listen while the argument swells, crests, and breaks without anyone coming to blows or agreement. Judith mutters, "Idiots." Then she turns back to Guy.

"Now, widen your daughter's lack of compassion to include her entire generation. They all, as a society, wish us well, but they'll do whatever it takes to keep us out of sight. The last thing anyone wants is to watch the police riot on grandmas and grandpas."

Guy starts to catch on. "Our job is to stay in sight."

Judith slaps him on the knee, just what he was afraid might happen. "Attaboy, Okie."

"When you call me Okie, you'd better smile."

Judith pats his leg twice, causing a mild gag reflex. "Political correctness went out with Jeb the Third Bush, Guy. Now, pay attention." She holds up four gnarled appendages that were once the fingers of a girl. "There are four primary means for us to communicate with the media." She drops fingers as she counts. "Cell. Wireless Internet. Fiber optics. Hologram imaging. At this moment, our friend Cyrus is going about shutting down each of those."

"How can he shut down wireless e-mail?"

"They have boxes, same as what they use to block cell phones in churches and concert halls these days."

Nicolas jumps into what Guy thought was

a private conversation. "Ray John has an amazing media database. He writes letters to the editor."

"Let's give old Ray John something to do," says Judith.

Nicolas smiles, happy to have come up with an idea. It makes him feel like a contributor to the cause. "What should he say?"

"Ray John's a smart boy. He'll think of something."

Guy's attention has drifted. He dreams of going over the wall. Or under it. Or maybe finding the secret passage Zorro used to escape from Don Whatever-his-name-was in the stories. As Guy recalls, the passage starts in the mission library and comes out in a peasant's fireplace, far away. If there is an invasion, they'll be after him more than the others. Instead of sticking around to face God knows what legal ramifications come from conking dogcatchers, Guy dreams of slipping away and hitchhiking to Oklahoma. He used to hitch quite a bit around Wilburton. He still has friends along the Red River who would hide him out. Guy can see no reason for sitting in an institution, either this one or prison, quietly awaiting death. It would be more fun to go out in a hailstorm of glory, carving little *Z*'s in the chests of those who would steal his freedom.

Twenty-Four

Dear Roderick,

Well, the inmates have taken the asylum. It was bound to happen, sooner or later. They were only waiting for an excuse and the new resident gave them one. He did what no one else around here has managed to pull off. He took action. Now, like a jump-started hot rod, this bunch of ancient activists is off to the races. They're up in their rooms, now, as I write, firing off e-mails and blog rants, trying to make certain the tantrum doesn't go unnoticed.

I'm afraid my message will be short today. Judith Frost has called a meeting of everybody — residents and staff — out on the quad. Sounds like she's planning a pep rally. Judith has risen from the dead, so to speak, to lead the operation. You have to admire her for being first to go through the tunnel and come back, but she still strikes me as creepy. I can't picture her as young, or even middle-aged. Everyone around here sees each other pretty much as they were, and not as they are, but, I swear, Judith sprung from her mother's womb post-menopausal. I don't trust her, Roderick.

The other thing that bothers me, besides Judith, about this little uprising is the motivation. Darcy Faye Gardiner called it a flashback festival, like we're organizing some kind of '60s theme party. It used to piss me off so much during the Vietnam War protests. While the cause was important, ninety percent of the protesters were out there to have a good time. They came for the music and pot and the thrill of flipping off National Guardsmen. They came because here was a cool excuse to cut class and we could break the law in public. They might even get self-righteously laid. Whoopie. Whoopie.

Chairman Mao said a revolution is not a tea party. But our revolution was. While boys were being killed because the grownups thought American pride was more important than ruining families.

And here's what makes it a heartbreak. We grew up thinking it would be different when the old farts died off. It wasn't. If anything, our generation is worse. We became the old farts ourselves, willing to send our neighbors' children — never our own — off to die simply because the United States doesn't lose wars and we'll be damned if it'll happen on our watch, even years after we realize the war is stupid.

Today, after Ray John recited the Port Huron Statement and only Judith and I knew what it was, the grief came washing over me, the whole last sixty years of crushed hope. And the jokers at lunch were laughing, "Just like the good old days." Well, we lost big-time in the good old days. Not one damn thing happened in the '60s that I feel nostalgic about. The drugs didn't take. The free love wasn't free and it wasn't love.

Christ, I must sound like a shrew to you, Roderick. And I'm sorry about that crack about inmates and the asylum. I sometimes forget where you are.

Let's talk about something more pleasant.

Like the new guy. Guy. He started this mess, but he acts as if he's unaware of what he's done. Maybe he's not acting. Maybe he's a for-real lost soul. He reminds me of the character Gary Cooper used to play in movies back during Depression I — sort of a well-meaning doofus galumphing through the chaos, while everyone around him is working angles, using him for their own ends. *Meet John Doe.* The man of rock-solid principles we admire even though we know all along he's not so very bright. Maybe Guy is bright. If so, he's gotten real used to hiding it. He kind of scares me.

Willow just stuck her head in the door and said the meeting is about to begin. I suppose now we've started the revolt, we should decide what we're revolting for. Or, at least, against. I hope we demand something more specific than world peace. That was a dud, last time.

Good night, my precious. Until tomorrow.

Ever,
Your mother

Rocky mouses the arrow over to Send and clicks. She waits, then waits some more.

A sign comes on the screen: DOMAIN SERVERS ARE NOT RESPONDING.

"Hell," Rocky says.

The library lights flicker and go out.

Mick adjusts the subwoofer and plugs in the monitor. "Power's gone."

Judith says, "Tell Wanda to fire the generator."

Mick leaves his sound board, half set up, and goes to find Wanda Bretschneider while Judith pushes her walker along in the wake of a groundskeeper named Leroy Love, who is spray-painting a stripe from the eucalyptus to the goose pond. Leroy shakes his can, rattling whatever it is they put in spray paint cans for whatever reason they put it there. He sprays down to within two feet of the pond.

"Not going to be enough paint to make it all the way," Leroy says.

"That's close," Judith says. "They'll get the idea."

Leroy's finished off two cans of white paint and one of red, so far, and he's out. Not once has he asked Judith why he's painting a stripe on the lawn. Leroy is fifty-two years old. Between the Army, the San Francisco City Parks department, Wal-Mart, and Mission Pescadero, he's never had a job where it's acceptable to question an irrational order.

Residents filter onto the quad in twos and

threes. Many bring lightweight lawn furniture. Some carry plastic, multipurpose stools. They have that expectant yet stoical look you see on the faces of people filing into a bluegrass festival. Winston and Hu are obviously stoned. Lucinda brings a box of donuts, which she shares with Willow and Sunshine #1. From up in the bell tower where she's stationed with Henry, Sunshine #2 calls down a plea for donuts of her own.

From Administration and Maintenance, housekeeping and the orderlies' break room, the staff appears. Alexandra hires by a strict system of racial profiling that makes sense to her and no one else. Once you learn the system, it isn't difficult to tell who holds down what job: housekeeping, Mexican women; dining hall waiters and bus help, Mexican men; cooks, white; gardeners, Asian; orderlies and janitors, black; laundry, Jamaican; maintenance, white males over fifty. The only manual staff members of mixed ethnicity are dishwashers, who can be any color as long as they come enrolled in a government-financed program for the physically or intellectually challenged.

Each group sticks tightly together, off to the statue side of the pond. The staff is doing whatever they can to remain noncommittal. While no one feels any particular loyalty to Alexandra or the cartel of Russian Hill doctors who own Mission Pescadero, neither are any of the employees in a rush to lose their jobs.

Judith hobbles in six-inch jerks over to the clutch of Spanish housekeepers. "Any of you girls named Inez Vasquez?"

The youngest of the bunch translates and the oldest holds her hand up breast high.

"This is Inez Vasquez," says the translator.

"Her grandson asked about her. Wants to make certain she's okay."

The translating housekeeper says something to Inez, who says something back. They keep this up through three exchanges, then the translator speaks to Judith. "She says she is fine."

"Have Inez give her grandson a call. She can tell him we're treating her well."

"The phones are out, Señora."

Judith puffs her capillary-sprayed cheeks. "That was quick."

On her way back to Mick, who is finishing his sound check — *Testing. One, two. Testing* — Judith stops to talk to the nurse, Kristen. Kristen is surrounded by nodding-out women in wheelchairs.

"You got everybody?" Judith asks.

"All except two bedridden patients we

shouldn't move." Kristen has one child in jail and another in rehab. She has no fear of Judith.

Judith starts to hobble away, then stops. "We should discuss the way you're medicating in Nursing Care."

"It won't do any good, talking to me. I follow Dr. Beaver's orders."

Judith ducks her head and looks up at Kristen from hooded eyes. "But you don't always agree with Dr. Beaver, do you?"

Kristen sees Angelica Rose is about to slide out of her chair. As she hefts Angelica by the armpits and lifts her up, back into position, she says, "It's not my job to say."

"What if crazed anarchists threatened your life unless you cut out unneeded tranquilization? What would you do then?"

Kristen pats Angelica on shoulders thin as shovel blades. She looks across Angelica's nearly bald head to where Judith stands with a sly kind of smirk on her face. "I'd have to do what the anarchists tell me."

"That's the spirit." Judith nods and puffs. She lifts the walker an eighth of an inch, then drops it. "Come see me after the meeting."

Twenty-Five

Guy waits, alone, tucked in, arms crossed over his rib cage, at the back of the crowd, almost to the Administration arcade. He tries counting heads, but it is difficult, as groups mingle and shift. He comes up with fifty-five or so Assisted Living, and maybe twenty-five Nursing Care, although there is a smattering of upright individuals he cannot place. He hasn't seen them in the dining hall, yet they don't act so far gone as to qualify for N.C., either. So, where have they been hiding?

Rocky pulls on a light sweater as she crosses over from the library to stand near Guy. Not quite next to. Near.

"Who're the ones over by the wheelchairs?" Guy asks. "They're kind of spry for Nursing Care."

Rocky looks at the six or seven men and women mixed in with Kristen and her charges. Two wear bathrobes over pajamas.

The rest are dressed more for winter up the coast than this warm November afternoon. They appear cogent, more or less, except they wear vulnerability like an open wound.

"Alzheimer's," Rocky says. "They're not so advanced as to be helpless, but as soon as Beaver diagnoses Alzheimer's he ships them through the tunnel."

"I'll bet that's what he has in mind for me."

Guy counts twenty he would call staff. Upper management and office types hover together around Glenda and Eldon, watching Judith with suspicion. The more menial employees wait in various degrees of boredom and restlessness. Not much overt curiosity. Some of the kitchen help smoke cigarettes in direct defiance of Mission policy.

Then there is Dixie Lichens, in a category all her own. Guy is surprised to see she's still on the property, still in silver lamé. She stands with her back to Guy, rising on her toes, twitching her shoulders. The crescent moon of skin visible above her leotard is both tanned and translucent. Her blond hair is tied in a ponytail set off the crown of her head, the way Guy remembers girls wearing their hair back in the '50s. He can plainly see that she is isometrically exercising her butt muscles.

Rocky knows what Guy is looking at. "I would never want to be that young again," Rocky lies.

Guy tells the truth. "Me either."

"People." Judith hunches over the microphone with both claws clutched to the mike stand, which is set at its lowest possible position. She chews and glares, willing the crowd to pay attention. "Let's start."

In the ensuing silence, Hu farts. Winston breaks up, as if Hu has pulled the most hilarious stunt imaginable. Hu falls out of his wheelchair.

"Someone stifle the loadies so I can talk," Judith says.

Sunshine #1 pats Winston on the arm, gently shushing him. Willow and Lucinda lift Hu back into the chair, where he fakes mortification.

Judith nods to Mick, who cranks the volume. She breathes in and out through her nose, causing an electrical whistle noise to reverberate through the speakers.

"People. We are alive!"

General cheers from the stoned gang. Stares from staff.

"Our children and our government, our conservators, our doctors, certainly the administration of this facility, all have conspired to make us believe otherwise. But, by our actions today, here at Pepper Land, we have proclaimed to the world, *We. Are. Alive!*"

More cheers. Henry and Sunshine #2 shout, *"Ho, Ho, Ho Chi Minh. AARP is gonna win,"* from the tower. Sausalito joins in, although more in the ironic party mode than genuine support. More *Go Girl!* than *Yes!* For the most part, New York looks grim.

Judith continues. "Dylan Thomas wrote, 'Do not go gentle into that good night.' I propose to you that we take his advice. I propose that we go kicking, screaming, and in Phaedra's case *biting,* into that good night."

Even the seniors who aren't on drugs cheer this one. Rocky thinks it's a nice touch to single out Phaedra. If Judith hadn't crawled out of N.C., no doubt Phaedra would have put herself in charge. And giving her credit strengthens Judith's power base.

"Look at the words written over the dining hall."

As one, the crowd turns their heads to look at the inscription they see every day.

"Independence. Dignity. Respect. Alexandra Truman has made a mockery of those words. She has twisted them into an *advertising* slogan. Today, right now, we shall give meaning back to the words we hold so dear. We shall stand up, and if we can't stand up, we'll sit up straight." Judith waits for the laugh she doesn't get.

"We shall shout to the world, *We are alive!*"

Guy has to admit, she's good. Back in his faraway youth, in Cotton County, Oklahoma, Guy's social life had revolved around revivals and fairs, and, except for her wounded bird voice, Judith is as rabble-rousing as any southern evangelist.

Now she narrows her eyes and leans forward, speaking in a personal, conspiratorial tone. "I won't lie to you."

Beside Guy, Rocky snorts, cynically.

"I won't lie to you. Our battle will not be easy. The men who control this country will use any means to keep us invisible. Those *men* have the power and they will not give it up willingly. We, the oldest and wisest Americans, must reach out and *take* back our freedom."

Judith clears her throat with a sound like a rock slide. She turns her attention to the employees. "And while we are not the helpless infants Alexandra, the conservators, and that bunch back there" — she gestures contemptuously at the office staff — "would like us to be, neither are we so arrogant as to refuse help when it is freely offered."

The low end of the workforce shifts from foot to foot as the youngest housekeeper translates Judith's words. They look at the ground. They look at the walls of Residency. They look anywhere but at Judith. The office staff, on the other hand, stares at her. They know when they've been insulted. Eldon drifts from Glenda toward the low-end employees as the orderly known as the Squealer drifts the other way, toward management.

Judith says, "We need some of you who perform necessary services to volunteer as hostages."

"Can there be a voluntary hostage?" Guy asks.

Rocky says, "I guess so."

"I cannot guarantee how management and the state will treat those who stay. You may risk arrest or even physical harm if the state uses force against us. You may lose your jobs. We *will* include amnesty for everyone, staff and resident, in our demands — and we *will* win our demands or *burn* the Mission down trying."

Guy says, "Burn the Mission down?"

Rocky says, "I think she means metaphorically."

"I'm not so sure."

"You can't burn rock."

"All of you have families on the outside. Think of your parents and grandparents. Would you want someone to stay with them?"

To Guy, this appeal to family after she's said our children want us dead seems contradictory. Same as you might lose your job but we will protect you. It appears Judith wants it both ways. But then, the minimum-wage caregivers she's making the pitch to are mostly Hispanic and black. There are no Hispanics and only a few blacks in A.L. or N.C. Maybe Judith is working the "Rich white kids ignore their parents but you're better" angle.

"I understand this is not your battle. You have responsibilities on the outside. Stay, if you will, but if you cannot, no one will think the worse of you."

Judith turns partway back toward the residents and holds her arms out like Jesus at the Last Supper. "The moment of decision is at hand. Those of you who are willing and able to stand by my side and fight for our independence, dignity, and respect, I ask you to step across the line. Those of you who are unwilling, or, in some cases, unable, to cross this line will be released. Residents and patients who do not stay will be taken care of at other facilities. The rest of you can go home."

Judith pauses to let her congregation murmur among themselves. She scans the faces, left to right, searching for the doubters and weak links. The pathetic geezers. Most of them have no idea what in hell they are starting. Out for a party. A good time at the expense of the Boss Man. Well, she's begun with less before, and it came out okay. Someone once said, "You go with the army you have, not the army you want."

Time for the big finish. "We must sell our lives as dearly as possible. I shall stay and fight until the last breath is pulled from my body. I invite you to stay with me. You have three minutes to decide."

Mick reaches across to the sound system and punches the Play button. "A Whiter Shade of Pale" by Procol Harum surges from the speakers.

Twenty-Six

Ray John is first across the line, looking angry enough to punch someone. Then the Haight women, both early and late, flowers in their hair, donuts in their hands. New York crosses en masse. Berkeley holds a meeting, votes, and comes across. Sausalito dances across the line, hand in hand, singing "We Shall Come Over" to the tune of "We Shall Overcome."

Rocky says, "I didn't get the part about 'We must sell our lives as dearly as possible.' "

"It's from the Alamo," says Guy.

"The movie?"

"Lily's cousins lived in San Antonio and whenever we visited they would drag us down there. I hated it. There's nothing worse for an Oklahoman than to find himself in the Alamo surrounded by patriotic Texans." At the memory, Guy takes a clean handkerchief from his back trousers pocket and wipes his forehead. "Most important story in Texas history: William Travis drew a line in the sand, with his sword. He said, 'We must sell our lives as dearly as possible,' and had everyone willing to die cross the line. They all died but the one man who wouldn't cross."

"I wonder how Judith would know the Alamo story," Rocky says.

"That accent of hers is strange, but I don't think she got it in Texas."

"Nobody knows where Judith is from. My theory is she emerged full grown from the belly of a whale."

A vicious argument breaks out between Georgia Rogers and Frances Ian.

Frances says, "I'm crossing."

Georgia clamps hold of Frances's wrist. "These people are our enemies. We hate them for what they did to us."

"What they did before doesn't matter now. This time, they are right."

"They could never be right. Anything they are for, we are against."

The women engage in bitter eye contact. "Let go of me, Georgia."

"You are betraying your husband's memory."

"The Vietnam War is over." Frances tears up. "Right now, today, I'm sick of being

cheated by insurance companies. Pharmaceutical companies. Lawyers and doctors. Government bureaucrats hiding behind policy. They stole my Social Security. Medicare turned into a front for drug Nazis, and I'm not going to take it anymore." She brushes the back of her hand across the tears on her cheeks. "Even if I have to go over to the side of the assholes."

Sunshine #2 and Henry pause on their passage from the bell tower to the line. Henry says, "Great speech. You're better than Judith."

Both women glare at Henry. Frances says, "Get lost, loser."

The women maintain tense silence as Henry and Sunshine #2 join their Haight friends across the line. Georgia says, "The Vietnam War will never be over until the last person whose life was ruined by it dies."

Frances pries Georgia's fingers off her arm. "I'm crossing."

As Frances walks away, Georgia says, "We can't be friends anymore, after this."

Frances stops and turns. "I never liked you anyway. I only sat with you in the dining hall because of our husbands."

Frances crosses the line.

"Are you going over?" Rocky asks Guy.

"I started it. I guess I have to."

"Don't flatter yourself, kiddo. They've been planning this for months."

Guy nods. "I suspected as much."

Eldon says, "You all going?" and the bus-boys and other orderlies look at the grass.

Eldon says, "I'm going."

Inez Vasquez says the Spanish equivalent of "Me too," and the low-end wage earners of Mission Pescadero cross the line, all at once, like calves spurting over a bridge. One housekeeper, Rose, with five kids under second grade and a mother who won't take care of them after six p.m., stays behind, along with the office crew and mid-level management. Head housekeeper. Head chef. The Squealer. Eldon is the only one with *head* in his title who crosses.

Imogene is the woman in charge of washing nursing patients' hair. She writes a note to give to Rose. "Call Cubby's day care," Imogene says. This sets off a whirlwind of borrowed paper and pens and note writing. By the time Rose goes to clock out, she has an entire evening's worth of phone calls to make.

Kristen bends close to Angelica Rose's face. "Angie, do you want to stay or leave?"

Angelica fights with her useless tongue. "Take me cross."

"I can't hear you."

"Across."

Eldon brings his orderlies back over the line to ask the same question of all the patients in chairs. Three are asleep and two stare straight ahead with no indication of comprehension.

Kristen says, "Leave the ones who can't give some sign they want to go over."

Catatonic Joe Bob, who isn't really catatonic, same as he wasn't really fairly fast before he went through the tunnel, sniffs and drools and makes a sound like a smothered animal.

"I think he wants to stay with us," Eldon says.

"Can you take care of him? There won't be any night shift relief."

"I'll take care of him."

Over on the line, Phaedra spins her chair about to block Dixie. "We don't want your kind," Phaedra says.

"What?"

"Teaching girls to breathe through their pelvis is not a necessary service."

"Diaphragm," says Dixie. "And teaching people to breathe properly is too necessary."

"Why don't you go be pretty down at the mall?"

Dixie's face flushes, turning her freckles into a light-on-dark pattern instead of dark on light. "That is the rudest thing I ever heard."

Phaedra's lip curls. Her eyes spark with a hatred far beyond anything Dixie could have provoked herself.

"I'm offering to help," Dixie says. "And you're judging me because of the way I look. You of all people should be ashamed."

Phaedra doesn't give a damn. Behind her, Suchada places a hand on the older woman's shoulder. "Why Phaedra of all people?"

Dixie says, "I heard Phaedra practically started the women's movement in the '60s."

"Screw *practically.* I *did* start the women's movement."

"Girls of my generation idolize you for fighting the kind of prejudice that you're dumping on me right now."

"Dixie's right," Suchada says. "We're judging her because she looks and acts like an airhead. She deserves a chance to prove us wrong."

Dixie says, "Totally."

Suchada says, "Let her cross."

Phaedra twists and shrugs and bobs her head. "The first time her hair gets mussy, we'll have to babysit her."

"Will not," Dixie says.

"If there's a fight and I'm in it, I'll have Dixie babysit you." Suchada signals Dixie to step around Phaedra.

Dixie says, "Thank you for letting me stay."

"Promise you won't make me look bad," Suchada says.

"Nothing you do could ever make you look bad."

Suchada takes that comment six different ways, then drops it.

A strangling sheep sound bleats from Nursing Care and Gap Koch rolls down the ramp. His shirt flaps loose, the bottom button stuck through the third-from-bottom buttonhole. He's pulled his pants up, covering his legs but not quite over his yellow boxers. One black sock, no shoes. He hits the bottom of the ramp making decent speed, and heads up the sidewalk toward Judith's line in the lawn.

"I thought he was too drugged to get out of bed," Kristen says.

"Looks like he was," Henry says.

Arms pump. Tongue flaps. Gap moves along fairly well, shouting unintelligible gibberish about pigs, napalm, and warm pussy.

But then the chair veers into the grass and bogs down. The front right wheel strikes an automatic sprinkler head and he bucks to a stop.

Gap shouts, "Brothers, come get me."

No one moves.

Gap's eyes skitter in something akin to a panic. *"I am a lawyer. Do what I say."*

The orderlies, as a group, can't stand Gap Koch. The lawyer thing is bad enough, although forgivable in the aged, but what's worse is Gap is a jerkoff. Always the insult. Always the sneer. Treats them like bumptious servants. While Hu and Winston are harmless brain-dead buffoons — practically charming in a Cheech and Chong way — Gap is seen as a mean-spirited, disgusting pervert.

No one crosses the line to give him a hand.

"Someone, get over here!" Gap yanks the wheel back. Up. More stuck than ever, he's fallen off to the side so his head hangs over the handrail. From twenty yards out, the residents smell the ammonia stink of dried urine.

Gap gets angry. "Chickenshit scumbags. Help me."

He begs. *"Please."*

He bribes. "I'll give you skag."

Gap howls, more like a dog than a coyote.

"Oh, hell," Rocky says.

"What?" Guy asks.

"Nothing."

Rocky walks to Gap. She says, "You're a prick, you know that?"

"Yes." Big leer. "And you're my sweet-ass honey pie."

"This is a mistake." Rocky lifts Gap by the armpits, fixing him into an upright position. She rocks the chair back and forth but it won't go until she realizes in his flailing Gap has set the brake.

"No wonder you're stuck."

"I knew you had to help me. I'm not resistible."

"Don't make me vomit on you."

Gap lolls his head back so far Rocky fears his neck might crack. "I'm having a problem with stiffies. Can you help me?"

"No."

"But you're my little fuckee."

"I'll make you walk from here if you don't shut up."

Rocky pushes Gap across the line, then she gets away from him, leaving Eldon and Kristen to deal with the mess.

Gap calls out, "Come back, little fuckee."

Judith turns away. "Time's up. Let's get to work."

Twenty-Seven

Midnight at the Mission. Flying specks of insects swarmed in the glow of the goose pond security light. Nicolas, on his walk to the bell tower, stopped to watch. The bugs hovered, shifting, floating like summer fog. Nicolas had lived seventy-five years within a hundred miles of this goose pond, yet he had no idea the names, either common or scientific, of the insects. He could identify maybe four trees, double that in wildflowers, most, but not all, the land and sea mammals, none of the clouds or stars, three types of fish, at best. All in all, Nicolas had an incredibly small store of information about the world surrounding his body.

Generally, this wouldn't bother him. His was the media generation. (He could tell you Beaver Cleaver lived in the same house as Marcus Welby, but he couldn't tell a California gull from a western gull.) Tonight, however, watching bugs in the dense sea air, he wondered how important computers are in the grand scheme called life. Do they matter? Is heaven a d20 role-playing system with multiple lives and levels, like the cyber-Buddhists claimed? Are humans bits of information on a web, or is the grand scheme itself a bad joke?

He found Ray John, staring morosely out the bell tower arch toward the sheriff's department SUV parked across the street from the front gate. Ray John, too, appeared engrossed in deep thought. Maybe it was going around tonight. Or maybe his upcoming deafness made him appear engrossed. People losing their hearing are often given credit for depth they don't necessarily feel.

"Any movement?" Nicolas asked.

Ray John jerked to attention. He hadn't known Nicolas was at his side. "One of them took a leak over by the parking lot a half hour or so ago."

"I always wondered about that, when I saw a stakeout on television. How they handle urination crises."

"At their age, urination isn't the crisis it is for us." Ray John stuffed both hands deep into his pockets. "I peed out the window myself."

Nicolas eyeball measured the thickness of the arch ledge. Ten inches, at least. No way could he get up the pressure needed to piss out that opening, not without soaking the sill.

"The Sunshines took them coffee a while ago," Nicolas said.

"I saw." Ray John drew one hand from his pocket and pinched the bridge of his nose. "I was thinking about when the Sunshines stuck daisies down the gun barrels of the National Guardsmen over at People's Park."

"I wasn't there," Nicolas said. "I had to study."

"The Guardsmen didn't know whether to shoot them or desert." Ray John sighed, a long, sad sound. "As I recall Lucinda talked a kid from San Bernadino into deserting."

Who made the best use of their tiny allotted time alive? The kids fighting the National Guard? The hippies exploring consciousness? The ones who studied? Or the National Guardsmen themselves? To Nicolas, it doesn't seem to matter now, what anyone did on a given day in 1969.

"We were all naive back then, don't you think?" Nicolas said.

"*Naive* is the fey word. I would call us stupid."

Ray John walked the circle of the bell tower loft. There never was a bell. The continuing care center is only mission-style, not a real mission, and the bell itself, which was included in the original plans, was sacrificed in the name of cost-cutting. Nicolas thought that with the cell phones jammed, it would have been convenient to have a bell.

"I wasted my life," Ray John said.

Nicolas looked up from the sheriff's department SUV. This sort of personal despair had always been off-limits with the coffee clique. Even Henry, who is as depressed as an aging actor, never actually spoke aloud in terms of misery.

"Everyone thinks that now and then," Nicolas said.

"I think it all the time." Ray John stopped pacing at the arch, looking inward, toward the quad. "I spent twenty-six years married to a woman who could barely stand me, working a job that didn't matter. While Judith was out making the world better."

"Do you think Judith made the world better?"

"She tried." Ray John leaned both hands on the window ledge. "Twenty-six years pretending to love a woman I didn't love, then five years pretending I don't love a woman I do love. That's thirty-one years of living lies."

Nicolas brushed his fingers along the wall

as he, too, circled to the quad side. The rock was cool and rough. It felt like a message in Braille. He couldn't help but think at least Ray John had a woman to pretend to love and another to pretend not to love. All Nicolas ever had was a team of coworkers.

"I've slept with eight women," Ray John said. "And every one of them would rather have been with someone else."

"Eight? I thought you guys over on Haight had orgies every night."

"Maybe Winston did. Most of us used free love as a line to throw at runaways from Iowa. It worked now and then, but mostly they wanted to smoke pot and meet musicians."

Nicolas's woman count was considerably less than Ray John's, which was embarrassing because single men are supposed to have more sex than married men, in the Bay Area anyway. Nicolas had been too busy doing something else to think about the relationship deal. There'd been the one thing, back in high school, but he didn't think about that. Nothing you do in high school counts.

"What about Lucinda?" Nicolas figured she's the second woman Ray John was talking about, the one he had to pretend not to love. "She acts like you're first choice."

"Lucinda loves everyone." Ray John

squinted up his eyes, making the pond wrinkle in space. Lately his night sight had been hampered by a spray of red dots at the center of his vision. It was easier to see objects without looking directly at them. "I strongly believe people who claim they love everyone don't love anyone."

"She seems to prefer you. Maybe at our age, being preferred is the best we can do."

"She prefers me so long as I don't freak her out." Ray John leaned over the ledge to look at the flagstones below. "I wonder if a person jumped from here, if it would kill him."

Nicolas came to the opening and looked down also. "More likely, turn you quad."

A bent figure darted from Residential, across the dark lawn and into the hedges that surround Contemplative Corner. The figure was wearing what can only be called a breechcloth. It appeared to be painted, although in the dark Ray John and Nicolas couldn't make out the color of the paint, or even for certain if that was what it was. Leather house slippers. Dark glasses. A long feather behind one ear. The figure crept around the hedge, then ran over to the tree and slapped it with both palms.

Ray John said, "Henry."

Henry ran into the pond. Knees pumping, he splashed out until the water lapped over his groin. He squealed a startled *Yelp!* Thrashing, he turned and fought his way back to shore. He held both arms over his chest and ran back into Residential.

Nicolas said, “You think we should tell anybody?”

Twenty-Eight

Guy sleeps six hours out of ten he's in bed, dreaming of pecan trees and old-style girls' basketball the way Lily played it in high school, three on three. He awakens fuzz-tongued, and wanders down to the dining hall, hoping the current crisis hasn't screwed up the breakfast schedule. He finds the residents clustered around Rudy Milovik, the TV nerd. Rudy stands on the rear-of-the-room stage, interviewing Marta and Ike Pitcairne. His hair is freshly spiked. He has a brass nose ring the size of a Cheerio.

"And why have you joined the revolt at Mission Pescadero?" Rudy shoves the microphone into Marta's face.

Marta licks her chapped lips. She looks from Rudy to Judith, who stands stone-faced behind her walker at the side of the stage.

"I don't want to make anyone angry," Marta says.

"Then why did you help repel Lieutenant Monk yesterday?"

Marta is in anguish, torn between offending Judith and the outside world. Visibly, she screws up her courage. "I'm tired of being treated like an old lady," which, of course, is what she is. "People act like I'm helpless. The man at the cell phone company cheated me. He said it was normal for my phone to die after a one-minute call. He thought I was too old to know better."

Ike nods. "Our landlord evicted us from the townhouse where we'd lived since the kids moved out. We never missed a month's rent, but he said I might fall down and he couldn't risk a lawsuit."

Marta says, "The people in there now use it for a meth lab."

Guy picks up coffee with half-and-half and a sweet roll, then he joins the crowd. He stands between Dixie and Sunshine #2. The frizzy-haired Sunshine. She is trying to catch the eye of the cameraman. Leo. Same coveralls, hearing aid, and attitude as yesterday. Leo is sure he's going to be fired for this. He views the seniors as whiners. Hell, he's sixty-eight himself and hasn't missed a day of work in his adult life.

"How'd they get in?" Guy asks.

"The hearse garage," Sunshine #2 says.

"The kid says Lieutenant Monk ordered his boss to ignore the story, but he thinks if he gets some good material, they'll have to run it."

Ike and Marta are helped off the stage, and Willow steps up, resplendent in a Mama Cass muumuu. "I gained fifty pounds and my daughter said I could no longer live independently."

Then Mick, who has moved on from Paul Revere. Now he's the Confederate General at Big Sur. "I was playing touch football and broke my ankle. A niece I'd never seen before flew out from Chicago. She insisted on having her name put on my bank accounts while I recovered. By the time I came off crutches, she'd cleaned me out."

Wanda Bretschneider: "I was forced to retire from Skywalker Ranch, then Bob died and I got depressed. Medicaid took my house and forced me into an institution."

Hu, red-eyed and smelling of medicinal weed: "My pension plan went tits up because the CEO gutted the company. He lives in Kauai now, and I'm here."

Chicken Little : "Dr. Symmes said skydiving is a symptom of senility."

Fairly Fast Freddy: "I got busted for importing AIDS medicine from Argentina. Same pills cost twelve times as much here and my markup was only half that. The judge had me choose between prison and assisted living. I wish I'd chosen prison."

"How about you, ma'am?"

"Don't ma'am me," says Sunshine #1.

"How'd a woman of your obvious vitality come to Mission Pescadero?"

Sunshine #1 touches Rudy on the sleeve. "My neighbor, Mr. Berson, was ninety and the sweetest gentleman you ever met. Nobody could say no to Mr. Berson."

Her eyes slide into memory.

"And?" Rudy prompts.

"While he was showing me the Engorged Horse, Mr. Berson all of a sudden crossed over."

"What exactly is *crossed over?*"

"He died. His wife blamed me, of course, they always do, and my lawyer suggested I check into the Mission for a while. My lawyer made it sound like a country club. He said I could leave whenever I wanted. The motherfucker."

Sunshine #1 smiles into the camera. Or at Leo, Guy can't tell which. "I think Mr. Berson died happy. His wife couldn't make him happy. If it was left to her, he'd have died of something long and lingering."

Rudy glances at Leo. "We'll edit that." He steps center stage. "Start tight and then go wide as I talk."

"I'll do my job. You do yours," Leo says.

"Okeydoke."

Guy says, "You think he's over twenty?"

Sunshine #2 shrugs. "I never can tell anymore."

Dixie says, "I knew Rudy in high school. He was goth, back then."

Rudy counts three, two, one on his fingers, then puts on his camera face. "We're talking today with the senior citizens of Mission Pescadero Continuing Care Center who have seized the property and evicted the management team." No one has told Rudy about Alexandra and Dalton in the dispensary. "I'd like to hear more from you folks. What do you hope to accomplish by your act of civil disobedience? What is it you want?"

As Leo pans across the crowd —

"Locks on the doors."

"Access to medical records."

"I want my Mustang back."

"No more forced retirement."

"My pension."

"Kill the conservators."

"The money I put in Social Security."

"World peace."

"Free chocolate."

"Amnesty for Henry and Mr. Scratchy."

"End the war in Vietnam."
"Medicare-financed Viagra."
"I want to be treated like a human being."
"Give me control over my own money."
"Control over my own body."
"Control."
"Make me young."

Leo swivels back to Rudy, who says, "That's all very interesting."

Henry bounds into the room, dressed as he was late last night except the breechcloth — two safety-pinned hand towels — is now worn over wool trousers. Same leather vest with no shirt. Same slippers. The chest paintings are supposed to be buffalo, petroglyph-style — brilliant red — but the legs are too long, making them look more South American tapir than bison. Henry's face paint is alternating stripes of red and royal blue with a black streak down the bridge of his nose. The feather tucked under his sunglasses earpiece is black, probably from a crow. He carries Mr. Scratchy draped across his bare left arm. The cat appears to be dead or drugged, but is neither.

Henry strides to the coffee station, taking particular care with his posture. The old Henry was slope-shouldered, beaten down by gravity. The new Henry walks proud and erect.

"That's Henry," Lucinda tells Rudy. "He's the one we're here to save."

"And that's Mr. Scratchy himself," Willow says.

Henry pours himself a mug of coffee. Today, he drinks it black. Like a warrior. Leo zooms the camera in on Henry's facial paint, then he tracks down to the sleeping cat. Rudy hurries around Leo, placing himself into a standard interview two-shot.

Rudy speaks into the mike. "I'm talking to Henry Box, whose cat, Mr. Scratchy, set off the chain of events leading to the seizure of Mission Pescadero."

Henry lifts his chin. "My name is Sioux."

Rudy pulls an on-camera double take. "Why Sue?"

"With an *x*. S-I-O-U-X. I have adopted my tribal name to honor the original minority cheated of their birthright by the United States government. We" — Sioux makes a sweeping arm gesture straight out of Chief Seattle, except Chief Seattle wasn't carrying a cat — "are the new Native Americans."

Guy says, "You'd have less to explain if you changed your name to Pawnee."

"I am one-sixteenth Sioux, on my mother's side. I am not Pawnee." Sioux takes off his dark glasses and squints into Leo's camera. "My forebears were incarcerated even though they committed no crime. It is my turn to suffer the same fate." He holds the mug up, as if he's gotten a product placement deal. "After I drink this Peet's coffee, I shall scalp the evil physician who labels us senile."

Henry hands Mr. Scratchy off to Rudy and digs into his waistband for a Swiss Army knife. In an attempt to flash the blade, he pulls out the corkscrew instead.

Judith slaps herself on the forehead.

Leo turns the camera to Rudy. Mr. Scratchy opens his yellow eyes and yawns, showing rotten tooth stumps. Rudy says, "We'll edit that."

TWENTY-NINE

A wicked sandstorm rages around Casey Kasandris's bed. Grit fills her eyes. A tumbleweed bounces off the wall-mounted television before tumbling away. From under the bed, Casey hears the scratching sounds of something trying to break into the room.

"I am frightened," she says.

An eerie Hawaiian version of "Somewhere over the Rainbow" plays in Casey's ears. *"Where pretty little bluebirds fly . . ."* She remembers it from her daughter's wedding. She regrets that her daughter can't be with her today. Mandy would enjoy the remembrance.

Katharine Hepburn steps from the blowing sand and takes Casey's hand. In that remarkable accent of hers, Katharine says, "Time's up, Casey. Your session is finished."

"Are you certain?"

"We need a fourth."

At Katharine's touch, the sand turns to Sugar Pops. A blowing storm of Sugar Pops pelting Casey on the face and arms.

Casey laughs. "The Nazarenes didn't tell me it would be like this."

"Nazarenes don't know everything." Katharine Hepburn leads Casey out of the room and down the hallway, past Gap Koch, who drools and nods.

"You're looking sweet, Casey," Gap says.

"I'm feeling sweet," Casey says.

"Will I see you later?"

Casey nods to Katharine. "You'll have to ask her."

"Who?"

Katharine takes Casey to a pair of silver-inlay bat-eye doors. "Through here."

"Are you taking me to meet God?"

Katharine Hepburn chuckles. "Darling child, I am God."

Then the collie from Casey's lost childhood leaps into her arms. Barking, scratching. Shivering from pure delight. Casey falls to her knees and hugs the collie.

"Toto Too. I can't believe it." Casey weeps. The moment of joy is unlike any she ever felt alive. It's as if her entire body were expanding.

"Didn't I tell you Toto Too would be waiting." Casey looks up to see her mother. Stirrup stretch pants. Turtleneck sweater. Smoking a Kool. "You never believed a word I told you."

"Mama!"

Casey's mother, Maureen, gives her a smile.

"I can't believe they let you smoke."

"God smokes. She couldn't very well stop the rest of us."

Casey stands, holding Toto Too like a stuffed bear. She looks across a vast plain, stretching to the horizon, filled with folding tables and chairs. Thousands upon thousands of people, mostly in their pajamas, are playing contract bridge. The table closest at hand is occupied by Maureen's sisters, JoAnne and Clarissa.

"We sent for you on account of we needed a fourth," Maureen says.

"I have to die because you're short a bridge partner?"

"This is more important than whatever else you were doing."

Casey takes her seat. "Who was here before?"

"Your grandmother Hopewell. She said *nigger* and they sent her to hell."

JoAnne shuffles. "Are we playing cards or talking?"

Casey refuses to let go of Toto Too. The

dog continues clawing at Casey's chest with her front feet. It tickles.

"I don't know how to play bridge."

"We'll teach you," Clarissa says. "There's plenty of time."

"Where's Daddy?"

"He's in the workshop. Clyde always said heaven would be a garage full of power tools, and sure enough . . ."

JoAnne deals. Toto Too scratches.

Maureen says, "Two spades."

"Is this real or some kind of Alzheimer's delirium?" Casey asks.

"It's the real thing," Clarissa says. "Three diamonds."

"So, I'm dead?"

"Not quite, dear." Maureen looks down at her Timex Ladies Classic. "Two, one." Toto Too digs both feet into Casey's chest. "Now."

Back in Mission Pescadero, Casey Kasandris's heart breaks.

"You wonder if they forgot us," Dalton Beaver says.

Alexandra sits balanced on an air mattress with her legs stretched in a wide V. "Don't you think it's funny? A bunch of hippies have us locked in a room full of drugs."

"I don't see anything funny about it."

"The one room they would have looted and they can't because we're in it. My bet is Judith Frost planned it this way, to keep the dope fiends in line." Alexandra leans down and touches her toes, or ankles, she can't quite reach the toes. "Another two hours and I'm going to start sampling."

Dalton gives her a look of distaste. You'd think a man and a woman needing an excuse to fool around would jump at the chance of being trapped with their lust object — the stuck-in-an-elevator fantasy, only with bedding — but twenty hours of togetherness has withered the romantic rose for Dalton and Alexandra.

"Melissa is going to ask direct questions, and I can't lie, whether she believes me or not."

"You won't have to lie, Dalton. We can get it notarized — nobody touched anybody."

Even though Dalton is bitterly disappointed, he still maintains the moral high ground. "I must be able to tell Josh and Ginger the divorce is Melissa's fault."

"Just don't come looking for me after it's final."

A double knock raps the door, then a key rattles in the lock. Dixie Lichens calls out. "Is everybody decent?"

Alexandra snorts contempt through her nostrils.

As the door swings open and Dixie bops in, Dalton says, "Nothing happened."

Dixie checks out the two air mattresses, as far apart as mattresses can be in a small room. The bedpans are tucked up on high shelves. The food trays are in opposite corners. "Too bad," she says.

"I'll need a witness," Dalton says. "When we get out of here."

Suchada fills the doorway, behind Dixie. "Who says you're going to get out?"

"She's only kidding." Dixie is wearing a white pleated skirt borrowed from Lucinda and a sleeveless T. "Dr. Beaver, you're supposed to come with us."

Alexandra pushes off the floor and shoves past Dixie, only to stop, face-to-face with bear spray.

"Make me pull the trigger," Suchada says.

Alexandra blows her bangs off her forehead. "If I don't get a shower today, all the Mace in California won't stop me from busting out."

"We'll see you get a shower," Dixie says. "Nobody's that mean."

"I am." Suchada can't help but wonder what Che Guevara would have made of Dixie.

"Suchada likes to talk tough, but she's a sweetie pie," Dixie says.

Alexandra stands closer to Dixie than is usually considered regular in the West. "Let me give you some advice, honey."

"I don't need advice from a woman who dresses like my mother."

"The old farts have nothing to live for. But you're young. You don't want a felony on your record."

"Lots of kids my age commit felonies."

"I'm trying to save you from ruining your future. This woman" — Alexandra nods at Suchada — "hates you."

"I don't think so," says Dixie.

"You're young, good-looking, and straight, everything she isn't."

Dixie digs for a comeback. "So?"

"She will use you and destroy you."

Dixie puts one hand on her cocked hip. "You're just bitter because of the hot flashes."

"I don't get hot flashes."

"Then you have no excuse, do you?"

Alexandra stalks back to her mattress and flops down. "Take the bedpans on your way out."

Dixie glances at Suchada. The idea that Suchada might not be straight explains a lot. And it must be true or Suchada would have made a denial. That's not the kind of thing you let slide when it's a lie. Dixie wonders why she didn't realize what was up sooner.

"Where am I going?" Dalton asks.

Suchada says, "Somebody died. We need you to sign the paperwork."

Dalton slides into his shoes. "It's not my fault."

"Nothing ever is," Alexandra says.

Dalton stands, ready to go. "You think I could use a phone? I need to call my wife."

THIRTY

The back exit was the kind of door with a crash bar so people couldn't get stuck inside even when the door was locked. Since it opened with a hip thrust, a person carrying things in their arms didn't have to put them down to go out, but a person coming in did. Guy and Rocky took on the job of creating a barricade. Together, they explored the furniture storage room in the basement. They hauled up whatever pieces looked solid yet not too heavy for the two of them to carry. They lined the hallway with various night tables, benches, bureaus, and bed frames, then stood back and considered placement, as if putting together a 3-D jigsaw puzzle.

"The door opens out," Guy said.

Rocky nudged a furniture pallet with her foot, visualizing it against the door. "All exits open out in California. They had a fire once and people crammed together so hard they couldn't swing the door open. They found all these bodies stacked up behind the door."

"Where was this?"

"Los Angeles, I think. Or it could be an urban myth. There's a lot of California lore people take for granted that isn't true."

Guy tested the crash bar. The door opened easily. "So the sheriff's department shows up with a key. They open the door, that way. Out. I don't see how a barricade helps."

Rocky bent at the knees to lift the pallet. "Take the other end of this." As they lifted, "It doesn't stop them. It slows them down. The Sunshines are up on the roof, with a walkie-talkie." She dipped her chin at the walkie-talkie in her sweater pocket. "When the lawmen arrive, the Sunshines or whoever is up there calls down, we all rush to the hallway, and by the time the guys with guns wade through or over the furniture, we've formed a human wall. If that doesn't do it, we pull out the bear spray and all hell breaks loose."

Guys with guns was a '60s term for police. It was considered more ironic than *fuzz.* Rocky's walkie-talkie made a static sound and Sunshine #1's voice came across. "How're you folks doing down there? Over."

Rocky and Guy set the pallet in place and

Rocky pushed the appropriate button. "We're working our tails off. How're you folks up there? Over."

"We're smoking weed. Did you know you can see contrails from the airport up here?"

There was a ten-second silence, then, "Oh, shit. I forgot. Over."

"Don't fall off the roof, now. Over."

"I won't but I can't speak for Kathleen. You know what her inner ears are like. These old women can't do things the rest of us can."

From the background, another voice said, "You're older than me, girl."

Rocky turned off the walkie-talkie. Guy said, "Who's Kathleen?"

"That's what Sunshine #1 calls #2 when she's irritated. It's her real name." Rocky lifted the ugliest pole lamp on the West Coast and positioned it on the pallet. "Those two loathe each other, on account of both claiming to be the original Sunshine."

"They act awfully inseparable for two people who loa —" Guy couldn't say *loathe*. It didn't sound like a real word people actually use. "Hate each other."

Rocky decided the lamp worked better on its side. "The key to longevity in institutional situations is to pair up with someone you can't stand. Someone you swear to God you're going to outlive. Old folks with a good enemy last forever." She put a finger to her chin and studied the lamp placement. Maybe upside down. "Of course, when one goes, the other has no reason to live and follows pretty quick."

They wrangled a chest of drawers to the pallet, then balanced a twin bed frame on the chest of drawers. Most of the smaller stuff — a microwave oven, two printer tables, a satellite dish, and a plasma TV — they piled on the pallet itself. By the time the junk mountain was in place, Guy found himself winded. After the last golf game, he hadn't been allowed any exercise to brag about. At his age, you lose whatever you've built up in no time.

"How often have you done this before?"

"The once." Rocky didn't mind a break herself, although she was proud he gave out before she did. "I was more freak than radical in the '60s, but in '73 I joined some women who took over the Playboy Club on Market Street. We held out six days. There was a story in *The Saturday Evening Post* with a picture of bras hanging out the third-floor window, like a flag." Rocky sat on a bench. Guy was tired and would have liked to sit, too, but that would mean touching hips and he was afraid she might think him sleazy. Lily might not like it, either.

"On the sixth day the state police came and kicked our heads in. They started a fire we got blamed for. I spent two months in the downtown jail."

"Was it worth the trouble?"

"At the time, I thought it was."

Guy straddled the end of the bench. The position spread his legs, facing her, but it seemed better than touching. Claudia had warned him, when he first moved to California, that behavior he'd been raised to think of as civil back home was considered creepy in California. She'd made him paranoid to show any level of friendliness for fear of being misunderstood.

"Jails scare the wadding out of me," Guy said.

"Ours wasn't as bad as I'd thought it would be."

"I can't even stand being stuck in here."

Rocky cut her eyes toward him, proper in his pressed shirt and slacks. She didn't understand why he was straddling the bench, teenager-style. He seemed like such an old-fashioned gentleman, and old-fashioned gentlemen don't straddle.

"Sioux told me you're an involuntary."

"Isn't everyone?"

"I'm not. Lots of us aren't. We could leave whenever we want, but where would we go?"

"What difference does it make where, so long as you have the freedom to get out?"

"I mean, we have nowhere to go if we leave for good. Everyone takes day trips into town."

"Not me. I'd give whatever money my daughter's left me for a day trip to town."

Rocky gave Guy a look. "Can you ride a bicycle?"

It turned out there was a second tunnel, besides the one to Nursing Care.

"I knew it," said Guy. "Every *Zorro* I ever saw has a secret tunnel out of the Mission."

"Nothing secret about it. The tunnel goes down to an entry pavilion at the Cabrillo Highway bus stop. The employees use it every day."

"And we can get out?"

"Nicolas left this morning. He went to Radio Shack and bought the walkie-talkies. Where'd you think they came from?"

"I figured you people had them all along, as part of the plan, knowing cell phones would be jammed."

Rocky laughed. "The takeover was planned. No one thought beyond that, except maybe Judith."

"And the police aren't watching the bus stop?"

"Nicolas says they're over by the parking lot, but they don't know about the pedestrian exit. Or maybe they know but don't dream old people can walk away. Ray John's out now, making phone calls."

"I don't have a bike."

"We'll borrow Sioux's."

THIRTY-ONE

Sioux's bicycle was a fairly new Stumpjumper with fat, lugged tires and a straight-across handlebar. Twenty-one standard gears. A half-dollar-sized mirror mounted on the left-hand grip. Even though Guy had not been on a bike for somewhere in the fifty-years range, and he had never been on a mountain bike, inside two blocks he was comfortable on this one. Beside him, Rocky rode an upright bicycle with U-shaped handlebars, something of a cross between road and off-road. The front tree sported a spring. Rocky had installed twin saddlebags across the back fender. She cut quite the figure in her wide-brimmed fishing hat, her arms draped over the handlebars and the cuffs of her slacks clamped tight by elastic bands. Blue Keds with white gym socks.

Guy felt compelled to speak. "It was good of Henry to loan me his bike. Sioux. I can't get used to calling him by a strange name."

Rocky had a hint of a smile on her face. The smile of being out. "Half the men in Pepper Land use nicknames. Sioux's no stranger than Mr. Natural or Chicken Little."

The street dead-ended and they rode across a beach parking lot with grass growing through tar cracks in the concrete. Rocky led Guy past a sign that said clean up after your dog and onto a pathway going up a gradual rise to the neon green bluff. Guy dropped behind Rocky. His gear-shift technique caused a momentary disconnected spinning of the pedals before he figured out that, like on the three-speed of his youth, the only way up a hill is to pump. He stood in the saddle, pumping, concentrating on Rocky's gray sweater and the band of skin between her collar and hairline. Unlike so many of the women at the Mission, Rocky wore her hair fairly short, the way older women in Oklahoma wore theirs back when Guy was younger. Unlike those old women, Rocky didn't tint her hair blue.

The bluff flattened on top. The pedaling got easy again. They rode between clumps of low weeds, past eucalyptus trees, while farther inland stood the Monterey pines. Toward the ocean lay sand dunes. The air flowing down Guy's throat was sharp with a touch of salt. He felt stronger than he had in . . . he couldn't recall how long. Surely, since Lily came down sick.

Ever since losing Lily, Guy had felt her presence, watching and protecting, yes, but more often criticizing. Especially his diet, which had gone to hell without her. Now, riding behind Rocky Gingrass, between mountains and ocean, Guy started to wonder if he literally felt Lily was beside him, or if he was using her as a method of not letting go. Was the real Lily really watching? Or was he cheating her memory, pretending she was some kind of spirit still interested in his welfare? Even to ask such questions amazed Guy.

They passed two women in boxy shoes and tucked-in lumberjack shirts, walking dogs on leashes. The women stopped, scowling, and protectively reeled their dogs in close. A dirt road cut off to the east. The track crossed from the bluff ledge to a slag pile where motor heads romped on dirt bikes and three-wheelers.

About the time Guy's legs started to give, Rocky pulled up next to a plywood shack with boarded windows. A sign read LOOMIS SNO KONES and listed at least thirty flavors of snow cone including nontraditionals such as peanut butter and licorice.

Rocky leaned her bike against the shack.

Guy was more than glad to stop. "What's this?"

"Wine and cheese break." Rocky unzipped the saddlebags and handed Guy a paper-wrapped wedge of Boschetto cheese, two artichokes, and a box of gourmet crackers. She kept the wine pack herself. "Come on." She led Guy around the shack to a picnic table embedded in a concrete slab.

"You come prepared," Guy said.

"I don't believe in exercise without refreshments. Never did." The wine was a Rosemount Shiraz 2016.

"Is that a good year?" Guy asked.

"Was for me."

He lined the cheese, crackers, and artichokes up on the table. To Guy, an artichoke was exotic food. He'd only tried a couple and felt he missed out by not knowing what he was supposed to do with them.

"I would have packed Vienna sausage and an apple," Guy said.

Rocky reached deeper into the pack for two disposable wine flutes and a maple-handled corkscrew. "This is how we ride bike here." She expertly peeled the seal, tilted the bottle to the correct angle, screwed in the corkscrew, and popped the cork. One smooth motion.

Guy sat on the opposite side of the table where he could look at the beach and bay behind and below Rocky. He knew she gave him the better view, on purpose. "You open wine like a pro."

"I am. Or, I was."

"Yeah?"

"I was a waitress. Didn't you know that?" She poured a swallow in her glass. "Forty-four years. Almost thirty at the same restaurant." Rocky swished, eyed, sipped. Satisfied, she filled Guy's glass, then her own. "My wrist went out — bursitis — and I couldn't carry a full tray. I asked for two months off to rest it and they said, 'Fine, take as long as you need.' "

Guy swished his wine. He knew there was a ritual to follow, but he wasn't sure what it was. "And when you were ready to come back, you no longer had a job."

"You've heard the story."

"Everyone's heard the story. I took a year off to be home with Lily while she was sick. After she passed, I couldn't wait to go back to work. I thought it would help me make it through the day." Fingertips on the glass, he spread his thumbs in what amounted to a hand shrug.

Rocky closed her eyes and drank. With her eyes closed, Guy looked at her closely. He liked the thin lines of her eyebrows. And the scalloped hollows along her temples. Nothing like Lily. Rocky opened her eyes and caught him.

He quickly looked away. "They said I couldn't relate to the modern athlete." Guy, too, drank. The Shiraz was tart, not as sweet as the Mateus Rosé he and Lily used to share on the anniversary of their first date. "I guess they were right."

Thirty-Two

Guy and Rocky polished off the Shiraz. It took the better part of a pleasant hour. Both were aware of the air and the water, the mountains close by. They were aware of where they were. And where they weren't, which was even better.

The first glass passed in small talk. Rocky showed Guy how to scrape meat from the artichoke leaves. He sliced cheese while she gave the Boschetto rap — mixture of cow milk, sheep milk, and truffles — then she had to explain truffles' mystique.

He told her about sports writing in Oklahoma, where nothing matters so much as football. While the rest of the country thought of 2020 as the start of Gulf War V, in Oklahoma the year was remembered for a national championship.

"Football puts me to sleep," Rocky said.

"Me too. Now." Guy didn't go into his transformation from sports obsessive to sports phobic. "Is the tide out?"

Rocky twisted in her seat. "Sure, look at all that beach." A man in oatmeal sweats threw some kind of rope toy for a chocolate Lab down by the waterline. Gulls wheeled and sparred. A large bird — a heron — flapped inland.

"We don't have tides on the Red River. Half the year, we don't have water."

The second glass of wine was spent in quiet, comfortable contemplation. Rocky looked into her wine. Guy looked at nature, seeing through the eyes of Lily. Ground cover on the hills was so green it looked fake. Oklahoma was never this green, even at the height of spring. Lily never cared for plastic flowers and Guy didn't think she would care for this.

Guy passed on a second refill and Rocky finished the bottle. Glass three took her so deep into contemplation she found herself with a need to talk. At first, Rocky resisted. Nothing much good comes from talking, in her experience, but wine-inspired curiosity finally got the best of natural reticence.

She looked straight at Guy. "When were you the happiest?"

Guy did what any man would when asked a direct question. He stalled. "What's that?"

"In life. We've both been around awhile.

Can you look back at one moment and say, 'This was my happiest'?"

Guy stared across the bay. Crab boats were coming in, moving north toward Pacifica, riding low in the water. Recreationists sailed the other way — out. No matter how often his granddaughter diagrammed the principle, Guy had never understood how sailboats sail against the wind. "The day Claudia was born. July 1, 1973. Waurika, Oklahoma. Back then men weren't allowed to watch the delivery, not in Waurika anyway. I don't remember any man wanting to watch. But afterward, the nurse took me down a hall to a glass window and she said, 'Your daughter.' Claudia had on a pink sock hat. She looked like a cartoon tomato. You know, with eyes and a mouth, but still a tomato." He paused, putting himself back in the spot. "I remember thinking how much I looked forward to the future. That whatever happened would be interesting."

"Did you think she might grow up to take your house, money, keys, and stick you in continuing care?"

Guy quick-checked to see if Rocky was being sarcastic. She wasn't. He said, "Yes."

They both smiled, each knowing he was telling the truth.

"Except they didn't call it continuing care

back then." Guy pushed his wineglass forward an inch, then to the right, then back. "That afternoon, driving home in an incredibly hot car without air-conditioning, I remember thinking, *This is the person who will break my heart.*" He looked up from his glass to meet Rocky's eyes. "But I knew whatever happened, she was worth the bother later. Even today, raising Claudia — and my son, Martin — was worth whatever I've let myself in for."

Rocky nodded. She had spent much of her imaginative life wondering what it would have been like to raise a healthy child.

"Your turn," Guy said. "What's your happiest day?"

She blinked into the remaining swallow of wine. "Same as yours, but for the opposite reason."

"You might have to explain that."

"There was no being excited about the future when Roderick came out. The nurses wouldn't look at me. I thought it was because I had no husband and my parents were ashamed of me, but they hurried the baby away without letting me see him, and I knew something was wrong." She finished the wine. "They didn't let me see him for four days. People treated me like I was the one dying."

"Where was the father?"

"Gap was long gone. A commune out by Joshua Tree, then when he was ready to move out of the tipi, his parents paid for law school and away he went. I'm still not sure if he knows he has a son."

"Gap is what they called the man in the wheelchair. The man you brought across Judith's line."

"Bingo."

Guy did the two-and-two math while Rocky put the wine flutes and corkscrew back into the wine pack. He studied her hands, or, more exactly, he studied the pattern of veins in bas-relief on the backs of her hands. Rocky's face and body could have passed for a woman younger than her age, but these were the hands of a working woman.

Not looking at Guy, she said, "Have you noticed that people only come alive during bad times. Not the boring-rut bad times, but the exceptional bad times." She sniffed the cork, then poked it into the empty bottle and the bottle into the pack. "I worked the floor the night after the '89 earthquake. The restaurant was packed. The customers and staff were operating at a level of attention they'd never had before. Their eyes focused, they talked to each other and they listened, even the ones on dates. They tasted the food. For the first time, ever, they saw me."

"Isn't that good?"

"Damn right, it's good. The tips were terrific." Rocky rewrapped the cheese and gathered artichoke leaves while Guy tried to understand her point.

He said, "I've heard New Yorkers after 9/11 were the same way. People ripped out of their insulation."

"Roderick's birth did that for me. The morning they brought my baby in, I saw how awful his life would be and how awful my life would be, loving him, and I was happy. For the first time in my life, I was happy."

"You're getting too complicated for a sports reporter."

"The peace, love, and everything-is-beautiful-in-its-own-way bullshit was blown to smithereens. My situation was not beautiful. I didn't have to feel like a failure any longer because I couldn't love, love, love. I was alive in the moment the way no free spirit could ever be."

Rocky and Guy gathered everything they had brought, put it all back into her saddlebags, and mounted up for the ride back. Guy studied his derailleur, not certain what gear he should be in going downhill after two glasses of wine. With a car, low gear acts as a brake. Bicycle gears didn't work that way in 1960, but they'd changed so much since then they should be called something else.

Next to him, her hands high on the handlebars, Rocky said, "Goddamn."

"What's that?"

"There's no point in telling a story if you leave out the part that matters." She glared at him, fiercely. "Between the morning Gap got me pregnant and five weeks later when I found out I was pregnant, I ate mescaline. A royal hit of purple haze. God knows how many micrograms and God knows what was really in the cap. I was so blasted and strung out I started throwing down tequila shots. I did a bunch of shots."

"And you take your son's problems as punishment."

Rocky broke the eye contact. "*Punishment* may be the wrong word. Responsibility. In the back of my mind — hell, in the front of my mind — I think I may have caused Roderick's terrible life."

Guy wanted to touch her, but he didn't. "You'll drive yourself insane if you think that way."

"No duh, dumbass, I am insane." She saw the hurt jump to Guy's eyes. "I'm sorry. I didn't mean it that way."

"I know."

"When Roderick was thirteen, I was forced to admit I couldn't take care of him anymore. He was a big boy. I couldn't control him and I had to put him into a place."

"So, there's the guilt of giving him birth made worse by the guilt of giving him up."

"You're perceptive, for a male."

"I have a fair amount of experience with guilt." Guy let that one lie on the ground between them. There'd been enough confession for one bottle of wine.

"Does it make you hate Gap?" he asked.

"Sometimes it makes me hate everyone. Even Roderick. And what it makes me hate most are mind expansion drugs and eighty-year-old hippies who talk about beautiful people and the summer of love. The Mamas and Papas. I hate the Mamas and Papas. I once threw up in my car when 'California Dreaming' came on the radio."

" 'California Dreaming' would make anyone throw up."

"Here's a secret you can't tell the guys at the Mission." Rocky leaned closer to Guy, who braced himself. He didn't like secrets. Rocky's breath had a sweet hint of wine. "I can't stand the Grateful Dead."

"Jesus," Guy said.

Rocky nodded. "It's true."

Guy looked into the little mirror on his handgrip. He could see the wavery SNO KONES sign in the glass. The journalist in him was repulsed by misspelled brand names. "Why are you at the Mission, then. Voluntarily. If you don't like the people."

"I like the people, enough, until they start with the *Far out,* and *Right on.*"

"But why Mission Pescadero?"

Rocky shrugged. "Gap was there. He doesn't know who I am, I don't think, and I don't want him to know, but he's my last link with home. Figuring one assisted living center is as good as another, I chose the one with the link."

She lifted her right foot to the pedal. "Let's see if we can still ride."

Guy considered the path along the bluff and down the hill to the beach. He could keep going. Ride Sioux's bike to Highway 1 and make real the hitchhiking-to-Oklahoma plan.

Rocky said, "At least it's mostly downhill."

Guy looked across at Rocky. In her floppy hat and blue Keds. One incisor notched over her lower lip. Eyes wondering if he was judging her on account of her past. This little woman was as far from Lily as Paris,

France, is from Paris, Texas. He wouldn't want to stop in France forever, but if you're there, you might as well see what it is. He could always go home later, after the siege ended.

"I'll follow you."

Thirty-Three

Mission Pescadero, also known as Pepper Land, boasted two resident lounges and a rec hall. The one lounge had evolved into a poker room, although besides poker it also had a pool table, a dartboard, and a chess setup that swiveled into backgammon. The other lounge was a television room with a bar. Mirrors and modern art. Chairs and sofas scattered about like the lobby of a high-end ski lodge. When Guy and Rocky returned from their ride, she went to her room for a nap and he headed for the ski lodge lounge, where the group was watching *KHMB News Watch at Five.* No one asked Guy where he'd been. No one except Sioux and Judith Frost knew he'd been gone.

As always, whenever three or more sophisticated people gather to watch local news, much sport was made of the talking heads.

"Phaedra's five-dollar rug is more natural

than that wig."

"I'll bet every penny I own she's not wearing underwear."

Nothing original. It was the spirit of trashing local celebrities that counted. The object of this fun at the expense of others was the politically correct anchor team — one black male, one Asian female, both coiffed to the nines — who were discussing a murder in Woodside. The CEO of an Internet start-up had electrocuted his auditor by throwing a Hubble Galaxie Gazer telescope into a Jacuzzi. The CEO's neighbors said he was a gentle man and they never saw it coming.

"You hate to see a Hubble treated that way," said the black anchorman.

The Asian anchorwoman turned to the second camera. "On a lighter note, residents of a Coastside assisted living facility are revisiting their past this week through a demonstration straight out of the wacky '60s."

Nicolas of all people was offended. "The '60s were never wacky."

"Amidst cries of peace and love, the aging hippies of Mission Pescadero Continuing Care Center are celebrating the glory of their younger days."

Hu said, "Let's hear it for us, people."

Suchada said, "Shut up, Hu."

The Mission dining hall appeared on the television screen. Rudy's voice said, "What do you people want?"

The camera panned across the old men in ponytails and Mexican peasant shirts and old women in flowing skirts with flowers in their hair.

"Free chocolate."

"End the war in Vietnam."

"World peace."

"Medicare-financed Viagra."

"They've edited out the stuff that mattered," Dixie said.

Suchada said, "No shit, Sherlock."

Henry — Mr. Scratchy on his right arm — dashed on screen, twitching, jerking, feeling his pulse with his left hand. The camera zoomed in on his painted face.

Rudy in voice-over: "I'm talking to Henry Box, whose cat, Mr. Scratchy, set off the chain of events."

Henry lifted his chin. "My name is Sioux." The television audience clearly saw eyebrow dandruff on Henry's dark glasses as he took them off and squinted into the camera. "After I drink this Peet's coffee, I shall scalp the physician who labels us senile."

Henry whipped out his Swiss Army corkscrew.

Back at News Nine, the Asian anchorwoman laughed, good-naturedly. "I just love it when cuddly old folks show their spunk, don't you, Darryl?"

Darryl, the black anchorman, said, "Those hippies just keep on trucking through the years."

The show cut to a commercial for a San Bruno plastic surgeon's breast reduction clinic. There was a before-and-after split screen. One side, a beautiful, healthy, happy woman with nice breasts in a vibrant job surrounded by good-looking men. The other side, a miserable, balloon-breasted woman in a sack of a dress, teaching elementary school.

The ski lodge lounge was silent for a few moments, then Ray John spit out, *"Spunk!"*

Hu said, "It's truckin', not truck*ing.*"

"They made us out to be senile," said Nicolas.

"Worse than senile, they made us look *cute,*" Lucinda said, pronouncing *cute* like the dirtiest word in English.

Phaedra growled. "That bastard lieutenant got to the station manager."

"I don't understand," Dixie said. "How can the news report a story that isn't true?"

Judith had Wanda help her out of a Barca-Lounger. Chewing like a jacked-up programmer, she shuffled to Guy. "Do you carry a pocketknife yourself?"

"Of course," said Guy. "I'm from Oklahoma."

"Come with me." Judith humped her way toward the door. "It's time somebody takes us seriously."

Guy holds the door for Judith as she pushes her walker through, then follows himself. It's a slower process than wheeling a chair, but Guy sees there must be a morale factor. *At least I'm not in a wheelchair.*

As if reading his thoughts, Judith says, "If you build a fire under a Parkinson's patient, even if he's been wheelchair-bound for years, he will leap from the chair. I read it in *National Geographic.*"

"I'd like to know how they tested the theory."

Judith bats her crinkle-lidded eyes at Guy. "Must have burned a few asses, finding out."

With something of a shock, Guy realizes she is flirting with him. Amazing. Judith could pass for a hard-living ninety. Women define themselves by their effect on men when they're young and never quite give it up. In fact, these California women are more aggressive about men in their seventies and eighties than the women back home were in their teens. Guy's been too busy the last few years to notice what old Oklahoma women are like now, so he doesn't know if the bawdy bias is an age thing, or regional.

They slowly cross the quad. Somewhere beyond the west wall, the sun is settling into the Pacific. The Mission grounds have been in shadow for two hours. The light is soft, filtered, like a forty-watt bulb seen through a silk shade. A flock of juncos flit hedge to hedge and a cricket cuts loose over by the chapel. Guy tries to picture what California was like one hundred years ago. Two hundred. It must have been a nice place to be an Indian. As opposed to Oklahoma.

Judith snorts, like a pony. "Tell me, Mr. Fontaine, what do you know about death?"

"I don't know one certain thing about death," Guy says. "Except that I know just as much as anyone else." It's an idea he came up with years ago, when dying wasn't an issue.

Judith can tell it's a line, and therefore meaningless. "Do you think the body is a temple, even after the spirit moves on?"

"The body is fertilizer, after the spirit moves on."

Judith's head quiver goes more up and down than side to side. Guy takes it as agreement. He wonders if he'll live long enough to develop the head quiver. He doesn't recall seeing it on old men so much as old women.

"You're the only one around this place with proper balls." Judith snorts again. "Except maybe Phaedra."

Guy doesn't know what to say to this. It doesn't sound as if she's still flirting. Sounds as if she's stating a fact.

"What we're fixing to do will take proper balls," Judith says.

She leads him through the dining hall, past the tables being set up for dinner, and into the kitchen. The cook, Tony, gives them a look that is not welcoming. The head chef left with management, and Tony has taken on the job. He sees this as an opportunity to prove Mission Pescadero needs a cook. Not a chef.

Judith doesn't acknowledge either Tony or the dirty look. Guy says, "Hey," because Oklahomans do not ignore anyone. Tony, who is from California, turns back to his soup. Judith winds through the stoves and stockpots.

She lifts a cleaver from the knife rack. "We may need this."

"Why?" Guy asks.

"Your Okie pocketknife may not be sharp enough." Judith keeps going, past the dish machine to the walk-in freezer. She stands there until Guy figures out she's expecting gentlemanly behavior and he opens the freezer door. Inside, he finds Casey Kasandris laid out on four cases of frozen French fries.

"That idiot lieutenant won't let the funeral home come in to get her. He thinks we'll buckle with a dead woman in our midst. Or maybe the stink will drive us out. God knows what he thinks." Judith lifts her walker the smallest bit and drops it. "I've come up against a raft of law enforcement in my days, some good, most bad, and I can tell you this Lieutenant Monk character is a royal dickwad."

Whoever moved Casey hadn't taken off her hospital gown, which is okay by Guy. Dead people are strange enough to look at, without being naked. Casey dead is the thinnest person he has ever looked at closely. A broomstick with hair. She's young, about Claudia's age. Her skin is the color of a dirty commode.

"Who is it?" Guy and Rocky left before word of Casey's death spread, so they are the only ones in the Mission who haven't heard.

"Casey Kasandris." Judith glances at the body, then away, at a bus tub of chickens.

She would never say it, but dead bodies give her the willies. "She was early-onset Alzheimer's."

Guy remembers where he heard the name. "Winston told me Casey was the most enthusiastic lover he ever had. He said she reached climax if you brushed the inside of her arm."

"This one won't be reaching climax anymore."

It's easy for Guy to picture Casey as sensual. Something about the tiny muscles that run from her upper lip to her nostrils. She probably enjoyed life immensely at one time, before she lost so much weight. "Do you know what she died of?"

"Beaver thinks heart attack or stroke. Maybe aneurysm. Basically, he isn't interested as long as he doesn't get the blame."

Guy thinks about seeing Lily dead. Lily had gone right at dawn, as the light was coming through the hospital blinds. To Guy, her face had a look of soft relief, as if she was free of pain. That's how Guy saw it at the time. Maybe she just looked gone.

"The media is going to say she died on account of us," Judith says. "They always do when you lose someone during an action."

"Did she?"

“I don’t see how. Wouldn’t surprise me if Beaver didn’t medicate her to death. That nurse, Kristen, tells me he kept Casey in a coma. On purpose.” Judith moves her hands from the metal side rails to the rubber handgrips. A few more seconds and she might have gotten freezer burn off her walker. “This Lieutenant Monk will make us out as killers. Beaver doesn’t know it yet, but he’ll go along. Last thing they want is an autopsy.”

Guy is cold. He wants to get away from Casey and Judith. They both make him feel clammy. “Why did you want me to see her?”

Thirty-Four

Thursday. Breakfast. The novelty of freedom is beginning to wear thin. The dairy truck wasn't let in yesterday, so there's no half-and-half for coffee. Only milk and nondairy, and the milk may well run out by the weekend. Nobody wants to fall back on nondairy.

Judith, in a red velvet Navajo skirt that would have been old-fashioned on someone's grandma in 1960, stands at her walker in front of the stage, frog-croaking into a microphone. Wanda Bretschneider is at her flank. Her audience isn't listening.

"Pay attention, people. We have to start conserving electricity. The generator won't last forever, especially if you keep playing your sound systems. Turn off the iPods and ZBoxes. We need the power to keep folks breathing over in N.C. We can't waste electricity on hair dryers."

This brings on a chorus of boos under-

lined by dark mutters.

A woman from Midwest, who hasn't raised her voice since coming to the Mission, shouts, "How long are we expected to live without satellite TV? This isn't fair."

Judith is astounded. "Fair?"

Sparkle Plenty — Billie Holiday down to the hibiscus behind her ear — says, "If my daughter doesn't hear from me every day, she worries."

"Want to bet," Suchada says. Dixie laughs.

"I supported this revolt," Mr. Natural says, "but I never dreamed they would take our wireless. I'm a day trader and you are affecting my livelihood."

"We must form committees," says Judith.

More groans.

"Do you want independence or not? We have to take care of ourselves and we can't do so without committees. I need volunteers."

The crowd develops a sudden interest in hash browns. Phaedra mumbles, "What a crock."

"I studied the American Revolution in high school and they had committees. I'm sure," Dixie says.

Dixie and Frances have joined Phaedra and Suchada's table. Phaedra acted massively put-upon by the imposition but, as

Suchada pointed out, if Frances can be seen with dykes, Phaedra should be able to tolerate reactionaries. Eldon the orderly, Kristen the nurse, and the housekeepers have taken over the Vietnam widows' table. At first, the housekeepers were shy about eating with the residents, but in no time at all they learned to boss busboys. By now, they're as demanding as New Yorkers.

Frances says, "In the '60s, you could kill a sit-in by cutting off the dope supply. These kids haven't changed a bit."

Up at the stage, Judith is reduced to begging for volunteers. "We need a statement of demands. Who wants to work on that committee?"

"I demand a ride to the mall," shouts a voice from North Beach.

"Cream for our coffee."

"Free Michael Jackson!"

Phaedra has had all she can stand. "Wheel me up there."

"This is Judith's trip," says Suchada. "Not yours."

"If we leave this mess to Judith, she'll bore the whole mob into Nursing Care. Wheel me up."

Suchada pushes Phaedra's wheelchair to the stage while Dixie watches and Frances doesn't. Most of the rest do. Phaedra is what we call a marker human. In a crowd, even the ones ignoring Phaedra know where she is and how she feels.

Judith sees them coming. "We'll need a compliance committee to encourage residents to save on electricity and toilet paper."

Sunshine #2 shrieks. "Toilet paper?"

"They were expecting a shipment."

Suchada brings Phaedra to a stop at Judith's elbow. The one woman is five feet, standing; the other woman is four feet, sitting. Between them, there's 170 years of meanness.

Phaedra says, "Give me the mike."

"What are you doing?"

"Saving your cute little tail."

Wanda steps closer to support Judith, but Judith shakes her off. Judith knows Phaedra is right.

She passes Phaedra the mike. "See if you can light a fire under these zombies."

Phaedra says, "Stand back and watch."

Phaedra has Suchada circle the chair clockwise till she's facing the dining hall. She clears her throat — imagine a loaded garbage disposal — and waits. The silence turns uncomfortable as it spreads back across the hall, from housekeeping to Midwest to New York and on into the Bay Area.

Winston is the last to stop tinkling silverware.

Phaedra's voice carries the power of passionate youth. She may have lost muscle tone and eyesight, but her lungs can still ripple hair on your head from thirty paces.

"Cream for coffee! Satellite TV!" She telescopes her milk-eyed glare toward the Midwest. "What do you mealymouthed half-asses think this is?"

Weight shifts from hip to hip. Faces are touched.

"What we are doing here is important, dammit. Haven't you water-heads figured that out? This isn't about a cat, or sock hop privileges. This is about freedom."

Winston lets out a sarcastic cheer. Sunshine #1 and Lucinda simultaneously kick him under the table.

"You people act like you're visiting the spa. I swear you expect a masseuse to come along soon, to rub your aching back. If all you can do is whine about *satellite TV,* you deserve to be treated like fifth-graders. Don't you people have any pride?"

Phaedra is pissing the crowd off now. Raining on the ironic, above-themselves attitude.

"Alexandra treats you like puppy dogs and you wag your tails and take it. You lick her hands. Hell, you lick her ass."

Guy checks out faces. The fifth-grade comparison holds well. He sees sulkers. Overreacters. Embarrassment. Rocky is watching him.

"Did you forget how it feels when she looks at you as if you're a pitiful, stupid loser? One mistake and she forces you to take an awareness test. A public awareness test. With her cooing" — Phaedra does a dead-on Alexandra doing a dead-on Mr. Rogers — " 'I will make your decisions because you are too *old*.' " Back to the Phaedra buzz saw. "Then if you don't clean your room she threatens you with the tunnel. If you say squat she has that quack doctor medicate you into oblivion."

Hu shouts, "I volunteer for that."

Phaedra ignores him. "How did we let ourselves be put in this position? No privacy. No locks. When you get laid she tattletales to your children." Phaedra breathes in and out, loud as an asthmatic. "Nicolas has been fishing in her computer. He tells me she reads your e-mails. She takes kickbacks from your conservators."

Nicolas nods, proud to have been singled out, although he didn't tell Phaedra what he found. He told Ray John and Henry who is now Sioux. They must have told someone who told Phaedra. Or what's more likely, she made it up, accidentally hitting on the truth.

"I am sick of being helpless." Phaedra throws Suchada a look. Nobody except Suchada and Dixie catches it. "I am sick of being treated like a victim. A harmless victim."

Phaedra winds up for the big finish. "Are you harmless?"

"No!"

"Are you angry?"

"Yes!"

"Wouldn't you love to make Miss Fancy Pants pay for the humiliation she dumps on you? The humiliation the world dumps on you."

"Yes!"

"She *humors* us."

Boos all around. For these people, *humored* is worse than punishment.

"When you complain, she says it is *your age.* Your complaints are *symptoms.*"

Ray John leaps to his feet. "Let's hang the bitch!"

Lucinda follows. "Hanging is too good for her!"

Even the housekeepers are into it. Most of them don't know the words, but they know the subject is Alexandra Truman, and if it comes time to hang her, they'll be glad to tie the knot.

Phaedra's voice booms. *"We are not children."*

Ray John shouts, "Break out the tar and feathers!"

"Right on!"

"You tell it!"

Lucinda grins at Ray John. They're on a roll. Together. Wrapped in the ancient buzz. She shouts, "We've got feathers! Where can we find tar?"

Ray John feels alive. He doesn't want it to ever stop. "We may not have tar, but we've got all the Vaseline petroleum jelly anyone could ever need."

Chicken Little is standing on the late Haight table, tracking syrup. "We'll ride her out on a rail."

Sioux rips off his ancestral blood cry.

Sausalito chants, "Burn the witch! Burn the witch!"

Everyone is up now. Or almost everyone. Guy, Rocky, Frances, and the chair-bound stay seated.

Eldon leans toward Kristen. "I can go along with Vaseline and feathers. If they set her on fire, I'll have to step in."

Kristen says, "I can live with that."

■ ■ ■ ■

In the dispensary, Alexandra lifts her head off her arms. "What's that noise?"

She and Dalton concentrate on the clamor outside. Dalton tilts his head, finding a better angle from which to listen. "Sounds like 'Burn the witch.' "

A key rattles in the door and the dispensary fills with senior citizens on a mission. Skittering eyes, grasping hands. Dalton covers his face with his forearms, fearful of being gassed again. Alexandra draws back to the shelving. She hisses like a trapped Mr. Scratchy. She strikes out, raking skin with her nails.

Willow yelps and slaps Alexandra in the jaw. Then anonymous hands lay hold of Alexandra and drag her, screaming threats, from the dispensary. The door slams shut. A key turns in the lock. A few moments later, silence settles over the room.

Dalton drops his arms from the eye defensive position. He stares at the door, which doesn't give answers. He makes a decision. For the first time since the hostage situation began, Dalton Beaver takes a well-known anti-anxiety remedy off the shelf and self-medicates.

Guy, Rocky, Eldon, and Kristen stand under the Administration arcade, out of the sun, watching the residents parade Alexandra up and down the quad. As they circle the eucalyptus, the residents sing a song Guy thinks of as "The Old Gray Mare, She Ain't What She Used to Be." He doesn't recall the official name of the song. It was his grandfather's favorite. Eldon drinks lemonade from a go cup. Rocky holds clip-on sunglasses in her hand, but she doesn't put them on.

Alexandra is stripped down to a demi-cup front-clasp bra with underwires and a low-rise thong, although the only skin that shows is a raccoon mask across the eyes. The rest of Alexandra's body is pasted over with pillow feathers supplied by the house-keeping ladies, who also tore the sheets used to tie Alexandra to the decorative ladder usually leaned against the chapel.

They first tried tying her to an IV drip pole but it was only long enough for one bearer on each end and there weren't two residents strong enough to haul Alexandra. Colin the maintenance man came up with the idea of the ladder any number could carry. Interestingly enough, Mission employees have been quite helpful in arranging Alexandra's demise.

The only person looking out for Alexandra's comfort is Dixie. She wouldn't let the party begin until she checked the wrist knots. Dixie worried about circulation. She convinced Alexandra to hook her legs through the ladder rungs and hold on with both hands.

"Close your eyes and breathe on the five count," Dixie said. "It'll be over before you know it."

Alexandra returned the concern by telling Dixie she was a "fuck-faced cunt." The bile in Alexandra's body focused on Dixie and no one else. She spewed verbal sewage with the eloquence of a Hollywood starlet.

Eldon sips his lemonade. "After today, I doubt if we'll have jobs."

"Small loss," Kristen says. "I'm burnt-out on keeping old folks stoned for the Beaver."

Rocky brushes bangs off her forehead. She isn't sure Alexandra's humiliation will be worth the trouble in the long run. "My bet is Alexandra will be the one looking for a job. The owners have a choice — evict every resident and start over, or can Alexandra and Beaver. You two will be fine."

"If I owned the place I'd remodel the

buildings into office space," Guy says.

Sunshines #1 and #2 lead the procession, lofting feathers from pillowcases, like flower girls at their big sister's wedding. Next comes Sausalito, who has switched songs to Petula Clark's "Downtown," which no one can remember the words to, so mostly they are singing, *"Dum, dum, dum, dum, dum-dum-dum-dum-dum-dum-dum, dumdumdum-dumdumdum, downtown."* Then come Alexandra and her carriers with Dixie alongside and Alexandra's head hanging down, twisted to the Dixie side as she curses. The remainder of Dixie's yoga class follows, amazingly enough, holding hands and skipping. More or less.

Lucinda leaves the party and crosses over to Guy and the group. She arrives as Rocky is saying, "I wonder if these yahoos ever think in terms of consequences."

"To hell with consequences." Lucinda touches Eldon's upper arm. "At our age, the consequence of everything is death, so you might as well feel good when you can." She gives Eldon's deltoid a squeeze, loaded with nuance. He has no idea what to make of it.

Out on the quad, Chicken Little and Nicolas carry their end of the ladder straight into the goose pond. They wade waist deep, then lower Alexandra under for a ten count. As they lift her back up, Sioux launches into what he sees as an aboriginal purification ceremony. Now Alexandra is covered by Vaseline and wet chicken feathers.

Her wrath turns from Dixie to Sioux. "Cocksucker. Your cat is dead, you hear me?"

Nicolas says, "Mr. Scratchy didn't cause your problems, Alexandra." He repeats the words she'd used on Henry. "You have no one to blame but yourself."

Alexandra spits feathers and calls Nicolas a fag.

Marta Pitcairne says, "Shut up, bitch, or we'll drown you like a rabid skunk."

Both Sunshines are aghast. #1 says, "Mar*ta.*"

Blood floods Marta's face. "I'm sorry. I don't know what came over me."

"Whatever it was, keep it there," Sunshine #2 says.

From the arcade, Guy calls, "That's enough. Time to cut her loose."

There are grumbles, especially from New York, but most of the revelers are ready for a nap. Winston pulls out his knife and cuts Alexandra off the ladder. She falls to the earth and lies on her back, sucking air, until Mick, Chicken Little, and Fairly Fast

Freddy pick her up and carry her to the gate. Judith Frost unlocks the double doors and stands back while Ray John Mancini opens them wide. Chicken Little takes the feet. Fairly Fast Freddy holds Alexandra under her armpits. They swing — *one, two, three* — then, much to the surprise of Esteban Vasquez in his cruiser, they heave Alexandra into the street.

Back under the Administration arcade, Rocky says, "Now we're in for it."

Thirty-Five

Twenty minutes later, Cyrus Monk attacks. Nicolas and Sioux who used to be Henry are in the bell tower, dicking around with the camera, reliving the old days when smearing a woman with Vaseline Intensive Care and feathers would not have been cool. In the old days, the protesters would have drawn up a petition. As a last resort, sat down in Alexandra's waiting room and refused to move till she accepted a list of grievances. Sioux, still face painted but now back in his long-sleeve Arrow shirt, Levi 501s, secondhand-store Adidas, black socks, and ratty sweater, tells Nicolas when his people wanted to shame an authority they spit in his shadow.

"Your people?"

"Native Americans. The first people forcibly ripped from a free life and stuck in a retirement community."

Cyrus's SUV comes screaming off the Cabrillo Highway and blasts up the hill, sliding to stop at the Mission gate. Cyrus piles from the driver's side, key in one hand, Taser in the other, gas mask strapped to his face. A praying mantis with a gun. Bobby Christmas jumps from the far side of the SUV, also in a gas mask, but he doesn't have the seal tight and he's tugging at the edges with both thumbs.

Nicolas says, "Holy cow."

Sioux forgets the walkie-talkie. Runs to the quad side of the bell tower and lets out an Indian war cry.

"Attack! Attack! The fuzz are coming in!"

Most of the residents have gone to their rooms to rest. A few are watching a non-satellite soap on the lounge TV because Judith won't let them turn on their own. Guy is in the laundry. Rocky, in the library. Dixie, exercise room. Guy hears the commotion and carries a clean shirt to the laundry room door in time to see Ray John and Suchada running across the quad, bear spray ready, followed by ten or twelve unarmed others. As Ray John reaches the gate, the doors swing open. Ray John lays down three seconds of spray and Cyrus Tasers him.

Ray John flops like he's lightning struck. A pair of wires snake from his chest to

Cyrus's gun. As Cyrus advances into the yard, he gives the trigger an extra squeeze, out of meanness. Ray John's body arcs.

Cyrus hands Bobby the Taser. "If he moves, fry him." Then Cyrus takes Bobby's Taser and points it at Suchada. "All right, hippie, up against the wall."

Suchada looks from the loaded Taser to the wires leading from Ray John to Bobby. "What wall?"

"I don't care what wall. Drop your weapon and assume the position."

Residents are pouring into the quad, drawn by Sioux's yell. At the sight of Cyrus, some turn and go back to their rooms, but most drift into the open, more curious than scared. Up in the bell tower, Sioux hears a siren and steps to the street opening. He sees more law enforcement vehicles squeal to a stop. Two police Impalas from El Granada and Moss Beach, Esteban's SUV, and a Jeep full of Butano State Park rangers.

The San Mateo Sheriff's Department main office knows nothing of Cyrus's insertion. He told them Mission Pescadero is holding a nostalgia festival and he may work traffic control. As a result, Cyrus couldn't put together but two gas mask rigs without alerting his superiors, which means Esteban runs to the open gate, hits the wall of bear spray, and falls back, eyes on fire.

He says, *"Chingado,"* and retreats to his SUV for a dose of Visine.

Back in the quad, Cyrus feels good. He pulls down his mask. "Who wants to go next?"

"You're a brave man when you've got a gun," Sunshine #1 says.

"You got it. Now, line your old asses up on the sidewalk here."

No one moves. Suchada thinks about rushing the bastard, making him use his last Taser on her so the others can overpower him. One look at Ray John laid out convinces her otherwise. Besides, Cyrus has a real gun in his holster. He'd no doubt switch off before any of these doofuses got it together to go after him.

Judith humps her walker out of Administration. She says, "There's no call getting wasted for a cat," and makes her way toward the sidewalk. Sunshine #2 follows, then Chicken Little and Phaedra.

Above and behind Cyrus, Nicolas says, "We better go down and do what the lieutenant says."

"Not me," says Sioux.

"He might shoot us."

Sioux stands erect, chin to the fore. "It is

a good day to die."

"I disagree."

"And the wires on that shock gun can't reach up here."

"But what if he gets mad and comes after us."

Sioux peers over the edge. "Then we jump."

Nicolas goes on down, leaving Sioux alone in the tower.

Cyrus, meanwhile, is stomping up and down before his lined-up captives. "Did you freaks think you could get away with ignoring the law? With ignoring *me?*"

"Shut up and do whatever it is you came to do," Judith says.

Cyrus whips around with such force his sunglasses fly out of his chest pocket. He says, "Pick those up, hippie."

Judith looks down at the glasses between her feet and the walker rod. They're the yellow lens type, preferred by lawmen worldwide. "Pick 'em up yourself. If I bend over, I won't be able to get back up."

Beside Judith, Willow starts to kneel down. Cyrus pushes the Taser toward Judith. "Her. The smart-ass has to do it."

Moving as slowly as possible, Judith stoops to retrieve the sunglasses. Blood goes to her head and she almost falls. Nicolas's hands take her left elbow, Willow's the right, and together they bring Judith back up. She passes the glasses to Cyrus, who one-hands them on.

He says, "You asked what I came to do —"

"No, I didn't," Judith says, but Cyrus doesn't care.

"I came to throw every one of you hippies in a cage where you've belonged since my father came back from Vietnam."

Judith nods. Thinks. Chews. "I wondered why you're taking it personally."

Cyrus looks across the flat gas mask eyes hanging on his neck. "You people killed my dad. That's how personal this is."

The silence is broken by the sound of Ray John dry heaving.

Lucinda says, "You didn't have to zap him the second time. Ray John never did anything to you or your dad."

"You volunteering to join your boyfriend?"

"He's not my boyfriend."

That's when Winston bursts from the chapel, shirtless, barefoot, hair flying, yelling gibberish.

"Jesus," says Bobby from inside his mask. "He's got a gun."

Winston screams out, "I'll kill the first dirtbag who flinches!"

Bobby freezes.

Cyrus drops the Taser and digs for the service revolver on his hip. Winston fires a shot into the air, then jerks back as if he didn't expect the gun to go off. "I'm on crystal and you know what I can do!"

Cyrus freezes.

Sunshine #1 says, "Winston, you asshole. Are you nuts?"

"You can't make waffles without breaking eggs." Winston points the barrel vaguely in Bobby's direction. "Throw down the peashooter, bub."

Bobby throws down.

"Now you."

Cyrus bends at the knees, as slowly as Judith retrieving his sunglasses. He gently sets the revolver on the sidewalk. "You have my promise. You will do time for this."

"You coppers'll never take me alive."

Out in the street, Esteban hears the gunfire. He takes a deep breath and a running start and jumps through the residual bear mist.

From his side of the quad, Winston sees a man in a uniform flying through the front gate. He snaps off a shot, missing Esteban by six feet and Ray John by one. Voices cry out from all sides, telling Winston to mellow out. Stop blowing it. Cool his jets.

Sunshine #1 has to be restrained from charging the gun-crazed chimney sweep.

Sioux spreads his arms wide and calls out, *"I will fight no more forever."*

Judith exhales buzzard breath into Cyrus's face. "I can't control him. You two should back off before someone gets hurt."

Bobby tears off his gas mask and flees past Esteban, who is confused, and Ray John, who is sitting up.

"Next time we use real bullets." Cyrus walks out with all the dignity a leader who has lost two revolvers and two Tasers can muster.

The oldest housekeeper calls to her grandson in Spanish. They exchange a few words, then Esteban jumps back through the gate. Even though the spray has dissipated, he's taking no chances.

Folding a shirt as he goes, Guy crosses to the library entrance. "I wonder what the old lady said to him."

"She told her grandson to quit his job," Rocky says. "She said the man he works for is crazed."

"You speak Spanish?"

Rocky says, "I was a waitress," as if that explains everything.

Thirty-Six

Tony the cook said they should save milk so there would be nothing to drink but coffee and tea for dinner, and Winston said in celebration of his driving out the invaders he would make a special outback iced tea. Several old-timers had wandered over from Nursing Care, where fifty-six hours without dumb drugs was causing a mass Rip Van Winkle syndrome. One at a time, they stumbled or rolled out of N.C., blinking in the sunlight, pulling at their own earlobes to prove their existence, trying to understand who and where they were. It came to them for the first time in a while that they were hungry, and they instinctively headed for the dining hall. So many left N.C. that Eldon and a couple of his orderlies set up another table between Phaedra and Housekeeping.

Mick said he couldn't fight the revolution without music, so Judith allowed one system for the complex. Mick and the Acid Reflux boys rigged an MP12 wireless for the hall, both lounges, the rec and exercise rooms, and the quad. They nailed speakers to the eucalyptus. The deal was considered fairly groovy until it came time to decide who controlled programming. Sausalito demanded Donovan, the album with "I Love My Jeans." Mick said they would listen to Donovan over his dead body. Sausalito said that was fine with them. The two camps compromised by playing Steve Miller followed by Spirit.

When Winston brought a tray of his Australian iced tea to the early Haight table, both Sunshines turned their chairs to face away.

"If I could, I would take back every hand job I've ever given you," said Sunshine #1.

Winston flashed a gap-toothed grin. "You say that now, but tonight in the hot tub, you'll forgive me."

Sunshine #1 twisted around to study Winston's eyes. She'd been around speed freaks enough to know who was flying and who wasn't. "You're not on crystal."

"I only said I was so the pigs would think I'm crazy enough to shoot them." He set the tea tray on the table and picked up his cane. "They'll screw you bald if they think you're sane."

Sunshine #2 turned back around. If #1 could face Winston, so could she. "Where'd you find that awful gun?"

"Hash dealer in Bombay gave it to me as a parting gift. Nineteen seventy-two. You could fly with a loaded pistol in your fanny pack back then. You want some tea?"

Willow held a glass to her lips and sniffed the rim. "You didn't give peace a chance."

"Hell," Winston said. "The man had a gun. He shot Ray John. People without guns never win against people with guns. Didn't you read about Montezuma and the Aztecs?"

"No, and neither did you." Willow simultaneously tore the tops off four packs of artificial sweetener and dumped the contents into her tea. "You heard about it on talk radio."

Sioux looked down on what he believed was supposed to be chipped beef on toast. He wondered if Mr. Scratchy would eat it. Ever since the trauma, Mr. Scratchy had been off his feed. He wouldn't come out of the closet, even though he was no longer locked in, and his litter box discipline had gone to heck. Pee all over the closet. The cat went so far as to take a crap on Sioux's headphones.

From Mr. Scratchy, Sioux's mind skipped to what happens to a person after he dies. Sioux definitely didn't want to die, but more and more these days the alternative was looking like a waste of time. He'd hoped being an Indian would change his outlook. So far all the war paint had done was scare Mr. Scratchy.

Ray John leaned across the aisle from Berkeley. "I wish you women hadn't thrown their firearms over the wall. With two more pistols and two Tasers we could have covered every exit."

"Oh, be quiet," said Lucinda, who, till then, had been as silent as Sioux. "You're bragging because you finally got wounded for a cause. Nobody wants to hear about it, Ray John."

"Who put a bug up your butt?"

"I'm tired of this attitude that California revolves around you."

Ray John said, "What?"

"The last thing we need here is more guns. Winston is bad hair enough without you going tough guy."

Ray John was torn between lashing back and crawling in a hole. First, the Taser, and now, Lucinda. Before he could decide, Winston said, "I resent the aspersion, coming from a twat," and Lucinda's line of fire swiveled to him.

"Winston, you are a clown. People making fun of the '60s look and talk like you."

Winston tapped his cane tip on the floor. "You're jealous because I'm the only one here who didn't change."

"What a bizarre thing to be proud of."

"I am proud I didn't sell out. You *girls* have gotten as uptight as a room full of copy editors. What you need is your doors kicked open."

"How dare you of all people call me uptight," Sunshine #1 said.

"Every one of you is living in a spiritual coma. It's time for someone to wake you up."

Sioux thought he'd heard the rap before, only he couldn't remember if it was recently or way back when. Maybe in an Alan Watts book. Or a Steppenwolf song. He finished off his tea and picked up his untouched plate. "I'm going to feed Mr. Scratchy."

"You do that." Winston sounded bitter. "Tell your cat he almost got me killed."

Lucinda said, "Bullshit."

Dixie stopped by on the way to her evening TM session. Although early Haight fairly crackled with tension, she missed it. To Dixie, this was the most together group in the world. She thought she'd discovered the mother lode of beautiful people.

"Loved the tea, Winston. Can I get the recipe sometime?"

Winston tucked his chin low and gave Dixie his Aqualung leer. "Nothing to it, Sheila. Lemon, ginkgo, cinnamon, anise, and green tea. Ingredients grown wild in the Aussie outback."

Sunshine #1 rolled her eyes. Lucinda muttered another "Bullshit."

"I'm assuming the green tea was decaf," Dixie said.

Winston affected hurt pride. "I've never taken a decaf substance in my life. I'm not starting now."

A cloud crossed Dixie's unlined face. "I hope it doesn't keep me up tonight."

"If it does, drop by the hot tub, Sheila, we're having a party."

"Okay," Dixie said. "Except my name's not Sheila."

"It's a Down Under term. What we use when men here would say 'Darlin'.' "

Dixie started to bounce away, then stopped. She beamed a happy smile at early Haight. "I can't wait till I'm old enough I can get away with saying whatever pops in my head. I want to grow up to be just like you folks."

Lucinda said, "I'm going to kill myself now."

At North Beach, the wheelchair table, Gap Koch placed one paper hospital straw into his iced tea and another paper hospital straw into an empty juice glass. He leaned forward, bent his straw joints to the proper angles, and inserted the tea straw into this left nostril. He then inserted the juice glass straw into his right nostril.

The truth was, no matter how sophisticated and lawyerly Gap had been behaving, the sight of Casey Kasandris walking out of Nursing Care with a movie star rattled his self-confidence. He'd seen so many others lose their minds and then deny the fact for months that there was a natural fear he had moved beyond observable reality.

Casey was the last woman Gap ever held in his arms. One night a year ago, after they first brought her through the tunnel, Casey crawled into Gap's bed. She chose Gap over the Parkinson's patient in the next bed who shouted advertising slogans in his sleep.

"Quicker picker upper!"

"Lucky Strike means fine tobacco!"

Casey and Gap held each other all night, in the innocent slumber party sense of holding. Gap owned a pharmaceutical sample case of pills, but none for sex, so instead of balling, Casey held him by the ears and whimpered as she rubbed her body against his. Gap had been certain he would never be touched by a woman again, and Casey's skin felt so wonderful that he wept into her bony chest.

She told him everything would be okay.

Gap said, "I don't think so."

At dawn, the orderlies prying them apart made disgusting comments, comparing Gap and Casey to stuck dogs. Gap spit in an orderly's face. Casey howled. Later that day, Alexandra had night restraints put on Casey's bed.

So, when Gap saw Casey upright, following a movie star whose name he couldn't remember, his faith in his concept of physicality had been shaken to the core. Especially when Casey walked into a wall and disappeared.

Now Gap felt a powerful need to prove himself. With his index finger, he closed off his right nostril. He sniffed iced tea up his left nostril, into his sinus cavity. Gap risked a glance around the table, checking the audience. Only Darcy Faye Gardiner was watching. She looked on quietly, her thumb massaging a fur patch on her chin.

Gap released his right nostril and tea

drained down into the juice glass. The trick worked perfectly. He was a man whose glass is half full.

Gap yanked himself upright and punched a fist into the air over his head. *"Yes! I haven't lost it!"*

Darcy Faye and Gap looked at each other across the table. Darcy smiled.

Over at Stanford, Guy worked out the nuances of standing by, folding a shirt while a hippie disarms a law officer who has Tasered a fellow revoltee. No one behaved the way Guy had been raised to think of as proper behavior. Ray John sprayed bear deterrent, Cyrus Monk fired a Taser, Winston threatened to shoot the peace officers. Everyone thought they were doing the right thing and no one was. Wars start that way. Guy had seen a streaker Tasered at a demolition derby once, twenty years ago. Fifty thousand volts in the naked butt. Guy interviewed the kid later, for a story the paper didn't run, and the kid said he'd rather have been shot. Guy came away from the interview glad law enforcement hadn't had Tasers when his son Martin was a teenager.

Judith's fork shook as she aimed Jell-O at her gullet. "I want a lock on those doors can't be opened with a key. One of those beam-and-slot deals like they used in frontier forts."

Wanda Bretschneider pulled out a notebook and took notes. "There's some three-by-sixes the gardeners use for hedge borders."

"Make it strong enough to hold off a battering ram."

Nicolas leaned toward his tray and looked up at Guy. "I'm not a fag, you know."

"Alexandra was venting," Marta said. "She didn't mean it."

"I have no gripe with people who are. Gay. I just happen not to be, that way."

Ike said, "We don't care, anyway."

Guy pushed back his chair and started to rise. Nicolas grabbed him by the elbow and said, "I'm not."

Guy shook himself loose. "It doesn't matter."

Guy walked to the dining room door, where he found Winston, a tray full of food and drink in his left hand, the cane in his right. Guy held the door open for him. "You need some help there?"

Winston lifted the tray an inch. "My turn to deliver the doctor his supper."

"How's Beaver holding up?"

"A bit lonesome, I would expect." Winston propped his cane on the door frame, blocking Guy's exit. "Some of my lady friends asked me to invite you to the hot tub tonight. We're having an intimate little get-together."

"It's been a long day," Guy said. "I'll probably hit the sack."

"The birds will be bummed out if you don't come. Here." Winston thrust the tray at Guy, who had to take it. Winston pulled out his billfold, dug under a flap, and produced a blue pill. "If you decide you'd enjoy socialization, take this an hour before you're ready to get into the tub."

Guy held the pill in his palm while Winston took back the tray. "What is it?"

"I call it the tablet of youth."

"I hate to bum out your lady friends." Guy thought it was kind of neat that he'd said *bum out* so casually. *Birds* was a bit much. "Youth is the last thing I want tonight."

Thirty-Seven

Cyrus found Alexandra in the back booth at the new Shari's in Pacifica. Clean and showered more than once. Dressed like an Alabama real estate agent, in dark glasses, hair up in a bun with a stick through it, spiking Diet Dr Pepper from a Jim Beam bottle.

Her first words were, "You always late for appointments?"

Cyrus slid into his side of the booth, seeing twin versions of himself in her sunglasses, wondering if she was worth the trouble of talking to. Esteban said coming out of the Mission, she was a mess. He'd helped her to the SUV with her railing at him all the way, blaming him for her state. Not a bit embarrassed to be on the street in thong and feathers. Cyrus had enough of the blame game from his wife. He didn't need a woman who couldn't control her hippies telling him it was his fault.

"I was tied up keeping the lid on your

screwup." He opened a plastic menu and looked at the Today's Special insert. Grandma's Meat Loaf. Why would a person eat out, then order food that tasted like it was cooked at home? "I've had calls from four newspapers, two TV stations, and a blog this afternoon. It's been a big-time scramble, but I've convinced every one of these news sleazebags that it's all a joke."

"You promised me they're cut off," Alexandra said.

"Somebody in there got to a phone."

"I don't give a damn about your newspaper lid, as long as the pencil-neck doctors who own the Mission don't hear about us." Alexandra lit a cigarette — long, skinny, brown thing. Phallic as the Washington Monument.

"You can't do that," Cyrus said.

"Arrest me, if you care so much."

Wren Waterford came up with a tray propped on her hip. "You going to let her smoke?"

"Looks like I am, now doesn't it," Cyrus said.

"No sweat off my buns. Are we eating or interrogating today?"

"Bring me a stack of blueberry cakes and a cup of coffee."

As Wren slouched for the kitchen, Alexandra blew smoke across her place setting, at Cyrus. "Pancakes?"

"You don't like pancakes?"

She shrugged and picked lint from her buff-colored filter. Her fingernails were the color of oxygenated blood. "I want you to give me Henry Box on a stick. You hear me, Deputy Monk?"

"Lieutenant."

"Whatever."

Cyrus took off his own sunglasses and rubbed his temples. The knee-jerk response to a civilian demand was to say something ugly. "Henry's the one with the cat?"

"I'll take Judith and the Okie, too, while you're busting heads. And the Jazzercise pixie. But Henry counts the most. I want him in jail the rest of his life, and not some New Age country club, either. I want Henry in a hole where they ass-ream the elderly." Alexandra downed a stiff slug of Beam and Diet D.P. "Can you do that for me, *Lieutenant,* or do I call the sheriff?"

"Hell, Alexandra, calling the sheriff is the last thing on your agenda, if you want old hippies reamed. You can't call anybody but me."

Alexandra carefully pulled off her sunglasses and leveled her PMS stare at Cyrus. The same stare that had once caused an

Alzheimer's patient to pee his pants.

"Sheriff Grady will go public with it. He'll negotiate with them." Cyrus said *negotiate* like it tasted bad. "He'll set a *paradigm* to air their complaints. He'll initiate a *conversation.* We don't want a conversation with these people. We want funerals."

Wren brought the pancakes and coffee at the same time. Cyrus hated it that way. He always wanted his coffee first, and she knew it.

"Anything else?" Wren asked.

"This is enough."

Wren looked down at Alexandra's Diet Dr Pepper. "I see you're getting your own refills."

Alexandra's fingernails beat a tattoo on the tabletop while Cyrus doctored up his cakes with butter and syrup. Elbows flapping like wings, he cut the cakes into perfect bite-sized squares.

"Is the Okie a hippie?" he asked.

"Are you kidding me?"

"They all looked like hippies, what I saw of them at the gate. But I would imagine a lot of old Okies never grew their hair out."

"The Okie is an Okie. What difference does it make?"

"Makes a lot to me." Cyrus forked a uniform gap around each uniform bite of pancake. His plate looked like it was covered by window frames. "You should know why I joined the Sheriff's Department of San Mateo County."

"Does this little story have squat to do with the scumbags who hijacked my care center?"

"Directly." Cyrus finally took a bite. He chewed and swallowed before going on. "When I went into law enforcement, my mother took me to my father's grave and had me swear an oath that I would bust hippies."

"You're kind of spooky about this."

"You ever hear of the Merry Pranksters?"

"Nobody could live here and not know about Pranksters. They put us on the map."

"Right. The Prankster cult was spawned up around La Honda." Cyrus pointed a pancake-laden fork at Alexandra's breasts. "This county is the source point for all the sewage that's swept over America since the Vietnam War. So this is where I have to be." He popped the bite into his mouth. "And now, there they are, one ugly band of hippies, holed up in your compound." He swallowed, jaws popping. "I'm not about to turn this fight over to a higher authority."

Alexandra stared at Cyrus through a veil of wisping smoke. The realization dawned that this man might be nuts.

Cyrus pushed a three-pancake-thick square back and forth through a pool of syrup. He glanced up at her, almost shyly.

He said, "Are you dating anybody?"

Might be, hell, he was nuts. "One step at a time, Lieutenant. You crack Henry Box's head and kill his cat, or, better yet, let me kill his cat while he looks on, and we'll talk about who I'm dating."

"I just wondered."

THIRTY-EIGHT

Rocky catches on first. In the shower, loofa working the elbows, a song she can't stand called "Where Have All the Flowers Gone?" rotates through her mind as she thinks about the blue chips in Guy's irises at the picnic table when she told him about Roderick. No judgment behind the eyes. No pity. Listening to what she had to say.

When a Freon rush rips up Rocky's spine into her brainstem, turning her sinuses into a pinball machine.

She staggers into the hot handle. Individual water drops spank her skin. Space and time between each drop. An invisible fist grabs her face.

"I'll kill the bastard."

The room tilts. Air thickens. Rocky towels quickly and dresses in nylon running pants and a pullover. In the stairwell, the wall contracts. A throat swallowing. She bursts out the door into the falling coastal light, which still hurts the eyes. The moon has risen over the edge of the back wall. A bloated aluminum foil of a moon, spider-webbed with blood. The Fugs howl "Strafe Them Creeps in the Rice Paddy, Daddy" from the eucalyptus tree. Laughter erupts from the picnic table, only not laughter she's heard since she was a girl. This is laughter from the head.

Barefoot Rocky cuts across the grass. She feels okay — maybe some low-grade anxiety disguised as heartburn — but she knows the evening is going to change for the worse. The security light is already separating from itself like a van Gogh star. She knows one thing and that is, she's screwed.

So Rocky blows on into the rec hall to find Fairly Fast Freddy sitting cross-legged on a pool table, staring at the back of his hand.

He says, "How did this happen?"

Rocky doesn't remember crossing the exercise room and on into the sauna. She's suddenly there, on the breathing tile, where Winston is lowering his skinny body into the froth. Sunshine #2 and Willow float, seemingly held aloft by their own breasts. Sparkle Plenty sits on the bench, pulling panties over ankles. Winston's dick looks like a wet sweat sock.

Rocky screams, *"Bastard!"*

She swings an open palm but slips on the wet tile and almost goes over into the tub, catching herself with an out-of-position hip. "You nasty prick."

Winston smiles. His head is a skull mirroring Grateful Dead bone tattoos on his arms and chest. A skeleton wrapped in skeletons. "Do you feel my gift?"

Rocky appeals to Sparkle. "He dosed us."

"Thank God." Sparkle gasps for air. "I thought I was having a stroke."

When Willow stands, a film of water courses down her slick fat. "Winston, how could you?"

"It's nothing you haven't done for fun, many the time."

"Not in fifty years, I haven't. You should ask people before sending them on a trip."

"Don't be so hung up. Let the love flow."

Sunshine #2 drops under the water and doesn't come back up. Rocky thinks, *Shit, she'll drown,* and reaches into the hot tub, grabbing frizzy hair, pulling Sunshine #2 to the surface.

Sunshine #2 sucks air, like breathing through a straw. "Get me out of here."

As Rocky beaches Sunshine #2, a mumbling voice is heard from the hallway. Sioux who was once Henry: "Betty Botter bought some butter, but, she said, the butter's bitter. If I put it in my batter, it will make my batter bitter, but a bit of better butter, will make my batter better."

"Poor Henry," says Sunshine #2. "He was on the edge already."

"It was in the tea, wasn't it?" Rocky says.

Winston grins, showing all his remaining teeth, and lowers himself down to the Adam's apple. He hums "Lucy in the Sky with Diamonds."

Rocky clenches both hands into a single fist and with all her might slams down on his bald spot. Winston laughs.

Rocky says, "There's people drank that tea have never tripped before. You asshole." She leaves to find Guy.

Mr. Natural crawls through the door, fear sparking from his eyes. "I'm about to fall off."

Rocky touches his shoulder. "Winston put LSD in the iced tea. You'll be through the bad rush in a couple of hours."

"But the Earth is leaving me."

"Ride it out, Mr. Natural."

"Soon as I can get up, I'm going to kill Winston."

On the quad, Lucinda holds Eldon's head

while he vomits.

"Come on inside. We'll brush your teeth and you'll be okay."

"Why am I so sick?"

"Acid hits black people different. I didn't know that till I saw Richard Pryor at the Cow Palace."

"What acid?"

"I'll guide you through it, if you'll let me."

Word spreads fast as crabs in a commune. Not a stroke. Not Alzheimer's, or a gas attack. Winston. There's a sharp split between those who welcome the renewal of experience and those who would rather have had boiling tar pumped up their anuses. The Sausalito girls run to their rooms for costumes. The Long Beach poets meditate on the size of the universe. New Yorkers dig out unfinished memoirs to record their impressions. The Midwest has no idea why their heads have gained so much weight all of a sudden. A couple of the men go paralytic, like black-widow — bitten squirrels. A pushing match breaks out at the MP12 player — the age-old trip battle between Pink Floyd and Moody Blues.

In Phaedra's room, Suchada holds both of Dixie's hands while Dixie's face splotches out. Her forehead stretches. Her eyeballs feel vacuumed. "I understand now. I get it, Suchada. The world is a beautiful island."

"Don't fight it. Let yourself flow downstream."

"Muscle tone is more than a symbol for true health. Don't you see? It isn't how flexible you are, physically, but spiritually, too. And intellectually, emotionally. Financially. Life is stretching. God is in the flex."

"Breathe, Dixie. Slowly."

"I teach breathing for a living."

"Well, you're hyperventilating now. Breathe on the five count."

"I can feel the earth rotating. I hear the sun."

"Get her the hell out of here," Phaedra says. Phaedra didn't drink tea at dinner. She snuck Black Velvet and has been at it ever since. Her hands are starting to curl into claws and she's likely to fall out of the chair if Suchada doesn't keep a lookout. Suchada knows she's in for a long night with Phaedra, but Dixie needs help and Suchada herself is rushing her brains away. Her gut feels the roller coaster drop. A thirty-pound chunk of lead balances on her forehead. White noise in the eardrums.

"I can't let Dixie out alone like this," Suchada says.

"Get yourself out while you're at it,"

Phaedra snarls. "I don't need you. I never needed you. I'm Phaedra Wallace. You're a puny snail beside me."

Suchada pulls Dixie to her feet. "I'll check on you later."

"Don't bother." Phaedra drinks and drools, pretty much simultaneously.

Dixie says, "The soul resides in the cheekbones. I see it clearly. Fat smothers the soul. We must tell Willow. And the dumpy woman from Kentucky."

"Come with me," Suchada says.

Two flights down, the dumpy woman from Kentucky rakes her belly with her fingernails and wails, *"Fat,* Charley. I'm *fat."*

Charley throws a blanket over his head.

Guy sits on his bed, lights out, afraid to move his hands or head. The television is on, against Judith's rules, but with the satellite out, he's watching shadows behind snow. Figures flit about, beneath the blizzard. Synchronized swimmers. He's sure he sees Lily, but it can't be. He thinks. A face glares out at him. A coach he knew forty years ago. Racist bastard who ran dogfights in the summer. Lily is behind him, signaling something Guy can't make out. Guy thinks about the Dutch painter who cut off his own ear. Understanding why.

Then the light flares, blindingly, and Rocky Gingrass is in the room.

"You're okay. Don't be afraid." She holds his head and, to Guy, it feels as if her hands are so hot they've fused with his bone structure. "Everything is okay."

He tries to speak. Soon, "I am in an attack."

"No, you aren't, Guy. This isn't dementia. Or maybe it is but it's artificial. Winston put LSD in the iced tea at dinner. We all feel like you do."

Guy sees Rocky's face as tongue-colored and wet. "Is this how you felt when you ate the mescaline, when you were pregnant?"

"I guess so. I don't remember. I remember wanting to stop it and drinking a lot of tequila, trying to bring myself down fast."

"Let's find tequila."

"I have a bottle in my room."

"You do?"

"Medicinal tequila, for when I can't sleep."

"That's nice." Guy finally turns his head. "Let's take it outside. There's no air in the building."

In the dispensary, Dalton Beaver bunches his fingertips together, thumb on bottom, four fingers on top. He holds them at arm's length, then he yanks his hand toward his eyes, stopping at the last moment. He drifts his arm back out straight, then zooms in on his face again. And again.

He ripple waves his hand from side to side. He snakes it to and fro, seeing his fingers in multiple positions at the same time. Dalton can bounce his hand off the wall. He can lash out like a frog's tongue gathering in a dragonfly in extreme slo mo. Then he pokes himself in the eye and it's the Fourth of July.

"Wow," he says.

Guy and Rocky go by Rocky's room for a fifth of Cuervo Silver. They start down the elevator, but as the doors meet, Guy decides the coffin thing is not for him, so they take the stairs, stiff-legged, holding the rail to keep from pitching forward.

"I don't recall an escalator," Guy says.

"That's your bifocals. Hold on to my shoulder."

Outside, the air is less like breathing through Styrofoam. The Butterfield Blues Band plays "Two Trains Running" from Mick's speakers. The six Sausalito women have changed into Victoria's Secret sleep-wear — nightgowns and teddies — and are dancing around the Greek statue. Imagine Shakespearean witches in Silk & Satin. The dancing isn't like anything Guy has ever seen, except maybe in a water aerobics video his daughter Claudia exercised to about thirty years ago. The Sausalito women weave their arms in, out, and around through waves of music. Chicken Little is way up in the eucalyptus, writing poems on index cards, folding them into airplanes, and sailing them into space.

Guy picks a card airplane off the flagstone and reads the poem written in tiny longhand, in blue ink.

My kids won't amount to a hill of beans
Cause I dropped acid on my jeans
It ate through my skin
And it ate through my bones
And now it's eating my chromosomes.

Guy doesn't show the poem to Rocky.

Darcy Faye Gardiner cries on a bench in Contemplative Corner.

Mr. Natural is trying to pee on the chapel and can't.

Sunshine #1 stands in the bell tower, her arms spread, her eyes closed. Crucified to the elements.

Rocky takes Guy to the coffee clique table

where Nicolas, Ray John, and Marta Pitcairne are watching the whole thing go down in harmony.

"I hated this stuff even back when I was supposed to like it," Nicolas says.

"Not me." Marta's grin is the so-called mile-wide variety. "I tripped every Friday for a year before I met Ike. My roommate Joy and I would go dancing at Apple Jacks and flirt with bikers the Pranksters left behind. I'll bet some of those horn-heads are still there."

"I can't picture you as a psychedelic wonder woman," Rocky says.

"Ike made me switch to chamomile."

Nicolas has never seen Marta without Ike or Ike without Marta. "Where is he anyway?"

Marta laughs, a high, strung-out cackle of laughter. "Ike drank a gallon of tea. He's hiding in the tippy-toe with the lights out. We won't be seeing him for another eight hours, I'm sure." She bats her false eyelashes. "I'm on my own tonight."

Rocky slugs down several swallows of tequila. Hot lava burns all the way down and halfway back up.

"Here." She hands the bottle to Guy, who takes his own extended hit.

"Pow." Guy shudders, then drinks more.

"You know what this tequila reminds me of? Of course you don't. Our dog Sooner got bit by a rattle-snake and my grandfather cut off his tail with an ax. Grandpa said Sooner might bleed to death, but he wouldn't die of snakebite."

Ray John says, "I get it."

Nicolas says, "I don't."

Dixie drags a mat onto the lawn and organizes a yoga session. "C'mon, girls, it'll be neat!"

The dancers ignore her while Suchada hovers, coiled, in the background. She seems a bit lost, without Phaedra, but lost in the good way, the way of unknown possibilities.

"We'll begin with a moon salutation." Dixie stands erect, her body and head straight, yet relaxed. "As you exhale, bring your hands into the prayer pose."

Suchada goes into the classic "Now I Lay Me Down to Sleep" stance. Darcy Faye Gardiner stops crying and wanders over to watch. Wanda Bretschneider follows a few steps back.

"Inhale and stretch your arms up over your head." Dixie curves way back into a shape spines aren't designed to go. Suchada keeps up, all the way. Tentatively, Darcy Faye raises her arms, too. Wanda isn't ready to commit.

"I wonder where Phaedra is," Rocky asks.

Guy closes his eyes and sees red, flashing grenades. Slime green wallpaper. Lily playing tennis at eighteen. As with every experience since she died, he runs the information through her eyes, not settling on his own opinion until he considers hers. Lily was more adventurous than Guy, in college, always talking about life outside Wilburton, wanting to see new stuff. She'd been intrigued by the Oklahoma version of hippies at Eastern State, like a girl intrigued by spiders. One October she went on a motorcycle ride with a long-haired kid from Shreveport. She was quiet for several days afterward. Guy himself is uncomfortable with head rushes and pulsating earth beneath his feet, but he can't help thinking the Lily of his youth might have made the trip into something fun. She could do that.

Ray John reaches toward the tequila. "Mind if I take a drink?" He's watching Lucinda, who is kissing Eldon Gaede. Eldon sits on a bench, one over from the bench Darcy Faye just left, with his shirt off. Lucinda stands between his knees, bent slightly at the waist, her arms around his shoulders.

Rocky says, "Uh-oh."

"What?" Guy turns to see where they are

looking.

Rocky touches the blue vein on the back of Ray John's hand. "I'm sorry, Ray John."

"What for?" He drinks deeply from the bottle, and only then moves his hand out from under Rocky's. He wipes his mouth. "More power to her, I say. We never had a monogamy contract." He drinks tequila again. This time, when he speaks his voice catches an edge. "You can't tame a coyote. Anyone tries is crazy."

Nicolas trips out on the moonlight on Eldon's back. He's never seen a pattern of flesh and shadow quite so beautiful. It glistens with a bit of sparkle, like living mahogany. Or molasses poured over neon. The color is unrelated to the person.

"Where you going?" Marta asks.

Nicolas rises and moves without will toward Eldon. He can see through Eldon's surface into another dimension. The life of sinew and muscle. He remembers a campfire from his childhood. After the flames died, the coals pulsed like San Francisco at night, seen from above.

Lucinda pulls out of the kiss. "What the hell are you doing?"

Eldon jerks, startled by Nicolas's touch. His face swings around. Misshapen. Frightened.

"This is a hetero situation, Nicolas," Lucinda says. "Go find your own kind."

"That's not what I —"

"Come on." Lucinda pulls Eldon upright. "We'll take this into the library. I've had dreams about that leather couch."

Blood flushes through Nicolas's face. "That's not what I . . . I mean." He looks down at the concrete bench. "You don't understand."

He feels someone at his side. A brush against his arm. "I understand." Marta touches his sleeve. He looks down at her. She's so short he can see wide gaps of skin between her hair patches.

"You know," Marta says. "We've been sitting at the same table for years, but we've never talked."

Nicolas says, "I'm not gay."

Marta laughs. "If you were gay, I wouldn't find you attractive."

"I'm having a bad trip now."

Marta turns Nicolas to face her, head-on. She holds his shirt with both of her hands. "If you want me to, I could love you, Nicolas Lessac."

Nicolas pulls her hands off his shirt. "Marta, look at yourself," and he flees into Residency.

Thirty-Nine

Sunshine #1, naked as the day she first took acid, strolls across the quad, stepping through dancers, yoga practitioners, and people standing frozen as statuary. She beelines for the table and the tequila. Without asking, she tips the bottle up and drinks.

"You and Sioux are supposed to relieve me at midnight," she says to Ray John.

"Is Sioux up there?" Ray John's voice crackles with lost love.

"No one's up there. That cop could march in and pop us all."

Ray John stands and puts on his fedora. "I'll go."

Sunshine #1 drinks till tequila runs down her chin and drips. "First the gun and now this. We have to do something about Winston."

"If this happened sixty years ago, we'd

throw him out of the commune," Rocky says.

"I'll tell you one thing. I'm not ever sucking the cocksucker's cock again." Sunshine #1 puts the bottle back on the table. "Fairly Fast Freddy is taking people in one at a time to see Casey's body," she says. "Either of you want to go?"

"No," says Rocky.

"No, thank you," says Guy.

"He's charging a dollar a minute to lock you in the freezer with her. Willow told me Casey's wearing mittens. Isn't that a trip?"

Sioux who was once Henry is lying back on a webbed lawn chair on the roof of Residency, over the rear exit. He pats a soft rhythm on Mr. Scratchy, who crouches on Sioux's belly, facing his face. Mr. Scratchy doesn't quite purr, although he makes a sound some would describe as wanting to purr. He flexes his claws, out and in, digging for waffles in Sioux's sweater.

The walkie-talkie is on and Sioux can hear two people making love in the downstairs hallway. Because of the overlying static he can't tell and has no interest in who, or even what gender, they are. He can tell one of them thinks he or she is at Woodstock. He or she keeps huffing about someone holding a place in line at the privies and they have to hurry.

"I don't want to miss Sly and the Family Stone."

After some time of this, Sioux cradles Mr. Scratchy in his left arm so he won't fall and, leaning over, picks up the walkie-talkie and tosses it off the roof. In the rare silence, he lies back again and rubs the cat behind its chewed-off ears. The stars spin and pulse, mutating from red to blue and back as the dome of sky breathes deeply. The rushes aren't so bad now. This is the part of the trip he used to enjoy, the part when you're flying, but able to function.

Sioux closes his eyes. He sees his mother's long, brown hair spreading over him like a curtain of rain. Her hair forms a secret enclosure that screens out all things not Henry and his mother. He inhales her powder smell. Jasmine. Peach. Pall Mall. She sings a song that goes, *"Too-ra loo-ra loo-ra, and a too-la-roo-la-ray, for you're Mommy's little baby, and I hope you stay that way."*

Henry's mother got the lung cancer when he was a high school sophomore. She took two bad years dying. The end finally came while he was in summer school, making up an English class. They buried her in a hilltop cemetery outside Havre, Montana, and, after the service, Henry didn't go back to the house with everyone else to eat the onslaught of funeral food. He walked out to Highway 2 and hitched a ride to the corner of Haight and Ashbury, where a man in cowboy clothes sold him a hit of LSD for two dollars and a cigarette.

Henry never went back. His uncle Newt would be dead by now, but he didn't know about the cousins. He'd always meant to find them, even went so far as to Google the names once, but nothing turned up. Henry's mother was the one who told him her great-grandfather had been Red Cloud, the Sioux chieftain. She'd said Red Cloud's blood flowed through Henry and someday he would grow up to be a man of distinction.

Henry/Sioux is pushing eighty and still waiting to be distinct. About all he can say is he survived two marriages. Maybe it would have been different if he'd had kids. Maybe there is time. Saul Bellow and Tony Randall both fathered babies when they were older than he is now. Of course, they were famous, so they had someone to love them.

Mr. Scratchy stretches and circles twice, counterclockwise. When Sioux opens his eyes, the sky has fallen low, like the black blanket he used to imagine hung over the world, with pinholes letting in sunlight from above. Sioux lifts his hand to touch the blanket. Distance and time have accordioned.

He thinks, *All my heroes are dead.*

Hu slithers across the floor of the exercise room, pulling himself from StairMaster to weight machine to treadmill to free weight rack to water cooler. Sweat soaks the bandanna tied around his head. He carries a steak knife between his teeth. Charlie Musselwhite plays on the sound system.

Hu pulls himself through the door into the cedar-sided hot-tub room where he finds Winston, alone, deserted by his women. Winston's eyes are closed. He leans his head back against the side of the tub. He's long since stopped resetting the jets' timer every fifteen minutes, so the room is quiet.

Without opening his eyes, Winston says, "Where'd you lose your chair?"

Hu takes the knife from his teeth. "I'm going to slit your throat."

Winston's eyes open, but he shows no alarm. "Whatever for?"

"You deserve to die. What kind of man doses old people and cripples?"

Winston appears to give the question serious thought. To him, it is not rhetorical. "They needed to wake up. You need to wake up."

"We deserved a choice."

Winston sits forward on the tub bench. "I remember a trip we took, fifty-seven years ago. Thanksgiving. Tish the Dish baked a turkey and you wore the carcass as a hat. You remember what you said? You said, 'I hope I always have the youth to do this once a year for the rest of my life. Even if I hit one hundred.' " Winston's eyes shift from the past to Hu spread across the floor next to the tub. "And look what you've become. You take anti-anxieties and tranqs. Painkillers. Any drug, so long as it represses awareness."

"Awareness is the enemy now."

"Don't you crave the days when LSD was our religion?"

"I could walk then."

"You could walk now, if you got high enough."

Hu lies with his cheek pressed to the cool tile. From an inch off the floor, the view is mostly grime. "No, Winston." Hu's voice comes as a whimper. "It doesn't matter how high I get. This stupid body will not walk."

■ ■ ■ ■

Lucinda makes the cardinal mistake of LSD. She looks in a mirror. She does not hallucinate, but the opposite of hallucination. She sees herself as she is, without the filter of self. Not the Lucinda she remembers or feels like or wants to be. She looks in the mirror and sees her self with no self-image.

How could her face contain these grotesque colors? She sees each worn-out pore and crack, not just around her eyes, but on her lips. Where has her chin gone? What are those twin cords running up her throat? Lucinda cannot fathom where this old woman came from and why she has stolen the body Lucinda loves. She knows to tear away, but can't. The acid won't let her.

Eldon walks the shelves, looking at books. He studies the Monet print until the shades of blue bleed together and separate again. The hard rush eases off and Eldon comes to himself, wondering why he's in this room, waiting to have sex with a woman forty years older than he is. He wonders why his head feels flayed.

"What are we doing here?" Eldon asks.

Lucinda doesn't answer.

Dalton Beaver lifts an oxygen tank over his head and throws it at the door. He screams. He scratches his face till blood runs under his eyes. Dalton realizes fully and completely that he hates his wife. He hates his children. The selfish bores stole the center of his existence and now it's too late. He's wasted his turn.

He could have gone to Florence and painted frescoes and made love to fire-eyed women on balconies. He could have danced in fountains at dawn. Instead, he tied himself to a spiteful harridan obsessed with shoes and fathered children who laugh at him. No one Dalton loved yesterday has the smallest use for him. No one knows him. The isolation is total.

He climbs the shelving, throwing pill bottles and needle packs, till he reaches his bedpan on top and he hurls that across the room into the door also. He curls up, fetal, on the top shelf, under the ceiling. He holds his head in his hands and sobs.

Forty

By four a.m. sobbing has replaced dancing pretty much all around. People with ten years or less life expectancy are taking honest looks at the past, present, and future, and not many like what they see. Mick has the Dead's "Dark Star" on the sound system. Suicide rock. The quad has the general appearance of the day after a natural disaster.

Rocky sits bent at the waist with her head between her knees and weeps, violently. Guy has no idea what to do. He places his hand on her back and waits, watching a woman across the quad practicing tae kwon do exercises. She faces the eucalyptus, her back to Guy. She's wearing a toga-style sheet. He doesn't remember seeing her before.

Rocky raises her head. Her fists are clenched. "I knew."

"What did you know?"

"I knew I might be pregnant."

Guy strokes her back. He hasn't touched a human with the palm of his hand in so long, it feels like a new experience.

"When I took the mescaline, and then the tequila." Her face is like a photograph that's been torn and taped back together. The parts are there but they don't line up. "I always told myself I didn't know, but I did."

"I don't understand."

"I knew I might be pregnant, but I ate mescaline anyway."

She bends double again, but she is no longer crying. She mumbles, "Poor Roderick," then doesn't say anything for a long time.

Guy looks at his hand on Rocky's spine, on her pullover, and he thinks about the last time he and Lily made love. It was a few days after they got the biopsy results. Before that, they hadn't done it in three months, maybe even four. Guy couldn't remember, it had been so long. That night, Lily went into the bathroom and stayed there for an hour while Guy waited in bed, reading a book on golf courses in Scotland. They don't water the grass in Scotland, so the fairways are yellow.

When he heard Lily come out of the bathroom, Guy said, "How would you feel about Scotland this summer?" He looked up and saw she had no clothes on. This was before she lost the weight. Before her hair fell out. Guy gasped, she was so beautiful. She was everything she had ever been. Lily's beauty peaked at seventy-one.

She said, "Guy," and he held back the covers.

The sex itself was awkward. He was afraid he might hurt her. She kept her face turned away. Neither of them climaxed, and by the time Guy gave up trying they both knew it would never happen again. Afterward, Lily lay on her side, facing away, while Guy held her.

Later, after Guy thought she was asleep, Lily said, "That was nice."

Guy didn't know if she meant that night's sex, or their whole life together's sex, or their life together in general. Or maybe she just meant her life. It didn't matter.

He said, "Yes, it was."

Rocky raises her eyes and looks directly into Guy's face. "Will you sleep with me?"

He isn't surprised. "I'm not sure I can."

"I mean sleep beside me. I want someone to touch me. Skin to skin."

"That sounds good."

"Not someone. You. We can have sex tomorrow, after we've slept. Right now I want to shower with you and brush my teeth and then I want to lie down between clean sheets and hold you."

"I've only done that with one woman before."

"I don't care."

As Rocky and Guy walk into Residency, they pass Gap, asleep in his chair in the lobby.

The key rattles and Ray John opens the dispensary door. He turns on the light.

"Jesus, Beaver, what happened?"

Dalton shields his eyes with the back of his hand. "I thought I was dying."

"You are." Ray John steps over crap and trash. "We all are."

Dalton turns and makes his way down off the top shelf. "Did that hippie who brought me dinner slip something in my food?"

"What was your first clue?" Ray John waits till Dalton's feet are firmly on the floor and Dalton has turned to face him. The doctor's hair is a matted, dead mass. His face has parallel red streaks from where he scratched himself. His shirt is torn and his fly open.

"Listen, Beaver, I came to apologize for zapping you with bear spray the other day."

Dalton is suddenly shy. Some people don't know how to handle apologies.

"That's all right."

"I got shot with an electric gun today, yesterday, and it's no fun. I shouldn't have sprayed you."

Dalton's eyes rove around the dispensary, registering the mess. "If you let me out of here, I won't go home. I'll fly straight to Florence, Italy, and become an artist. My passport is in my office desk."

"Okay."

"You will?"

"I'll let you leave, but my advice is for you to go home and sleep. The third rule of tripping is don't make major decisions until you've slept."

"What're the other two?"

"Don't look in a mirror and don't make long-distance phone calls. Some people have a fourth rule, which is don't eat Mexican food."

Ray John considers suggesting Dalton take a shower before he gets on a plane, but he decides not to. If the man has the momentum to change his life, Ray John knows better than to slow him down with details. "You can leave by the Residency fire escape."

They both think about shaking hands, seeing some kind of ritual is needed to get out of the room. Finally, Ray John says, "Good luck in Florence."

"Good luck with Alexandra. She's a bitch."

Ray John nods. Dalton nods. They go their own ways.

Up on the roof, Henry/Sioux feels a body settle into the other chaise longue. He glances over at Sunshine #2, then back at the graying glow of dawn. Because of the Santa Cruz Mountains there behind the Mission, the sky lightens through shades of charcoal and ash for some time before the sun makes a visible appearance.

Sioux and Sunshine #2 spend a half hour in comfortable silence, before she says, "Do you remember the Mothers concert?"

"Where we balled under the stage?"

"I was thinking about later, when we took the first cable car down to the wharf and walked over to Coit Tower at sunrise."

Mr. Scratchy moans in his sleep. Dreaming or arthritic, Sioux can't tell which. "I didn't think you remembered that night."

"Why shouldn't I?"

"It was a long time ago." Sioux remembers every detail of the night, down to a policeman who watched them kiss by the tower. The policeman had a mustache, made you think of the bass guy in a barbershop quartet. "Why didn't you ever say anything about it? Later."

"You got married, then divorced. Then married again. I got married and had kids and a job. I always wanted to get back to knowing you, but life came up."

"Oh."

"I thought you'd forgotten."

Sioux considers the consequences of telling Sunshine #2 that night was the defining moment of his days. It was the one time he was not only happy, but he knew he was happy. Most of his good times had only been verifiable in retrospect. The night of the Mothers concert with Sunshine #2, he had known, this is what makes dying worth the grief. Sioux figures most people have moments such as this, with relative strangers. He's fairly sure you're not supposed to tell the person fifty years later that all hours since have been measured against an hour the two of you spent together. It might freak them out.

He says, "I haven't forgotten."

Sioux feels Sunshine #2 reach across Mr. Scratchy and take his hand. Her fingers are dry. "We can know each other now," she says.

With his other, free hand, Sioux touches a scab on Mr. Scratchy's hip. He doesn't even try to figure out what she means by *know.*

In his sock feet, Ray John walks from the elevator, down the hall, and stops before Lucinda's door. He leans in from the hips, ear to wood, listening. He doesn't hear any sounds, but, nowadays, that doesn't mean much. There are a lot of sounds Ray John doesn't hear.

He knocks. Waits. "You alone?"

A light comes on, under the door.

"Lucinda?"

"I'm alone."

"You mind if I come in?"

"Suit yourself."

Ray John finds her lying under the sheet with the blanket and spread bunched at her feet. She keeps the sheet pulled to her neck. The pupils in her eyes are dilated, covering the entire iris — huge black holes a man could disappear into. Her expression gives nothing away.

"You all right?" Ray John asks.

"I'm ready to murder Winston."

"You'd have to stand in line." Ray John moves to the chair.

Lucinda doesn't invite him to sit down. "How was your night?" she asks.

"I spent most of it up in the bell tower, watching tracers on the Cabrillo Highway.

The light had a time-lapse thing going, especially the police flashers."

"Groovy." Lucinda drips sarcasm.

"Nicolas relieved me at six. He's been hiding from Marta. She has the hots for him."

"What a bizarre concept."

Ray John reaches into his back pocket and pulls out five twenties. "I guess you won the bet."

Lucinda doesn't say anything.

"Here's your money."

She stares at him, unblinking.

"Where should I put it?"

"On the bureau there, next to my love beads."

Ray John stacks the bills, Jackson faceup, all turned the same direction. "You coming down to breakfast?"

"I'd rather die."

Ray John nods, waiting for something he knows won't happen. Finally, "I'll see you later."

Lucinda lies flat and closes her eyes. Ray John quietly leaves.

Forty-One

Guy awakens to the sound of Gap Koch struggling with his wheelchair, banging it through the door designed for accessibility. He hears Rocky's voice, not so much angry or even surprised as mock outraged. "Gap, you sleazebag. Wheel your butt out of here."

Gap's sweat-soaked pajamas are bunched at the sleeves and ankles. He hasn't been shaved since the revolt started. He hasn't been given his drugs since the revolt started, either, and he's come to with the feeling he missed the middle hour of a two-hour movie.

"Roxanne is my old lady. Porking another dude's old lady is bad karma. You're supposed to ask me before you dick her."

"I haven't been your old lady since 1968," Rocky says.

Gap bobble-heads. "And what is it now?"

"Two thousand twenty-two. November."

Disbelief crosses Gap's face. He looks

down at his wheelchair as if he's uncertain how this old man took over his body. He speaks of himself in the third person. "Once Gap Koch owns a woman, he owns her for good. When doesn't matter."

Guy sits up. In no time, he adjusts to being naked in a bed with a naked woman other than Lily. "You want me to take him outside?"

Rocky reaches for her glasses on the nightstand. "I'm curious to see how much he knows."

Gap leers. "I know you write letters to a dead boy." He turns to Guy. "We were in physical therapy, and Hu told me how Rocky sits over there in the book room, writing her son letters. Every day a letter. Only Hu doesn't know the boy died or I'm his daddy. Nobody knows I'm the real father."

"You didn't know," Rocky says.

"Yes, I did. I was waiting to see how long you'd go before you told me."

Gap pops his chair across the room, over the oval area rug, and into the side of the bed. "An orderly at that place where she had him stashed away put the boy in a tub and turned on the water and went out to download porn. The boy — Roderick — turned the water to hot but he was too stupid to turn up the cold or get out of the tub. They found him boiled red. He lasted four days of killer pain before he went."

"Where were you those four days?" Rocky asks.

"My personal assistant was there, at the hospital."

"Your personal assistant?"

"The doctors were talking to me when they weren't talking to you." Gap's head ducks and grins. He exhales rotten shrimp breath in Guy's face. "I found her when she was fifteen and giving head so's to keep her virginity pure. The least I deserve is sloppy seconds."

Guy rises from the bed, lifts Gap out of the wheelchair, and carries him tucked against his chest, like a baby, into the hall.

"You can't treat me like this," Gap says.

"Seemed easier this way."

He props Gap upright on the floor, leaned against the wall, goes back into the room, and returns with Gap's chair.

"If you bother Roxanne again, I will break your nose," Guy says.

"That's not cool."

"No, it's not. But it is true."

When Guy returns to the room, Rocky is sitting on the side of the bed, the sheet across her lap, her breasts exposed. Her voice shows surprise. "Guy?"

"What?"

"You."

He follows her line of sight down his body. "That happens when I'm asleep, sometimes. I can't control it."

She pats the bed by her side. "Let's not waste a good thing."

"Was what he said true?"

Rocky's hand goes to her lips. She studies Guy, standing at the door, watching her, expecting an answer before they go on. "Yes."

"Your son is gone?"

"I don't know how Gap found out, but yes."

Guy processes the information. "Why do you write e-mails?"

"For the same reason you're going to tell Lily about sleeping with me. It doesn't make us weird, Guy. It makes us human." She slides back into the bed and holds the sheet open for Guy.

Her skin is an unknown texture. The feel of her breast against his breast, his leg against her thigh. Her bones are so much smaller than the body he spent a lifetime touching. She holds her hands on his hip instead of around his neck. The angle into her isn't the same.

Rocky breathes in short gasps, not loud but certainly not the silent concentration he's heard every time he's been with a woman. The strangeness is as extreme as last night's trip. Not what he thought possible. He hears a keening sound he's never heard before and only later does he realize it was the sound of her release.

Later, they lie on their sides, foreheads touching, his arm across her shoulder, her hand on his rib cage. Guy thinks he should say something, but he doesn't know what. She has experience at this. He hasn't slept with a woman he wasn't married to. He wonders if he's supposed to tell Rocky he loves her. When he starts to speak, Rocky puts a finger across his lips. Guy falls asleep, not thinking of Lily.

Forty-Two

"You take Gandhi," Judith says from her red love seat with the matching ottoman. She passes the joint to Sunshine #1, sitting with her legs crossed, on the end of the bed. "The man capable of bringing freedom to a nation but he couldn't keep his loincloth shut to save his soul."

"Who?" Dixie sits spread-legged on the floor, leaning eagerly toward Judith. This is history and Dixie has never been close to history.

"Mahatma Gandhi. Indian leader."

"Oh. He was a Native American."

"Jesus, Suchada, where did you find this one?"

Suchada takes the joint from Sunshine #1. There they are, hanging out in Judith's new room — old room if you think in terms of two weeks ago — four girls smoking pot and shooting the bull. They could be eighteen, except they aren't.

From the desk chair on wheels, Suchada looks down at Dixie at her feet. "I didn't find her, she wandered in all by herself."

"My mama told me never feed a lost kitten, or you were stuck for life," Sunshine #1 says.

Dixie doesn't mind being compared to a lost kitten. It makes her feel like part of the group, and this is the coolest group she's ever been part of. If teasing is the price, she's happy to pay. Heck, she deserves teasing from these women.

"Isn't pot supposed to make me feel funny?" Dixie drinks from a Diet Jolt. "I don't feel any different."

"Boo at this stage of the trip doesn't get you high. It takes the edge off coming down," Sunshine #1 says.

"We're smoking pot so we'll feel normal?"

"Now you get it."

Judith chews her own lips and continues the lecture. "Every world-saver I ever met thought they were above the rules. Kennedy, Martin King, both Clintons, all those hypocrites you see praying out loud on TV. Even that old goat Castro. There wasn't a one thought the bonds of marriage applied to them."

"Phaedra claims she slept with Kennedy," Suchada says.

"Phaedra proves my theory," Judith says. "Fight for the little people. Trash your mate."

Suchada gives Judith what would be called a hard look. "What makes you think she trashes her mate?"

"I may have cataracts, but I'm not blind." Judith hits the joint for all her limited lungs are worth. She passes a roach soaked in sticky drool to Sunshine #1, who gives it to Suchada, who gives it to Dixie. Unity of women be damned, neither of the older women is willing to suck Judith's spit.

"Sleeping with a Kennedy doesn't exactly make a girl unique," Judith says. "There's an Internet discussion group for women who claim they've slept with a Kennedy. One woman down in San Diego says she got nailed by Kennedy and Clinton." Judith snorts air out her nostrils. "It's never been authenticated."

"How about Bill Gates?" Sunshine #1 asks.

"He was a twerp," Judith says.

"I met him once and he seemed monogamous. There was a time I had an instinct for those things."

"Bill Gates doesn't qualify as a world-saver. I'm talking about idealists."

"He made a lot of money."

"Men who make over a hundred billion dollars hardly ever fool around on their wives," Suchada says. "That's a known fact."

"If these people are so famous, why haven't kids my age heard of them?" Dixie asks.

Judith's head quivers, as if she's taken a blow. "Good Lord, Twinkle Toes, how old are you?"

"Twenty-four. Next April."

"How did you survive so far into life with so little information?"

"I was raised in California."

Something strange is going on with Suchada. She looks down at the fine peach fuzz on the back of Dixie's neck. Dixie splays her feet out, in, out, constantly on the move. The heterosexual airhead child is everything she and Phaedra feel superior to. Suchada has been making fun of the Dixies of America forever, but this Dixie is the only one she's gotten to know. Suchada finds herself enjoying the break from relentless anger. Phaedra would be appalled.

Suchada looked in on Phaedra a few hours ago. She'd found her asleep, slumped forward in her chair with her wig pushed crooked, revealing her white, dead skull plate. Phaedra'd spilled Black Velvet on her lap. Suchada cleaned her up and dressed her in pajamas. She replaced Phaedra's pouch, which was full to bursting with strong tea-colored urine, and carried her to bed.

At Dixie's age, Phaedra had been more beautiful than Dixie dreams of being. She had towered over other women, alert and alive, with a shining will stronger than any man's. People were drawn to her, like a fire in winter. But last night, looking down at the snoring old woman, sleeping with her mouth open, Suchada felt the guilt of revulsion for the person she loves most.

Sunshine #1 says, "I made it with a televangelist once, the cute one with the hair implants. He couldn't get off unless I read the Beatitudes aloud while yanking his crank."

There is a knock and Willow opens the door.

"That sheriff is at the gate. He wants to talk to you."

"He's not a sheriff," Judith says. "He's a lieutenant."

"Whatever."

Dixie makes it to her feet. "Willow, if you have a minute, I'd like to talk to you about diet and exercise."

Forty-Three

Morning found Governor Daisy Barrymore on a specially rigged Amazon massage table, having herself shiatsued by a man named Antonio who used to be a woman named Peach. Peach was especially talented at loosening chi in the gallbladder, which, for some reason having to do with a stunt in *Boys on the Side II,* was the place where Daisy's stress went to roost. A two-ounce crystal shot glass of wheatgrass juice sat on a table at Daisy's elbow, next to a silver goblet of strawberries and an antique snuff tin filled with brown sugar. Koop played from speakers positioned for maximum yin/yang balance.

This was Daisy's sacred renewal hour, before the battle began. In spite of a strict self-discipline regimen requiring that she not dwell on problems before eight a.m., Daisy couldn't help but think about the Christ First Republicans who had artificially driven the price of gasoline to fourteen dollars a gallon in hopes of scaring California's citizens into demanding oil fields in Yosemite Valley. Then there was the Evian water war, the San Diego Spanish-language initiative, the gay rights in salmon fishing issue. Humboldt County had seceded from the state. Feng shui cultists were suing to cut the top off Mount Shasta. 50 Cent had proclaimed himself king of Anaheim and was giving away lots in Disneyland. Running this state had turned into a thankless chore, and Daisy was looking forward to the presidential campaign, when she could at least get the hell out of Sacramento.

So, when the intercom buzzed, Daisy was not in the mood. She pressed a button built into the side of the massage table, next to her hand, and said, "What?"

"I'm sorry to interrupt your session."

"Nancy, it's too early for a crisis."

"I'm down in the mail room and we have a package you should see."

"If it's a bomb, call the bomb squad. If it's anthrax, call the anthrax squad."

"It's not a bomb and it's not anthrax."

"Then bring it up."

"I'm not certain you want that."

"Bring it to me, Nancy, or wait till Antonio has turned me into a new woman."

"It can't wait that long."

Six minutes of Antonio digging his or her elbows into various meridians later, Nancy Juvenile walked in with a FedEx Pak. Nancy was an ultra-competent blonde who hadn't gained an ounce since middle school. She'd been with Daisy for thirty years. "You should dress before I show you this."

Governor Barrymore rose up on her elbows. Antonio slapped her butt cheek, ignoring Nancy, the Pak, and even Daisy herself. Daisy said, "Put it on the table there."

Nancy moved the wheatgrass juice aside and dumped the Pak contents onto the tray.

Daisy bit her lower lip. "Is that?"

Nancy nodded. "Yep."

"Are they real?"

"I'm afraid so."

Daisy fought an irresistible need to touch the two fingers on her tray — a ring finger and a pinkie. The ring finger had a wedding ring between the first and second joints, not where a person normally wears a ring. Three-quarters of a carat in an oval silver setting encircled by tiny diamonds. Gold band. The pinkie nail appeared to have been chewed.

"Thank you, Antonio."

Antonio stepped back and gathered his oil

and hand towel. He didn't give the fingers so much as a glance. Antonio saw nothing, knew nothing. Fox News enforcers could torture Antonio for days and have no information to show for the trouble.

Daisy sat up and swung her legs to the side of the table. Like Nancy, Daisy's body hadn't aged since *Charlie's Angels.* "Any idea who sent them?"

"The return address says Pepper Land, Half Moon Bay."

The irresistible need to touch proved irresistible. Daisy poked her finger into the pinkie, on the nail, away from the ragged, cross-section end. She more than half expected the finger to crawl across the tray, like in the old *Hand* movie. Or was it *Addams Family?* Maybe a Yellow Pages commercial.

"You'd better call Paul," by which she meant Paul Whiteside, the California state attorney general.

"He's on the way."

"I should get dressed."

"You probably should."

Daisy stepped from the table and moved across the room, toward the governor's private shower, originally put in by Arnold himself, before the steroid scandal. She couldn't take her eyes off the fingers. "Let's find out if the woman they belong to was alive, or whatever, when they . . . came off."

At or near that same moment, August St. John, who had been in the *San Francisco Chronicle* mail room for six years and fully expected to live and die there, dipped into a wire basket and plucked out a FedEx Pak from Half Moon Bay. Since the tainted alligator clip crisis of 2015, employees in his position had worn latex gloves and a paper mask when handling packages. Editors no longer opened their own mail. If someone was to die, it must be someone not covered by company insurance.

August slid the Pak under the FedEx UltraSound Foreign Substance Detector. He studied the image, then flipped it ninety degrees to the right. He bent toward the screen. His upper lip curled. He said, "Yuck."

KTLA-TV, Los Angeles, the *New York Times,* New York, CNN, Atlanta. Variations of the scene repeated themselves as Casey Kasandris spread across America, two fingers at a time.

Forty-Four

Vanilla Fudge feedback bled from the eucalyptus as Judith walkered her way out of Residency. Under the arcade, she passed by Hu, Phaedra, and Gap, their chairs lined up like handicap row at a church picnic. Hu was naked, nothing but a catheter bag taped to his inner thigh and the tube leading to his dick. Phaedra — in green pajamas and the iron wig — wasn't unconscious, but close. A drool strand hung off her lower lip, like a stalactite. Gap was wide awake, happy telling the others what an important lawyer he was.

"I never call ahead for reservations. I walk my butt in and snap my fingers. They give me the best table in the building." He tried snapping fingers and failed.

Hu said, "You are Satan made flesh."

The quad itself was awash with trash and clothes. The toga woman danced at the feet of the statue, only not to Vanilla Fudge.

Frances Ian had her watercolors and easel set up and was painting the chapel. Frances was one of the lucky half dozen who'd skipped the tea. The poet Chicken Little slept high in the eucalyptus, a broken hip waiting to happen. Sioux and Ray John conferred over by the gate. Sioux sported a silver lightning bolt from his forehead across his left eye, with the point on his lymph node. He cradled Mr. Scratchy in his arms.

"The frigging sheriff wants to talk," Ray John said.

"He's not a sheriff. He's a lieutenant."

"He says he's in charge."

Guy looked over from the bell tower, saw Judith, and walked down the steps. "He guarantees not to touch us if we come out to talk."

"Which us?" Judith asked.

"He used our full names — Guy Fontaine, Ray John Mancini, Henry Box, Judith Frost."

Judith closed the one lizard eye to focus the other on Guy. Her head quivered, more vertical than horizontal. "Is that how he worded it? The names, exactly."

"He wants to hear our demands."

"We don't have any demands yet," Ray John said.

Sioux rubbed his cat's neck. "Amnesty for

Mr. Scratchy."

"We should want something more noble than that. Let's hold out for an end to the conservator system," Ray John said.

"The demand has to be something your negotiator has the power to deliver. Especially if you're running out of fuel for the generator." Judith puffed her cheeks and chewed, lifted her walker and dropped it. Blinked. "He listed the names, first and last?"

Guy said, "He swore on the grave of his Vietnam veteran father that no harm would come to anyone with those names."

"He probably knows my name is Sioux now," said Sioux. "He'll shoot me on a technicality."

Judith turned her walker ninety degrees, taking in the quad, the Mission buildings, and the few residents about. "Send Sunshine #2 up in the tower with the camera. We'll have to walk into the street, so she can film us."

"Should I bring bear spray?" Ray John asked.

Judith shook her head. "This asswipe is looking for a reason to go off on us. Let's not give him one."

Sioux left Mr. Scratchy with Sunshine #2. Judith took her walker. Together, they walked four abreast across the tile entryway and into the street. The old woman with the ancient, puckered lips and breasts. The little man in a tacky sweater and a lightning bolt streaking across his left eye. The grizzled man in a black turtleneck and fedora. The Oklahoman, in pressed slacks and a tucked-tight dress shirt. Leaders of the revolution. Cue the soundtrack.

Sioux snuck a look up at the bell tower, where Sunshine #2 manned the movie cam. It occurred to Sioux that he'd made a wrong turn and spent fifty years in someone else's life. His only desire now was that it not be too late to make a correction.

Ray John's eyes darted along the cars at the back of the parking lot, searching for snipers. He'd seen the face-off scene in too many Westerns, as a boy, not to expect a dry gulch.

Guy, for his part, couldn't help but think, *What the heck am I doing with these people?* He looked across at Cyrus, hands on hips, flanked by Esteban Vasquez and Bobby Christmas. Bobby had a toothpick hanging out of his mouth. Esteban chewed gum. Those were Guy's people. Law-abiding, working-class rednecks. When had he changed sides of the fence?

Cyrus sneered. "This has gone far enough.

It's time we put an end to the foolishness."

Judith's lips cracked when she spoke. "That's up to you."

"Let's hear it. Tell me what you freaks want."

Ray John glanced at Sioux, who glanced at Judith. Guy kept his eyes on Cyrus.

Judith raised her walker off the asphalt, then dropped it. "We demand a direct conference with the governor."

Sioux said, "We do?"

Ray John looked at Judith. "That's brilliant."

"That's ridiculous," said Cyrus. "The governor doesn't care about old farts. I talked to her office yesterday and they said Governor Barrymore would be happy if I burned down the compound."

Judith's tongue darted out, licking her cracked lips. "I've met my share of liars in law enforcement, and you have the least talent for it of any cop I've come up against. The governor's office doesn't know about us, not from you anyway. You've been busting your balls to hog this party for yourself."

She focused the evil eye on Esteban. "Have you kept the real sheriff informed?"

Esteban shrugged.

"I suggest you give him a call before this idiot gets somebody killed."

"My men do what I say," said Cyrus.

"That may be true, but if one of you doesn't bring the governor here soon, I cannot guarantee the safety of our hostage. The four of us are civilized people, except maybe him." Judith nodded toward Sioux. "But I've got radicals in there, itching to Mace the doctor again. It was such fun last time."

Ray John shifted his weight, uncomfortably. He pulled at his earlobe. He hadn't told the others Beaver had moved along. Evidently, Beaver hadn't checked in with anyone on the outside, either. Maybe he actually did strike out for Italy.

Cyrus said, "Listen good, hippies. I'm only going to say it the once."

"I'm not a hippie," said Guy. "I've never been a hippie. Last night was the first time I took LSD in my life."

"You took LSD last night?" Bobby asked.

"Everyone did."

"Well, shoot," Bobby said. "What was it like?"

"Shut up." Cyrus could see his authority slipping. He wanted control. "What time is it, Vasquez?"

Esteban checked his Swatch. "Eight-oh-eight."

"You have twenty-four hours to give up the nonsense. At eight-oh-eight tomorrow,

I'm coming in. Hippie blood will flow."

"I told you, I'm not a hippie," Guy said.

"Every head you crack will be recorded." Judith motioned toward Sunshine #2 in the tower. "If your senior abuse ends up on TV, the consequences won't benefit your self-interests."

"Tell you what, Rachel, I don't care." Cyrus and Judith went into an intense eye lock.

Ray John said, "Who's Rachel?"

"Cuff her," Cyrus said.

Bobby Christmas stepped across the gap. He grasped Judith by her upper arm and gently turned her around.

Sioux's sense of fairness was outraged. "What happened to swearing on your Vietnam veteran father's grave?"

"That was for Judith Frost. This is Rachel Sulzer."

The name meant nothing to Guy, but Ray John and Sioux reacted as if they'd been struck by Sioux's lightning bolt.

Ray John said, "No way."

Judith glared back across her shoulder at Cyrus. "You ran prints off the sunglasses."

Cyrus smiled.

She turned to her friends. "Have Wanda cut the generator at night. Turn out the Nursing Care patients who can't get by without electricity. Tell Phaedra she and Ray

John are in charge."

Ray John started to speak but Judith cut him off. "Don't fight her. As soon as she sobers up, she'll know what to do."

Bobby held the cuffs for Cyrus to see. "Her wrists are too small. They slide off."

"Throw her in the cruiser, then, and if she runs for it, shoot her."

"Do I look like I could run for it?" Judith asked.

"The walker is a cover, Bobby. This is the most dangerous woman alive."

Bobby looked down at Judith. She didn't look like the most dangerous woman alive. She looked like someone he might help across the street, which is what he did.

Cyrus pointed a finger at Ray John. "Twenty-four hours, hippie. Then you're dead."

Cyrus and Esteban climbed into the front seat of Cyrus's county SUV, leaving Judith and Bobby in back, behind the cage. Cyrus said, "We'll call a press conference tomorrow afternoon, after we've dealt with this bunch. Meanwhile, keep your mouths shut. The both of you."

Bobby checked Judith's seat belt. Esteban looked out the window at the three old men left standing in the street. Maybe it was time to call the sheriff. Near as he could tell, either way — call or not call — his job was toast.

Guy said, "Tell me."

Sioux turned to see if Sunshine #2 was still filming. She held Mr. Scratchy to her chest and, with her hand, waggled a cat's paw wave at Sioux. He said, "I am blown away. Rachel Sulzer was right here and we didn't know it."

"Who?"

Ray John could scarcely believe Guy's level of ignorance. "Rachel Sulzer. SDS. 1970. She and two other outside agitators bombed the Madison Induction Center. A recruiting sergeant was killed. The others were busted within hours but Rachel has been a fugitive ever since."

"I thought she was a mythological figure," Sioux said. "Like Robin Hood."

Ray John took off his hat and stared at the SUV going down the hill. "I cannot believe Rachel Sulzer walked among us."

They watched as Cyrus passed a parked state ranger sedan and turned left at the bus stop, onto the highway. The rangers eased up the hill, toward them. Ray John turned back toward the Mission. Sioux and Guy followed.

Guy said, "What are we supposed to do now, without her?"

Forty-Five

Up in the tower, Fairly Fast Freddy gazed through Bosch binoculars off across the bay while Guy and Sunshine #2 tried to prove to themselves that the camcorder was, in fact, recording. When Fairly Fast Joe Bob was taken through the tunnel he left the camera behind without instructions as to its use, and there were several buttons and doodad deals neither Guy nor Sunshine could find a function for. Much depended on this camera doing what it was supposed to do.

"I haven't seen a VCR in years. I don't know how we can test it," Guy said.

"Mr. Natural's got one," Sunshine #2 said. "He uses it to watch his classic porn collection."

Fairly Fast Freddy focused on a pair of surfers in wet suits out beyond the seawall. One of them stayed upright all the way in, but the other disappeared in a wall of foam.

"The best waves on the West Coast come in out past those rocks." Freddy licked his lips. "When conditions are perfect, they'll be fifty feet, crest to trough."

Guy glanced over at the line of rocks extending out from Princeton. Yachts and sailboats on the right, green ocean on the left. A small fleet of crab boats was moving to the south, although Guy didn't know they were crab boats. To him, they were quaint local color placed there to entertain tourists.

"Did you surf?" he asked Fairly Fast Freddy.

Freddy's eyes took on a gleam that Guy knew meant he'd touched the thing that mattered. As a sportswriter, Guy discovered each one of these old men, and possibly the women, too, had one shining moment in their lives that mattered. The secret to understanding the man was to find the moment.

"I rode a forty-footer out there once," Freddy said. "The takeoff was straight vertical. If you paddle to the head of the wave and panic, you die."

"Is that supposed to be fun?" Sunshine #2 asked.

"The adrenaline was so extreme, made last night's LSD feel like baby aspirin." F.F.

shifted the binoculars to track a Volkswagen bug turning up off the highway. "Anyone expecting a visitor?"

Sunshine #2 nodded toward the bug. "I had a car like that in college. Herbal Essence Shampoo paid me two hundred dollars to paint it psychedelic wacko, but then Neil the Seal sat in the backseat and crushed the springs down on the battery and started a fire. Burned the car down."

The bug sounded like the muffler was full of holes. It coughed to a stop behind the state rangers' cruiser.

"Neil the Seal weighed three hundred pounds back then," Sunshine #2 said. "He got a stomach-stapled operation and lost a hundred. But then he died."

From their angle, Guy, Fairly Fast Freddy, and Sunshine #2 could see a pair of hands on the steering wheel.

"That's a '71 Super Beetle," Freddy said.

"Not a year newer than '70," said Guy.

"The front end is wider than a '70. The suspension is totally different."

"Those bugs all looked the same to me," said Sunshine #2. "Either way, it's more than fifty years old."

"Old VWs last forever," said Freddy.

"Mine didn't. It caught fire."

A man got out of the bug — Hawaiian

shirt, baggy canvas cutoffs, leather sandals. His hair was Rastafarian, not the '60s look at all. He had a mustache and a shaped beard reminiscent of Sam the Sham.

"My son wore dreads in college," said Sunshine #2. "I hated them. I told him mites lived in the mats."

"Too bad kids these days don't wear their hair like we did," Guy said.

"He looks Buddhist," said Sunshine #2.

The man turned and flipped the lever causing the front seat to fold forward. He leaned in, reaching into the backseat.

"What does a Buddhist look like?" Guy asked.

"An egomaniac with a subsumed ego."

Fairly Fast Freddy said, "Subsumed my butt. He's an old street freak."

The man pulled out a sign nailed to a survey stake. He walked over in front of the park rangers, sat on the curb, and crossed his legs, right over left. The sign read: GLORIFY YOUR ELDERS.

"What's that all about?" Fairly Fast Freddy asked.

Guy borrowed the binoculars and gave the picketer a close look. His face was set, expressionless. The eyes of a Cotton County dirt farmer. He had the body language of a man in for the long haul. "It means the word is out. Someone knows we're more than cuddly old folks showing our spunk."

A spanking new bio-diesel–powered Ford Galaxy turned and came up the hill. San Mateo Sheriff's Department, Redwood City unit. The driver eased past the fifty-year-old Volkswagen and the rangers, parked, and got out. He was a short man, shaped like a third-trimester pregnancy. No hat. He glanced at the demonstrator, read the sign, and walked to the ranger car. He leaned one arm on the roof, over the open window, and bent to speak to the rangers.

"That's the sheriff," Fairly Fast Freddy said. "I forget his name but I saw his picture in the Palo Alto paper. He's running for reelection."

"I got the idea the piddle-face who took Judith didn't want the real sheriff here," Sunshine #2 said as she theoretically filmed the new arrival.

"We should tell someone," Guy said.

Sunshine #2 took her eye from the viewfinder and looked across at Guy. "I wonder who all's in charge, now?"

Ray John climbed up to take a look. He carried a walkie-talkie for keeping Phaedra abreast. She was still drunk, but, upon being told who Judith was, where she'd gone, and what she'd said before they hauled her away, Phaedra was making a remarkable recovery. Most folks will rise to the occasion if they have a reason to.

Her voice crackled over the walkie-talkie. "Talk to me, Ray John. What're they doing?" Phaedra didn't mess with the *Over* nonsense.

Ray John pressed the Talk button. "California Highway Patrol is coming up the hill." He held the binoculars to his eyes with his free hand, but they weren't needed. "Two patrolmen." Standard-issue sunglasses. Hats on square. They walked bowlegged, like weight lifters. Guy wondered if either one was the officer from his golf cart experience. If this had been Oklahoma, it would be likely. In California, the odds ran against encountering the same stranger twice.

"I think there's a question of jurisdiction," Ray John said.

Phaedra's voice came from the walkie-talkie. "Two highway patrolmen trump a county sheriff."

"The sheriff doesn't see it that way." A Lexus SUV crossed through Ray John's binocular field of vision. "Who are these guys?"

Two men in white short-sleeve shirts and black ties got out. They stood talking, looking over the Mission, waiting for the gathered law enforcement professionals to join them. One had a clipboard, the other a hands-free cell phone.

"The world's oldest Mormon missionaries," said Sunshine #2.

Finally, the two men gave up and walked down to the congregated group.

"State attorney general's office," Fairly Fast Freddy said.

"How would you know?" Ray John said.

"I was arrested a time or two."

"That doesn't make you an expert. Everyone was arrested a time or two."

"I wasn't," said Guy.

The highway patrolmen walked back to their cruiser and opened the trunk. They pulled out reflective road warning triangles and set them up, effectively closing the road. The AG officer with the hands-free phone took out the earpiece and flicked it with his index finger. One of the park rangers pointed to the cell and satellite jammer box on the sidewalk, beside the parking lot entrance. The AG officer showed signs of distress.

That's when the black Lincoln arrived.

"FBI," said Fairly Fast Freddy.

"FBI," said Ray John into his walkie-talkie.

"That makes no sense," Phaedra said. "What have we done federal?"

"What have we done federal?" Ray John asked the others in the tower, as if he were the only one who could hear the walkie-talkie.

Sunshine #2 and Fairly Fast Freddy looked at each other for answers. Guy drew his handkerchief from his back pocket and cleaned his glasses.

He said, "Judith had me FedEx some packages. A couple crossed state lines."

The others turned to stare at Guy, waiting.

Sunshine #2 said, "What packages?"

Before Guy could answer, a CNN news helicopter blasted across the compound, coming from the San Francisco side, over the quad, then over the tower, blowing a whirlwind of dust and noise, drowning out Guy's answer.

FORTY-SIX

They filed out of the employee break room, four housekeepers in street clothes, skittish as deer in hunting season. The orderlies came from Nursing Care. Gardeners from the maintenance shed, waiters and busboys from the dining hall, none of them in uniform.

Rocky said, "Uh-oh."

She and Suchada were working on Phaedra, washing her face with Wetnaps, holding her coffee between gulps, dealing with the walkie-talkie. Their aim was to turn Phaedra from pitiful senility back into a leader.

"They sent fingers to the *New York Times,*" Phaedra said, part disbelief, part admiration.

Rocky nodded toward the oncoming staff. "Looks like a mutiny."

Suchada said, "That was bound to happen."

The youngest housekeeper, whose name

was Rita, scanned the quad, figuring who was in charge, and led the assembled menial labor staff toward Rocky, Suchada, and Phaedra.

Phaedra barked. "So the rats are leaving the ship."

Suchada touched a drop of coffee hanging off Phaedra's lip. "Let's hear them out."

Rita and the housekeepers shuffled to a stop with the others spread in a fan to the rear. Rita gathered her courage. It wasn't easy, telling Phaedra something she didn't want to hear. "We stayed to help you in your battle for freedom."

"And we appreciate that," said Suchada. Phaedra glared. An owl sitting in judgment of a mouse.

Rita went on. "Then last night, you tricked us into taking drugs. You made us feel sick."

"I wondered where you folks were last night," Rocky said.

"We stayed in the tunnel." Rita gestured toward the entire staff. "All of us stayed together so you elderly patients could not abuse us the more. You did a bad thing, and now we are going home."

The staff who spoke English nodded. The ones who didn't speak English just looked angry. Phaedra looked angry, even though she had no idea what Rita was talking about.

Suchada said, "We were slipped drugs without our consent, the same as you. No one meant to harm you."

"Someone of the residents tried to make me crazy."

"That was a single man. Winston."

One of the black orderlies spoke up. "The demented longhair who hits on the girls?"

"That's the man."

Rocky did not see Eldon or Kristen among the group waiting to leave. Or Colin the maintenance man. At least something was okay.

Inez Vasquez spoke in Spanish. Rita translated. "We would have had to leave today anyway. We have families. Children. They need us."

Suchada started to speak, but Phaedra gripped her wrist with claw fingers, so Rocky went through the motions instead. Someone had to say it.

"Thank you for staying as long as you could. No one thinks the less of you for leaving."

"I do." Phaedra's eyes cut narrow and milky. "If you minimum-wage lackeys are so cold as to abandon your responsibilities, at least do us one courtesy before you go." Her fingers left Suchada's arm and tapped a beat on her chair. "Two. Two courtesies. You owe me that."

"We already did you a courtesy and you poisoned us," Rita said.

"I didn't poison you. Suchada didn't poison you." She turned on Rocky. "Did you poison the help?"

Rocky didn't feel like answering Phaedra. Her policy with bullies was to ignore them. From the corner of her eye, she saw Guy and Sioux looking down on the scene. Rocky couldn't help but wonder what Guy was thinking today. You never know, the day after a first night. Was last night a one-shot aberration brought on by psychedelics mixed with tequila, or the start of something regular, and, if she had her choice, which would she want it to be? It'd been a long time since she'd shared more than her body with a man. Hell, a long time since she'd shared her body. She had learned how to be comfortable with solitude, not an easy skill, and not one she was in a rush to lose. But touching skin had been nice. Pretty damn nice.

"First," Phaedra said, "don't leave for five minutes. We need to tell the policemen out front you are coming so they won't start shooting."

This caused a rustle of unease among the English speakers, soon picked up by the others. Rita said, "They would shoot?"

"They might if they thought you were us. And, second, everyone goes out the front gate. We don't want anybody leaving by the bus stop tunnel."

"But I ride the bus home."

"It's a nice day," Phaedra said, although her body was so sensately isolated, it's hard to say how she knew. "You can walk to the bus stop."

"I am not wearing the sunscreen."

Only Suchada understood the act of will it took for Phaedra not to browbeat. The old lady ducked her head and breathed in and out through her nose, whistling like a teapot. She said, "The police are not aware of the tunnel yet."

"Everyone knows about the tunnel."

"The police don't. And when they come in here to kill us, we need a place to run."

The orderly spoke up again. "You are old. The police won't kill you."

"You can ask Sioux up there in the tower. The lieutenant told Sioux, in twenty-four hours he will kill us."

"Then why are you not leaving now?" Rita asked.

Rocky wondered that herself.

"My people are not afraid," Phaedra said. "If we must die, the newspapers will tell our story and other seniors may benefit. We are not selfish ingrates who run at the first sign of inconvenience. Like you."

The housekeepers had another conference. The men behind them shifted their weight from hip to hip and smoked. They seemed content to wait and see what the women decided.

Finally, Rita turned back to Phaedra. "We will wait five minutes and leave by the front gate, only if the *hijo de puta* apologizes."

Phaedra spun her chair ninety degrees. She called to the loafers under the Residency arcade, "Where's shit-for-brains?"

Hu looked up from his pecker. "The bastard is holed up in the chapel. He hides in there, to smoke pot."

Rocky said, "I'll get him."

Suchada said, "Winston won't want to apologize. It goes against his code."

"He will this time, or he'll never get laid again. That goes against the code, too." Rocky left for the chapel.

Phaedra said, "I need a piece of paper. Who's got paper and pen?"

Tony the cook had a pen. Suchada found a Chicken Little poetry plane on the flagstone and gave it to Phaedra, who hunched over, her eyes an inch above the card, writing furiously. As Phaedra handed the note back to Suchada, a crash came from inside the chapel. Sounded like a falling pew.

Suchada read the card: IF WISHES WERE FISHES, WE'D ALL SMELL LIKE THE GIRLS' LOCKER ROOM.

"The other side," said Phaedra. "Go up top and read it to the FBI."

"We could try to bargain, hostages for electricity."

"And what would we do when they said no?"

Suchada mounted the steps to the bell tower.

"Is the help pulling out?" Fairly Fast Freddy asked.

"Looks that way."

"Who will feed me?"

"Life's tough," Suchada said. "You may have to fix your own lunch."

The FBI, state AG officers, highway patrol, sheriff, and state park rangers had been joined by three newspaper reporters, CNN, MTV-News, and Rudy Milovik from KHMB-TV. One of the rangers was being sent down the hill to direct traffic. Rudy's cameraman Leo of the coveralls had his camera aimed at the lone demonstrator, waiting to see if the guy could breathe. The CNN crew was working on a satellite hookup, but because the cops didn't like the media, no one had told them about the blocker box.

Suchada stood beside the adult diaper turned into the Pepper Land flag and cupped her hands around her mouth. She shouted, *"Hey, you. FBI grunts."*

The gathered cops and reporters looked up at her. None of them spoke.

Suchada read the card: "We welcome you and thank you for taking the place of the evil Lieutenant Monk. We trust you are not here to see us all dead, as he was." She glanced down. No reaction. Except for the CNN engineers, who worked silently with their backs to her, Suchada was talking to statues.

"As a gesture of our goodwill, we the liberators of Mission Pescadero, also known as Pepper Land, will now release our hostages."

Law enforcement didn't say a word. They simply stared, as if Suchada were speaking Flemish. The demonstrator didn't react. Leo swung his camera around to take in Suchada. CNN was too busy with technical details to care about the actual story.

Suchada said, "Henry."

No one in the bell tower moved.

She said, "Sioux."

Sioux walked to the inner side of the tower. He saw Winston speaking to the staff. Winston's arms were out and he leered, obviously jiving. From above, he came off as a teenager talking his way out of a jam.

Rocky looked up at Sioux. Sioux flashed her the peace sign. Rocky spoke to Phaedra, who nodded. Rocky pointed toward Mick and Wanda, who raised the new bar lock Wanda'd installed on the double doors.

From his station in the tower, Guy watched the staff file out.

Forty-Seven

Lunch is grim. Tuna salad on white fixed by a solid Midwest woman who spent last night's acid adventure cleaning her room. Residents speak in low tones or not at all. Many chairs remain unoccupied. At the vegan table, two old women stare at slices of white bread on their plates.

Winston sits alone at early Haight. Sunshines #1 and #2 have moved back to the abandoned housekeeper table, Willow sits at Berkeley, taking the place of Ray John, who has moved to Stanford, along with Rocky, to confer with Guy and Nicolas. Lucinda hasn't come down from her room, and Sioux appears to have permanently installed himself in the bell tower.

Even the tables near Winston — late Haight and mixed San Francisco — shift their chairs around so no one is close enough to be touched by the renegade chimney sweep. Winston ignores the ostracism. He eats his tuna with exaggerated relish, as if it has a taste, tapping his cane and carrying on a conversation with imaginary mates.

One of the reasons for the subdued mood, besides the obvious, is the effect of having Rachel Sulzer in their midst and then not having her there. It's the feeling of having been in a movie theater during a tornado, not knowing what is up, then emerging into the light to see the results. Wanda Bretschneider feels vaguely betrayed.

"We were best friends. I thought I knew Judith."

"Nobody knows anybody," Ray John says. "Each of us is a planet, light-years from other life forms."

"You're using the defense of hyperbolism against your own problems," Rocky says.

"Whatever gets you from lunch to dinner."

Nicolas, over on his side of the table, remembers eating in a restaurant in Los Angeles — Barney's Beanery — with his mother and sister. He must have been fourteen. After the people at the next table paid their bill and left, the waitress told Nicolas's family they had been sitting beside John Wayne. Nicolas nearly drove himself nuts trying to recall details of a man he'd barely noticed. The anecdote of a lifetime and he'd missed it.

And now, it's happened twice in a lifetime.

The single bright spot at lunch comes when Mr. Natural's phone bursts into the theme from *Close Encounters of the Third Kind.* Mr. Natural fumbles the phone from his linen vest pocket.

"Hello."

It's a telemarketer, offering Mr. Natural the opportunity to invest in his children's future through *Hooked on Phonics.* When he hangs up, a small yet deeply felt cheer rings out in the dining hall. Sparkle and a dozen others dig for their own cell phones.

"They don't need us cut off anymore," Ray John says. "I wonder if they'll give us electricity next."

Rocky says, "This just proves the power of the media out front. They didn't turn off the blockers for our convenience."

Rocky sits in Marta Pitcairne's old seat, next to Guy. After an initial nod, they haven't spoken to each other or looked in one another's direction. Rocky sees this as classic courtship ritual. Guy sees it as regret on Rocky's part. The sexual tension hangs over the table, visible as fumes over spilled gasoline.

From mixed San Francisco, Fairly Fast

Freddy whines, “I can’t believe I have to clean up my own room. I can’t remember how long it’s been since I cleaned up my own room.”

“I can.” Sparkle was Freddy’s old lady in 1970. She still holds the ugly breakup against him. “You have never once, in seventy-three years, cleaned your own room.”

Down the line three tables, Phaedra consults with Kristen. “I say we evict the rest of Nursing Care. We’ll lose electricity tomorrow, and they’re taking up space.”

Kristen kneels on one knee, between Phaedra and Suchada, putting her at Phaedra’s eye level. “Almost all of them in N.C. are better since we stopped the tranqs. It’s amazing, the difference. I had an advanced Alzheimer’s gentleman make a pass at me this morning.”

“He must have been demented.”

Kristen laughs as if Phaedra were making a joke. “There’s two on ventilators. They’re the only patients who need steady electricity, and neither wants to leave till they have to. This revolt has given them a reason to stay alive.”

Ike Pitcairne appears at the door, neat, tidy, and small in his blue suit from the Target boys’ department. His bald head is its usual cue ball white, but his cheeks are a splotched American rose color, as if he's been crying. He blinks quickly and zeroes in on Stanford.

Rocky finally speaks to Guy. "This might be entertaining."

Ike stands next to Nicolas's chair, too shy to interrupt while Nicolas fork-shapes his tuna salad into a pyramid. Like a stone tossed into the goose pond, a silent wave ripples from Stanford, across the dining hall, until even Phaedra and Kristen leave off their discussion of Nursing Care to watch Ike watch Nicolas.

Thirty seconds past the time when Ike can no longer be ignored, Nicolas fakes surprise. "*Ike.* How's it hanging?"

Ike clenches his little fists, then unclenches. "Marta informed me of the truth."

Nicolas loses control of his hands. They tug at his hair. His ears. His nose. They're all over the place. "I'm sure she didn't mean whatever she said, Ike. It was the acid talking. Not Marta. She flew too high and got carried away."

"She said the two of you have shared an unspoken passion for many months."

"Oh, *God.*"

"She said she must explore the possibilities, she cannot reach the fullness of her potential unless she is free to follow her path."

Nicolas's complexion drops through the whiter shades of pale. His lips tremble.

Ike begins to weep; then, through heroic effort, he gathers himself. "I love my wife. I shall not stand in the way of her happiness."

"Ike, you should stand in the way."

"No. Marta is my beautiful canary. She must be set free in order that she may sing. I, myself, shall pray that someday, somehow, she may return, of her own choice."

Nicolas swallows vomit.

Ike says, "I can't say the best man won because I will never believe the best man would lure Marta into leaving her marriage. I will say, you won. I will not deny the truth."

Nicolas sneaks a peek at the faces around the table and the room. Public sympathy is not flowing his way. The general attitude seems to be one of disgust, aimed at him. He desperately tries to think of an honorable way to nip this thing in the bud. Not speaking up right now, this instant, puts him at risk for years of grief. But, instead of crushing Ike humanely, Nicolas waits a moment too long.

"Be forewarned, Nicolas Lessac, if you ever by word or deed do anything to hurt my Marta, I will track you down and I will kill you, as sure as I stand here now."

Ike walks across the dining hall and out. The only sound is the hollow clomp of his footsteps, followed by the shutting of the door.

From three tables down and one across, Sunshine #1 says, "I hope you're satisfied."

Nicolas groans. He repeats, "*Oh,* God."

Almost immediately, Marta enters and beelines for Stanford. The diners go back to eating. They have no interest in this part of the soap opera. Ike was noble. This is tawdry.

Marta takes Nicolas's hands in her own. "I'm so relieved you are safe, darling."

Nicolas says, "What?"

"Ike is an animal when he is angry. I feared he would create a scene. I should have known Ike is man enough to face the reality of our love."

Without waiting for Nicolas to confirm or deny, Marta turns to Guy. "I was waiting in the rec lounge, watching television. As soon as they come back from commercial, they're going to interview your daughter."

Guy says, "Claudia?"

"Is that her name?"

"Where is Claudia?"

"I guess she's out front. They have a

bunch of relatives out there. They're interviewing her next."

Guy stands. "I should see this."

Marta says, "You mind if I borrow your chair? Nicky and I need to make plans."

Seen through wire-frame glasses, Claudia's eyes appear swollen — the fishy look of rickets-ridden Guatemalan children painted on velvet.

"Daddy suffers from multi-infarct dementia. That wasn't my father who attacked the animal control officer. It was the horrid monster who has stolen his mind."

Rudy Milovik's nose ring bobs up and down, sympathetically. He is the one reporter in frame, but six more microphones besides Rudy's are thrust at Claudia's face. Guy sees she's wearing the aquamarine cardigan Lily knitted the last Christmas Lily was in shape to knit. Her hair is held back by tortoiseshell barrettes.

"Daddy is being influenced by atheists. Somebody in that place has taken control of his will, I'm sure. One of the deputies told me they are giving him mind-altering drugs."

Claudia turns her eyes to stare directly into the camera lens. She lifts her right hand, palm up, beseeching.

"Daddy, if you can hear me, please put an end to this terrible ordeal. Come to your family. Please. We love you, Daddy. We only want what is best for you."

Rocky touches Guy's arm, below the elbow, above the wrist. She says, "I'm so sorry."

Ray John says, "Next time I hear 'We're doing what's best for you,' I'm going to buy a shotgun."

Guy stands with his arms crossed, looking at the television where Willow's daughter is begging Willow to remember her insulin. He bites his lower lip. "You know the sad thing about what she said?"

"It's all sad," Rocky says.

Guy nods, although she isn't sure if he heard her. "The sad thing is, I don't know. I think I know, but I'll never be sure that what Claudia says isn't true. I may be demented."

Rocky says, "Oh, Guy." On the TV, Willow's daughter tells the reporters Willow suffers from obesity.

Willow squeals, "You're not the one to talk, bitch!"

Guy leaves the room.

Out there on the street, each network interprets events to fit their own philosophy. Fox News says the residents are terrorists and homosexuals. ABC says they are victims of a soulless government that uses its senior citizens and tosses them in the waste heap. CNN concentrates on Naomi Boudreaux — Sunshine #1 — who was once a supermodel celebrity and therefore counts while the other residents don't. Only Rudy Milovik of the spike hair, nose ring, and pimpled neckline reports on the story as being more important than his view of it.

Forty-Eight

By mid-afternoon the shadow line slid down the west wall onto grass no one had cut since Wednesday. Contemplative Corner would soon be in shade, then the goose pond. The geese were napping, if that's what geese do on a warm November day when they aren't scouting for food. Most had flown south. Only the older, more obstinate honkers stuck around Half Moon Bay all winter.

Helicopters crisscrossed over the compound, *whock-whock*ing so loud even the more deaf residents had been driven inside. Only the guards on the tower and Residency roof remained outdoors. And the revolt leaders. Although no one called a meeting, Ray John, Phaedra, and Guy gathered at the picnic table to figure out what should be done. Without food, electricity, or Judith, morale was bound to slip over the next few days.

Phaedra chewed sunflower seeds, a habit she'd picked up at fourteen, grown out of at eighteen, and rediscovered at eighty. She puckered her floppy lips and spit seeds with all her might, only she didn't have enough spit might to clear her footrests. Seeds that made it past her lap ended up on her white shoes.

She spit and talked. "Those reporters outside file two stories a day, whether there's news or not. The longer we hold out, the more coverage."

"Until we use up their attention span and they leave," Ray John said. He took his hat off and glared up at an INS helicopter, aware of what easy targets the three of them made. "What we want is to go out in a hailstorm of police brutality, like we did in Berkeley. Get ourselves dragged through the gates, one at a time, by our heels, our heads bouncing off the flagstones. They'll show it on every network and we can start a movement. Wipe out the conservators. Punish insurance companies that claim every disease comes from a preexisting condition. Put an end to lawyer rape. We can make a difference."

"You're preaching to the choir," Phaedra said.

"If we hold out till the Man turns violent,

we can preach to the nation."

Guy didn't much like where this was headed. He'd paid some attention to the news, while writing sports for the newspaper, and, as he recalled, whenever law enforcement turns violent the people end up on the short end of the stick. Not only physically, as in beaten to smithereens, but also public opinion, always, every time, sides with the beaters.

"Too bad they took Judith," he said. "She would know what to do."

Phaedra made her patent snort-down-the-sinuses sound. "To hell with Judith or Rachel or whatever she calls herself. We don't need anybody but me."

Guy didn't quite buy that, but he was willing to go along. From mother to wife to daughter, women had controlled his life. He was used to following the feminine.

Ray John said, "Okay, Phaedra, you want to be boss. Tell us what to do. Tomorrow, we'll be out of fuel oil for the generator. We've lost the housekeepers, cooks, and orderlies."

"We don't need cooks if we're out of food," Phaedra said.

"I have a call in to the Daughters of the Gray Panthers."

Guy said, "Who?"

"Support group for Panther political actions."

Phaedra spoke to Guy, as if he were the child of hick parents. "The Gray Panthers — radical senior citizens. I doubt if they had them where you came from."

"We had Daughters of the Confederacy. I don't remember panthers."

"The Panther Daughters say they'll make a food drop tomorrow," Ray John said. "A ton of Cheerios and powdered milk."

"That'll go over big in the dining hall," Guy said.

Phaedra snorted again. "Tell them we'd rather have chai mix. Sausa-lito will dance on out of here if I feed them Cheerios and powdered milk."

A Coast Guard helicopter lifting over Residency from the ocean side nearly collided with the KTLA Traffic Watch coming through from the south. Only skillful piloting avoided tragedy, and as they separated, the occupants flipped obscene gestures at each other.

"What was all that about?" Ray John asked.

"Sunshine #1 and Lucinda are on the roof, combining guard duty with nude sunbathing," Guy said.

"Lucinda is up there?"

"I told them it was too cold but they laughed at me."

Phaedra spit a seed clear over her lap and onto the table. "A tit shot from those two isn't worth dying for."

"Dixie is with them."

"That explains it," Ray John said.

"There's a positive action we can take," Phaedra said. "Lock up the yoga princess. We need a new hostage, after Ray John turned loose the one we had."

"Dixie's been changing bedpans in Nursing Care," Guy said. "We need her too much to lock her up."

Ray John said, "She's pitched in as much as anybody. More than most."

"What typical males you are. You'll defend any girl with a tight ass."

"Alexandra had a tight ass," Ray John pointed out.

"How would you know?" Phaedra popped a handful of seeds in her mouth. Her chewing sounded like chickens scratching hardpack. "I don't trust the teenybopper. What's she doing here anyway? This isn't her fight. If we don't lock her up, we should boot her little fanny out the door. Her and a bunch more. Let everyone more interested in satellite TV than social justice go on home."

"Home?" Guy said.

“Wherever.”

Ray John’s mind clicked back on the *Manual of Civil Disorder.* He quoted, “ ‘Unity is the linchpin of any action.’ ”

“Yeah, yeah,” Phaedra said.

“Why don’t we ask the police or FBI or whoever’s in charge out there to turn on the electricity,” Guy said. “Now that Lieutenant Monk is gone, they might be understanding.”

Phaedra swiveled her head toward Guy. She looked as much like a construction crane swinging its bucket as a woman. “Where have you been this millennium?”

“Oklahoma, mostly.”

“I don’t know how Okies operate, but in real America decisions are based on muscle. Threats and bribes get results. Asking without leverage is a waste of energy. You’ll be a laughingstock.”

Guy watched a black, unmarked helicopter hover over Residency. The glass was tinted so he couldn’t see who was doing what inside. He wondered where Rocky was. He’d last seen her in the library, writing Roderick an e-mail she couldn’t send and he couldn’t receive. Guy was curious as to what she wrote today. Yesterday afternoon, he hadn’t given a hoot for what happened in the future. The past was what counted.

Guy figured if his life was a movie, this would be the part where they roll the credits. Today, his world has been turned inside out. Oklahoma was farther away than ever.

He said, "When I was a young reporter, just starting out, I had a goal and that goal was to grow old without becoming cynical or bitter."

Phaedra rolled her Ping-Pong-ball–cast eyes at Ray John, who snickered. She said, "You were an idiot."

Guy says, "That's true."

Phaedra humped up and down, working herself into a state. She craned her neck to the side to glare at Guy. "Every man and woman in this dung-heap has four things they deal with, every single day." Phaedra held up the fingers. "Regret, isolation, physical pain, and the knowledge we'll soon disappear."

Guy said, "You mean die?"

"Don't pretend to be stupid when I know you're not."

Guy nodded. "That's reasonable."

"Cynicism and bitterness are the natural results of aging. They can't be avoided, and those walking Happy Faces who tell you different are either young or lying."

"Well, I'm going to ask. What have we got

to lose?"

"Asking will prove to them you're senile," Ray John said. "You want that?"

Guy stood. "I'd rather die senile than cynical."

Chaos on the street grows exponentially, by the hour. Scores of reporters and cameramen. Satellite trucks. Streaming Webcams. Caterers and porta potties. Makeup trailers for the stars. There's news networks out there Guy has never even heard of. Far as he can guess, they're German or French or something. One crew has on Arabian-looking gowns.

More deputies have come in, more park rangers, but to Guy they don't seem poised for a raid on the Mission so much as there to keep the pro–old folks and the anti–old folks from ripping into each other. The pros gather off to the left, south, of the media pool, hoisting signs that read BALD POWER and MENOPAUSE: IT'S NOT FOR SISSIES. EUTHANASIA KILLS. They're having fun, laughing, taunting the antis. The GLORIFY YOUR ELDERS man sits plug in the middle. He hasn't moved.

The antis cluster around a clot of bitter-faced VFW types old enough to be residents. The antis don't smile. They're spoiling for a fight, only their rage is aimed more at the pro–senior demonstrators than the actual seniors looking down from the tower. They only have the one sign: THE BOOM WAS A BUST.

Guy sees Alexandra, in a green pantsuit and running shoes, standing near a short-waisted woman with a larger-than-you-would-expect head. He doesn't see Claudia.

"You think my daughter is still down there?" he asks.

Sioux says, "I do not know your daughter."

Guy has joined Sioux, Sunshine #2, and Mr. Natural in the tower. As they pass around the binoculars and a bag of organic Chee-tos, Sunshine #2 points out her daughter.

"She's the one in a sweatshirt and cutoffs. You'd think if she's going to be on TV, she would have dressed nicer."

Sioux has fashioned a copy of *Modern Maturity* into a makeshift megaphone. He uses it to call down to a heavy-breasted black woman carrying a laptop and talking on a hands-free phone.

"You're fired! I'm not paying you by the hour to hang out on the street!"

The black woman smiles and sends Sioux an A-okay sign.

"She's my conservator, too," Mr. Natural

says. "She's happy on account of she's double billing us, and she knows we can't fire her. She's court appointed."

"Crap." Sioux mutters to himself more than the others. "Now I have to die. I'll never be able to pay for this."

It's the first time Guy has been in tight circumstances with Mr. Natural, and he finds Rocky was right about the roadkill breath. He has trouble believing Mr. Natural doesn't know he's knocking people down.

Four men in dark suits are circled around a street map laid out on the hood of the Lincoln. Those would be the FBI and state AG officers.

"Which one is in charge?" Guy asks.

Sioux uses his magazine as a pointer. "Red-faced white man with the bullhorn. Says his name is Roger Cole. He wants us to surrender."

"Here." Sioux gives Guy the *Modern Maturity* megaphone. "When the demonstrators get wound up, it's hard for anyone to hear you."

Guy calls down, *"Yo, Roger."*

The red-faced agent looks up. All the agents and officers look up. The anti-senior contingent *boo*s and throws eggs, but none come close to a target.

"We've got incapacitated people in here,

breathing oxygen from tanks. We know you're not villains. You're just doing your job. How about turning on the electricity?"

TV cameras swivel from Guy to Roger Cole, who lifts the bullhorn to his red face. "Bring us proof the hostage is healthy, we'll give you power."

Guy turns to Sioux. "What's he talking about?"

Sunshine #2 says, "You think a busboy stayed behind?"

"The nurse maybe," Sioux says. "Or Eldon the orderly."

Guy calls down, "We cut the hostages loose already. Nobody stayed but a nurse and orderly who offered to help the bedridden."

"And Dixie," Sunshine #2 adds.

"And our yoga instructor," Guy calls. No one remembers Colin, the maintenance man, drinking in the tunnel.

Roger confers with the other agent, then speaks into the bullhorn. It is physically impossible to sound compassionate when talking through a bullhorn. "Show us that Dr. Beaver is alive and well, and we'll return the electricity."

Mr. Natural says, "Bummer."

Guy calls, "Beaver left this morning. He isn't here."

Roger the FBI man calls back, "You can't possibly expect us to believe that."

"He was upset, so we let him go at dawn."

The woman with the oversized head yanks the bullhorn from Roger's hands. "What have you done with my Dalton?"

"Who's that?" Sunshine #2 asks.

"Nothing," Guy calls back. "Almost nothing. He got fed some LSD, accidentally. We all did. It frightened Dr. Beaver, so we sent him home."

"Wouldn't I know if my husband came home!"

Mr. Natural says, "Double bummer."

Alexandra cups her hands around her mouth and shouts, almost as loud as the woman with the bullhorn. "Don't lie to me, Okie."

The bullhorn woman glares at Alexandra. Guy can see that, even though they share a mutual concern for Dr. Beaver, the two women are not allies.

Roger wrestles the bullhorn back from Dalton's wife. "You heard Mrs. Beaver. Now, if you cannot prove the doctor is unharmed, we're going to assume he isn't."

"Did you follow that?" Sunshine #2 asks.

"Isn't what?" Sioux says.

Guy calls, "Let me get back to you." He walks to the quad side of the tower, pushes a button on the walkie-talkie, and has Phaedra give her end of the set to Ray John. Meanwhile, a group of anti demonstrators has taken advantage of the distraction to sneak around the media. They fall upon a kid in baggy pants and steal his *ANCESTOR* IS NOT A DIRTY WORD sign. A struggle breaks out and the state park rangers rush to separate the factions. Reporters charge into the fray like blowflies on a carcass.

Guy returns to the bell tower archway. "The man who set him free says Beaver experienced a life-changing illumination last night. He left, saying he was flying to Italy, where he would become an artist and adopt the romantic lifestyle."

Melissa Beaver screams, "Rubbish!" overlapped by Alexandra's "Bullshit!"

"Dalton can't be an artist. He's color-blind," shouts Mrs. Beaver.

Alexandra yells, "Dalton is no more romantic than dirty underwear."

"What?" Melissa says.

"You heard me, Hobbit."

Roger speaks into the bullhorn. "Stop with the lies and produce the doctor."

Guy shouts, "How can we prove someone isn't here?"

"This conversation is now over. When you are prepared to be reasonable, we will discuss electricity." Roger passes the bullhorn to his minion agent and turns to Melissa Beaver, who is shrieking at Alexandra Truman, who is on the edge of coming to blows.

Guy gives the *Modern Maturity* magazine back to Sioux. Britney Spears is on the cover, showing eight inches of puckered skin between her navel and the top of her capris.

"So much for understanding," Guy says.

"I can see their point," Sunshine #2 says. "Why wouldn't Dr. Beaver tell his wife he was released?"

"Because Beaver is a dipshit," says Sioux.

"At least this Roger fella is more human than Monk. He would have shot us out of the tower." Guy studies the faces spread out below. "I wonder where the mad lieutenant went?"

"Down there." Sioux passes Guy the binoculars. "Look at the line south of the bus stop."

Because the demonstrators have been forced to park down below and walk up, the highway shoulder is jammed with cars, trucks, and SUVs. A few bicycles. Harleys. Guy focuses on the bus stop, then scans south. The fourth vehicle down, he finds Cyrus Monk, looking back at Guy through his own government-issue binoculars. They stare at each other. Cyrus raises an arm, the back of his hand forward, his middle finger extended.

Sioux says, "He tried coming up a while ago, but they stopped him."

"Goes to show you," Guy says. "Things could be worse."

Forty-Nine

Ray John spends the late afternoon, through dinner and into the evening, at the picnic table, looking at his thumbs against the wood, looking at the sky, looking at geese on the pond. He goes inside to the bathroom, but then he comes back out and resumes looking. He's been Tasered and dosed with LSD. He hasn't slept in thirty-six hours. The woman he loves has slept with another, and the odds are fairly high tomorrow will lead to arrest or hospitalization. Most likely both. Ray John sits and thinks for hours, and this is what he comes up with:

Beauty is heartbreaking. Happiness is heartbreaking. Beauty and happiness are both doomed. The sole way happiness can make a person happy is by ignoring the future when it will surely be lost. This might work for a fourteen-year-old kid, but, at seventy-six, a man cannot ignore reality.

Whatever beauty I see today, I won't see soon.

The guy Guy had said, "I'd rather be senile than cynical," and, at the time, Ray John took the words as somewhere between silly and stupid. Hours later, he isn't sure. What if senility is built into the DNA as a defense against crushing despair? Animals, babies, and advanced Alzheimer's patients are unaware of death. Everyone else should be suicidal.

Ray John groans.

Then, there is the question of heartbreak itself. Heartbreak is life-affirming. Pain proves a person is alive the same as absolute lack of pain proves he's dead. There's nothing like a hammer blow to the thumb to make a person realize life is not a dream. Along about dark — even darker than usual because the lights are out in Residency — Ray John's racing thoughts round the fourth bend in the track. Beauty is heartbreaking and heartbreak is life-affirming, therefore beauty is a heartbreaking form of life affirmation. We're onto something now. Happiness is the same as whacking your thumb with a hammer. Next question: Which hurts the east?

Lucinda walks out of the dark Residency wearing a brown shift of a dress. The Indianmaiden look, down to fringe and a leather headband. She carries a beaded bag. Ray John's one hope is she hasn't changed her name to Mohawk.

Lucinda sits across from Ray John, reaches into her bag, and pulls out ten twenty-dollar bills, which she separates into two stacks on the table.

She says, "I didn't sleep with Eldon."

Ray John looks at the money.

Lucinda fingertips the stacks toward him. "You won the bet."

"When you left the bench over there, it looked like you were taking him to bed."

"I was." She keeps her eyes on the money, as if that's what this is all about. "I could have. He was willing."

"Was the bet that you could sleep with an orderly, or you would?"

"I don't remember."

"Why don't we call it even." Ray John picks up one stack of twenties and stuffs it into his shirt pocket. He pushes the other stack back to Lucinda. She drops her five twenties into the beaded bag. Now, money out of the way, they are free to talk about what matters.

"If you could have slept with Eldon, I don't understand why you didn't."

"Don't make me say it."

"Fine."

"There was no point."

Ray John studies initials carved into the table, waiting. He's certain if he looks at Lucinda, she'll stop telling the truth.

"I couldn't see the point in having sex with another man I'm not emotionally close to. There were so many before I got married, then I spent forty-two years of macrobiotic sexuality. When my husband died, I swore I'd go back to the way I was before, only last night I didn't feel the same as I did at twenty."

"You lost the libido for sleeping with men you don't like."

"I like Eldon, but I love you."

Lucinda has told Ray John she loves him many, many times, but before it was in the vein of "I love Ben & Jerry's ice cream," or "I love the Youngbloods." This one time, he hears a specificity in the statement that wasn't there in the past.

Ray John says, "That's nice."

"I don't mean that in the good way."

"I didn't realize there's a bad way to love."

"Sure there is." Lucinda's hands curl into themselves, fists, only with the thumbs tucked inside the fingers instead of outside. "I don't want you balling other girls."

"Okay."

"Okay, what?"

"I won't ball other girls, whether you ball other guys or not. I'm too old for the I-won't-if-you-won't balderdash. I won't. You do what you have to do."

Her voice catches — almost a sob. "That's not good enough."

Ray John finally looks directly at Lucinda. Her eyes are laced pink, the eyelids translucent. Her neck cords are strung tight as piano wires. "But I thought that's what you want."

"I want you to care if I sleep around."

"I care, Lucinda. I just know better than to demand promises from you."

"But I want to make promises."

"Jesus Christ."

"I know. Isn't it awful?"

Ray John quickly looks back down at the redwood table. It was once painted brown, but the paint blistered in the fog, and over the months of coffee cliques, most of the paint has been picked away.

"I don't think I can sleep with men other than you," Lucinda says. "Or women. Or anybody. You've ruined screwing around for me."

"I'm sorry."

He feels rather than sees her smile. "I don't believe you. I think you're proud of yourself."

"I can be sorry and proud of myself at the same time. Does this mean we're going steady?"

"I don't know what it means." She reaches across the gap and takes his hands in hers. "I was raised to see monogamy as a form of failure. Proof a girl can't take care of herself."

"Monogamy isn't so bad."

Lucinda sniffs. "Do you really believe that?"

"We'll make it fun."

FIFTY

Suchada and Dixie lift weights by candlelight. Dixie on the quad machine, kicking sixty pounds, fifteen reps a set. Suchada bench-pressing. Out of exercise courtesy, Dixie doesn't look to see how much weight Suchada is pushing, but when Suchada finishes a set, the bars drop with a solid *clang.*

Dixie runs a towel along her arms. Six candles wax-stuck to paper plates light a cozy clearing around the machines while the corners of the room and the doorway remain in darkness. Something, the soft lighting or the lack of sleep or the endorphin rush, something gives Dixie license to pry.

"I don't get it, Suchada. You're younger than any of the women in this place."

"[illegible]t much younger." Suchada breathes [illegible]y, deeply, and starts her second set. [illegible]ooked on fifteen pounds more than her usual, to impress the girl, which means she's maxed out on an eight-rep set. She hopes Dixie doesn't think she's interested in bulk, but then it hits her like a brick to the brainpan that she even cares what Dixie thinks. What's going on here? Dixie is young enough to be her whatever. The girl has Saran Wrap depth. She's straight.

"In attitude, you are. You're still vibrant. The other women around the Mission act like it's last stop on the bus ride."

Dixie kicks into her third set, giving it all the power she's got. She loves exercise. The buzz of it. The single-mindedness. Everything else is so complicated. You can't ever do one thing without thinking about how it affects the other parts of your life, especially when it comes to men. Men never tell you where you stand or what they mean in spite of what they say. Dixie sees no connection between what men do and what they want, which is usually sex.

"Alexandra said you're a lesbian."

Suchada glances over at Dixie. The candles do interesting things to Dixie's legs, softening them, yet casting shadows of definition. "That's what she said."

"Is it true? I mean, I don't want to hurt your feelings if it's not. I just wondered."

"It's true."

Dixie's professionally darkened eyebrows furrow, bringing down her forehead. Bottom-lit, her face takes on force. "What does it feel like, being lesbian?"

Suchada sits up. "It feels like I'm a woman attracted to women. I have no idea what it feels like, being straight, so I can't say if there's a difference or not. I suspect I lead a richer life, loving a woman and not caring what men think."

"Do you think you're strange?"

"I'm comfortable being me."

Dixie swings her left leg across the quad bench and drops to a stretching pad, on the floor, between the candles. "I don't know if I could be that way."

"Have you ever tried?"

Dixie giggles, like a girl. "Once in middle school, Mimi Johnstone touched my breast."

"And?"

"It felt weird." Dixie does splits on the floor pad, her toes pointed in opposite directions. She lies forward, across her right leg, her arms extended, chin to knee, hands over toes. "I wonder sometimes if kissing a girl feels so different from kissing a guy. My ex-boyfriend Bryce was like kissing cardboard. We never kissed after the first date. We always screwed instead."

Suchada places her hands on her thighs,

affecting extreme calmness. She closes her eyes, counts five, considers consequences, then opens her eyes and says, "Would you like to know what it feels like? To kiss a woman."

Dixie turns her head ninety degrees, ear now to knee, face to Suchada. "I think so."

"Would you like to kiss me?"

Dixie raises her trunk upright, spine straight, the posture of a dancer. "Should I come over there or would you rather come here?"

"Why don't you come here?"

Dixie stands, drying her hands, trying not to think about what she's doing. She walks across to where Suchada sits with her legs off the end of the bench, Suchada wearing baggy sweats and an EMILY'S LIST T-shirt with the sleeves cut off, Suchada breathing through her mouth, watching Dixie.

Dixie has to bend over toward Suchada. She places the palm of her hand on Suchada's bare shoulder, more for balance than affection, and they kiss.

Dixie is surprised to find Suchada a good kisser. She is old, after all, and a lesbian, but then it makes sense a lesbian can kiss since they don't do the other. Suchada is simply astonished that she's crossed the line. That this young girl would want to kiss her. She's shaking from the unlikelihood of it all.

From the darkened doorway end of the room — "You ungrateful *cunt!*"

Phaedra wheels into the circle of light, her head thrust forward, her mouth a gash. "You bitch. You *slut* of a woman. How dare you destroy what has taken us forty-three years to build."

Dixie's not certain which of them Phaedra is talking about. With the white-blue eyes, she can't tell who Phaedra sees.

Phaedra rolls up in Suchada's face. "I made you, you butch bitch. I cre*at*ed you. You are nothing without me."

"That's not true," Suchada says.

"I gave you a name, a personality. You're famous because you're mine, and I can take it all back. I don't need you."

Suchada says, "I didn't ask to be famous."

"You cruel, useless, senseless *pig.*"

Dixie's had enough. "Shut up."

"What?"

"Suchada is nice. You let her alone."

"Nice!" Spittle sprays from Phaedra's lips. "You killed our love for a pair of boobs and a crack that says *Nice.*" Phaedra twists her head to Dixie. "You don't even exist in our world, you stupid child."

"That's enough," says Suchada. "This isn't about Dixie."

Phaedra slaps Suchada, the sound of bone on flesh. "Go to your room, young lady."

To Dixie's amazement, Suchada rises from the bench and walks out.

"You didn't have to be so mean to her," Dixie says.

Phaedra swings her chair around to look toward the dark door where Suchada was last visible. Energy rushes from her worn-out body. Phaedra is exhausted at a level she never thought existed. She says, "You don't know a single thing. You're nothing but a baby, destroying its toys."

"I know Suchada isn't a toy."

Phaedra lowers her head to her chest. "You can go to hell."

Dixie takes two candles and leaves Phaedra sitting alone, her plowed earth-face bottom-lit by the other four candles. She crosses the quad, seeing Ray John and Lucinda over at the picnic table, enters Residency, and goes down the hall to the room where she's been sleeping, or not sleeping, depending on which night she's thinking of. Dixie leaves one candle on the TV and moves into the bathroom with the other, deciding she'll take a bath. Normally, Dixie showers. It's been years since she's taken a bath, unless you count hot tubs, which are more social than cleanliness. Tonight seems the night to do things in a new way. Lord knows she's off to a fast start.

The thing that surprises her even more than the kiss — heck, the kiss didn't surprise her; Dixie has been around long enough to know when someone is angling for action — is that when Phaedra said, "Go to your room," Suchada went. Dixie thought Suchada was tougher than that.

But then, Suchada hadn't told her about the forty-three years. That's longer than Dixie's parents have been together. Dixie has a strict rule against messing around with married guys, not even flirting, no matter how good-looking or funny they are. One out-of-line crack and Dixie nips it in the bud. Her rationalization for tonight is that Suchada slipped up on her. Dixie didn't think of her as married till it was too late. She knew Suchada was lesbian, even before she'd asked, and she more or less knew Suchada and Phaedra were a pair. It's just that Phaedra is so incredibly *old.* Dixie thinks of Suchada as Phaedra's keeper, not her lover. How could anyone do it with a person that old anyway? Where would you put her?

Dixie turns on the water, lets it run a few seconds, and flips the plug lever. She undresses by the light of a single candle on the back of the toilet. The thing is, the kiss changes the whole deal. The kiss makes it not matter if Suchada is married, legally or morally. Dixie can still feel it on her lips. Boys don't kiss like that. A boy kisses you, you stop feeling his skin against yours in five minutes. Suchada's wasn't a romance novel kiss — none of that tingly, moist stuff — but it wasn't like any kiss Dixie'd ever had before. It made her lips breathe.

Dixie sticks her wrist under the water stream and finds it cold. She realizes the water heater, wherever it is, must run on electricity, and other residents have drained off the last hot water. It doesn't matter so much. Dixie sits on the side of the tub, facing the bathroom mirror she can dimly see in the candlelight, thinking about the kiss. Wondering how old Suchada actually is. Wondering if the kiss means she's turned into a lesbian, or maybe she'd been one all along and hadn't known.

The knock Dixie has been expecting without knowing she is expecting it comes at the outer door. She considers not throwing on a towel, then decides she'd better. Just because Suchada is a woman instead of a man doesn't mean the boy-girl rules against showing excessive eagerness don't apply.

Suchada stands at the door, as Dixie expected, but she's dressed for outside in shoes and socks, wool pants, an embroidered jeans jacket. She carries an overnight bag.

"Are you moving in?" Dixie asks.

"I'm out of here. You want to come?"

In the darkness, Dixie can hardly see Suchada. The body language isn't that of seduction, but for all Dixie knows lesbians have a separate system. "How can we leave?"

"I'll show you, if you want to go with me."

Dixie moves back into the room, letting Suchada in. Dixie is suddenly shy to be wearing a towel while Suchada is dressed for an excursion. She moves across to the closet and pulls out a miniskirt Sunshine #1 loaned her. Sunshine #1 and Lucinda are the only women in the compound Dixie's size, but their clothes reflect a style popular fifty years ago. Dixie feels like she's playing dress-up.

"I want to go with you, Suchada, only I can't promise I'll be a lesbian. I don't know yet."

"Let's take it one step at a time. First step is to leave Pepper Land before the S flies into the F and we're stuck."

It takes Dixie a moment to catch on to *S in the F.* Even when she gets it, she isn't sure if Suchada is talking about Phaedra or the FBI. "What about your forty-three years?"

"Phaedra's right." Suchada stares at Dixie's body in the time between the towel dropping and the miniskirt going on. "I'm an ingrate and she doesn't need me."

Power is still on in the kitchen. Got to keep that refrigeration humming as long as possible. We have to eat. The freezer is down to cases of French fries, frozen stew vegetables, and Casey Kasandris in her mittens. No one wants to thaw Casey.

Nicolas sits on a dining hall chair behind the gun-barrel-gray dish machine where the mentally challenged, federally funded boys usually stack the glass racks, reading *Trout Fishing in America* and eating frozen grape juice straight out of the can. He's hiding from Marta Pitcairne, who, last time he saw her, was dividing up his bureau so she'd have two drawers for herself.

"Only fair," she said. "It's how Ike and I do it."

Nicolas moaned and said it was his shift on the back exit. She said she would join him, as soon as her milk of magnesia set her free.

The truth is, Nicolas is at the end of his rope. Ike's been seen weeping in public. Marta told him to have the good sense to stay in his room, but he said it was lonely there. He's over in the rec lounge, crying like a lost child in a room filled with candles and sympathetic women.

Sunshine #2 told Nicolas he was a home wrecker. When he denied an interest in Marta, Sunshine #2 said, "You better not toy with her. She's given up a lifetime of companionship, on account of your leading her on."

The dining hall double doors swing open and Nicolas draws back into the shadow of the silverware sorting table. Suchada and Dixie walk the length of the kitchen, past the salad station and the grill, past the dish machine, where they come within ten feet of Nicolas's hiding place.

He hears Dixie saying, "Why the flashlight?"

Suchada says, "It's dark in the tunnel."

"Tunnel?"

Nicolas leans out to watch them from the back side. Suchada is carrying a suitcase. He can't be certain in the glow of security lights, but they appear to be holding hands.

"Here." Suchada stops at a door beside

the employee time clock. "I'll go first." She and Dixie exchange a look.

"Last chance to back out," Suchada says.

"Let's boogie." They slip out the door.

Nicolas spoons frozen grape juice into his mouth. He thinks, *There's an option I hadn't considered.*

Cyrus Monk prays: "God, if you exist and there's any justice anywhere, bring me a helicopter so that I may swoop down and annihilate my father's enemies."

He leans forward, his arms drooped across the steering wheel of his three-ton, American-built truck, smoking a Tiparillo. He stares at the little city of lights up the hill. There's bonfires burning on either side of the klieg lights. The FBI is playing retro hip-hop loudly, in hopes of driving the seniors to distraction and surrender. The FBI has used the obnoxious music tactic in every siege situation since Waco, Texas, back whenever that was. Sinatra in the ghetto, country at the colleges. Show tunes in Baghdad. The bad idea hasn't worked anywhere. All it leads to is distracted FBI agents.

Cyrus knows by now they will have people on the back side, ruling out the fire escape attack. A helicopter could go in over the top, but where's Cyrus going to get hold of a helicopter, if God doesn't provide it? He's no longer in the department. *Temporarily relieved of duty pending further investigation.* Bastards. He captured Rachel Sulzer, for Christ's sake. How many decades had the FBI driven themselves sick chasing her, and he, Cyrus Monk, Jr., captured the most wanted woman in the world. When the Fucking Blind Idiots came to his substation and hauled her away, not a one of them said, "Good work, Cyrus. We couldn't have done it without you." He deserves the thanks of a grateful nation, not *Temporarily relieved.*

Cyrus blows smoke into the windshield, knowing his wife will throw a fit over him smoking again. He doesn't care. Hippies have destroyed him. They have taken his livelihood. They have caused the law enforcement community to shun him. All he ever dreamed of was to be a cop. That and busting freaks. Cyrus is seriously considering the Slab City alternative, once this is finished. It was good enough for Dad. Good enough for a man to abandon his only son to run off and live in filth no better than the very hippies who had brought him down. Cyrus draws deeply on his Tiparillo, wondering if his mother lied. Was it hippies who drove her husband to Slab City, or the prospect of raising Cyrus Jr.?

Later, Cyrus would speculate as to what, at that moment, drew his eyes to the corrugated tin building north of the bus stop. A subliminal noise, perhaps, or maybe superhuman intuition born from years of law enforcement. It's not that Cyrus was unaware of the building, before that moment. Once, when he was out of the truck, taking a leak, he even walked over and tried the door. He assumed the building was highway department storage — lawn mowers or orange traffic cones. Parking signs for the summer rush when Pillar Point Harbor becomes a circus. Who would look at a tin building next to a highway and think *tunnel?*

So he's more than mildly surprised when the door opens and a flashlight beam shines across the highway. The light goes out and two women slide from the building. Cyrus recognizes the old bat right away — the crew-cut Asian dyke who laid a brick into his face. The other one is a girl, young, in a miniskirt and midriff-baring top. Could pass for a San Francisco State Tri Delt moonlighting as a Geary Street hooker. From Alexandra's description, he spots her as the yoga babe.

They come out the door, shut it behind themselves, and relock it with a key. Then, not looking at the cars and trucks parked along the ditch, they start walking north toward the brewpub lights a quarter mile away.

Cyrus's impulse is to jump from the truck and bust their butts. The dyke assaulted an officer. His forehead is still sore. The young one aided and abetted. But Cyrus doesn't jump from the truck. What's he going to do, shout "Citizen's arrest!" and chase them down the road? Cyrus is more interested in how the women came to be in the shed than he is in the women themselves. He arcs against the seat, tailbone to shoulders, and digs into his back pocket for the key. Rachel Sulzer had a key in her housecoat pocket when Cyrus arrested her, a key he didn't mention to the FBI.

Cyrus holds the key in the palm of his hand and stares at the shed. Maybe God exists, after all.

FIFTY-ONE

Rocky lit an oil lamp and Guy took the blue pill Winston had given him the night before. It was a decorative lamp, the housewarming present you never expect to use, with a red fake-crystal hood and a quart bottle of green-tinted oil. Once Rocky figured out the proper height for the wick, the lamp gave a nice, rosy glow to her room.

Guy had debated with himself some time before taking the pill. Sleeping with Rocky at dawn had been an interesting experience that brought on emotions and sensations he wanted to explore. Sex had never been an all-consuming part of Guy's experience, even early on with Lily when it should have been. Sex was important, God knows, looked forward to and enjoyed. Two children had come of it, but Guy had never wasted time considering methodology other than the one way he thought of as normal.

Frankly, sex had never dominated spectator sports.

Now he found himself intrigued. Fascinated. Only if this new experience was to be pursued, he wanted some control over performance. He didn't want to depend on waking up with an erection.

He and Rocky made love as slowly as possible, like old friends out for a walk in the woods in October, taking their time, feeling each step fully before going on to the next. Much to Guy's surprise, he came, not long after Rocky. Afterward, they lay on their backs with Rocky's head on Guy's shoulder hollow, his arm holding her to his side. It was the same position Lily had lain in, afterward, but Lily's body fit against his so differently. Lily had been taller. More there. The word *cuddle* came to mind with Rocky as it hadn't with Lily.

"I was afraid I would have to seduce you tonight," Rocky said, "but you were raring to go."

"I ate the pill Winston gave me."

Rocky raised her head and turned to look into Guy's eyes. "You planned this? Ahead of time?"

Guy nodded. "I didn't want to spoil it by being embarrassed."

Rocky lowered her cheek to Guy's skin.

"Every time I think I know who you are, you surprise me."

"Is that a good thing?"

"I wouldn't care to be with a man who can't surprise me. What would be the point?"

Guy thought about the number of times he and Lily bought each other the same Christmas presents. The way they finished each other's sentences. The last few years, they knew each other so well they hardly needed to talk.

"I don't think I surprised Lily, not even in high school."

"I'll bet you did, at least once."

Guy tried to remember the once. Their first date had been orchestrated by a friend. She was the one who proposed to him. Both babies had been planned.

"You know what is important to me?" he said. "I want to remember her, and us, the way we really were. The more time passes since she died, the harder it is to see her face and the more I think of us together as being this happily-ever-after-till-cancer love affair." Without knowing he's doing it, he stroked Rocky's hair. "The thing is, I don't even know if she was happy with me or not."

"How you think of her is more important, now, than how she was."

"You think so?" Guy remembered an argument he and Lily had, over a rodeo he'd covered in Big Spring, Texas, the night of Claudia's prom. Lily had been disappointed in him, much more than Claudia was. "I was gone a lot, especially during football season. And I know she didn't enjoy the trips where I took her with me. She said she'd rather stay home and watch TV than go to another fishing derby on Lake Texoma."

Rocky fought off a laugh. "If you took your wife to a fishing derby and she didn't divorce you, I'd say you married a saint."

"One morning I came home when she didn't expect me — I'd left my notes on the SMU recruiting class on the kitchen table and I needed them to write the story — and I found her in the bathroom, crying like she'd lost hope."

"All women do that sometimes."

"Lily didn't cry in front of me. Not once. Not even when Martin said he could never forgive us for bringing him up in Oklahoma, surrounded by rednecks and Republicans."

"That's a strange reason for turning on your parents."

"*Turn* is the word. Till Martin was fourteen, he thought Lily and I hung the moon. He followed her around the house like a puppy. He told his eighth-grade teacher I was the most important man in the world."

"You were lucky."

"But then he started reading books about New York and Paris. He saw wealthy, sophisticated people in the movies and on TV, and he felt cheated. At fifteen he stole a car and tried to drive to Manhattan. We kept him in Waurika by force till he got out of high school, but that was the end of it. When Martin left, he wrote a note saying Lily and I were losers and making him grow up in a small town was child abuse."

Rocky snuggled in closer, moving up Guy's body to brush her lips across his neck, then under and over the chin and on to his lower lip. She felt the vibration in his throat as he continued to speak.

"I know Lily grieved for Martin. It took me a week to track him down after she died. He missed the funeral." Guy dipped his head to kiss her. Her breath comforted him. He already held dear the smell of her hair. "How could a child treat his parents like that?"

Rocky kissed his eyes closed. "My child wasn't given the choice, so I don't know."

"I wish I knew if Lily regretted marrying me."

"Guy, you take the life you have. Getting

to be our age and hurting yourself with what-if and what-was doesn't make anyone feel better."

"Feel better? It keeps me awake at night. When I do sleep, I wake up terrified, as if I've had a horrific nightmare, then I'm crushed by a flood of nausea when I realize it's not a nightmare. Lily is gone. I'll never see her again."

Rocky slipped a leg across Guy and sat on his belly, leaning forward with her hands on his shoulders. She looked him in the eyes. "Okay, I wasn't going to spring it on you yet, but I have a plan. A way to live without going insane."

Guy smiled. "I'd like to hear this."

"Here's what I think. I think you and I should have sex as often as we possibly can with what time we have left. We'll beat back the regrets by making love. It may not be the best way to come to terms with the sorrow and wonder of life, but it'll be fun."

"You want continuous sex?"

"As continuous as we're capable of. We'll get more pills from Winston or whoever. I'll buy ointment. We'll hold on to each other, Guy. We'll screw away the terror."

Guy was silent for a while, considering sex as therapy. "You think it will work?"

"It didn't when I was nineteen, but there

were issues then I don't have now. I think we should give it a try. What have we got to lose?"

Guy laughed.

Rocky said, "What?"

"I can't help wondering what my daughter would say, if I told her I was going to copulate constantly until I die."

"To hell with what anyone thinks. Which sounds like more fun — loneliness, depression, despair, and night terrors? Or frequent humping?"

"Lily would say it's a no-brainer. She talked that way, sometimes."

"By the time we hit eighty, we'll be setting records."

"They'll put us on the cover of *Modern Maturity.*"

"Whenever you get scared, you come to me."

"And I'll do the same for you."

Rocky stuck out her hand. They shook. She said, "It's a deal."

Sioux left Darcy Faye Gardiner and Mr. Natural in the tower, throwing pennies at the circus across the street, and took his flashlight over to his room to feed Mr. Scratchy. All Sioux had left was Sam's Club canned tuna. He'd never been able to keep real cat food for fear the housekeepers would find it and tell Alexandra.

Mr. Scratchy soundlessly hopped from the closet to sniff his dish, but he didn't eat. Instead, he gave Sioux a sour look, along the lines of "You can't expect me to eat *this.*" Sioux dumped the tuna in the toilet and filled the food bowl with fresh water from the sink. He knelt on the bathroom floor, dipped his hand into the bowl, and let the cat tongue water drops off the tips of his fingers.

"That's fine, Mr. Scratchy," Sioux said. "If water is all you want, it's good enough for me. I haven't eaten much myself of late."

In truth, Sioux hadn't taken in solid food since the sunshine muffin Tuesday. He hadn't slept since then, either. The lack of food and sleep gave him a clear head, or, at least, the illusion of one. He felt on top of things — the man who knew what to do next, which was the way he used to feel fifty years ago when he went days without sleep.

He pulled out his watercolors and stood before the bathroom mirror, balancing the flashlight in his rinsing cup, freshening his lightning bolt. The corners had started to run. His facial art looked more like the yellow brick road than a lightning strike from heaven. He washed the silver off his brush and stirred a few drops of water into the blue. Working backward from the mirror, he painted a Z on his left cheek, a CB on his right. Then he held the flashlight like posing for the Statue of Liberty only with the light aimed down instead of out at the masses and stared at himself in the mirror. Take away the dandruff on his glasses and he was fearsome.

He walked into his room. "What do you think, Mr. Scratchy? Savage warrior, right? Not a man to be ignored."

Mr. Scratchy jumped on the unmade bed and peed.

Back in the tower, Sioux found Darcy Faye and Mr. Natural waving the Pepper Land flag and singing Country Joe and the Fish's "I-Feel-Like-I'm-Fixin'-to-Die Rag," to the collected groups in the street.

"Be the first one on your block to have your boy come home in a box."

Not that anyone on the street could hear them over that horrendous racket the police were listening to. Sioux had no clue what it was. It sounded like teenage children screaming as they drove cars into telephone poles.

Darcy shouted, "Screw you, Agnew! Go tell Nixon we'll be here long after he's nothing but a bad dream!"

"Get out of Vietnam now!" Mr. Natural yelled. "Down with pigs! Up with people!"

Sioux held one hand over his face as a shield against Mr. Natural's breath. "They're not pigs anymore," he said. "We call them peace officers."

"What's so peaceful about a man with a gun?"

"Don't sell out, Henry." Darcy clutched at his shoulder. Since Sioux had last seen her, Darcy had grown a new fuzzy mole on her upper lip. "We have to bring our boys home."

"The name is Sioux. With an *x*."

Sunshine #2 climbed up the steps, wearing what in Sioux's youth had been called a granny dress and go-go boots. Her hair was up in a big, frizzy bun. "I'm your relief," she said to Darcy Faye and Mr. Natural. "You kids go get some sleep."

They tottered down the steps, arm in arm to keep from falling, singing, *"Tin soldiers and Nixon coming, la la la la la la la . . . four dead in Ohio."*

Sunshine #2 reached into her fanny pack and pulled out a pint of sour apple schnapps. "What's with those two?"

"They think it's 1970 and we've taken over the dean's office."

Sunshine #2 sipped schnapps and watched the old couple sing their way through the moonlight into Residency. She said, "Cool," pronouncing it in two distinct syllables — *"Coo-ul."*

"What's it like in the rec rooms, in the dark?"

"Same old same old. Orgies and pot parties." Sunshine #2 stood close to Sioux, gazing into his face. "I know the Z is for Zappa, but the CB goes over my head."

"Captain Beefheart."

Sunshine #2 nodded, getting it. "And his Lost Planet Airmen."

"That's Commander Cody. Captain Beefheart is the Magic Band."

Sioux and Sunshine #2 moved across to stand at the outer arch, side by side, looking down at the police, protesters, and reporters, and beyond them the highway and the moon on Half Moon Bay. Sunshine #2 drank from her bottle. She offered Sioux a snort but he said he was high on life.

"What is that awful noise?" Sunshine #2 asked.

"Modern music, I think. They must like it."

"One man's runny crap is another man's gravy."

Sioux considered the appropriateness of

that remark, coming from a schoolteacher. If he planned on pairing up with Sunshine #2, he was in for a lesson in tolerance.

"You know what tomorrow is?" Sioux asked.

Sunshine #2 thought. "Saturday."

"November 27. If he'd lived, tomorrow would be Jimi Hendrix's eightieth birthday."

Sunshine #2 took another drink. She wiped her mouth with the back of her hand. "That's hard to wrap your mind around."

"Yeah."

"Seems like Monterey Pop was yesterday."

"I heard this hundred-year-old piano player on *Prairie Home Companion.*"

"I remember. It was a radio show."

"And Garrison Keillor asked him how it felt to be a hundred. The piano player said he couldn't believe how the time had gone by so quickly."

Time had always been a mysterious concept to Sioux. Nothing about time made sense, and all the world's religious and scientific beliefs only worked if there was no such thing as time. Except, a person had to be goofy to deny that time exists. Any idiot could see it flying by. He remembered an old Rolling Stones song called "Time Is on My Side." Had to be the most arrogant statement any rock star ever made. He guessed time showed those bums.

Sunshine #2 said, "I met Jimi Hendrix, back in '66. I was working at the Git Shit in Cow Hollow and he came in, loaded, four in the morning. He bought Screaming Yellow Zonkers and a banana Popsicle."

"He must of had the munchies."

"When he paid, Jimi called me a fox."

"Not foxy lady?"

"Just fox." Sunshine #2 's eyes took on that slightly out-of-focus dilation eyes do when people think about a distant brush with immortality. "I was a fox back then, too. Dammit." She hit her bottle, hard. No delicate sipping this time. "Jimi went into this rap for like ten minutes and I didn't understand a word of it."

"I was told Jimi mumbled when he was stoned."

"For all I knew, he could have been asking me to run away to Rainbow Bridge and be his bride. I'd have gone if he asked." She came back to the tower, slowly, easing in from the memory. "After a while the Popsicle started melting and he left."

Sioux wished he'd run into famous people in the '60s. There'd be so much more to talk about. The closest he ever came was once when he asked Ken Kesey for spare change. Kesey told Sioux — who was Henry at the time — to get away from him.

"I wonder what Jimi would think of the world now, if he'd lived," Sioux said.

"He would be appalled. Nowadays, strangers hate each other. Normal people are mean as badgers. That's not the Hendrix Experience."

Sioux looked down at the lawmen and the supporters dancing around their fire and the ones who were out to get him passing a bottle around their fire. The media reporters on cell phones in the middle of the night.

"Peace and love have turned into bad jokes," he said. "No one dreams that stuff might be real."

Sunshine #2 threw her bottle at the klieg light, missing by a good twenty feet. She said, "The Boss Man won."

Fifty-Two

Jimi Hendrix's birthday. Eight-oh-eight a.m., gunfire erupts from the kitchen and the Midwest woman who hadn't been fazed by LSD screams.

Guy's sitting with Rocky at mixed San Francisco, eating shredded wheat in reconstituted artificial creamer. Not many others are awake yet, sleeping in to make up for the late night the night before, and the ones who are awake aren't in the mood for Coffee-mate on shredded wheat. Sunshine #1 sits with Mick and Fairly Fast Freddy. Hu eats like he's starving, his spoon clutched in his fist. Gap is there, three days without drugs, wearing a decent suit. He's hitting on Darcy Faye Gardiner, impressing her by turning his eyelids inside out, driving Mr. Natural crazy from jealousy.

Phaedra sits alone, like something thrown up by a predatory animal. Hunched over a bottle of Black Velvet, not blinking, chewing, bobbing, or any of her usual tics. There's some chance she's had a stroke. No one has the nerve to get close enough to feel for a pulse.

Rocky is talking about teeth. She says when she was a girl, the old folks had false teeth they took out at night. She remembers her grandpa in Alabama, putting what he called his "choppers" in a glass of water by the bed and teasing her with stories of the teeth wandering in the night, biting little girls who weren't good.

"So far as I know," Rocky says, "there isn't a single set of dentures in Pepper Land."

"People get root canals now," says Sunshine #1 from late Haight.

"Proof civilization has moved forward in the last sixty years," Mick says, then shots — five rapid-fire *bang*s from an automatic weapon — come from the kitchen, followed by a scream and the Midwest woman being shoved through the swinging doors.

Cyrus Monk follows her into the dining hall, armed like he's off to invade China. Antique M16 in his hands, ammunition belt across his chest, grenades on his hips, nine-millimeter Glock in his waistband. He's wearing what would later be discovered as his father's uniform. He fires off another burst, aimed vaguely at a seascape of the

Pigeon Point Lighthouse.

"Everybody outside."

When no one moves, Cyrus lowers his sights to just above head level and squeezes off another burst. A bullet goes into the coffee machine, sending a spurt of hot, black liquid across the aisle.

"Anyone not outside in fifteen seconds, I kill."

It takes more than fifteen seconds but the dining hall clears as quickly as can be expected, considering the age of the diners. Sunshine #1 takes off, first and fastest. Mr. Natural pushes Gap's chair. Guy holds Rocky by the arm, leading her through the checkerboard of tables. At the door, she goes out and he looks back to see Cyrus in front of Phaedra, the only resident who hasn't obeyed his order.

Cyrus pokes the M16 into her scalloped gizzard. "You coming, or would you rather die?"

Phaedra raises her head to look at him. She comes across as a turtle, one of those big ones kids ride at petting zoos. Her milky, hooded eyes never quite focus. She mumbles something Guy, from across the room, doesn't catch.

"I didn't hear that," Cyrus says. "What did you say?"

Loud this time. "I said, your father was a baby killer."

Cyrus shoots her in the head.

Guy goes out the door, catches Rocky and says, "We better open the gate."

Sunshine #1 takes cover behind the hedge in Contemplative Corner. Everyone else scatters into Residency, Administration, the rec lounges, the workout room, anywhere there might be a place to hide. Ray John comes out of the chapel, with Lucinda a shadow back at the door. Winston appears from the gardener's shed.

Guy shouts to Ray John, "Open the gate," but Cyrus kicks through the dining hall doors and fires a burst in Ray John's direction, driving him back inside.

"Freeze, Okie, or I'll drop you where you stand."

Guy and Rocky freeze, midway between the dining hall and the front gate. Guy feels Rocky's hand on his arm, tensed for the bullet they both expect.

Cyrus calls, "What're you doing, hippie?"

Cane in hand, eyes straight ahead, Winston gimps around the wall, toward the gate. He's wearing swim trunks and a blue San Francisco Warriors basketball jersey, number 13, which Guy knows was Wilt Chamberlain's number about sixty years ago, back when the San Francisco Warriors were a team.

Cyrus fires into the wall ahead of Winston. Winston keeps going. Doesn't even glance over to see what Cyrus is up to.

"Freeze. Now!"

Winston reaches the gate. His hand moves to the bar and Cyrus pops a round into his leg. Winston emits a cut-short squeal, hits the ground on his side, and rolls, holding his knee, onto his back, his silver hair spread like a halo on the tiles.

"Stupid piece of shit." Cyrus stalks past Guy and Rocky, ignoring them. "Did you think you'd get away with disarming an officer of the law, taking my Taser, making me look bad in front of my men?"

Winston squints up at Cyrus, backlit by the morning sun. "That was my good leg you shot, mate."

"You won't be needing it much longer." Cyrus steps forward and sticks his M16 to Winston's temple. "What I can't understand is how my dad died and you got to live."

Winston shrugs. "Luck is all. You weren't there. Anybody died, it was luck. Anybody lived, it was luck."

"Your luck just ran out."

Winston looks up along the barrel of the gun, waiting for whatever is going to happen. To Guy, he doesn't seem frightened, more accepting, unaware even, like a pet being put to sleep.

Rocky tightens her grip on Guy's arm. "Do something."

"What?"

Cyrus moves the barrel from Winston's temple to the spot known as the Third Eye. He says, "This is for Dad."

An Indian war cry echoes across the quad and Guy looks up to see Sioux launch himself from the tower. He flies, arms spread wide, silver lightning bolt glinting in the sunlight, mouth open, screaming. Sioux's body seems to hang in the air, with Sunshine #2 behind him, her arm extended down, as if she tried to grasp Sioux as he jumped.

Cyrus swings the gun up, firing. Sioux flips his head down into a high dive and crashes into Cyrus, knocking the ex-lieutenant to the earth, spiral-fracturing his leg from knee to ankle, breaking his collarbone, and sending the M16 cartwheeling toward Sunshine #1.

Guy runs to Sioux and checks his pulse. Sunshine #2 comes down the steps so quickly it's almost as if she jumped, too. Rocky heads for Sunshine #1, who points the rifle at Cyrus on the ground.

"I'm going to kill him," Sunshine #1 says.

Rocky says, "No."

"I changed my mind about nonviolence. I'm going to kill this bastard." She calls to Cyrus, "Reach for the pistol, Buster. I dare you."

Rocky is at her side, gently easing the barrel upward. "We don't have to kill him. He's through."

Then Ray John is over Cyrus, taking the Glock from his waistband, carefully unclipping the grenades. Cyrus whimpers and blinks. He is bleached white from fear.

Guy is aware of the others, Nicolas, Willow, Gap. They form a circle, watching Guy and Sunshine #2 work on Sioux. Sunshine #2 holds Sioux's head off the dirt with her right hand. Her left touches dandruff on his eyelashes.

She says, "Henry, you jerk."

Guy stands. "Open the gate."

Rocky says, "Is he dead?"

"He's dead." Guy looks at her. "Open the gate."

Fifty-Three

The next five minutes are predictable. Law enforcement floods in followed by media, followed by rednecks hoping to beat up a senior citizen and liberals planning to adopt one. Then law enforcement realizes people it doesn't want are coming in and people it does want may be going out, so much is made of securing the area, establishing who is authorized and who is not, trying to force the unauthorized back out.

Guy and Sunshine #2 are slapped in handcuffs. Sioux is covered with a government-issue body tarp. Gap Koch collars the Fox News reporter and tells her he was ringleader of the rebellion.

"I'm an attorney," he says. "These fine people are my clients. We're going to file a billion-dollar suit against the owners of this internment camp."

MTV gets a nice sound bite of Sunshine #1 handing the M16 to Esteban Vasquez.

The reporter — white male, good teeth, fair hair, no brain — calls Sunshine #1"Naomi Boudreaux, former supermodel turned radical terrorist."

Rocky walks over and stands next to Guy, but they don't talk. They both look down at the tarp over Sioux. Guy starts to put his hands in his pockets, then realizes he can't.

After a while, Rocky says, "Hell."

Guy says, "Yes."

The FBI refuses to believe Dalton Beaver isn't on the property. Roger Cole radios for a body-sniffing German shepherd. Alexandra throws such a fit ABC News confuses her with Melissa Beaver and interviews the wrong woman. Hu is caught in the Administration washroom, flushing two pounds of marijuana down the toilet.

That's when the helicopter comes over the north wall. A Bell 407, great seal of California embossed on the tinted Plexiglas hull, it circles twice and settles on grass between the eucalyptus and the goose pond. Conversations do what they usually do when a helicopter lands close by, as do toupees and skirts. There's nothing subtle about a helicopter coming to roost in your courtyard.

The pilot they can't see through the smoked windshield cuts the engine and the rotors wind down to slow *whock-whock*s.

Residents, cops, and media turn as one, like Muslims facing Mecca.

Ray John says, "What now?"

Lucinda, who taught creative writing in another lifetime, says, *"Deus ex machina."*

Ray John gives her the look and she says, "God in a helicopter."

The door pops from the bottom and a twenty-something-or-another toady appears in the opening, one hand on his hair, the other on his tie. He lowers the steps and stands back. Satellite news cameras zoom in. One of the state AG officers groans.

And Governor Daisy Barrymore makes her entrance. Dark green over-the-knee skirt, white ruffled blouse under a knit jacket, square-toed black pumps, speaking into a cell phone. As Daisy walks toward the FBI agents and Sioux's body, the rotor blades glide to a final *whock.* Daisy's voice can be heard throughout the quad.

"You send in the National Guard, Jenna, and I'll stand with these elders of our nation to the bloody end. Let your goons stomp little old men and women. And me. See how that plays on the evening news."

Daisy stops to kick off her shoes. She proceeds barefoot across the grass, past the half-naked Greek woman statue, listening. When she walks by Sunshine #1, Daisy looks her in the eyes and winks.

"*Ms.* President," Daisy says, "you are a bloody bitch. Your daddy was a cunt. Your granddaddy was Satan. I'm going to run against you next year and kick your sorority sister fanny back to Texas."

Daisy smiles into the CNN camera. "You get that?"

She clicks the phone off and tosses it to the trailing toady, who, since he's carrying her shoes, drops the phone.

"What're these people doing in handcuffs?" Daisy turns on Roger Cole. "Where do you think you are? This isn't Oakland."

"Yes, Governor."

"Cut those people loose."

Nancy Juvenile has followed Daisy out of the helicopter and across the grounds. Daisy speaks to her next. "I don't want a one of these sweet folks charged with any crimes whatsoever. You arrange it. If they broke the law it was because they had to to make us listen."

Daisy walks directly to Ray John Mancini, as if he was her destination from the moment she left home. She holds out her hand. "I heard you want to talk to me."

Fifty-Four

The dining hall — Sausalito table — is set up as a conference room and the rest of the morning Governor Barrymore sits, barefoot, listening to complaints. The toady, whose name is Benjamin, types the residents' statements into his Apple laptop. He is a fast typist, able to get down every word without impeding the flow of conversation.

Some of the complaints are legit — landlords evicting tenants because of their age, conservators, Medicaid stole my house, my pension plan evaporated. Others are less crucial — no separate line for seniors at Starbucks, alien brain implants. Daisy takes each complainant seriously. She listens with compassion and a straight face.

Even Ray John is impressed. He tells Nicolas, "If she's blowing smoke up our butt cracks, she's taking the time to do it right. No one even faked listening to us before."

Nicolas doesn't pay Ray John any mind. He has problems of his own.

Nancy Juvenile cleans up the mess, dealing with the media frenzy and multi levels of emergency personnel. She moves Winston out, after giving him her private phone number. She moves Cyrus out, telling him Daisy's blanket pardon does not apply in his case. She makes arrangements for Henry/Sioux's body. Amazingly enough, Phaedra isn't dead. The bullet hit her hard skull and skipped like a stone tossed across Golden Pond.

Phaedra is, however, disoriented. She calls the EMT Suchada. Tells him panty hose are misogynist.

"I didn't raise you to dress like a Fillmore streetwalker."

The EMT says, "We need a morphine drip on this one."

The power comes on. Food arrives. Toilet paper arrives, in the nick of time. The Saturday housekeepers walk up through the tunnel and clock in, as if nothing's happened. They're hoping for overtime because their last shift went forty-eight hours.

Late that afternoon, as the sun dips behind the west wall, Governor Barrymore stands at the eucalyptus, facing Lucinda and Ray John while the residents and staff spread out across the lawn. Daisy says, "Will you, Lucinda, love, respect, and at least listen to Ray John from now on, so long as you stay together?"

"I will." Lucinda is wearing a traditional white Duchess Satin wedding gown with a chapel-length train loaned to her by Willow, who weighed seventy pounds less when she bought it. Ray John wears the charcoal suit he keeps dry-cleaned for funerals. Eldon the orderly gives Lucinda away. Sunshines #1 and #2, Willow, and Kristen the nurse act as bridesmaids. Nicolas is best man.

"Will you, Ray John, obey Lucinda, stay true to her, and never take lightly the things she cares about?"

"I will."

"Will you swear never to take her to a Riverdance concert, so long as you both shall live?"

"I don't remember that one in the contract."

"Will you?"

"I will."

"Will you get rid of that ridiculous hat?"

Ray John turns to Lucinda. "You're already trying to change me."

"So?" Lucinda smiles.

Ray John looks at her a moment, then faces back to Daisy. "Okay."

"I now pronounce you woman and husband."

Rocky and Guy stand at the back of the gathered crowd. Guy says, "Is that the California way to get married?"

"Lucinda wrote their vows this afternoon, over a bottle of Pinot. We all helped her. River Dance was my idea."

"Can you picture yourself ever getting married?"

Rocky holds his arm with both her hands and snuggles up against Guy's side, feeling his size against her. "Not if I live to be a hundred and two."

At the end of the ceremony, Marta Pitcairne pushes Darcy Faye Gardiner to the ground and snags the bridal bouquet.

Fifty-Five

No one is there to meet Sioux at the gate. No Welcome Wagon. No maître d'. No guy in a choir robe balancing sins against righteous deeds. Mostly, it looks like a million card tables, each seating four women in sundresses and men in silk pajamas. Sioux wanders the aisles until he finds Casey Kasandris.

Casey says, "Hey, Henry."

"I changed my name to Sioux. With an *x*. You weren't around when I changed it, so you wouldn't know."

The woman sitting opposite Casey says, "They've got a special shampoo up here for that flakiness."

"This is my aunt, JoAnne." Casey nods toward the woman who gave him grief about his hair. "And this is Clarissa, my other aunt, and my mom, Maureen." Maureen is smoking a Salem. "My grandmother Hopewell went to hell."

"She said *nigger,*" JoAnne says.

Casey rubs the ears of a dog lying in her lap. The dog reminds Sioux of Mr. Scratchy and he feels a moment of loss. Casey says, "You want to play? They're opening new tables."

Sioux cleans his sunglasses on the tail of his shirt. He notes, interestingly, that while he died in Levi's, he's now wearing Wranglers. He wonders about the symbolic significance. "Is that what people do all day, play cards?"

When Casey shuffles, Sioux can't help but stare at her fingers. "There's different departments for different ideas of death. It comes down to whatever you thought heaven would be like, you know, down below."

JoAnne says, "God smokes the atheists."

Casey's mother shrugs her shoulders in the direction Sioux thinks of as west. "The Happy Hunting Ground is off that way, but I heard it's gotten awfully commercial. The real Indians are moving into computer gaming."

Henry puts his sunglasses back on and squints toward a large building with black marble walls and Greek columns. Looks like the Palo Alto Smith Barney Investment Center. "I'd mostly like to find my mom."

Casey shuffles without looking down at her hands. She never could shuffle cards when she was alive, not even before she got sick. She's learned several new skills since she died, and it's only been four days. She looks forward to the future. "There's a database in the library." She stops shuffling to point toward the building with black marble walls. Katharine Hepburn sits on a salon chair out front, having her hair tinted.

"The database is way behind," Clarissa says. "They have me listed in quilting."

Sioux feels his neck for a pulse, but he can't find one. "Why is Katharine Hepburn laughing?" he asks.

The dog stands in Casey's lap and circles clockwise before settling again. Casey rubs its forehead and says, "Someone down below must be praying for money."

"Or to win a war," JoAnne says. "That always cracks her up."

Sioux watches as Katharine Hepburn blesses her hairdresser. He says, "I suspected she might be God, when I saw *Philadelphia Story.*" Four people are lined up at what appears to be a sheet metal outhouse. Sioux's voice takes on a note of dismay. "I hope we don't have to pee. The one thing I didn't mind about dying was that I wouldn't have to pee afterward."

"I'm new here myself," Casey says. "Mama, what's that line for?"

Before Casey's mother can answer, JoAnne butts in. Sioux is starting to tire of JoAnne's know-it-all attitude. "That's the ones want to go back."

"Oh." Sioux studies the four in line, wondering why anyone would want to go back. They're all young and white. Maybe that explains it.

"I think I'll walk around, look for Mom."

Maureen, who came from the last generation with manners, says, "It was nice to meet you, Henry."

"Sioux, Mama," Casey says. "He wants to be called Sioux."

JoAnne says, "A few years up here and he won't care what he's called."

Fifty-Six

When Rocky walks into the rec hall that night, Acid Reflux is pounding out "Magic Bus," Tom Gypsum wailing the vocals — *Yoo hoo, Magic Bus* — banging the drums, almost but not quite sounding young and pain-free. Rocky never did understand the bus culture — the Pranksters, the Beatles, the Who. Everybody on the bus or off the bus. Transportation as metaphor. Rocky doesn't get it, which makes her feel like she never was on the bus.

Tom is dressed in English foppery. He sports granny glasses, a satin shirt with puffy sleeves, and velvet tights tucked inside boots that stretch to his knees. The others have gone Seattle grunge from whenever grunge was cool. Rocky remembers it as the bass fishing look in Opp, Alabama, back in 1961.

Rocky works her way down the east wall to where Sunshine #2 sits in a black Allman Brothers T-shirt and black bell-bottoms. Mr. Scratchy sleeps in her lap. Sunshine #2 's frizzy hair is up in Princess Leia twin buns, only with lots of loose strands coming out the sides, giving her a wispiness like she's been walking through cobwebs.

Rocky says, "How you doing?"

"I'm bummed." Sunshine #2's voice is flat. No emotion. "Henry and I spent all those years alone and with the wrong people when we wanted to be together, only not knowing the other one wanted it, too, then we took acid and figured out what we both want, which is each other, and a day later Henry jumps off the bell tower." She scratches Mr. Scratchy. "It's like an Oxygen Network made-for-TV movie. I can even picture who would play me. One of those girls was on *Dallas* way back when. I can't remember her name."

"The one who shot J.R."

"I always forget which one that was." Sunshine #2 pulls the neckline of her T-shirt up to her nose and damps back tears. "I'd lots rather Winston got killed than Henry."

"Henry died a hero."

"I wish he was still depressed and meek."

Pretty much everyone who can dance is

dancing. Sunshine #1 is wearing a peasant blouse and a skirt made from cutting the inseams and resewing a pair of blue jeans. Frances Ian has given up on polyester in favor of green cargo pants and a paint-spattered Sorbonne sweatshirt. Willow sticks to her tie-dyed muumuu. Lucinda has changed out of her wedding gown into a yellow silk dress with a fringe hem. Bare shoulders and arms. Green wreath on her head and hordes of Mardi Gras beads. She's barefoot. Beside her, Ray John grins like somone's popped him between the eyes with a Wiffle bat.

Ike Pitcairne dances with Willow, Eldon the orderly with Kristen the nurse. Darcy Faye Gardiner and Mr. Natural dance by rubbing their backs against each other.

"What's that dance?" Rocky nods toward Darcy Faye and Mr. Natural.

Sunshine #2 blinks away her tears to study the dancers going at it like bears scratching themselves on a fence post. "It's how a woman romances a man with death breath."

"Or how a man romances a woman with fur on her face," Rocky says.

"Magic Bus" ends and the band kicks into "Country Comforts." The Sausalito girls whip Hu's chair one way, then the other, playing Spin the Bottle. Hu sings along loudly, pretending he's twenty-five and Rod Stewart.

"Hu told me Winston got caught smoking weed in his hospital room," Sunshine #2 says. "He claimed it was medicinal, but the police said medicinal pot laws don't apply to gunshot wounds. They're going to arrest him when he's healthy enough to go to jail."

"I can't think of a better place for Winston."

Besides Rocky and Sunshine #2, the only other residents not dancing are Nicolas and Marta. They sit, alone, up the line of chairs. Marta clutches Nicolas's hand with both of hers. She's got him in an old suit that must have belonged to someone else. Rocky remembers a neighbor boy back in Opp who, at thirteen, was forced to attend his first cotillion. His mother made him take his sister as a date. Rocky can still picture the mortified look on that boy's face. She sees it now on Nicolas.

After "Country Comforts" Mick hunches up on the microphone, practically spitting on it. He says, "And now for a special treat in honor of Ray John and Lucinda's getting fused" — big cheer — "and Henry changing sides of the curtain" — bigger cheer, whistles — "We'd like to introduce the newest sensation in girl groups." Mick holds his arm out, hand pointed to the side door. "It's Sparkle and Daisy!"

Sparkle Plenty and Daisy Barrymore bounce through the door and bound onto the stage. Or Daisy bounds onstage, then she stops to give Sparkle a hand up. Nancy has sent the helicopter to Sacramento and back to fetch the governor's evening wear — a black circle skirt and a cap-sleeve top with halter straps that shows a hint of skin at the belly. Sparkle is channeling Alice Cooper, the drag queen, with face paint Sunshine #2 found in Henry's room when she went to pick up Mr. Scratchy.

They approach the microphones happy as two girls on a Make a Wish trip. Daisy shouts, "I am so honored to be here tonight."

Sparkle shouts, "I'm honored to be anywhere. This time yesterday I wasn't sure I would be."

Tom rim shots his snare drum. "One, two, three, four," and Sparkle and Daisy launch into "White Rabbit."

"One pill makes you bigger and one pill makes you small . . ."

Rocky squinches her eyes almost shut, which makes Daisy look more than a bit like Grace Slick in 1967 — same basic posture and silhouette. Rocky thinks about how arrogant they were back then, she and Grace and the whole tribe, how they knew old people were wrong and what the kids were doing was right and that it would never end. Of course, here they are, fifty-five years down the road, doing the same damn thing, so on one level it had lasted, in a twisted way. The difference is the love children never expected to grow old. Rocky supposes no one expects to grow old, but the children of the '60s were worse than other generations. Old age came as such a shock. You'd think sooner or later someone would tell the young what to expect and the young would listen. But then what? The social contract would crash and burn if the young knew what was in store for them.

Right about the time the girl singers start trading off *"Feed your head! Feed your head!"* Sunshine #1's peasant blouse flies onto the stage. Rocky checks her watch and says, "Crap." Willow *whoop*s and hugs Sunshine #1.

Willow gushes. "I have never won anything before. Not once in seventy-four years. Doesn't it go to show. It's never too late to win."

"If you're such a winner, show your own tits," Sunshine #1 says.

So Willow's muumuu comes off over her head.

"Bras don't count," Sunshine #1 says.

Willow's cavernous bra flies into Hu's face, and there she is, a fat, happy seventy-four-year-old woman in cotton panties, prancing around the dance floor.

Daisy loses it. She laughs so hard she hangs on to the mike stand to stay upright. "You people are a trip. If I'd known old age was this much fun, I'd have put myself in a nursing home years ago."

"We like to call it continuing care," says Sparkle.

"Whatever you call it, you people sure don't act your own age."

The residents freeze in place. Rocky touches Sunshine #2 on the wrist. "She didn't have to say that."

Sunshine #2 passes Mr. Scratchy from her lap to Rocky's. "It was bound to happen." Sunshine #2 stands and advances toward the stage.

Daisy whispers to Sparkle, "What'd I say?"

Sparkle says, "Watch."

Sunshine #2 walks right up to the stage, directly under Daisy. She turns around, facing her gathered friends, rivals, and extended family. She says, "Let's show Henry how much we love him," and she drops her bell-bottoms to the floor. A second later, black, thigh-cut panties land at her feet.

Mr. Natural says, "For Henry," and he drops his white linen trousers and pee-stained boxers.

Frances Ian, who has changed more in a week than anyone else in the room, turns and drops her cargo pants. "For Sioux!"

Sunshine #1's not wearing panties, so she has a head start. "For Sioux!"

Lucinda, "For Sioux!"

Ray John, "For Henry!"

Sparkle and the band go all together. Darcy helps Hu. Eldon and Kristen drop their drawers. Nicolas has to fight off Marta, but he gets his suit pants down. Then, out of loyalty to her man, Marta follows.

Rocky thinks, *Oh, shit,* and stands, holding Mr. Scratchy along one arm. "For Henry!"

Thirty seconds later, Daisy looks down on the exposed butt cheeks of Pepper Land. The sight is so beautiful, sad, wonderful, heartbreaking, and bizarre, tears come to her eyes. She takes the microphone off the stand and holds it gently in her right hand. Her left-hand fingers feel for the elastic waistband on her skirt.

"For Sioux!" And the governor of California bares her ass.

FIFTY-SEVEN

The immediate aftermath of any large-scale mooning is awkwardness. What next? Covering yourself feels anticlimactic, but who wants to stand around socializing with their underwear at their ankles. Luckily, the guys in Acid Reflux had experience at this sort of thing. They knew the way back into normalcy is through rock and roll.

The band pulled up their grubby jeans, or in Tom's case velvet tights, Mick said, "Hit it," and they broke into a spirited rendition of "Somebody to Love." Sparkle and Daisy followed the boys' lead and in no time the dance floor was once again abob with gyrating bodies. Pretty much the entire crew knew the words.

"Don't you want somebody to love? Don't you need somebody to love?"

It occurred to Rocky that Guy should be here by now. She'd last seen him in the dining hall when they separated, going to their own rooms for showers in recently restored hot water. Guy said he would meet her in the rec hall in an hour or so, and it had been an hour or so. Since Sunshine #2 showed no sign of coming back off the dance floor, Rocky took Mr. Scratchy down to Nicolas.

"Can you keep an eye on Henry's cat while I find Guy?"

Nicolas reached for Mr. Scratchy, but Marta pulled down on his arm. "Nicolas is allergic to cats."

"You're thinking of Ike," Nicolas said.

"I am not." Marta appealed to Rocky. "He always throws Ike in my face. I can't help it if I have a past." She turned back to Nicolas. "Besides, Ike isn't the one allergic. You are."

Nicolas took the sleeping Mr. Scratchy from Rocky's arms. "I would know if I'm allergic, by now."

"You don't know what you are," Marta said.

Rocky discovered Gap under the Residency arcade, leaning off toward the Pacific, his suit a stained wreck, his eyes watering.

He said, "Peace, Sweet Cheeks. How about a hand here?"

Rocky pushed him into a more or less upright position. "Tuck away your sausage, Gap. You won't be needing that little thing again in this lifetime."

Gap said, "You've turned mean since you left Alabama."

Rocky was surprised he remembered Alabama. You never could tell what Gap knew from day to day or pill to pill. "I thought you were back among us. How'd you get stoned again?"

"They had this doctor in, picking up the lesbo with the bullet through her head. I told him you people were hiding my medication, on account of you hate lawyers." Gap's chin dropped to his chest. He looked up at her, his pupils hooded by his upper eyelids. "How'd you like to give a dying man his last blow job?"

Rocky came close to laughing. She still didn't like the old doper Gap, but she had to admit he was more entertaining than the alert lawyer Gap. When this Gap made lewd propositions, you could think he was a jerk because of the drugs. The lawyer Gap had no excuse.

"Maybe later." She glanced behind him into the Residency door. "I'm looking for someone who isn't brain-dead, but if I need a village idiot, I'll keep you in mind."

Guy leered up at her. His lips appeared to grow bluer as he spoke. "If you're looking for that old man you dumped me over, you better look in Nursing Care yourself. He's more demented straight than I am medicated."

"I'll keep that in mind."

"Last time I saw the crankcase, he was crawling through the dirt, over by the back wall."

Rocky peered across the moonlit quad. For some reason, when the electricity came back on, the security light went out. She could make out a dark hump of a shape, low on the ground, in front of the chapel.

Gap said, "You ever stop to think that any man you ball ends up stupid."

Rocky found Guy squatting on his haunches on the plank porch in front of the chapel, facing the door. His arms dangled across his thighs. His head was tipped forward, as if listening.

She said, "I missed you at the rec hall."

Guy looked up at her. She could see his eyes in the moonlight. "Martin locked himself in the bathroom."

A chill jumped up Rocky's spine. She dropped to her knees and touched his arm. "Guy?"

He leaned forward to rap his knuckles on the chapel door. "Young man. I've had just about all of this nonsense I'm going to take."

He blinked quickly, listening. Rocky found

herself listening also, watching Guy, hoping an answer didn't come, or if it did, they both heard it. With a grunt, Guy settled back to sit directly on the planks. "I don't know what to do about that boy."

"Martin is okay, Guy."

"A certain amount of rebellion is expected at his age. Heck, I wouldn't want a son with no spirit, but sometimes I think Martin hates me."

Rocky lifted Guy's hand into her own. "Martin doesn't hate you. Leave him alone. He needs time to sort himself out."

"Lord knows what he's doing in there."

Rocky's voice was gentle. It was the tone she'd learned on Roderick, when it became clear he wasn't like other boys. "Come with me, Guy. They're having a party in the rec hall."

He cocked his head to the side. "I heard the pep band."

Rocky helped Guy to his feet. Upright, he leaned against her, his big body on her small one. He sniffed her hair. "You smell nice tonight, Lily."

Rocky held Guy around the hips, hugging with both arms. She buried her face against his chest.

He said, "I love you now, even more than the day we got married."

Rocky spoke into his shirt. "I love you, too, Guy."

"There'll never be another girl for me."

Guy and Rocky walked hand in hand across the quad, past the goose pond and the tree, drawn toward the sound of the music.

"You know what I think?" Guy said.

"What's that?"

"I think Martin is abusing himself in the bathroom."

Rocky stopped outside the rec hall door. She looked up into Guy's face. "If he is, that's okay," she said. "It's all part of living and dying."

"I'm surprised to hear you say that," Guy said. He opened the door for Rocky. "Somebody to Love" washed across them, the band stretching it into your standard half-hour rock-and-roll live-show big finish. Guy followed Rocky into the room he saw filled with boys in crew cuts and flat-tops, high-top tennis shoes, white socks and T-shirts, girls in sweaters and pep club skirts, hair sprayed against the Oklahoma wind.

Guy put his hand into the small of Rocky's back. He said, "How about it, hon, you want to dance?"

ABOUT THE AUTHOR

Tim Sandlin is the author of seven novels, including the GroVont trilogy and *Honey Don't.* He lives a full life in Jackson Hole, Wyoming, with his wife, son, and daughter.

The employees of Thorndike Press hope you have enjoyed this Large Print book. All our Thorndike and Wheeler Large Print titles are designed for easy reading, and all our books are made to last. Other Thorndike Press Large Print books are available at your library, through selected bookstores, or directly from us.

For information about titles, please call:

(800) 223-1244

or visit our Web site at:

www.gale.com/thorndike
www.gale.com/wheeler

To share your comments, please write:

Publisher
Thorndike Press
295 Kennedy Memorial Drive
Waterville, ME 04901